W9-BYD-852

She Had It Coming

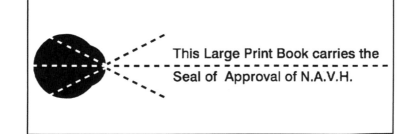

This Large Print Book carries the
Seal of Approval of N.A.V.H.

SHE HAD IT COMING

MARY MONROE

THORNDIKE PRESS

A part of Gale, Cengage Learning

GALE
CENGAGE Learning™

Detroit • New York • San Francisco • New Haven, Conn • Waterville, Maine • London

GALE
CENGAGE Learning‍™

LIBRARY OF CONGRESS CATALOGING-IN-PUBLICATION DATA

Monroe, Mary.
  She had it coming / by Mary Monroe. — Large print ed.
    p. cm. — (Thorndike Press large print African-American)
  Originally published: New York: Dafina, 2008.
  ISBN-13: 978-1-4104-1078-8 (alk. paper)
  ISBN-10: 1-4104-1078-1 (alk. paper)
  1. African American women—Fiction. 2. Adultery—Fiction. 3.
  Large type books. I. Title.
  PS3563.O528S54 2009
  813'.54—dc22   2008045203

Published in 2009 by arrangement with Dafina Books, an imprint of Kensington Publishing Corp.

Printed in the United States of America
1 2 3 4 5 6 7 13 12 11 10 09

ACKNOWLEDGMENTS

To the wonderful national and international book club members (especially Louise Cook in Richmond, California, and Marsha Thomas in London, England), the bookstores who promote my books, and to the loyal fans who read my books: this one is for you. I sincerely appreciate your comments, support, and suggestions.

A very special thanks to the staff at The Ivy restaurant in Beverly Hills for always giving me A-List attention.

Get ready for next year's *God Ain't Blind,* the fourth book in my *God Don't Like Ugly* series.

Please continue to send your e-mails and letters and visit my Web site at *www.Mary monroe.org.*

Peace and blessings!

Mary Monroe
Oakland, California
September, 2008

CHAPTER 1

I saw my best friend kill her vicious step-father on the night of our senior prom. While our classmates were dancing the night away and plotting to do everything we had been told not to do after the prom, I was helping Valerie Proctor hide a dead body in her backyard beneath a lopsided fig tree.

Ezekiel "Zeke" Proctor's violent death had come as no surprise to me. It happened sixteen years ago but it's still fresh on my mind, and I know it will be until the day I die, too.

Mr. Zeke had been a fairly good neighbor as far back as I could remember. When he wasn't too drunk or in a bad mood, he would haul old people and single mothers who didn't have transportation around in his car. He would lend money, dole it out to people who needed it, and he never asked to be repaid. He would do yard work and other maintenance favors for little or no money. And when he was in a good mood, which was rare, he would host a backyard cookout and invite everybody on our block. However, those events usually ended when he got too drunk and paranoid and decided that everybody was "out to get him."

When that happened, barbequed ribs, links, and chicken wings ended up on the ground, or stuck to somebody's hair where he'd thrown them. People had to hop away from the backyard to avoid stepping on glasses that he had broken on purpose. There had not been any cookouts since the time he got mad and shot off his gun in the air because he thought one of the handsome young male guests was plotting to steal his wife. In addition to those lovely social events, he'd also been the stepfather and husband from hell.

Valerie's mother, Miss Naomi, bruised and bleeding like a stuck pig herself after the last beating that she'd survived a few minutes before the killing, had also witnessed Mr. Zeke's demise. Like a zombie, she had stood and watched her daughter commit the granddaddy of crimes. Had things turned out differently, Miss Naomi would have been the dead body on the floor that night, because this time her husband had gone too far. He had attempted to strangle her to death. She had his handprints on her neck and broken blood vessels in the whites of her eyes to prove it.

To this day I don't like to think of what I witnessed as a murder, per se. If that wasn't a slam dunk case of self-defense, I don't know what was. But Valerie and her mother didn't see things that way. They didn't call the cops like they'd done so many times in the past. That had done no good. If anything, it had only made matters worse. Each time after the cops left, Miss Naomi got another beating. They also didn't call the good preacher, Reverend Carter, who had told them time and time again, year after year, that "Brother Zeke can't help hisself; he's confused" and to be "patient and wait because things like this will work out somehow if y'all turn this over to God." Well, they'd tried that, too, and God had not intervened.

"None of those motherfuckers helped us when we needed it, now we don't need their help," Valerie's mother said, grinding her teeth as she gave her husband's corpse one final kick in his side. She attempted to calm her nerves by drinking vodka straight out of the same bottle that he had been nursing from like a hungry baby all day.

Miss Naomi and Valerie buried Mr. Zeke's vile body in the backyard of the house that Miss Naomi owned on Baylor Street. It was the most attractive residence on the block, not the kind of place that you would expect to host such a gruesome crime. People we all knew got killed in the crack houses in South Central and other rough parts of L.A., not in our quiet little neighborhood in houses like Miss Naomi's. Directly across the street was the Baylor Street Mt. Zion Baptist Church, which almost everybody on the block attended at some time. Even the late Mr. Zeke. . . .

The scene of the crime was a two-story white stucco with a two-car garage and a wraparound front porch that was often cluttered with toys and neighborhood kids like me. The front lawn was spacious and well cared for. A bright white picket fence surrounded the entire front lawn like a houndstooth necklace. Behind the house, as with all the other houses on the block, was a high, dark fence that hid the backyard, as well as Valerie's crime.

Miss Naomi's house looked like one of those family friendly homes on those unrealistic television sitcoms. But because of Valerie's stepfather's frequent violence, the house was anything but family friendly. He had turned it into a war zone over the years. Valerie's baby brother, Binkie, referred to it as Beirut because Mr. Zeke attacked every member of the family on a regular basis, including Valerie's decrepit grandfather, Paw Paw, and even one-eyed Pete, the family dog.

Even though there was blood in every room in that house, that didn't stop me from making it my second home. Over the years I had learned how to get out of the "line of fire" in time to avoid injury whenever Mr. Zeke broke loose.

That night, I had innocently walked into the house and witnessed Valerie's crime. As soon as I realized what was happening, I threw up all over the pale pink dress that had cost me a month's worth of my earnings. I continued to vomit as I watched Valerie and her long-suffering mother drag the body across the kitchen floor to the backyard so casually you'd have thought it was a mop.

Before they reached the gaping hole in the ground that had several mounds of dirt piled up around it like little pyramids, they stumbled and dropped the corpse. There was a thud and then a weak, hissing sound from the body that made me think of a dying serpent. Somebody let out a long, loud,

11

rhythmic fart. I could smell it from where I stood in the door like a prison guard. And it was fiercely potent. I couldn't tell if it had come from Valerie, her mother, or if it was the last gas to ooze from the asshole of the dead man. It could have even been from me, but I was such a wreck, I couldn't tell. I squeezed my nostrils and then I froze from my face to the soles of my feet.

I held my breath as Valerie stumbled and fell on top of one of the mounds of dirt. Miss Naomi, breathing hard and loud, fell on top of Mr. Zeke's corpse. One of us screamed. I didn't realize it was me until Valerie scolded me. "Dolores, shut the fuck up and help us." Why, I didn't know. With the tall dark fence protecting the backyard like a fort, none of our neighbors could see her. "We need to get him in this hole *now*," she said, huffing and puffing. I couldn't believe that this was the same girl that Reverend Carter had baptized less than a week ago, in the church across the street from the scene of her crime.

CHAPTER 2

The Los Angeles experience was like something out of a movie. Literally. Things just didn't happen in L.A. Being that this was where Hollywood was located, even night didn't just happen in L.A. It made an *entrance* the same way Gloria Swanson did in that old movie *Sunset Boulevard.* Just like the demented character that she had so brilliantly portrayed, this particular night was *ready for its close-up.* And I was right smack-dab in the middle of it. I was not the star, but in a way I had a strong supporting role. It was not where I wanted to be.

I grabbed a flashlight from the kitchen drawer and stepped into the backyard. Even in the dim light, I could see that the hairdo Valerie had spent a hundred dollars on was ruined. Her usually glorious mane, matted with dirt and saturated with sweat, looked like a sheep's ass. With every move she made, the long curls that she was so proud of flopped about her face like limp vines. She leaped up from the ground, pulling her mother up by the hand. They then continued to slide Mr. Zeke into his final resting place. Well, it was final as long as some busybody didn't dig him up.

"Lo, you need to hold that goddamned flashlight straight," Valerie informed me, speaking in a voice I hardly recognized. There was a desperate look in her eyes that I had never seen before.

I was temporarily unable to speak. I moved my mouth, my tongue, and my lips, but nothing came out. All I could do was try to hold that fucking flashlight in place. Even with the porch light on, and the beam from the flashlight in my hands, everything seemed so dark, including my beautiful light pink dress. And nothing seemed real.

"Aren't y'all supposed to wrap him up in something?" I asked in a trembling voice. It seemed almost disrespectful not to include a shroud. I even snatched a towel off the kitchen counter and held it up, waving it, hoping they would at least wrap up his head and cover his eyes. But Valerie and her mother ignored me. Mr. Zeke went into the ground with just the clothes on his back. Almost every single inch of the white shirt he'd died in had turned red with his blood.

14

Valerie and Miss Naomi put together didn't weigh as much as that loathsome body that they had dropped into a hole that had already been dug. I don't know how I managed to stand there holding the flashlight in my hands, both of them shaking hard. I had to use both to hold the flashlight in place so Valerie and her mother could see what they were doing.

Mr. Zeke had dug the grave himself the day before and told Valerie's mother that she'd be in it by the weekend. No, he had promised her. Ironically, he'd dug it long and deep enough to accommodate his six foot four, 270-pound frame.

The murder weapon, a butcher knife that could have passed for a sword if it had been any longer, was on the kitchen table with half of the blade missing. I'd find out later that the missing part of the blade had been buried with Mr. Zeke, still planted in his chest like a spike. This was a horrible way for a horrible man to die, and for some reason I felt unbearably sad. Despite everything he was and had done, he was still somebody's son. Having never known my blood relatives, family had a special meaning to me.

In the kitchen, the blood on the floor was so thick it looked like you could dip it up with a spoon. There was a large puddle in front of the sink that covered the floor like an area rug, and a wide trail that looked like a thick red snake that led to the door. The spot in front of the stove was where Mr. Zeke had issued his last threat, and breathed his last breath. Pete, the dingy black mutt that Valerie and I had rescued from the street, had already started slipping and sliding across the floor, lapping up blood like he was at a hog trough. Pete stared up at me with his remaining eye. Mr. Zeke's blood was dripping from his tongue, whiskers and nose.

Besides Valerie and her mother, who died from natural causes herself about a year later, and Valerie's one-eyed dog, I was the only other individual who knew what had happened to Mr. Zeke. That night, I promised Valerie that I would carry her secret with me to my grave. And one thing I knew how to do was to keep a promise.

I had kept that promise for sixteen years. And it had not been that hard for me to do. I knew that my knowledge of the crime, and not reporting it, put me somewhere in the vicinity of the guilt. Since Valerie never talked about Mr. Zeke's murder after that night, I didn't know if she had shared her

16

secret with anybody else. And I didn't want to know.

Even though I knew that Valerie's mouth was one of the biggest things on her body, I shared secrets with her, too. A lot of people did. When I shared something with Valerie it was usually something petty — something that a lot of our friends already knew anyway, or would hear from me eventually. But not this time.

Not only was Valerie Proctor my best friend and former roommate, she was one of the most popular bartenders I knew, because her ears were even bigger than her mouth. She was the one person I knew who'd be more than a little interested in my confession, and the only person who would have any sympathy for me. But even before I spilled the beans, I had to ask myself, "Should I be telling this woman my business?" I didn't even have to think about my answer. I had to tell somebody. This was a load I could no longer carry by myself. Besides, what were best friends for?

"Now what's so important you had to drag me away from the comfort of my own place of business, and a possible date with one of the hottest men on the planet this side of Denzel? And it better be good," Valerie warned, her voice half serious, her eyes wide with curiosity. "Girl, I've been itching to hear some juicy news all week. I want to hear some news that is going to make my ears ring."

"Well, I've got some . . ." I said, speaking with hesitation. "And, it's real juicy . . . I think." We occupied a patio table at The Ivy in Beverly Hills.

"Who about? Paris Hilton? Nicole Richie? Lindsay Lohan? Beyoncé? Will Smith? Star Jones? Big-mouthed Rosie O'Donnell?" Valerie served drinks to a lot of celebrities who visited Paw Paw's, the bar she owned in West Hollywood. And it was profitable for her in more ways than one. A lot of the things she heard from the famous and not-so-famous patrons had ended up on the pages of the tabloids. She was well paid by her media contacts, even for something as petty as one of the Lakers leaving a five dollar tip on a hundred dollar tab. "Who? Who?" she said, sounding like an owl. And the way her eyes were stretched open, she looked like one, too.

"Uh . . . me."

Valerie reared back in her seat so far her neck looked like it belonged on a goose. *"You?"* From the expression on her face, there was nothing I could have said that would have disappointed her more. She let out a disgusted sigh and rolled her eyes. "Shit," she mouthed.

"Uh-huh," I muttered. "Me."

"Oh. Whatever, whatever," Valerie said with an exasperated shrug. "Well, what did *you* do, mow somebody down with your Honda and flee the scene?"

I shook my head. "Valerie, I need to talk to you about something I've done. But you have to promise me that you won't ever tell anybody. I . . . I can't keep this to myself any longer," I said, speaking in a low voice. "This is serious. Real serious."

I was glad to see that Valerie seemed more interested now. She held her breath and stared at me for a moment. "Please don't tell me you've got some fatal disease," she squeaked, her eyes full of tears and her lips quivering. "I don't know what I'd do without you!"

I shook my head again. "I'm not going to die," I assured her.

"All right then. I'm listening," she replied, letting out a loud sigh of relief.

CHAPTER 3

Not only was The Ivy our favorite restaurant, but it was a regular hangout for celebrities from the A list to the D list. The only thing that Valerie and I ever ordered was the grilled garden salad. We washed it down with several glasses of Chardonnay. This was the only time that I'd pushed my salad away after just a few bites, but I'd already sucked up two glasses of wine and had just started on the third.

It was April. Even though there was plenty of sun that afternoon, the weather was cool enough for a light jacket. But I had removed my light blue Windbreaker and laid it across my lap. My body temperature always rose when I got nervous, upset, or scared. I was all three. In the hour since we had arrived, I had already soaked up four napkins wiping sweat off my face. This annoyed Valerie.

"Your makeup is beginning to look like a mud pie. Your wig is on sideways, and it looks like a baboon's armpit," Valerie informed me with a smirk. She reached into her straw purse and fished out a small mirror. She held it up to my face, but I waved it away. The way I looked was the least of my concerns.

"So what? Why should I care?" I snarled. I ducked when she leaned forward and tried to straighten the wig on my head.

"Because this is Beverly Hills, not South Central," Valerie snapped. "You can't roam around this neighborhood looking like Aunt Esther from *Sanford and Son* and get away with it."

I ignored Valerie's comment because this was one time that I didn't care what I looked like. "Valerie, I know how hard it is for you to keep secrets. So before I tell you this, I have to know if I can trust you to keep it to yourself."

"Will you stop beating around the damn bush? Now either you shit or get off the toilet. Don't keep me in suspense. Spill the wine, girl! And it better be as sweet as this," Valerie teased, waving her wineglass in my face. She peered into her mirror and patted her hair, securing a few strands back into place with a long bobby pin. "What's the worse thing that could happen . . . if . . ." She stopped and stared at me. She sniffed and returned the mirror to her purse, her eyes still on my face.

"If you blab?" I had to take another sip of my wine before I could continue. Then I said something that really got her attention. "If you blab, they could put me up under the jailhouse. I could even get physically hurt, real bad. If this information gets to the wrong person, my life is over."

I knew that the mention of jail would peak Valerie's interest. She let out a loud gasp and then looked at me as if I were about to reveal the secrets of the universe.

"Jail? Did you kill somebody, too?" she whispered, blinking so fast and hard that her left contact slid to the corner of her eye.

Any reference to killing usually made Valerie nervous. And since jail was one subject that she avoided, I was surprised that she was the one who had brought it up. "No," I mumbled. "I could never do something like that." My answer seemed to relieve her. She exhaled a loud sigh of relief.

"Yeah, I know." Valerie cleared her throat and gave me a pensive look. "So what did you do, Miss Muffet? Uh, are you fucking some other woman's man?" She paused and swooned with anticipation. "You nasty 'ho! No, that's not it! That's not like you. I know! I know! I bet you stole some money from your job!" she hollered, shaking a finger in my hot face. I didn't like the fact that Valerie was not taking a more serious position, and I gave her the kind of look that let her know that. It made her give me an apologetic look. Then she rubbed her contact back into place and continued, talking in a slow, controlled voice. At least she was truly serious now, and that made me feel somewhat more at ease. "Girl, what have you gotten yourself into?"

"That's what I'm trying to tell you," I whimpered.

Valerie swallowed hard and shook her head. "I won't tell anybody. Honest to God," she said, glancing around, then leaning over the table. I could see that she was getting impatient.

"I got married a few months ago," I said, spitting the words out like vomit.

Valerie reared sideways in her chair and gave me an incredulous look. "*Is that all?* Is that what you dragged me over here to tell me? You got married. So what?" she shrieked. "A lot of people renew their vows. How come you are just now telling me this? How come you didn't tell me about this when you did it? Was it Paul's idea?"

"This doesn't involve Paul," I muttered. "Well, in a way it does . . ." I said with a sheepish grin.

"Look, Lo, I don't know about you, but there are a lot of things on my agenda for today," Valerie said, looking at her watch, and then back at me with her eyes narrowed. "One thing I don't have time for is playing games. What you have said so far doesn't make a whole lot of sense. At least not to me. You married Paul umpteen years ago. I was there when it happened. Now did you get a divorce and not tell me? Did you marry somebody else — and not tell me that either?"

I shook my head. "You remember Floyd?" I asked in a stiff voice. I had a hard time getting the words out of my mouth. "He was the brother who was going to take me to the prom . . . that night."

Valerie gulped so hard she shuddered. Then she cleared her throat and dabbed at her lips with her napkin. Her eyes darkened, and her jaw twitched. She blinked and lifted her chin until she was looking at me with the lids of her eyes half closed. "Does this have anything to do with what happened on . . . *prom night?*" she whispered, leaning over the table so far her titties touched the lettuce on her plate.

I shook my head again. "Valerie, we are not supposed to talk about that," I reminded, still shaking my head. "I know you don't want to, and I don't want to either. Never," I said. She looked even more relieved. "This has to do with Floyd."

"Floyd Watson that used to live on Baylor Street?" Valerie gave me a confused look and a tentative nod. She coughed to clear her throat, and then she blinked hard a few times. "That Floyd?"

I nodded. "That Floyd. The one that went to . . ."

It took a lot to make Valerie uncomfortable, and it bothered me to know that when that happened, I was usually the one responsible. She sucked in a loud breath and finished my sentence. *"Jail."* It was one thing for me to mention jail. That was painful enough for Valerie. But when she mentioned the word herself, her face looked like it wanted to crack. "He's in jail for life."

I shook my head. "Not anymore. He was innocent. Just like he said he was, and just like I tried to tell everybody. He didn't rape and kill that girl, because he was with me when it happened. DNA got him off, and he will be getting paid big time by the state for all those years he spent locked up. It was all over the news. He will be getting out of prison soon; maybe even tomorrow." I didn't know why I was whispering. Other

than our waiter, nobody else seemed interested in Valerie and me, anyway.

"What about Floyd? Why are you bringing him up after all these years?" Valerie
sighed and looked around. With her head
tilted to the side, she looked at me out of
the corner of her eye. Even when she was
angry, with a scowl on her face that could
scare the devil, Valerie was one of the pretti-
est black women I knew. And L.A. was full
of pretty black women. A stunning up-and-
coming model and two glamorous actresses
from a popular television show occupied a
table just a few feet from ours. But neither
one of them was as attractive as Valerie. The
thick black hair that she usually kept in a
ponytail like her favorite singer, Sade, was
all hers. But she had purchased the green
eyes from Bausch & Lomb and her tall,
sculptured body from three different Beverly
Hills plastic surgeons. With her sparkling
white, capped teeth and a face that any
model or actress would have died to have,
she still was not satisfied with the way she
looked. She had recently started threatening
to get her nose done. I didn't tell her but
she already looked more like Tyra Banks
than Tyra Banks. People told her that all the
time. But she was still the most insecure
female I knew.

I didn't look like a famous model or any one of the beautiful Hollywood actresses we had to compete with, but I was happy with the way I looked. I watched what I ate and I ran five times a week, so my body was in pretty good shape. I had no need for plastic surgery, but I did own several Wonderbras. My hair was a little too thin and unruly, so I owned several wigs and hairpieces. My paper-bag brown face was average without makeup, but I knew how to work with what I had. Despite my shortcomings, I had enough confidence for myself and Valerie. She never had a bad time when she was with me. Which was one of the many reasons we had been best friends for more than twenty-five years.

I poked my fork around in my salad. My lips were pressed together so hard it felt like they'd been glued shut. My hesitance was causing Valerie even more aggravation.

"Look, woman, I love you to death and you are my girl, but you are working my last nerve up in here today. You better hurry up and tell me the whole story." Valerie paused and looked at her watch again. "In about forty-five minutes I'm going to give up and go on back to my own bar where I can get me some real drinks." She frowned and took a sip from her wineglass.

"I married Floyd," I said sharply.

Valerie's mouth dropped open and her eyes got wide. She suddenly looked so stiff, it looked as if everything on her had turned to stone. Even her eyes. She didn't even blink as she stared at me for several moments before she spoke again. "The same man who went to prison for life for rape and murder?"

I gave her a sheepish look and a nervous nod.

"Uh, I don't think I heard right," Valerie said, slapping the side of her head with the palm of her hand. "Can you say that again?"

I folded my arms and tilted my head to the side as if preparing myself for a verbal showdown. "I married Floyd," I repeated. This time I made the statement with a little more conviction. "The same man who went to prison for life for rape and murder."

CHAPTER 4

"I did hear you right the first time?" Valerie tossed her napkin onto the table and stared at me in slack-jawed amazement. "Girl, what's wrong with you?"

"Nothing is wrong with me," I insisted, giving her the most defiant look I could manage. "I married a man I love."

"When?"

I dipped my head and hesitated. Then I blinked hard and looked up at Valerie, forcing myself to smile. "I'd been visiting him in the prison almost every month since he went in. Uh, he was that 'sick friend' in that mental clinic you and everybody else thought I was visiting. There was no sick friend in a mental clinic," I admitted with a heavy sigh. "A few years ago he hooked up with a new lawyer and he set it up for us to get married in the, um, prison chapel. At the time I thought it was the least I could do for Floyd to make his situation a little better. It was what he wanted . . ."

"Shit!" Valerie shook her head and slapped the side of it. Mumbling gibberish, she dipped her napkin into her water glass then used it to dab at her forehead. "Girl, you've got me sweating like an ox up in this place!" she exclaimed.

"Well, I can't help that," I mumbled, tapping the tips of my fingers on the table. I had to take a few deep breaths to restore my composure. I couldn't feel anything from the waist down. I rearranged my numb ass in my seat and crossed my legs. Next thing I knew, I was itching and sweating just about everywhere. I wiped my face with my napkin.

Valerie continued to stare at me with her mouth hanging open and her eyes stretched open so wide, I thought her contacts were going to pop out. "You married Floyd Watson. What I want to know is *why?*"

"You know how it was before he went to . . . uh, got in that trouble. He was the only man I'd ever been with at the time, and the only one I ever wanted to be with for the rest of my life. We were going to get married."

"What about Paul? How did he take it? And when did you get a divorce? How come you are just now telling me?" Valerie asked, speaking so fast her sentences ran together.

"Paul doesn't know about this! I still love him and I don't want to lose him. . . ."

"How in the fuck did you think you could pull this off, girl?"

I shrugged. "I didn't think that Floyd would ever get out of prison!" I wailed. "And . . . and other prisoners were getting married left and right. Even that Richard Ramirez — the Night Stalker! He really did kill somebody — tons of people! And was happy to admit it! I thought that if a devil like Ramirez could hook up a marriage, why couldn't an innocent man like Floyd enjoy the same privilege?"

Valerie looked at me with such a horrified expression on her face, you would have thought that I'd just sprouted a beard. "I can't believe my ears. You are married to two men at the same time!" Valerie hollered. The people at the tables on both sides of us turned to listen. "That's bigamy, girl. You could . . . Do you know what could happen to you if you get caught?"

"I know," I said with my head bowed and throbbing. "But I won't get caught. Not if I watch my step and you watch my back. I just had to tell you because, uh, things are getting kind of messy. It looks like I am going to need you to help me pull this off."

"What . . . what do you want me to . . . to do?" Valerie stuttered. She hunched her shoulders and gave me a hopeless look. She lowered her voice to a hoarse whisper. "How can I help you pull off this mess?"

"Don't worry. I am not asking you to do that much, yet. Right now, all I need is for you to help me make it look like I've moved back into your house. That's all. I need a decoy place to hide in case Paul surprises me with one of his visits, like he did last month."

"You need a what?"

"A fake residence."

"What the fuck is a fake residence?"

"A place that looks like I live there. Look," I said, holding up my hand. "If you don't want to get involved in this, that's fine. I understand."

"You stop right there," Valerie ordered, holding her hand up like she wanted me to talk to it. "I'm already involved." I was surprised, but happy when she flashed me a smile. "You are still my girl, for better or worse," she told me, shaking a finger in my face.

"That works both ways you know," I said with a quick nod.

"What about your place on Manchester? The one you share with your, uh, other husband, Paul."

I let out a deep sigh and a groan. "I'll keep some of my shit there and some at your place."

"And you will keep some of your shit up there in the Bay Area condo that you share with Paul, too?"

"That's right."

"Look, I don't know if you are clowning me or what. But if you are telling me the truth, I'd like to know how long you think you can get away with this?" Valerie let out a sharp laugh, then she gave me one of the most serious looks I'd ever seen on her face. "You are telling me the truth, aren't you?"

This time I looked at my watch. "Like I just said, if you don't want to get involved, just say so. I'll figure out something. But I have to know now. Paul and Floyd are both getting a little too nosy. They want to know all my business about what I do when I'm not with them. I've had a few close calls. If I don't watch my step, and get you to watch my back, things are going to get real messy."

Valerie reared back so far this time, the chair almost tipped over. Then she clucked her tongue like a setting hen and looked at me in such a peculiar way, it seemed like she could see straight through me. "I got news for you, Dolores Reese, or whatever the hell your last name is these days." She paused and gave me a hot look. "From what you've told me so far, it sounds like things are already messy," Valerie informed me with a nod.

CHAPTER 5

I had been acquainted with Valerie Proctor longer than any of my other friends. She was the first one to welcome me to the neighborhood when Viola and Luther Mason took me into their lovely home on Baylor Street in one of L.A.'s nicest mixed, lower middle-class neighborhoods. I was seven at the time. Valerie was just a couple of months older than me. But she seemed a lot older. She had a mature quality about her that my foster mother called "disturbing." She even went so far as to predict that Valerie would be my downfall some day, if I didn't "feed her with a long-handled spoon." But my foster mother's words went in one ear and out the other. Valerie was my best friend forever, my BFF, as they say in the tabloids that she was so fond of. As for her leading me to my downfall, well, as far as I was concerned, my birth had been my downfall. The only direction I could go was up. Before Valerie entered my life, all of my friends had been foster kids with issues only other foster kids could relate to, like me. It was refreshing to have a friend who was part of a "real" family.

I never knew exactly what Valerie's mother did for a living other than the fact that she worked in a bar in West Hollywood called Paw Paw's that Valerie's grandfather owned. But everybody knew what her stepfather did. Mr. Zeke was a policeman, and he was one of the scariest men alive — the boogie man in living color. His head was big and round. It seemed like the perfect place for his homely moonface and jowls so plump it looked like he had a permanent case of the mumps. On top of all that, he had the nerve to wear a goatee sometimes — which didn't make him look any better, or worse. His mother was a humongous black woman from the hills of Mississippi. She'd met Zeke's father, a Samoan man who was even bigger than she was, when she was working for the Peace Corps and stationed in the South Pacific. According to Mr. Zeke, his father had come from one of the most war-like tribes in Samoa. I had decided that this information vaguely explained his violent nature.

After Mr. Zeke's daddy died, his mama

returned to the States with Zeke and raised him on her own. Being the son of parents who were one step from Bigfoot, it was no wonder Zeke was so humongous. The man was so tall he had to lean forward every time he walked through a door, and when he sat down, his legs looked like logs. His hands looked like little shovels. He had skin that was so rough and weather-beaten that it was hard to tell his original shade. But I realized that at one time he'd been very light skinned. One day when I was being nosy, I peeped through our bathroom keyhole when he was visiting my foster parents and I saw him standing over the commode holding a dick that was so fair in color it looked like it belonged on a white man. His shiny black eyes were so tight I used to wonder how he could see out of them. They looked like slits.

"Whatever you do, don't make Zeke mad, or he'll get crazy," Valerie warned me. It was a few days after she'd come to my new home to introduce herself and invite me to splash around with her in the paddling pool that Mr. Zeke had put in the backyard. She lived two doors down from where I lived with the Masons.

The Masons had a nice house, a two-story beige stucco with a lemon tree in the front yard. But it was nothing compared to the

37

large white house Valerie lived in. That had a lot to do with the fact that I chose to spend so much time there.

"You call your daddy by his name?" I asked, excited because I'd been anxious to make some new friends. "I wish I had a daddy," I whined. "If I did, I wouldn't call him by his name like you do."

"*That man* is not my real daddy! Zeke adopted us a long time ago and changed our last name from Burriss to Proctor," Valerie said quickly, and with a severe scowl on her face. "My real daddy got hit by a train coming home from work one night. His name was Alex, and that's the name I'm going to give my first child, whether it's a boy or a girl." It was so hot that day that I remember watching beads of sweat slide down the sides of Valerie's angry face like little pebbles. "Where your real mama and daddy at?" she asked, wiping her face. Her long honey brown legs looked good in her crisp white shorts. I felt pretty dowdy standing next to her in my baggy blue jeans with the legs rolled up to halfway my knobby, ashy knees.

I shrugged and turned away so that she could not see the tears in my eyes. I had very little memory of what had happened in my life before the Masons rescued me. But

I'd heard enough to know that I was lucky it was all behind me now.

My missing-in-action biological mother was raised in a house where everybody from her grandparents to her and her siblings drank alcohol like it was water. She took off when she was fifteen and lived on the streets before turning herself in to the authorities. While she was in one of many foster homes, she got pregnant with me. I was born in the backseat of a car that she and her boyfriend had carjacked earlier that night. I spent my first four months living in that car with my mother and her man. I knew all of this because before she disappeared from my life, she told me certain things that she thought I should know. Most of the information she shared with me did me more harm then good. I probably would have enjoyed life more had I not known some of the details of my early life.

Anyway, Mama told me that from the stolen car, we moved into somebody's garage where we lived until somebody burned it to the ground. From there we moved into an abandoned school bus that sat behind an old warehouse in East L.A. I can remember guzzling beer from a baby bottle, and then pissing so much that my Pampers had holes in the crotch by the time somebody changed me.

One morning, still slightly drunk, I woke up in a bed in a room with so much white — the walls, the bedding, the white people standing over me dressed in white — I thought that I had died and gone to heaven. It didn't take long for me to realize I was in a hospital room. And from there, a foster home.

I never saw my mother again until several years and a couple of foster homes later. It happened one Saturday afternoon when I was out shopping in a mall with Viola for some feminine products that I needed. I'd just gotten my period for the first time and was looking forward to a new phase in my life. I felt good about everything and myself that warm sunny day, until I spotted my mother. I couldn't even remember her name, but she had a face that I could never forget. Because I saw that same face every time I looked in a mirror — the large, sad brown eyes and shy smile, a smile that only made cameo appearances at the time.

The years had not been good to Mama. She was still a young woman in her early thirties, but with her glassy eyes, stringy hair, wrinkled face, and scattered brown teeth she looked like an old crone from a mummy's tomb. Somehow she had developed a noticeable hump on her back. She had gained at least sixty or seventy pounds. Compared to the last time I saw her, the extra weight made her look well fed if nothing else. Being so plump seemed like an odd thing for a homeless person, especially with the way they ate things they fished out Dumpsters or off the ground.

Dressed in rags and holding a tin can with a hand that looked like a claw, my mother wobbled up from a bench at a bus stop and staggered over to the shiny new Buick Viola and I had just climbed out of. I hid behind Viola as she dropped a few coins into the can. I never shopped in that mall again, and I never saw my mother again after that painful day. But I saw her in my dreams, and every time I looked in a mirror.

CHAPTER 6

Despite my traumatic early years, I had an outgoing personality, so it was fairly easy for me to make friends. In addition to Valerie Proctor and a few other kids in the neighborhood, I had a lot of friends who were also in foster care. That was important to me because I liked knowing kids who had endured experiences similar to mine. I bonded faster with them than I did with kids who lived with their biological families. Valerie was an exception. It didn't take long for me to feel as if I'd known her all my life.

The Masons were elderly people who had never been able to have children of their own. I was the only foster child in their home. But before me, they had opened their arms and hearts to half a dozen other neglected and abused kids. And they associated with a lot of other couples who took in foster kids. I preferred the company of other girls, but there was one boy I'd met at church who stayed on my mind for days after I'd met him. His name was Floyd Watson, and he was also in a foster home.

Floyd was an average-looking boy with bronze skin and curly, reddish brown hair. But when he smiled he looked quite handsome with his round brown eyes and full lips. The problem was, he rarely smiled. Like me. Knowing that we had something in common made me smile. Unfortunately, from what I'd heard, he didn't have much to smile about. I knew from Valerie, the church gossips, and my foster parents that Floyd had been horribly abused throughout his fifteen years. The first time I saw him, he had a cast on one arm and bandages practically all over his face from injuries that he'd sustained during a stay in a previous foster home.

"His mother was a prostitute and his daddy was one of her tricks. She lived with a drug dealer for a while, and they used to make Floyd do drug runs, wearing a bulletproof vest," Valerie whispered to me in church one boring Sunday afternoon. Floyd sat on the end of the pew across the aisle, looking like he didn't have a friend in the world. "And that frump sitting next to him is his latest foster mother, Glodine Banks. She's a bitch on wheels," Valerie hissed.

"Damn," I mouthed. "Well, at least Miss Glodine seems like a nice-enough woman. Bringing him to church and all," I added. *Nice* was one word that was rarely used to describe Glodine. Not only was she a nosy busybody, she talked about everybody she knew like a dog. Unlike Valerie, who ran a close second to Glodine as the biggest gossip in our neighborhood, Glodine was a straight-up troublemaker. She had been known to call up the welfare people and report the cheats. And even I knew that the only reason she took in foster kids was to get paid. But according to Viola, there was a reason for Glodine's bitterness. She had lost all three of her children a few years ago. While she was enjoying a cookout at a neighbor's house, her kids had hidden themselves in an abandoned refrigerator while playing hide-and-seek with the neighbor's kids. When the kids never came out from their hiding place, everybody started looking for them. Three hours later, they found them in the refrigerator, dead from asphyxiation. Glodine had had a hysterectomy, so she couldn't have any more children. Viola insisted that Glodine's nasty ways were how she hid her grief and shame. I felt sorry for the woman, but Valerie still thought she was a witch.

"That witch? Nice my ass. She is a sex-pot!" Valerie cupped her hand to whisper in my ear. "I heard she used to sell pussy when she was young. I guess now that she looks like the Creature from the Black Lagoon, she has to get her nookie anywhere she can. That thang she married must be sleeping on his job."

"What do you mean by that?" I asked.

Valerie rolled her eyes, rotated her neck, and gave me an exasperated look. At the same time, she seemed to be enjoying her position. "Everybody knows that Glodine gets jiggy with her foster sons. Just the big, cute ones, though. She must be in hog heaven with a hunk like Floyd living under her roof. And from what I can see when he wears them tight jeans, he's got a big dick that any grown woman would like to get her skanky hands on. That nasty-ass bitch." Valerie snickered, covering her mouth with both hands and flashing me a smug look.

I gave Valerie a sharp look and shook my head. "Miss Glodine molests her foster sons? Floyd is kind of cute, though, so I can understand her not being able to keep her hands off him."

"Uh-huh." Valerie nodded. "I heard that from three or four different people, so it must be true. That many people wouldn't go around telling the same lie."

"Can't she go to jail for that?" I wailed. Two middle-aged sisters in front of us turned around and gave us dirty looks so we lowered our voices.

"Girl, please," Valerie quipped, snapping her fingers. "Black kids don't have a chance in this world. I live in the same house with a cop, and he is just as bad as any of these other motherfuckers, if not worse."

"Dang. It's bad enough when a girl gets molested, but it must be hella bad for a boy," I said with a muffled groan.

"And that husband of Glodine's has his way with all the foster girls. Everybody on the block knows about it. The last three girls that was there, all three of them got pregnant with his babies and Glodine fixed them up. I heard that heifer used a coat hanger."

"I didn't know any of that shit," I admitted. "Can't somebody do something to make her stop? Like calling the police?"

"Well, I know it hasn't been going on for too long. At least not with Floyd. That brother is hardly some everyday punk. That boy is from Crenshaw, and he's still in touch with some of his boys. Sooner or later, they will take care of that old bitch. You know the Crips don't play. And if I was you, I wouldn't get involved with somebody that's got so much going against him."

I didn't hear the rest of Reverend Carter's sermon that day, and I had stopped listening to Valerie. But as soon as church let out, I went up to Floyd and invited him to my house, which was a few doors down the block and across the street. I couldn't tell if he was surprised or annoyed because he looked at me with such contempt I flinched.

"Boy, where your manners at? Be nice!" Miss Glodine barked, giving Floyd a nudge with her elbow. He looked down, so I looked down. Seeing his cheap pants with the legs several inches too short and his shabby shoes, I truly felt sorry for him.

"Any dudes over there I can kick it with?" he muttered, chewing on a toothpick. Behind Miss Glodine stood her two cute but sad-faced teenage foster daughters and her lanky, mule-faced husband. In his vomit-colored suit and greasy hair, he looked like a snake-oil salesman. From the smug look on his face and the way he seemed to be guarding the two girls, I had no trouble believing that he was a pervert.

"Not yet. But I got a lot of games and stuff," I said proudly. "You like Pac-Man? I got that."

Before responding, Floyd looked at Miss Glodine and she answered for him. "This

47

boy got enough of a mess on his hands without you getting him caught up in some of your mess," she said. "I know how you little heifers pick out a handsome boy like Floyd so you can get yourself pregnant and on the welfare. Floyd, don't you be no fool. Do you hear me, boy?" I couldn't believe that this was the same woman who had just told Floyd to "be nice" to me.

"Yes, ma'am," Floyd muttered.

I gasped. The two teenage girls gave me pitiful looks, and Glodine's husband snickered and moved even closer to the older of the two girls.

"Come on, Lo. It stinks up in here," Valerie said, pulling me toward the door. "Let's go to my house where we can have some fun."

I followed Valerie to her house, dragging my feet like they weighed ten pounds apiece. But I didn't stay long. Mr. Zeke was on a rampage. As soon as we entered the living room, we saw him dragging Miss Naomi across the floor by her hair like a caveman.

"You son of a bitch! Turn my mama aloose!" Valerie screamed. Then she shot across the floor like a bullet and started beating Mr. Zeke on his back and head with her fists.

"Girl, have you lost what was left of your

mind or what?" he roared. With one hand still holding Valerie's mother by the hair, he raised his other hand and hit Valerie hard across the face. She stumbled and crashed into the wall with so much force that every picture on the wall, and a huge wall clock, crashed to the floor.

CHAPTER 7

An ambulance took Valerie's mother to the hospital that same evening, and I didn't see Valerie again for several days. Neither she nor her two younger siblings came to school, or even out of the house. When I finally did see her in church the following Sunday, I was stunned and upset by what she told me, and by what I saw.

"Zeke made Mama say she fell down the steps," Valerie sobbed through clenched teeth. Her left eye was swollen and bloodshot. I didn't ask and she didn't tell me, but I knew that she'd also taken a few more hits from Mr. Zeke for trying to help her mother.

Valerie and I usually occupied the same pew every Sunday, but this time Floyd and his foster family had beaten us to it. We sat behind them, whispering as Reverend Carter preached so hard that the veins in his neck and forehead looked like coils. I enjoyed going to church every Sunday, but not for the same reasons as most of the congregation. The choir had so many people singing off-key, it was a real treat to hear them. It reminded me of *The Gong Show* reruns. When our frenzied preacher's preaching got real intense, he flapped his arms as if he was about to take off flying. So that was another treat. And attending church gave me a chance to gaze at Floyd Watson.

"What about you? I know you didn't tell them that you fell down the stairs," I said to Valerie, looking at the back of Floyd's head out of the corner of my eye. He was chewing gum so his ears were wiggling, until Glodine gave him a mean look.

My foster parents occupied the same pew with Floyd and his family. I had to talk in a real low voice because the one thing Viola and Luther didn't tolerate was me being disrespectful in the Lord's house.

"I didn't tell anybody anything. It only makes things worse. Last week Zeke slapped my little brother so hard he vomited. All because he didn't take out the trash when he was supposed to. I told my gym teacher. A social worker came to the house and took Zeke and Mama into the kitchen and talked to them. I don't know what all they talked about, but they came back into the living room laughing and slapping each other on the back. 'You know how clumsy kids is . . . and how they like to tell lies to get attention,' Zeke was saying to the social worker. My little brother is just nine years old and just learning about things. There is nothing a child that young can do to get beaten like that."

"But what about your mama? Can't she say something to get people to believe her?"

"He's a cop, Lo. He's got guns, and handcuffs, and pepper spray and shit. He can do whatever he wants to do to me, my mama, and anybody else. Last night during dinner when my little sister Liz took a pork chop without asking, he handcuffed her to her chair. She was still there when we got up this morning."

"Shit! She slept handcuffed to a chair all night?"

Valerie nodded. "She couldn't get to the bathroom during the night, so she wet herself. She got a whupping this morning for doing that!" Valerie paused and stared off into space. From the look on her face, there was no telling what kinds of thoughts were running through her head.

Still staring off into space, she started talking again, speaking real slow. "Nobody can speak against him and get away with it. He brags about all the heads he's cracked when him and the rest of those rogue cops go after somebody. One time I heard him talking out on our back porch with some of his cop buddies. He was bragging about how he makes the hookers that work on his beat suck his dick and break him off a few hundred dollars a week. A lot of the cops in this town do that same shit. They plant drugs and stolen property on gangbangers, and they even shoot the ones they really want to get rid of."

I gave Valerie a thoughtful look. "Has he ever . . . you know?"

"I know what?"

"Has he ever done anything nasty to you or your little sister?" From the look on Valerie's face I had a feeling that my question offended her.

"No. Hell, no," she said quickly. "What makes you think he's ever done that?"

I gave my shoulders a hearty shrug. "He's done everything else. I figured if he's so mean and nasty that he makes prostitutes suck his dick, what's to stop him from doing the same thing, or something worse, to you and your baby sister."

"Well, all I can say is that he hasn't. At least not yet." Valerie reached for a hymnal in the pocket on the back of the pew in front of us and started fanning her face. She glanced at Floyd and nudged me with her elbow. "Guess what? Your boy busted Rosie Graham's cherry at Bobby Baker's birthday party last night."

I stared at Valerie with wide-eyed interest. "It should have been me." I swooned.

Valerie jabbed me in my side with her elbow. "Don't worry. Your day is coming. Anyway, Floyd did the deed like a pro. They were all over that couch in Bobby's rec room."

"Who told you that he did that?" I asked with a hopeful sigh. Three old ladies gave me dirty looks and motioned for me to shut up. "Who told you that?" I whispered, leaning so close to Valerie I could smell her sweat. That, combined with her cheap perfume, reminded me of a fragrance my mother used to wear called Bitches Brew. I remember her spraying my soiled ass with that shit when I was a toddler when she didn't feel like washing me properly. All of a sudden my nose started itching and I let out a few sneezes that were so aggressive, it felt like somebody had punched me in my nose.

"I was there and seen the whole thing. Me and Iris Cunningham followed them when they left the party room. I guess after he's had to wallow up on top of Glodine's nasty lumpy body, getting some pussy his own age must be a real treat to him. You don't watch your step, he'll be busting you, too."

I shook my head and giggled. "I don't think so."

"I wish you would make up your mind! I thought you just said it should have been you he busted at that party," Valerie snapped, covering her mouth to keep from laughing.

"Oh! I did say that, didn't I? Oh well. But I don't care what I have to do, I am not going to end up the way my mama did. Or like a lot of other women like her." I turned to look in Floyd's direction. At about the same time, he turned to look at me and our eyes met. He was looking at me like I was the most beautiful girl in the world. And for the first time in my life, that was exactly how I felt.

CHAPTER 8

Floyd and I were the same age and we attended the same school, but he was not in any of my classes. His two foster sisters were so mentally slow that they had to attend special education classes in a school halfway across town. They rode on a short, bright orange school bus that picked them up at a spot in front of my house. Some days Floyd escorted the two girls to the bus stop and then waited with them until they got on the bus. He did that to protect them from the neighborhood bullies who had already knocked them down and snatched their lunches from them a few times. Knowing that Floyd cared about people enough to fight for them made me want him even more. Every morning before I went to school, I watched from my upstairs bedroom window as all three of them lugged their cheap, shabby backpacks decorated with outdated cartoon characters and jelly stains to the bus stop. The backpacks were bad enough. But they all carried greasy brown-bag lunches because that greedy-ass Glodine was too stingy to spend more of the money she got from the state on them.

My dear, sweet old foster parents led such dull lives that they got slaphappy whenever somebody came to visit them. Three days before my sixteenth birthday, I galloped downstairs and there was Floyd, sitting at the dining room table playing Chinese checkers with Luther. As soon as his eyes met mine, I started trembling in my tracks.

I was surprised to see Floyd spending his time with a man old enough to be his grandfather. The fact that he did something this ordinary and *uncool* made me like him even more. I expected a boy like him to be somewhere kicking it and getting whacked on weed with his homeboys. That was the moment when I realized I had a serious crush on Floyd, and I planned to do something about it.

Viola was beside herself. Judging from the sweet aroma coming from the kitchen, I knew that she had baked some of her ten-minute tea cakes. And I knew that she was going to practically shove a few of those damn things down Floyd's throat. She didn't know, and I wasn't going to tell her, but my foster father had told me several times that Floyd had to force himself to eat those damn tea cakes. The boy had my sympathy because I went through the same thing at least three times a week. Every time I emptied the trash can in my bedroom, it was usually half full of stale tea cakes.

"Dolores child, Mother said to tell you to fold and put away the laundry before you leave this house," Luther told me, not even looking up from his game. Luther didn't shave every day or comb what was left of the wiry gray hair on the sides and back of his head. He had a few suits and other nice pieces of clothing that he wore only to church and when he had to pay a visit to one of his three doctors. He wore a red-and-black flannel shirt and overalls most of the time, and a pair of old house shoes. He looked like a bum sitting next to Floyd, who had on a crisp white shirt and black pants. If Valerie had not told me, I never would have suspected that Floyd was being abused by his foster mother. With his strong-looking young body, he looked like he could whup Mike Tyson with one hand behind his back.

"Hey, Lo," Floyd said with a smile and a wave. "Wassup?"

"Um, nothing," I muttered dumbly, shuffling my feet like a stooge. "I see you in school and in church all the time," I added, stumbling through the room trying to get to the laundry room without running into a wall. "Uh, can I go to Valerie's house when I finish the laundry?" I asked my foster father, my eyes still on Floyd.

"You can go anywhere you wanna go as long as you do what Mother said for you to do," Luther said, still not looking up from his game. This was as stern as Luther ever got with me. He had never looked, touched, or said anything inappropriate to me. I knew other girls in foster care who had been raped so many times by the men and boys in some of the houses they landed in, they thought it was normal. Sweet Luther was everything that I'd wanted in the father I never had. I was more than a little blessed. It saddened me to know that Valerie had to live with an asshole like Mr. Zeke when I had a man like Luther — and all to myself at that. The only good thing about Luther and Viola being so old and worn out was that they didn't think they could handle but one foster child. "And don't worry about them tea cakes. Me and Floyd will leave you a few," Luther assured me with a devilish grin. He couldn't stand those damn things any more than Floyd or I could, but nobody had the heart to tell Viola.

"That's nice," I muttered. It pleased me to see Floyd shoot me a conspiratorial glance as he nodded toward a saucer on the table with pebble-size crumbs scattered around on it like a beaded halo. He cleared his throat and nodded toward the waste-paper can in the corner by the living room door. The more I saw this boy, the more I liked him.

I was glad Luther didn't look at me because I didn't want him to see me walking backward, grinning at Floyd until I got out of the room. Floyd's eyes stayed on me until I was out of sight.

I folded and put away the laundry and by the time I got back to the dining room, Floyd was gone. Luther was outside fiddling around under the hood of the old Ford he'd bought from one of his friends, and Viola was across the street at the church for choir practice.

Luther looked up as I skipped across the lawn toward Valerie's house. "You take care of that laundry like I told you?" he wanted to know. He didn't even give me a chance to answer. "You better get back in the house before dark. This is a school night." I didn't bother to respond because he had already returned his gaze to his car. "And if that Zeke gets loose, you better get to running,

60

girl," Luther advised, trying to sound harsh, which he could not have done convincingly even with a gun aimed at his head.

Despite his gentle nature, Luther tried to be "tough" with me from time to time, but it wasn't necessary. I did everything I was supposed to do, and I had enough respect for him and Viola to hide the things I did that I knew they wouldn't like, like smoking an occasional joint in the backyard or sucking up a few beers. The only thing they had a problem with was my frequent visits to Valerie's house because of Mr. Zeke. Everybody on the block knew what a monster Mr. Zeke was when it came to Valerie and the rest of her family. And, according to Valerie, he had more enemies than Saddam Hussein. The running joke was that if something fatal happened to Mr. Zeke, the list of suspects would be as long as a yardstick. And he knew that. As a matter of fact, he made jokes about it, too. "If a civil war ever breaks out in L.A., they'll be shooting at me from every side." He always laughed when he said stupid shit like that, but he was probably right.

With the exception of Mr. Zeke, Luther and Viola got along well with everybody, as far as I could tell. They had a few relatives who they enjoyed spending time with, which to my everlasting horror included a nephew who was more interested in what Viola and Luther were going to leave him when they died. Since they'd never had any children of their own, they had a soft spot for this nephew. And that sucker played those two kind and wonderful people like a piano. I knew for a fact that everything except the house — which the greedy nephew was going to inherit — was to be divided equally among all surviving relatives. The house was no palace, and with the exception of the new bedroom suite that they'd bought for me, all the rest of the contents were almost as old as Viola and Luther. Sadly, I'd overheard a few rude relatives admit that there was nothing in the house that they'd want. As far as I knew, I'd get nothing other than what was already mine. That didn't bother me because I didn't expect anything, anyway. I had no right to. The Masons' love, and the fact that they had given me a nice home, was more than enough.

I enjoyed living with Viola and Luther and I prayed that I'd be able to live with them until I turned eighteen and could do as I pleased. I wasn't worried about the social services removing me and placing me in another home, even though that was a possibility. My biggest concern was the fact that the Masons were in their midseventies and not in the best of health. I didn't know if they'd be around for another two years. Sadly, I found out a couple of hours later that Luther wouldn't.

It was Floyd who came to Valerie's house to tell me that he had returned to my house to deliver some tools that Luther wanted to borrow. He'd found Luther stretched out on the ground in the driveway, clutching his chest.

"I hope he's going to be all right. He's the closest I ever came to having a daddy," I moaned, trying to sound brave as Floyd escorted me back to my house. Instead of walking on the sidewalk, we trespassed on the elderly Scotts' property, trampling the neat lawn that they spent a lot of their retirement money and time on. Out of the corner of my eye I saw Mr. Scott peeping out of his upstairs window with a horrified look on his face. As usual, I ignored that old man. There was another old man on my mind who was a lot more important to me. "I don't know what me and Viola would do without him," I added.

I didn't realize that Floyd had his arm around my shoulder until we reached my front porch. The paramedics had already come and gone with Luther's body in tow.

Sister Oralee Crockett, a stout motherly woman from the church, was in the house, crying and about to dial the telephone. She put the telephone back into its cradle as soon as she saw me. It was a struggle for Sister Oralee, but between sobs she managed to tell me that Luther's sudden passing had upset Viola so much, a second ambulance had been called for her.

"Lord have mercy! We gwine to have to dig *two* graves!" Sister Crockett wailed.

"They're both dead?" I cried, pulling away from Floyd. He was right behind me, stepping on my heels as I ran across the living room floor. "What's going to happen to me now?" I hollered, looking at Floyd. I was frantic, and it showed on my face. My reaction startled him. "I have nobody now," I said in a hoarse voice. "Where will I go?"

Floyd looked at me. Then he put his arms around me and started rubbing my back. I knew right then and there that this was real love, and it was mine for the taking.

CHAPTER 9

Viola survived the mild heart attack that she'd suffered immediately after she'd been told about Luther. However, she was in no shape to attend his funeral. But the way some of their relatives behaved, you would have thought that she had died, too. As soon as they had been notified, they descended upon the house like locusts. Vehicles with out-of-town license plates sat in front of the house in a crooked line that stretched two blocks long. This clumsy caravan included everything from a shiny, new, white Cadillac from Texas to a low-riding, fish-tailed jalopy with an Arkansas license plate, with a piece of wire holding one door shut.

I already knew that Viola's relatives didn't get along that well with Luther's relatives. The tension in the house was as thick as a bowl of paste, and I was stuck smack-dab in the middle. Me, an outsider if ever there was one. None of the relatives had accepted me. If anything, I was treated like a servant. One greasy-mouthed relative after another ordered me to perform one menial task after another. I had to trot into the kitchen and bring this one a glass of water and that one a piece of pecan pie. I had to sew a button back onto one's coat. I even had to "smash" some potatoes for one of those greedy bitches who hadn't stopped eating since she walked in the door.

One of the reasons I looked forward to getting married and having a family of my own was so I could truly feel like I belonged somewhere, and to somebody. I knew from talking with other foster kids that until we had real homes of our own, we would always feel like intruders on some level. Despite my situation, I was one of the lucky ones. Before Luther and Viola I had experienced two other foster homes. I had never felt comfortable in either one of them. Even though I had not been neglected or abused, I'd felt displaced and in the way. Like an ugly old piece of furniture that nobody wanted but kept because they didn't know what else to do with it. And even having to deal with the fools that I had to deal with now, I was still in the best place that I had ever been before in my life.

One of the things that made my current

situation so bearable was right across the street. And that thing was Floyd. I prayed that the case workers would leave me alone. I didn't know what I would do if they snatched me away from Viola and dumped me into another home. That's why I promised myself that I would tolerate Viola and Luther's crazy relatives no matter what.

The situation that was playing itself out in Viola's house like a warped record reminded me of a visit to the San Diego Zoo with my previous foster parents. I felt like I was in the wild kingdom. A jungle. One of the more beastly inhabitants was Noble Coleman — and what kind of name was that? — Viola's greedy, scheming nephew. He was without a doubt the biggest thorn in my side. That thirty-year-old booger had been sitting around for years waiting for Luther and Viola to die so he could get his claws on the deed to their house. He had the nerve to mosey on over a few hours before Luther's funeral to go through Luther's clothes. "I might be able to get a few pennies for Uncle's suits at the flea market," Noble announced, his voice sounding like a frog's croak.

"What about that old La-Z-Boy he was so fond of? And them end tables he made? You want that, too?" asked Glodine, wearing a tight navy blue dress and a matching turban. As big a bitch and sex fiend as Valerie claimed Glodine was, the woman was always available to jump in and help out when it came to a church member's funeral. As a matter of fact, she was always available to help with any other neighborhood tragedy, too. She had come to the house with Floyd and his two foster sisters to help some ladies from the church and a few of Viola and Luther's relatives get the house ready for the rest of the mourners. With the exception of a few garishly dressed individuals roaming throughout the house looking for something else to take, everybody else was in the living room. I didn't care about anybody else, but I was glad to see that Floyd and Valerie were present.

"I want that La-Z-Boy and them end tables!" yelled Rudy, one of Luther's cousins from Dallas.

"And you can have it! I know y'all don't think I'm about to drag a U-Haul down that freeway back to San Diego with *all* of this junk up in here!" Noble shouted, standing by the window holding up two pieces of silverware to the light. He had a plain, pinched, reddish brown face and no neck. It looked like his chin, jaws, and chest were all one big separate slab of meat. He looked like a penguin in his tight black suit and white shirt. This gargoyle had the nerve to be married to a very attractive, young Mexican woman. She was sitting by the door on a hassock looking like she wanted to make a run for the border.

"Noble, you can put that silverware right back where you got it from! That belongs to my auntie and last time I checked, a few minutes ago, she was still breathing," hollered one of Viola's other nephews, a bucktoothed security guard named Lenny from Compton. The relatives all started talking and fussing. There were so many hot conversations taking place at the same time that within seconds it sounded like one angry voice. I wanted to hide in my room, but some teenage relatives were swarming around in every room upstairs looking for their own treasures to take. I let out a loud disgusted sigh when I spotted one of the Arkansas relatives who they called Sister come wobbling down the steps. That bold heifer was clutching a boom box that Luther had promised I could have when he passed.

"This is the only thing I want out of all this mess," Sister muttered, struggling to sit down with the boom box on her lap. I had a feeling that Luther's spirit was outraged. It must have broken his heart to hear the things he'd cherished for so many years being referred to as "mess." Sister unbuttoned the two top buttons on her stiff black cotton dress and started fanning with her hand. "And I ain't going to sit up in this stuffy barn all day without no beer." She stopped fanning. Then she looked around the room, her hand shading her beady black eyes. "Otis Lee, tote this thing out yonder to the car," she ordered, holding up the boom box. A long-headed teenage boy shot across the floor and snatched the boom box out of her thick hands. I ignored the smirk on her face.

"That's mine," I said under my breath, just loud enough for nobody but me and Sister to hear. Not only had that bitch taken the boom box from my room, she had also helped herself to a handkerchief that Luther had given me on my last birthday. She used it to blow her nose. She glared at me in a way that made it seem like she was daring me to complain, but I knew it was to my advantage not to.

"You all right, Lo?" Floyd asked, sitting close to me on the lumpy plaid living room sofa that Luther had always been so fond of. Hell, no, I was not all right. But feeling Floyd's hand on my shoulder made me feel somewhat better.

"I'm fine," I managed, knowing that I had

no say-so in who took what. "Floyd, thanks for being here. I don't think I could get through this without you and Valerie," I told him. "I'll be glad when things are back to normal."

"Same here. Listen, when things do settle down, let's me and you hook up and do something. You know, movies or something. You cool with that?"

"Yeah," I mumbled, praying that Viola would be all right so that I'd still have a place to call home.

I hadn't told Valerie about my feelings for Floyd lately. With the way things were with her, I didn't think that was something she wanted to hear, anyway. She had enough to deal with. The same day that Luther died, Mr. Zeke beat Valerie so brutally for stealing money from his wallet, he'd broken her arm in two places.

CHAPTER 10

A few of Viola's relatives stayed with me until the hospital released Viola three days after Luther's funeral. Once home, Viola tried to behave like it was business as usual. Even though she was mourning her husband, she hobbled into the kitchen to bake some tea cakes. For the first time in years, I actually ate every single one that she piled onto a large plate and handed to me with a warm smile. It was the least I could do. Hurting the feelings of somebody I loved was one thing I tried to do as little as possible. So in addition to allowing Viola's dreaded tea cakes to wreak havoc with my bowels, later that night I helped Valerie capture a stray dog that was running around in the middle of the street. Since Valerie's arm was in a cast, I helped her bathe the homely, one-eyed mutt in Viola's kitchen sink. She named him Pete, her grandfather Paw Paw's real name.

The first time Pete pissed on the floor in Valerie's house, which was a few days after we'd rescued him, Mr. Zeke gave her a mighty punch in the face with his fist. Then he kicked Pete halfway across the floor with his steel-toed boot. If anything, the dog just seemed dazed. Valerie seemed twice as dazed, even though this type of violence had become routine for her. She already had a broken arm in a cast, but that injury no longer fazed her. She took her latest assault in stride, shielding her head with her arms as I stood by and watched. She was lucky this time. The cast on her arm had protected her somewhat, so all she got was a busted lip.

"Mr. Zeke, please don't hurt her too much," I begged, standing a safe distance away. Unlike a lot of the neighborhood kids who had stopped coming to Valerie's house, I didn't feel that I was in any real danger. Mr. Zeke seemed to be the kind of brute who knew where to draw the line when it came to other people's kids. "You can't keep beating up people the way you do!" I yelled.

"Dolores, I advise you to vacate the premises," Mr. Zeke warned. "I done put up with you sassing me one time too many. If I wasn't a gentleman, I would have cold-cocked your fresh ass a long time ago! Now you get the hell out of my house while you still able!"

He didn't have to tell me to leave but one time. Something told me that the line Mr. Zeke had never crossed was getting thinner by the minute. As I shot across the floor toward the door, I noticed Valerie's younger brother and sister, William and Elizabeth, called Binkie and Liz, crouching behind the door leading from the living room to the kitchen. I ran and I didn't stop running until I was in the Scotts' yard. Old man Scott, a mole-like geezer who usually kept to himself, ran out on his front porch. He was waving a broom, fussing and cussing at me for trampling his lawn — again. I took off running some more, and I didn't stop until I was in Viola's house, in my room with the door locked, praying that Valerie would survive the night.

I could not believe that Valerie and the rest of her family let Mr. Zeke get away with so much. But strangely enough, nobody in the neighborhood wanted to talk about it much. Not even Viola.

"What goes on in that house ain't none of our business. There's a lot of mens like that Zeke and there always will be as long as there are women desperate enough to groom 'em," Viola managed when I gave her an update. Her hair looked like a thorny gray helmet. There was a look of despair in her small black eyes that hadn't been there before Luther's death. She smelled like Bengay and sweat, but that didn't bother me. I was just thankful that she had survived her heart attack. And if Dr. Miller knew what he was talking about, she'd be around for at least another ten years.

Viola was on the living room sofa in her gown, covered up to her chin with a thin blanket. The night before, as she lay in the bed she'd shared with Luther for more than fifty years snoring like a grizzly bear, Floyd had taken my virginity on that same couch.

It had lasted only two minutes, but it had seemed more like an hour. I didn't enjoy it. And the way Floyd took off running afterward, with his pants still unzipped, made me assume he didn't enjoy it either. But he called me when he got home later that night and told me that I was special and that we would have a special relationship. That made me feel somewhat better for the moment, but when I didn't hear from him for the next two weeks, I didn't know what to think.

I was glad that I had Valerie to talk to about it, but she was so preoccupied when I told her that when I mentioned it to her again a day later, she acted like she was hearing it for the first time. Viola was doing much better, and one of her church sisters had volunteered to come stay at the house until Viola was her old self again. So I didn't have to miss much more school or hang around the house.

Even with Viola recovering so rapidly and somebody in the house to help out, I was nervous about leaving the house for more than a few minutes at a time. For some reason I was afraid that something would happen to Viola while I was gone, just like it had with Luther. But spending time with Valerie was one of the few things I enjoyed and one of the few distractions I had in my life. Anything that helped me keep my mind off what would happen to me if Viola died was a blessing. Besides, my sex life was one thing that I wanted to discuss with Valerie in person. Mr. Zeke often eavesdropped on her phone conversations, anyway, so I was not about to go there on the phone.

"Well, now you know why the rest of the world is so crazy when it comes to sex," Valerie told me, scratching the skin on her arm at the bottom of the cast. She had told everybody else that she had fallen down some steps. The last time she had injuries to explain she told everybody that she had run into a wall, just like her mother did a few times a month. And so did everybody else who lived in that house when they had injuries to explain. Even though nobody believed them, nobody wanted to talk about it. But everybody agreed that they were either the clumsiest people in town or the most stupid.

Six months earlier Valerie had confessed to me that she'd fucked some boy from Compton for the first time on the ground in Griffin Park for giving her a ride home from a party. Unlike me, she claimed she'd enjoyed her first sexual experience, but she also made it clear that it was not her favorite subject to discuss. "Some people say that money is the root of all evil. That's a damn lie. Sex has caused more problems for some people than money. Like my mama," she told me with a tired and heavy sigh. You would have thought that we were discussing something as unpleasant as cramps, the way she kept screwing up her face and rolling her eyes as she spoke.

"Your mama can get another man. Why does she put up with Mr. Zeke and his beatings?" I asked, more interested in talking about Valerie's business than my own. "Is she that big of a fool for a man?" I asked boldly. I could tell that Valerie didn't appreciate my choice of words, and I immediately wished that I could take them back. But she just rolled her eyes again and shook her head with the most disturbing look I'd ever seen on her face. She looked like she had given up on life completely, but something told me that Valerie was going to come out blasting with both guns some day.

CHAPTER 11

"My mama was a damn fool when she first got involved with Zeke. But she was lonely and didn't want to raise three kids by herself," Valerie told me. "But she's not a fool now because she sees him for the asshole he is." I was glad to see that the expression on Valerie's face had changed. Her eyes had softened and the scowl had disappeared.

"Then why won't your mother get a divorce? Or at least kick him out of this house," I said, making a sweeping gesture with my hand. Valerie's bedroom was almost twice as big as mine, but she shared it with her little sister, Liz. Her brother, Binkie, occupied one of the other bedrooms by himself. And her grandfather, Paw Paw, who had never fully recovered from a stroke a year ago, occupied the bedroom next door to Valerie so she could keep an eye on him.

Waiting on Paw Paw hand and foot was

bad. He used a bedpan, but when he couldn't get to it, he soiled his underwear like a newborn baby. Valerie never complained about having to clean him up. She just started putting diapers on him. I'd actually seen her smile as she emptied his bedpan and clipped his long, lethal-looking toenails. I admired her for being so caring.

What Valerie did complain about was the fact that Mr. Zeke was just as mean to his elderly father-in-law as he was to the rest of the family. He had sucker punched the old man's face that morning for interfering when Mr. Zeke had lined up all the kids for a whupping to make sure he got the one responsible for drinking one of his beers. It broke my heart to see that eighty-year-old man propped up in his bed with two black eyes and other injuries. "Vally, one day Zeke will get what he deserves. Sooner or later, that devil will meet his match," Paw Paw mumbled through a swollen and busted lip when Valerie and I delivered his dinner tray.

"And it will be sooner than later if I have anything to do with it," Valerie vowed, helping the old man sit up.

"I still say your mama should just get a divorce," I insisted, opening the window at the top of Paw Paw's bed, which was cluttered with old magazines and newspapers.

Thanks to Valerie, the rest of the room was as neat as a showroom. Despite the old-fashioned oak furniture, the bright white walls and stuffed animals strewn about gave the room a youthful look. It had belonged to Valerie before Paw Paw moved in.

"I wish," Valerie said with a heavy sigh, punching the sides of Paw Paw's pillows. "It's not that simple anymore." Valerie flinched and so did the old man when she checked a large Band-Aid on the back of his neck.

"If I were a younger man, I'd get me a gun and blow his brains out. Or" — Paw Paw paused and took a sip of coffee from the cup on his tray, then a sip of Pepto-Bismol straight from the bottle on the same tray — "if I could get around better and if somebody was to help me get my hands on a piece, I'd do it now." Paw Paw's face was lopsided from his beating, and because one side of his mouth was full of buttered bread. The pink Pepto-Bismol outlined his thin lips like cheap lipstick. Valerie and I looked at each other, but neither of us acknowledged Paw Paw's comments.

Paw Paw was doing better by now. He was snoozing like a baby when we checked on him. Afterward, I followed Valerie back downstairs where we resumed our conversation about the Mr. Zeke situation. Even though we were in the living room alone, we kept our voices low and we looked around every few moments to make sure that slimy devil had not slipped up on us.

"Your mama can't get the cops to get him out of this house? And him being a cop, can't she go to his boss or somebody down at the precinct and tell them what's going on? He's getting away with all this shit because she's letting him. What if she packs you all up and leaves town? Let him stay in this house by himself if he doesn't want to leave!"

"Dolores, my stepdaddy told me, my mama, and all the rest of my family that if Mama leaves him, she better take every single person in her family with her because *everybody* she leaves behind will die. I got my sixty-year-old auntie Valerie living on Crenshaw with her cats. She's in the middle of all that gang activity, but she doesn't want to leave. We've got cousins in Compton and Glendale. And what about Paw Paw? We can't leave him here, and trying to run away with a sick old man that can barely walk . . ."

"I get the picture," I said, holding up my hand. "Well, at least when you graduate in a couple of years you can get up out of here,"

I offered.

"Girl, are you crazy? There is no way I am going to leave Mama and the kids, and Paw Paw, here to fend for themselves with that sick motherfucker. As long as he's here, I'll be here," Valerie vowed. "Everything I love is in this house." The mutt that had already caused Valerie to have a showdown with Mr. Zeke limped into the room and leaped up on her lap.

I promised Valerie that I'd help her housebreak Pete because Mr. Zeke had advised her to be prepared to suffer more consequences every time he stepped in some dog mess in his own house. And that was another thing. The house that he had a habit of referring to as his actually belonged to Valerie's mother. Paw Paw had signed it over to her and had made her promise that she would keep it in her immediate family after he died. He had even made her make Mr. Zeke sign some kind of prenuptial agreement before she married him. This was to make sure Mr. Zeke would never get his hands on property that he didn't deserve.

Mr. Zeke was coming in as I was leaving. He had the nerve to have on a Bob Marley T-shirt and a pair of short baggy shorts. The kind that only boys my age should wear. With his thick, high butt and his long legs, he looked like a stork. "Girl, don't you never stay home?" he asked, breathing through his mouth. His snake eyes looked tighter than they'd ever looked before. As a matter of fact, they looked like they were closed. I didn't know how the man could even see me. But this man saw everything he wanted to see. When he got a few feet in front of me he stopped, placed his hands on his hips, and looked me up and down. "Girl, you need to go home and wash your dirty neck. I could plant a tree up under your chin." Mr. Zeke shook his head and laughed. That was the only way I knew he was just teasing me. But even when he was trying to be funny, he was a fright.

"Uh, I just came over to see how Valerie was doing," I managed, rubbing the side of my neck. He was right. My neck was dirty, and it usually was. It was the place on my body that I paid the least amount of attention. I could hear Valerie's siblings scrambling around, running for cover.

A few seconds later, something happened that took me completely by surprise. As hard-hearted as Mr. Zeke was, for the first time since I'd met him, he seemed to soften before my eyes. Suddenly, he didn't seem like such a physical imposition anymore. He cocked his head and smiled at me. If it was possible for him to behave like this, it was possible for me to change my opinion of him — for the better. Even though I knew what a monster he was most of the time, I felt kind of sorry for him, anyway. He was the only person I knew that *nobody* liked. And I knew some gangbangers over in South Central who would torture their own mothers, but a lot of people still liked them. One thing Luther and Viola had taught me was that it didn't take any more energy to love than it did to hate.

"How you doing in school, Dolores? You better keep your nose in them schoolbooks and not up some boy's butt. You don't want to end up married to no booger like me." Despite his brutal nature, every now and then, Mr. Zeke seemed like a normal person. "That's how stupid women end up." He laughed. I laughed, too, but it saddened me to hear him refer to Valerie's mother as stupid. However, I couldn't stop myself from wondering why the woman had not come up with a plan to get out of her messy marriage. Maybe she really was stupid.

"How's Sister Mason?" Zeke asked, tilting his big head even more to the side. I was glad to see that he was still smiling at me. As long as he did that, he didn't seem so threatening and ugly.

"She's fine, sir," I said as graciously as I could while trying to move past Mr. Zeke and get out the door.

"Tell her if there's anything she need done around the house, just call me and I'll take care of it. Old Luther was a good old brother, and I still owe him a few favors."

A week later Mr. Zeke got fired from the police force and things got even worse for Valerie's family. The same day he got fired he stormed the house that evening and lit into Binkie with a belt just for giving him a mean look. As soon as Liz entered the living room, he grabbed her and boxed her ears so hard she heard a ringing noise for the next two hours.

Valerie knew that if she interfered it would only make matters worse for everybody. She stayed in her room and prayed for herself and her family. "He didn't even give a reason as to why he attacked little Liz," Valerie lamented to me when she called me up later that night after Mr. Zeke had passed out drunk on the living floor. Valerie wore a pair of dark glasses to school the next day to hide a black eye that she *swore* she got when she tripped over her dog and stumbled into a door. I didn't know if any of the other kids believed her, but I didn't. She didn't want to tell me what had really happened, and she didn't have to. I already knew. As it turned out, I was wrong. Miss Naomi and Valerie's siblings backed up her story. But that still didn't make me feel any better about what Mr. Zeke was doing to that family.

One of the reasons that Mr. Zeke got away with so much was because the family made excuses for him: "He's depressed. He's confused. Nobody understands him. He's weak." There was no excuse for the excuses they made for that man. And it was not because they cared about him, it was because they were so afraid of him at that point that they didn't know what else to do. I couldn't even imagine what he would do to them if they stood up to him more often.

Valerie's mother sometimes worked up to twelve hours a day running the bar. But when Mr. Zeke was unemployed, she had to come home every day around noon to fix him some lunch. Some days he'd still be in bed when she got home. The first time she stepped into that house with a box from Kentucky Fried Chicken, he snatched it and flung all twelve assorted pieces around the kitchen. Then he bounced the empty container off her head. He was very picky when it came to his meals. A big ox like him didn't even deal with typical lunch items like sandwiches. Miss Naomi had to fix him whatever he wanted, and it was usually something elaborate and time-consuming. One day she had to prepare him some barbequed spareribs, turnip greens, yams, cornbread, garlic mashed potatoes, and peach cobbler.

It did no good for Valerie to volunteer to take care of Mr. Zeke's lunch. Even though it would have meant she had to take an extra-long lunch period from school herself. Mr. Zeke made it clear that if Miss Naomi didn't come home every day to take care of him, she'd suffer.

When Floyd finally did get around to calling me five days after Mr. Zeke was fired, he was appalled when I told him the latest about Mr. Zeke.

"That nigger's crazy," he snarled. Then he mumbled a few cuss words under his breath. "Just like my old man." I didn't encourage Floyd to reveal any more details about his own daddy. I already knew all I wanted to know about that man, anyway. I felt the same way about the sperm donor who had helped create me. What I really wanted to discuss with Floyd was us. I wanted to know where our relationship was going. Right after I asked him he got quiet for a few moments, and that made me nervous. "Girl, you don't have to worry about our future. It's already been set up." That was all I wanted to hear. If he thought that and it was good enough for him, then it was good enough for me.

CHAPTER 12

Floyd didn't like condoms, but I made it clear to him that if he wanted to keep fucking me he was going to wear them. "I'm clean, baby. Other than a slight case of the clap a couple of months ago, I ain't never had no diseases," he insisted. We were on the well-used couch in Viola's living room as usual. I was glad we didn't have to worry about Viola's interference. That woman could sleep through Armageddon. We could hear her snoring all the way from upstairs to the living room downstairs, but we whispered and spoke in low voices, anyway.

"I'm glad to hear that. But catching a sex disease is just part of the reason you're going to wear protection if you want to be with me," I told him, giving him a hard look. "The last thing I need complicating my life right now is a baby."

"Girl, stop tripping," he said, dismissing my outburst with a wave of his calloused hand. "I know how to pull out the dragon in time. You don't have to worry about getting pregnant. At least not by me. . . ." He put on the condom anyway.

Unlike Valerie and some of the other girls I knew, I didn't have to worry about stretching out in the backseat of somebody's car, or on the ground, or helping some boy scrape up enough money to rent a cheap motel room. Viola usually went to bed as soon as it got dark. So when Floyd wanted to spend some time with me, we made our plans earlier in the day. We'd agree on a certain time and then I'd call him up at an alternate phone number that he'd given to me. That worked for the first few weeks until that bitch Glodine found out. As it turned out, that phone number was a second line that she had recently installed in her house. I almost had a fit when she picked up the phone one day and started fussing as soon as she heard my voice. "Girl, if you want to snuggle up and do whatever it is you and that boy do, you better figure out another way to hook up with him. And if I was you, I'd be a little pickier about the dudes I keep company with. You can do a lot better than Floyd. His family tree didn't grow nothing but thugs and lowlifes. And he didn't fall too far from that tree. He is going to cause you some serious grief someday. Do you hear me?"

"Yes, ma'am," I mumbled. I didn't have enough nerve to ask Floyd's foster mother what she meant by her last comment. I didn't even want to think about it. But when I didn't hear from Floyd for the rest of that week, Miss Glodine's mysterious comment was all I could think about.

L.A. was a big city but there were a lot of small circles of busybodies that carried news from one end of the city to the other, and beyond. It was a boy I knew only casually from school who told me that Floyd hung out with members of the Crips. I didn't ask Floyd about it the next time I saw him. I didn't have to.

About a week later he got picked up for questioning by the cops along with half a dozen confirmed gang members. Three members from the deadly Bloods, the Crips' worst enemy, had turned up dead in an alley behind a bar a few blocks from our neighborhood. Floyd had fought with one of the dead boys over some weed that one of Floyd's close friends had stolen. Some bigmouth had started a rumor that Floyd had been involved in the theft. Whether that was true or not, nobody was able to prove it. But Floyd's run-ins with the cops didn't stop there.

Some of his friends stole a car, and when the cops located it, abandoned on a street in Brentwood, a jacket that belonged to Floyd was in the car. It was easy enough for him to explain to the cops that the jacket had been stolen from his locker at school. It seemed like every other week Floyd got caught up in something that involved the cops. How he managed to stay out of jail was a mystery to me.

"I know you are crazy about your boy, but sooner or later his luck is going to run out and you'll be visiting him in County," Valerie commented.

"I don't think so," I said without hesitation. "I think I know the boy better than you do. Floyd just got a job at that new movie theater at the mall and he'll be working six nights a week, so I don't have to worry about him spending too much time with his homies. With school, his job, and spending time with me I don't think I have to worry about visiting my man in County, or any other jail," I said.

Valerie looked at me with a lot of doubt on her face, and she wasn't the only one. Viola had some concerns about how my association with Floyd was going to impact my future. "I didn't raise no fool, so I know you got enough sense in your head to keep your nose clean. But sometimes just being around the wrong person can land you in a mess of trouble," Viola told me.

Floyd managed to keep his nose clean for the next few months, and as far as everything else was concerned, it was business as usual. The day before Christmas I went to Valerie's house to drop off some gifts that Viola and I had picked out. Since Viola was on a fixed income and the people I babysat for from time to time didn't pay that much, if they paid at all, we rarely purchased anything expensive or fancy. We usually bought all of the females on our list a scarf, some handkerchiefs, or cheap cologne. The males all got socks, some undershirts, or cheap cologne. This year we had a few extra dollars left over from the money that Viola got from Luther's life insurance, so we got a little more creative: gift certificates from various discount stores for everybody. Even Mr. Zeke.

"You back again?" Mr. Zeke said with a smirk before I could even get in the door. He seemed to be in a good mood. And he had to be, because Valerie told me that he was massaging her mother's feet when I'd called her up earlier. But I knew from experience that his good moods could change in the twinkling of an eye.

"Uh, I just came over to drop off a few things from me and Viola," I told him, talking fast. I looked past him, hoping to see Valerie or anybody else who lived in this sad house. As mean as Mr. Zeke was to everybody, as far as I knew the only people he ever beat on were Valerie's family. I had heard the rumors about him beating up people when he was still on the police force. But since I'd never seen him do it, I didn't count that. Just like I didn't believe that Floyd was having sex with his foster mother. And that was one thing that I wouldn't believe unless I heard it from him, or saw him fucking her with my own eyes. It was the one thing that I would never ask Floyd. If it was true, I didn't want to know. Hearing something and seeing something were two different things, and I applied that to everybody I knew. Especially Mr. Zeke. However, despite how nice he was to me just then, there were times when he looked at me like he wanted to slap the shit out of me. Like at that moment. His attitude had changed just that fast. He had replaced his smile with a scowl.

"Can I put everything under the tree?" I asked, still rotating my neck so I could look past him. He opened his mouth, but before he could say anything else, Miss Naomi limped into the room on the same feet that Mr. Zeke had massaged. She was wiping blood off her face with a damp washcloth. I looked from her to Mr. Zeke.

"Hi, Dolores," Miss Naomi muttered, her voice sounding like it was about to crack in two. "Uh, you can leave that stuff on the coffee table there."

I was glad when Valerie eased into the room and beckoned for me to follow her to her room upstairs. "How come the house is so quiet?" I asked. "It feels like a funeral parlor up in here," I said as soon as we got inside Valerie's room and shut the door.

"One of these days . . . one of these days I am going to make that bastard wish he was never born," Valerie assured me with a firm nod. It was only then that I noticed the most recent wound on her lip and scratches on both sides of her neck.

"I saw the cops over here again last night when me and Floyd passed by," I said, sitting down next to her on her unmade bed.

"For all the good it did. Mama told him again that she was going to have him removed. And he told her again that he would crucify her, and then beat the dog shit out of the rest of us. She called the cops anyway, and all they can say is they can't arrest a

96

man for what he *might* do. Tell me something," Valerie said, pausing to catch her breath. "What good is the law if they can't protect us from something that somebody might do?"

I shrugged. "You are asking the wrong person, girl. By the time the cops do something to help, it might be too late."

"They keep saying that they can't do anything to him until he does something. If you ask me, a threat is *something*. If somebody threatens the president, they throw them up under the jail and throw away the key."

"Well, what about the beatings? If that's not something, I don't know what is."

"Yeah, right! Mama is so scared that he will do something really crazy, she never goes all the way and presses charges." Valerie stood up and started pacing back and forth at the foot of her bed. It made me sick to see such a pretty girl with such a look of despair on her face.

"Look, if the social services people even think that a child is being abused, they remove the kid until they investigate," I offered.

Valerie shook her head, and I could tell that with the scratches on her neck it was painful for her to do so by the way she flinched. "That's not enough. Been there, done that. They didn't do anything that other time but give us lip service when I told my gym teacher about what Zeke did to poor Binkie. After that, Zeke said if we ever tried to sic the white folks on him again for mistreating us kids, it would be the last thing any of us ever do."

"I noticed that your mama was limping when I came in. . . ." I mentioned.

"Oh that," Valerie said with a sigh and a shrug. "He told her to take down the Christmas tree 'cause Binkie and Liz didn't clean off the back porch like he told them to do. When she didn't take it down fast enough, he knocked it down. It fell on her legs and pinned her to the floor until me and Binkie helped her up," Valerie explained.

"Oh. Well, I left the gifts for everybody on the coffee table," I mumbled. "By the way, just how old is Mr. Zeke?"

"What?" Valerie stopped pacing the floor and stood in front of me with her arms folded and a puzzled look on her face.

"How old is your stepdaddy?"

"Why? What's his age got to do with anything? Young asshole, old asshole. The only difference is years. What's your point?"

"Just answer my question," I suggested.

"Fifty-something now. Why?" Valerie

asked, giving me a thoughtful look.

"He drinks a lot, and that can't be too healthy for him. He smokes. He won't live forever at the rate he's going," I said in a serious tone of voice. I noticed a strange look appear on Valerie's face, like she was in a trance. "Did you hear what I said? I said, Mr. Zeke won't live forever at the rate he's going."

"Paw Paw drinks and smokes and he's eighty," Valerie reminded me. We paused when we heard a fresh commotion being played out downstairs. Something hit the living room wall with a loud thud. Somebody screamed. Pete was barking up a storm. Mr. Zeke was cussing so loud, his voice was the only one we could hear. We looked toward the door at the same time; we shook our heads at the same time.

"Yeah, but most people are not as lucky as Paw Paw. I don't think that Mr. Zeke will be as lucky as your grandfather," I stated, my eyes still on the door. Locking it did no good. Mr. Zeke broke through locks like he was breaking rubber bands. But Valerie locked her door all the time anyway. If nothing else, it slowed him down when he stormed her room.

"No . . . he won't be," Valerie said in a hollow voice. Despite the ruckus taking place downstairs, she smiled for the first time in days.

CHAPTER 13

Except for the ongoing violence in Valerie's house, things were fairly quiet in my life. The days, weeks, and the months drifted by, taking me closer to my uncertain future. As much as I wanted to enhance my education, I didn't have any plans for college. For one thing, I knew Viola couldn't afford to send me, and I didn't expect her to, anyway. Another thing was the fact that she had more than a few relatives who thought it was their business to remind me that I was not a blood relative. And my grades were not that great, so I knew that there was no chance of me getting a scholarship. But I had some reasonable career goals. I wasn't exactly sure what it was I wanted to do with my life. But I knew what I didn't want to do. I didn't want to end up like my mother and so many of the other kids who'd started life in the same boat with me.

Graduation was still six months away. But

I had already filled out several applications for jobs. But the jobs I applied for were ones that nobody else I knew would take, even if they came gift wrapped. Like stocking shelves at a nearby Walgreens, a boring security guard job at an office building downtown, and even a position in a car wash working the cash register.

I already knew what Valerie's plans were. She would eventually take over running the bar that her mother had inherited. That was all she wanted to talk about when the subject of jobs came up. She totally ignored the fact that a lot of folks had told her she should pursue a modeling career. I'd even told her myself. "I don't think so. I don't want to be a small fish in a big pond. By being my own boss, I will be the biggest fish in a small pond," she told me with so much conviction I knew she was serious.

I eventually stopped trying to tell Valerie what to do with her life. My only concern, and the main thing that she was concerned about, was how she was going to deal with Zeke when she took over the bar. In addition to his many other flaws, that man was about as self-centered as a pimp. Not only was he a brute who thought the world owed him something, he was a lazy-ass brute. After he lost his job on the police force, he didn't even pretend to be interested in trying to get it back.

He screamed when Miss Naomi offered to let him work in her bar as a bouncer. He made it clear that the only job he would accept in her "Mickey Mouse" bar was manager, and head manager at that, which meant he would supervise Miss Naomi and everybody else. Miss Naomi refused to let that happen, telling him that it was bad enough he was running the show in her house, she wasn't going to let the same thing happen with her bar. Mr. Zeke whined and wheedled and she still refused, even after he threw a telephone book at her. As far as him getting another job someplace else, that didn't even register with him. When he was not at one of the Indian casinos gambling away money that Valerie's mother brought into the house, he was in the living room slumped in a chair in front of the TV with the remote in one hand and a bottle in the other.

Then there were the other women. According to Valerie, her stepfather had women coming out of both his ears. I had no idea what women saw in Mr. Zeke. He had nothing I would want. He was not a good-looking man. He didn't look like a baboon or anything like that, but he was no Denzel.

He must have been *real* good in bed because I couldn't see any other reason why Valerie's mother married him in the first place. With so many stupid women in L.A., he would have no trouble at all finding him another meal ticket. I brought up the subject to Valerie on a regular basis, and her response was usually the same: "Zeke's gotten too old and too comfortable to try and find him another nest with a goose that lays golden eggs like my mama does," she told me, with a look of extreme disgust on her face.

One thing that I was sure of was that Floyd was the *only* man I wanted in my life. Despite his minor brushes with the law, he was smart and he had a lot of ambition. "I can't think of a better way to jumpstart my future than to get what I can out of the military," he told me, more excited than I'd seen him since, well, since the last time we had sex. His plan was to enlist in the military and soak up as many benefits as possible. I was proud to share this information with everybody who would listen. Knowing how limited our options were, Floyd even suggested that I pursue a future with the military, too. "If nothing else, you'll get a chance to see the world at Uncle Sam's expense."

"I'd like to see the world. But if I do it at

Uncle Sam's expense, I probably wouldn't get to see the places I want to see. And all the rest of that military rigmarole is too rigid for me," I said. I laughed but I was serious.

As much as I loved Viola, I couldn't wait to get out of school and into a place of my own. I wanted something that I could call mine. I wanted to have some control in the next place that I called home. It made my blood boil when Viola's relatives came to visit. Those people had no shame. They did whatever they wanted to do in Viola's house, and that included my bedroom. Things disappeared from my room so often you would have thought that I'd been burglarized. One day I came home as one of Viola's nieces was leaving the house wearing one of my best blouses, even though it was two sizes too small for her. Another one of the reasons I felt such a need to have my own place was because I'd never had a blood family that I could call my own. Once I got a good job, whether I had a husband or not, I planned to have several children.

Floyd was the one who had first brought up the subject of us getting married. "I don't care what I have to do to keep my family together. As long as I got a breath in my body, I will never allow a child of ours to end up in foster care like us," he vowed.

We talked about where we wanted to live and how many kids we wanted to have. The only thing we didn't have on our agenda yet was our wedding date. There were other concerns, though. Not on my end; my mind was made up. But every time we talked about getting married, no matter how well the conversation was going, Floyd would always sink into a slump of uncertainty and paranoia. "I just hope things don't change while I'm in the service. The last thing I ever want to get in the mail is a 'Dear John' letter from you. I don't know what I'd do if you found somebody else."

"You don't ever have to worry about me backing out. I wanted to get married to you the first time I saw you," I confessed with a laugh. "I thought you'd never get around to asking me," I told him. "Even if you decide you like the military life and want to stay longer than a few years, I'll wait for you."

"I am going to make you real happy, Lo. I swear to God I will," Floyd assured me. I was convinced that he was sincere. No boy or man had ever looked at me the way he did. And despite what Valerie and a few other girls had told me about how I would never know for sure if I was getting fucked right unless I tried a few other men, the sex life I had with Floyd was good enough for me.

"But you are only seventeen, Dolores. Give yourself some time," Viola said when I told her that Floyd and I had decided to marry in a few years. "I didn't tie the knot until I was twenty-five." We were in her living room with me rolling her hair with large, pink sponge rollers. I stood over her as she sat on the same couch that Floyd and I still rode each other on when he didn't have motel money.

I gasped. "I can't wait that long!" I hollered, dropping two rollers to the floor. "I don't want Floyd to get away," I added, leaning over to pick up the rollers.

"Get away from what? You? If you think that boy truly loves you, why are you worried about him 'getting away' from you? Ow! Don't roll my hair too tight."

"Poor Floyd. He thinks I might run off with another man while he's in the service, but I won't. But I don't know about some other woman snatching him up. Something else might make him change his mind," I admitted with a worried tone of voice.

"That's all the more reason why you should wait. Date a few more men for a few years, and if you feel the same way then, and if Floyd's still in the picture, marry him then."

I hurried to finish Viola's hair. Even though I dismissed her comments, and I knew that I was going to do what I wanted to do anyway, I respected her opinion. I was going to marry Floyd and that was that. Other than death, nothing was going to make me break my promise to him.

CHAPTER 14

Living in the same house with a fool like Mr. Zeke had a strange effect on Valerie. At least that was the way it seemed to me. As good looking as she was, that man had that poor girl believing she was ugly. "Mornin', frog eyes" was how he often greeted her, just because she had big eyes. "Is it just my imagination, or are you uglier today than you were yesterday?" Mr. Zeke's assessment was the furthest thing from the truth!

It helped when I told Valerie she had the same eyes that Diana Ross had. People sometimes stopped my girl on the street and asked if she was a model. When she told them she wasn't, they told her she should be. None of that seemed to matter. Valerie hated herself and had a hard time believing that she could be loved. Boys approached her all the time because she was so pretty, but the minute they realized how needy and insecure she was, they fled the scene. However, there were always a few horny boys willing to do anything to fuck Valerie, so she really could have looked like a frog for all they cared. A hasty fuck was all she got from them. But once they got what they came for, those boys fled the scene, too.

I used to think that any boy would be glad to have a trophy like Valerie on his arm. I was wrong. If her experience with the opposite sex was not proof that looks weren't everything, I didn't know what was. She had been fooling around with the same three boys off and on throughout our last year of high school. When it came to our upcoming prom, neither one of them asked her to go. And when she asked one of them to go with her, a week before the prom in the middle of lunch one day, he was horrified. "Girl, I know you don't think I'm going to walk up into that prom with your used-up whore pussy self on my arm!" Rudy Morgan told her to her face, right in front of me and a couple dozen of our classmates. "And another thing — get your black ass outta my sight and stay out!" I could not believe that anybody could be so callous. I couldn't figure it out. It was not like Valerie was some wart-faced frump that no boy wanted to be seen with. There were a few other girls whose track records with boys were just as bad as hers, and they were even more insecure and needy than Valerie. But those girls were not nearly as good looking as Valerie. I couldn't believe that being insecure and needy could ruin a girl's life in such a profound way. And Valerie couldn't either. Poor Valerie slunk out of the school cafeteria that day with her feelings so hurt, she didn't come back to school for two days.

As tight as my relationship was with Floyd, there was never any question about who I was going to go to the prom with. As a matter of fact, I was now spending more time with him than Valerie. We walked to school together, spent all of our spare time at the movies or hanging out at a mall, and fucked our brains out any and every place we could. We even went to church together, and that kept Glodine and Viola happy.

I was excited about the prom, even though I knew I wouldn't really enjoy it knowing that Valerie was sitting at home that night, probably caught up in another one of Mr. Zeke's attacks. She had been talking about going to the prom since tenth grade, and that made it even worse. She wanted to go more than I did.

As it turned out Valerie asked some cock-eyed, homely boy from church who had never even had a girlfriend to go with her.

And as hard as it was to believe, that knuckle-head had the nerve to let her know in advance that he expected her to be "nice" to him afterward. "The only body part on me that that sucker is ever going to see is my black ass, and that'll be for him to kiss it!" Valerie yelled into the telephone as she shared her story with me. She canceled that date.

"Well, you can always ask one of your cousins, or even your little brother," I told her.

"I'm not that desperate." She laughed. "I'd ask one of Floyd's homies first." And that's just what she did. She asked Floyd's best friend, Ollie Reed, to take her to the prom. He was no prize, but he had a nice body, and Valerie had already told me that she wouldn't mind getting some of that body. Ollie agreed to be Valerie's date, but it was not just because he knew he was going to get some pussy. She paid for his tux and "loaned" him a few dollars to put gas in the car he was going to borrow for the night. But the main reason Ollie agreed to give up a rap concert to go to the prom was because Floyd and I practically begged him off and on for two days before he agreed to do it. Everything was all set. Or so I thought.

"I can't go to the prom," Valerie told me

an hour before Floyd and Ollie were supposed to pick us up. I already had on my low-cut, off-the-shoulder pink dress and had started peeping out the window in my bedroom, anxious to see Floyd trot across the street when it came time for him to pick me up.

"Oh, hell no! You better have a damn good reason for backing out this late in the fucking game, girl!" I screamed. I stumbled from the window to my bed and plopped down so hard I almost fell onto my back. I clutched the cordless telephone with both hands. I blew on my nails to help dry the pale pink polish that I had applied a few minutes earlier.

"My stepfather is drunk," Valerie revealed with a heavy sigh.

"So what else is new? *The man's been drunk for ten years!* What's that got to do with you not going to the prom? How much longer are you going to let that motherfucker ruin your life?" I yelled, blowing on my nails some more. It had taken two trips to two different malls for me to find nail polish the same shade of pink as my dress. I wanted everything to be special and perfect tonight. "Look, girl. I don't care what you have to do, you are not going to let that motherfucker ruin this night," I vowed. "I wouldn't put up with that shit for one minute if it was me! Mr. Zeke doesn't own you!"

"You ain't got to worry about putting up with none of my shit, you black-ass bitch. I wouldn't have your skank ass if you was served up on a platter!" I had not heard Mr. Zeke pick up the extension, but I wasn't surprised. His voice was already like the roll of thunder. It sounded even worse when he got mad. Well, madder than he usually was. Lately it seemed like every single time I saw that man he was mad. "Get your ass off this phone!" he roared. I didn't know if he was talking to me or Valerie.

"Mr. Zeke, can I talk to you for just a minute? I don't know why you won't let Valerie go to her own prom, but her going means as much to me as it does her," I wailed.

"That heifer ain't going noplace with her ugly self!" he roared, talking so hard and loud he had to stop to cough and catch his breath.

"You're not her father!" I reminded, rising from my bed so angry my legs buckled and I almost hit the floor. "I don't know who in the world you think you are, mister!" I knew he couldn't see me, but I was shaking my fist at him even though it caused me to smudge several of my freshly painted nails. That aggravated me even more because now I'd have to remove the polish and paint them again.

"Girl, as long as you live on this planet — don't you never sass me again. This is my house and what I say goes!"

"Nuh-uh, Mr. Zeke. That's Miss Naomi's house," I reminded.

"What's hers is mine! And — what the fuck business is that of yours? You ain't nothing but a damn teenager! You ain't got no business getting up in my business in the first place! Get your ass off this phone, gal!"

"Mr. Zeke, I didn't mean to sass you," I muttered in a meek voice. "But just this one time, let Valerie go with me to our prom. *Please.* This is a once-in-a-lifetime thing. We've been looking forward to it for a long time."

"Now if Valerie knew how to show some respect for me, she could do whatever she wanted to do. Anytime and anyplace. But I ain't no fool. I know she been humping everything but that fire hydrant out there on the street. This out-of-control heifer been getting dick-slapped ever since she figured out what her pussy was for! I let her get away with a lot of stuff 'cause, I knew she was going to do it anyway. Well, this is one

115

thing she ain't going to do."

"But why? This is our senior prom. Don't you realize how important this is to us? All kids want to go to their prom!"

"Prom shrom! Fuck that shit! I didn't go to no prom!"

"I'll call you in the morning, Lo. You can tell me all about the prom. Tell Ollie I'm sorry," Valerie whimpered. "Bye —"

"Don't you hang up this phone, girl!" I screamed. I didn't realize how loud I was talking until Viola came stumbling into my room in her nightgown. Her large, pink sponge rollers decorated her head like rocks.

"Who in the world are you talking to, Dolores?" she asked, walking up to me. I gave her an exasperated look, held up my hand, and shook my head, but I kept talking into the phone.

"Mr. Zeke, can I come over and talk to you? If you won't do this for Valerie, please do it for me. I swear to God I'll never ask you for anything else as long as I live," I hollered. Mr. Zeke responded by slamming the telephone down on me so hard my ears rang.

"What in the world is going on, child?" Viola demanded, her hands on her hips.

"Mr. Zeke said Valerie can't go to the prom," I said in a weak voice, blinking so

116

hard my eyes stung. I was so angry it was a struggle for me to keep talking. "I'm going over there," I said, dropping the phone onto my bed.

"No, you ain't! That nigger's crazy. It's bad enough he uses his own family for a whipping post, but I'll be damned if I allow you to go over there at a time like this. It sounds like that man's on a rampage. There ain't no telling what he might do." Viola placed her hands on my shoulders.

"You don't have to worry about me. I can take care of myself," I insisted. "This won't be the first time I went over there during one of his rampages. He's never raised a hand to me and I know he's not stupid enough to start doing it now." I was so angry I was trembling. I gently removed Viola's hands from my shoulders. "If Floyd calls, tell him I'll be back in a few minutes." I smoothed down the sides of my dress and glanced at my watch.

"I don't want you going over there, Dolores. Now I ain't never had no trouble with you minding before. Don't start now," Viola pleaded, shaking her head so hard her pink foam rollers were dropping off her head like leaves. She followed as I ran from my room and downstairs toward the door. Not only did her heavy bare feet sound like a mule

117

running across the floor, she was huffing and puffing like one, too. Because of Viola's declining health and age, I didn't like to upset or excite her. But this was one time it couldn't be helped. "Dolores, just be careful," she wheezed as I ran out off the porch.

"I'll be right back," I hollered over my shoulder, running across our yard and then the Scotts' yard next door. Instead of using the sidewalk, like the elderly Scotts had told me and the other kids time and time again, I galloped across their neat lawn, trampling old lady Scott's rose garden — which shouldn't have been in the middle of the yard in the first place.

I didn't know what to expect when I got to Valerie's house. Her brother and sister were spending the night with relatives. Lately they had been doing that a lot more than usual. To me that was a sign that things were getting worse in that pretty white house directly across the street from our church. All because of Mr. Zeke.

Even though it was none of my business, I was glad to know that those kids had other places to go where they would be safe. Too many times Binkie and Liz had gotten caught in the crossfire during one of Mr. Zeke's tirades when it didn't concern them. I had never heard him as mad as he sounded on the telephone tonight. There was no telling what he was going to do this time. My hope was that with me in the house, he wouldn't do too much damage to Valerie and her mother.

I knew that other than Valerie, her mother, and that punk-ass Mr. Zeke, Valerie's grandfather was the only other person in her house. I prayed out loud all the way over there that Paw Paw was somewhere in the house where he wouldn't get hurt.

The house was quiet when I stumbled up on the front porch, and for a minute I thought it was deserted. But the lights were on and the door was unlocked when I turned the knob. Even though I wore the dress that I was wearing to the prom, I had on the well-worn flip-flops that I usually wore around the house. "Val," I hollered as I padded across the living room floor with my shoes flapping. I almost stepped on a broken wineglass in the middle of the floor. The television was on, but it had been muted. I stopped for a moment, looking toward the staircase that led to the rooms on the second floor. I gasped when I saw what appeared to be a bullet hole in the wall by the doorway leading into the kitchen. Then I heard what sounded like somebody choking. It was hard to tell what direction it was coming from, but I moved toward the kitchen anyway.

I was glad that I was still young enough to blame my stupidity on my youth. First of all, under the circumstances, I should not have entered that house. Seeing that bullet hole in the wall and hearing somebody being choked in the kitchen and me still staying on the premises said a lot about me. Either I was too stupid for my own good or I was willing to die for my best friend if I had to.

I froze. I knew right then and there that in a few moments somebody was going to die in that kitchen that night, and it could be me.

CHAPTER 15

The way that Hollywood depicted black neighborhoods in L.A. like ours, you would have thought that black people were used to seeing people get killed. I wasn't. I could not stand the sight of blood or anything that involved violence. The few times that I'd been challenged to fight, I had chosen to walk away. I had seen a lot of violence at school, and at some of the rowdy rap concerts, and parties I'd attended. Not to mention the wrath of Mr. Zeke. But I had never witnessed a fatal situation until now.

I don't know how long I stood in the kitchen doorway unable to speak or move. But it could not have been more than a couple of minutes. The first thing that stunned me was Mr. Zeke's appearance. At first I didn't recognize him. I honestly thought that some other thug had got loose and stormed Valerie's house.

Since the last time I'd seen Mr. Zeke, he

had shaved all of his hair off the sides of his head and was now wearing a Mohawk. A *Mohawk!* I didn't care what anybody said, that was one hairdo that I didn't think looked good on anybody. Not even Mr. T or the Mohawk Indians, who should have been the only ones wearing it in the first place as far as I was concerned. Mr. Zeke was already ugly, and had been since the very first time I laid eyes on him. Now he looked so straight-up fierce that it almost hurt my eyes to look at him. His eyes were hidden behind a pair of long, wraparound sunglasses. On one side of his bald, shiny head was a loathsome tattoo of a snarling pit bull.

Mr. Zeke was straddling Miss Naomi's chest, with his long legs splayed as if he were on a horse. His massive hands were wrapped around her neck so tight, it looked like they were growing out of her body. Valerie was stretched out on the floor herself, on her back with her eyes closed. I didn't know if the girl was dead, unconscious, or just playing possum. But she was not moving at all. The only sound in the room was Miss Naomi gasping for air and trying to pry Mr. Zeke's hands from around her neck.

"Oh my God!" I didn't realize I was the one talking until I bit into my tongue. I was surprised that I was finally able to speak again. Mr. Zeke took his time looking at me. "Mr. Zeke, please stop that!"

"Get the fuck up out of here, girl," he ordered. I couldn't believe how calm he sounded. But the look on his face was demonic.

"Do you realize what you are doing?" I hollered, hopping from one foot to the other.

"I realize you might be next!" His chilling threat made me shudder even more. His dark glasses fell off as he whipped his head back around to face Miss Naomi. He was choking her so hard, her body was jerking and trembling as if she were being electrocuted.

"I'm calling the police!" I yelled, running to the phone on the wall by the stove.

"Naomi, I done told you, and told you to stop pushing my buttons, and you wouldn't listen. Look at you now! You bitch!" Mr. Zeke suddenly stopped choking Miss Naomi, and he stopped talking. He took a few deep breaths, and then he started mumbling gibberish under his breath between growls. He shook his head so hard that sweat dripped off his forehead like raindrops. I stood there in slack-jawed amazement when I realized he had only paused to rest for a moment, and to catch his breath. He glanced up and ignored me. Then he put both hands back on Miss Naomi's neck and started choking her and talking again.

"You brought this on yourself so you ain't got anybody to blame but yourself. I told you that I was going to bury your black ass before the weekend was over! Why — why won't you die, bitch?" As hard as it was to believe, Mr. Zeke tightened his grip on Miss Naomi's throat even more, until she was purple in the face. Her eyes were rolled back in her head and her tongue was flapping out the side of her mouth like the tongue in a loose shoe.

"Oh Lord, Mr. Zeke! Please don't do this!" I shouted. It never occurred to me that I was in danger of getting choked myself. My mind couldn't process that thought. My only concern was getting some help.

As soon as I picked up the telephone Valerie started coughing and sitting up. First she looked at me, and then she looked at Mr. Zeke still sitting on her mother's chest choking her. Miss Naomi had stopped struggling and gasping for air. It took about two seconds for Valerie to get up off the floor, grab the biggest knife on the counter, and plunge it into Mr. Zeke's chest. The whole scene played out like a scene from a bad movie. It didn't seem real. I covered my eyes for a moment, but when I opened them nothing had changed. This was as real as it got, and I was smack-dab in the middle of this mess!

"Valerie . . . no," I managed, placing the telephone back on its cradle. She pulled the knife out but she didn't stop stabbing. I was too disoriented to count, but the knife went in and out of Mr. Zeke's chest several times. I didn't even realize Miss Naomi had stood up until it was all over. Valerie ran and grabbed her mother around the waist, and they stood there crying for the longest time.

"He won't hurt us anymore," Valerie finally said. She let out a loud breath and released her mother and then turned to me. *"You didn't see anything,"* she told me.

I couldn't talk. All I could do was shake my head, but I couldn't take my eyes off Mr. Zeke lying there on that floor in a pool of blood that was getting wider by the second.

Floyd answered the telephone huffing and puffing like he was out of breath. "Hey, baby. I know, I know," he said, laughing and gasping for air. "I just ran a few laps on the basketball court and lost track of the time.

125

But don't worry, we'll pick you and your girl up on time. And don't you laugh when you see me in that damn tux because I'm telling you right now I look like a fucking penguin." He paused and laughed. Somehow I managed to laugh along with him. "Now I hope y'all ain't expecting corsages, too. I forgot all about that little detail —"

"Baby, stop talking and just listen," I said in a low but firm voice. "You and Ollie don't have to worry about taking me and Valerie to the prom now."

Floyd took his time responding. In the background on his end I could hear Glodine bitching at her husband and her foster daughters about a mess in the living room. Then her voice got louder as she addressed Floyd. "Boy, get your nasty self off that phone and get ready for that damn prom." Floyd ignored Glodine like he usually did. I waited until I heard her voice moving farther away.

"Did you hear what I just said?" I asked. It was not easy for me to remain composed. And I was anything but that. But I had to make Floyd think I was.

"Oh? Y'all can't go to the dance after all, huh?" He didn't even try to hide how relieved he was. "Uh, somebody sick or something?"

"Something like that," I said, almost choking on my words.

"Well, what do y'all want to do then?"

"I'm going to stay with Valerie until she feels better," I said stiffly.

"Baby, you sounding mighty funny? Where are you?"

"I'm at Valerie's house. She's, uh, real sick." There was a long moment of silence before Floyd spoke again.

"You know my boy wasn't too crazy about going to no prom in the first place, but he got used to the idea. Valerie is kinda cute and, well, you know . . . Um, we thought that afterward, we'd cruise around for a little while and, you know, get into something. Get a motel room and some beer. My boy's counting on having a good time. Is your girl too sick to do *that* later on?"

"Uh-huh." There was more silence. "She's too sick to do that, too."

"Oh. Listen, why don't you call me when you get back home. Me and you can hook up and do something on our own. I know of at least three parties in the Valley. And I think I got enough to get us a room. . . ."

"I'm going to spend the night at Valerie's," I said quickly.

"Damn. Is she that sick?"

"Uh-huh." I coughed. "And I don't feel

127

too good myself. . . ."

Floyd sighed. From the way he did that, I could tell that he was highly disappointed. But this was one time that I didn't care. "Later on then. Give me a call back when you get a chance. If you ain't too sick.. . . ."

I hung up without saying another word. Miss Naomi handed me a damp washcloth to wipe the front of my dress where I'd thrown up. I felt like I was about to throw up again so I ran to the sink and did it there this time.

"Is Mr. Zeke really dead?" I managed, not turning around, my head still hanging over the lip of the sink. I don't know why I had to ask. If that pool of blood on the floor had been any bigger, I could have gone swimming in it.

"Dolores, you need to pull yourself together. We need your help," Valerie informed me. I stood up straight and spun around. "Listen to me," she said, whispering. "It was either him or me. You know that, don't you?" Valerie didn't give me a chance to answer. "And my mama. After he got on my case about me going to the prom, Mama told him she'd filed divorce papers yesterday. That's when he really snapped. He grabbed a shovel out of the garage and ran in the backyard and dug a . . . a . . ." Valerie paused and swallowed so hard her eyes crossed and looked glassy, like the eyes on a cheap doll. *"He dug a grave out there in the backyard."*

I gave Valerie a puzzled look. "A grave? What do you mean he dug a grave?" I asked, my jaws tightening like somebody had slid my head into a vise.

"You heard what I said. You know he didn't play," Valerie replied, blinking hard. "He started threatening to bury my mama a long time ago, but I didn't believe he'd go through with something that crazy. I realized I was wrong when he dug that grave. But I tell you one thing: there was no way in hell I was going to stand around and let him finish off my mama. This whole family has suffered enough on account of that man."

I looked past Valerie at her mother. She stood over Mr. Zeke, looking down at his body with a look on her face that sent shivers up and down my spine. There was a wild-eyed, desperate look in her eyes. Like a deer caught in the headlights of a truck. I couldn't tell if she was sorry, glad, mad, or what about what had just happened. She looked up at me and exhaled. Then she started blinking like she had something caught in her eye, but I realized she was doing that to keep from crying when she snatched a dishrag off the counter by the stove and wiped her eyes and nose. The front of her dress was ripped almost down to the waist.

Bruises were all over Miss Naomi's neck, and I could see bald spots on her head where her husband had pulled out clumps of her hair. "Dolores, we need your help," she told me.

CHAPTER 16

There was a lot going on outside Miss Naomi's front door. It seemed like a whole different world, and I guess it was. Old Mrs. Scott next door was yelling about somebody trampling her lawn and rose garden again. A dog was barking as though it had cornered a squirrel in a tree. A cat was screeching like somebody was beating it. And somebody was gunning the motor in a loud car. This was one time that I wished I was on the other side of Miss Naomi's front door.

Viola took her time answering the telephone when I called home. I breathed a sigh of relief when she finally picked up on the eighth ring. I didn't know anybody who shut down as completely as Viola did at the end of each day, now that Luther was gone. It was almost like she ceased to exist after a certain hour, which was usually around eight o'clock. Other than her wheezing and heavy breathing, there was absolutely no background noise on her end of the line. I knew that she had already turned off every single light except the one in her room, where I was sure she was right now. "Gal, how do you expect to get ready for that prom the way you lollygagging and dragging yourself around all this time? I can't stay woke waiting on you to be on your way so I can lock up. I was just fixing to call over there," she told me. "That Zeke done calmed down?"

"You might say that," I said. Since there had never been any love between Viola and Mr. Zeke, I knew that it would please her to hear that he had calmed down *forever.* Not to say that she wanted to see him dead, though. Viola was the kind of sanctified old sister who had too much respect for life to even think about something that morbid. What I could tell her and what I couldn't depended on Valerie and her mother and how they wanted to finish this thing they had started. They stood side by side, a few feet in front of me, with folded arms and impatient looks on their faces. Miss Naomi's blue plaid dress and Valerie's white terry cloth housecoat were almost as bloody as Mr. Zeke's shirt. "Uh, I just called Floyd and told him I can't go to the prom," I said into the telephone in a stilted voice.

"What do you mean by that, girl? As soon as you made it to the twelfth grade, which was a leap some folks never thought you'd never make, all you talked about was going to that prom." Viola let out a short laugh that sounded like a chicken clucking.

"I know, I know. But something came up and I don't want to go now," I said, my voice cracking. "See, Valerie is real sick and I need to stay with her."

"Done finally got herself pregnant, I bet," Viola insisted, clucking some more.

"Uh, not nothing like that. She ate something earlier today that didn't agree with her and she's been throwing up ever since. And on top of that, she's real constipated . . . uh . . . and has been for three days."

"Well, where is her mama at? Where is them other two kids of Naomi's at? Binkie and that little sister of hissen. Why you got to be the one to stay with her? And anyway, you ain't no Dr. Feelgood. What she expect you to do about her being constipated — escort her to the commode and squeeze her butt?" Viola was not the kind of woman to make fun of people, but every now and then she said something about somebody that made me laugh. She laughed long and hard at her last comment. Under the circumstances, I was glad that I was able to let out a little laugh myself. I didn't want her to notice anything different about my voice.

Miss Naomi, her eyes still looking like they were going to pop out of her head and roll across the floor, motioned for me to get off the telephone. "Uh, Viola, can I call you back in a little while?" I was also anxious to get off the phone so I could return my attention back to the scene of the crime.

"You can call me back but it better not be tonight. As soon as I hang up this phone, I'm getting in my bed. And you know once my head hit that pillow, I wouldn't know if the house was on fire."

"I'll see you in the morning then." I hung up before Viola could say anything else. "What do we do now?" I asked, looking from Valerie's face to her mother's. Then I looked at Mr. Zeke on the floor and shivered. And then something strange came over me. For the next few moments I felt profoundly sad. There was something about death that made everybody seem equal. It was the only thing that every living thing would experience on the same level. And that was: once it was over, it was over. No ifs, ands, or buts about it. One body couldn't be more or less dead than another. However, in Mr. Zeke's case death seemed to take on a whole new meaning. For Valerie and her family, it meant life. My main concern was what kind of life it would mean for them now. Freedom or jail? What if it meant Valerie and her mother would develop such remorse that their guilt would eventually destroy them, anyway? I couldn't figure out why I was thinking about these things when there were other things that I needed to focus on first. "What do you want me to do?" I whimpered.

"All you need to do is be a lookout. Make sure nobody comes into the house. And if they do, don't let them past the living room," Valerie informed me. "Binkie might show up, and he got a key. If he comes home, you keep him in that living room even if it means you got to sit on him. Paw Paw might wake up and holler for some water or help to get on the bedpan. Other than that, we don't have to worry about him."

"What are you going to do?" I asked, looking toward the door.

Valerie didn't answer my question. Instead, she looked at her mother. Before I knew what was going on, Valerie lifted Mr. Zeke's legs and Miss Naomi lifted him off the floor by his shoulders. And then they hauled him toward the back door.

With my arms wrapped around my chest

I went into the living room and tried to act normal. I made sure the door was locked and then I turned off the light. I sat on the sofa in the dark, shaking so hard my teeth clicked and clacked like castanets at a salsa party. I don't know how much time passed, but eventually Valerie came into the living room.

"Lo, can you come out to the backyard?" she asked, looking toward the room her grandfather occupied.

"What for?" I asked, my breath fluttering around inside my throat like a loose kite.

"We need you to hold the flashlight. That's all," Valerie told me, wiping sweat off her forehead with the back of her hand. "That bastard weighs a ton, and we want to make sure he's, uh, all the way, uh, you know . . ."

"Valerie, I can't believe this is happening," I said. "I don't want to be any more involved in this mess than I already am," I bleated. "We could all go to jail, and to be honest with you, I don't think that what you and your mama are doing is the right thing. You can't get away with this."

"We already have," Valerie assured me with a nod. "Only four people know what happened here tonight, and one of them is dead. Nobody else will ever know . . . unless *one of us* tells them." Valerie paused and gave me a look that scared the daylights out of me. "Do you understand me?"

"I understand," I managed. Then I followed her to the backyard where Mr. Zeke's body lay on the hard damp ground at the edge of the grave that he'd dug with his own hands.

CHAPTER 17

I knew that almost everybody who knew Mr. Zeke disliked him on some level. He had a few brooding male friends who came around and went to the bars to raise hell with him. But Mr. Zeke was the kind of man who didn't have a lot of use for other men.

However, he loved the ladies, and he didn't care who knew it.

Even the other women he claimed he fucked whenever he felt like it. The problem with that was that these women didn't realize what an asshole he really was until it was too late. By then they couldn't get rid of him and had to put up with his mess until he decided to move on. There was a Mexican woman in an East L.A. barrio that he'd been fooling around with right up under Miss Naomi's nose. Every time I ran into that woman at the nail shop we both went to, she talked about him like a dog — in English and Spanish. Miss Naomi didn't even try to break up that relationship. "Every minute that Zeke spends with one of his whores is one less minute that I have to spend with him," she'd said.

What I couldn't understand was, if there was another woman crazy enough to get involved with Zeke, why was it so hard for him to leave Miss Naomi? Why would any man in his right mind want to hang around a woman who hated him, especially when he had another woman he could pester?

Despite the fact that I was scared shitless and desperate to leave, I stayed at Valerie's house the night that Mr. Zeke died. As hard as it was for me to believe, he was buried like an old bone in the backyard under the fig tree next to the barbeque grill. The same barbeque grill that Mr. Zeke had kicked over the weekend before because Miss Naomi had burned the ribs and chicken wings.

They had asked me to help them scoot him into the grave, but I had promptly refused. Just being at the crime scene was bad enough. Had I touched Mr. Zeke's corpse I would have felt even worse. I already felt like I was in a trance as I watched Valerie and her mother mop Mr. Zeke's blood up off the kitchen floor. I had also refused when they asked me to help them clean up his blood. Every time I got too close to that bloody mess I started gagging. I had already thrown up so much that it felt like my insides had been turned inside out.

As soon as they had finished mopping and sopping up blood, they continued to work on the linoleum floor with Mop & Glo. By the time they finished, that floor was shining like gold. Then everything that Mr. Zeke owned was stuffed into large garbage bags. They disposed of his clothes, shoes, and other knickknacks, like tools and his collection of Miles Davis albums, in Dumpsters all over L.A. They made several trips in Miss Naomi's station wagon, and by morning they were still dumping. They had even thrown out every single picture that included Mr. Zeke. The last thing to go into a garbage bag was a half-empty bottle of beer that he'd popped open with his teeth and left in the refrigerator the evening before.

I didn't sleep at all that night on the couch with the pillow and blanket that Valerie had tossed into my lap. For one thing, I couldn't stop thinking about the fact that there was a dead body in the backyard. Not that I believed in ghosts, but I almost jumped out of my skin every time I heard a creak or any other odd noise. At one point during the night, I dozed off for just a few moments. I woke up real quick when I thought I heard a man's voice whispering my name.

When Binkie and Liz came home the next morning, the first thing twelve-year-old Binkie wanted to know was why I was sitting in their living room at nine o'clock on a Saturday morning. Valerie and Miss Naomi had just left to dump the last of Mr. Zeke's belongings. I still had on my soiled prom dress, but I had on one of Valerie's robes. The strange thing about that was I didn't even remember putting the robe on.

"What you doing here?" Binkie asked with a stiff smile, strutting across the living room floor with Liz, who was just ten, a few steps behind him. Both kids, who looked like younger versions of Valerie, clutched their sleeping bags and backpacks. They looked around the room with curious looks on their faces. Their demeanor was so poised it seemed staged. It seemed as if they thought that they were being observed by hidden cameras that had been planted throughout the room by their cruel stepfather. And knowing Mr. Zeke, that sounded like something he would do. But not anymore. . . .

I knew that these two kids were more interested in trying to determine where their mean-spirited stepfather was lurking than they were curious about my presence. Liz, with her hands trembling, leaned forward and tilted her braided head toward the kitchen, cupping her ear. A loud crash made us all jump, but it was just Pete. He came trotting out of the kitchen with a dog biscuit in his mouth, something he had never been allowed to get away with when Mr. Zeke was alive. Then it dawned on me that the dog had witnessed the murder and the burial. I didn't know how intelligent dogs were, but I had a feeling that Pete knew that he no longer had anything to fear in this house.

"Uh, I came over to keep an eye out for Paw Paw until Valerie and your mama gets back from taking Mr. Zeke to the bus station," I said. Binkie and Liz let out mild gasps at the same time and gave me puzzled looks. Pete ran up to Liz, dropped his dog biscuit, and started wagging his tag and sniffing her leg. The way he always did when he was happy.

"The bus station?" Liz asked, leaning down to rub Pete's head. "Where is Zeke going? To Mississippi where his mama's folks live? Or maybe to Samoa where his daddy came from?" There was a hopeful and anxious look on her face that I hadn't seen since she was a toddler.

"I don't know where he went for sure," I said. "He mentioned a bunch of places he might go. Even out of this country. And, uh, Samoa was one of them. All I do know for sure is that he packed up all his stuff last night and told Miss Naomi he wasn't coming back. He even slapped her one last time before he left." I paused and sniffed. The one thing that Miss Naomi had emphasized the most was that we were not to mention any one particular city, on the slim chance that somebody might check. But more important was the fact that we were to make it clear that we had not seen Mr. Zeke actually purchase a bus ticket, period. That way in case somebody was concerned enough to check there'd be no record on file with a ticket purchased to anywhere in Mr. Zeke's name. Even I knew that people went to the bus station planning to go somewhere all the time and changed their minds once they got there.

"He won't be coming back?" Liz asked in a pleading tone of voice and an anxious look on her face. "For real?"

I looked at the floor before I answered. Then I looked up at Liz's face. I nodded my head so hard that my neck felt like somebody had tried to choke me to death, too. "I'm sure," I said. "He's gone for good."

Now that Mr. Zeke was "gone for good," it didn't take long for me to find out just how unpopular he really was. Only a couple of his drinking buddies came to the house looking for him. "The only thing they seemed concerned about was the fact that he'd skipped town owing them some money," Valerie told me.

Valerie also told me that when Zeke's relatives heard he'd run off, they had no interest in his whereabouts or his welfare, either. To make the story seem more plausible, Miss Naomi called up Mr. Zeke's mama in Gulfport, Mississippi, and asked her if she'd seen her son, sobbing to the woman that Mr. Zeke had packed up and left, hinting that he was going to "hook up" with a woman who knew how to treat a man. "No, I ain't seen that mannish rascal and I don't care if I ever do again." That old woman went on to say that if, and when, Mr. Zeke wanted to talk to her, he knew where to find her. She was not about to try and track him down, especially since the last time he'd visited her he'd slapped her because she refused to give him money so he could visit a nearby casino.

Other than God, who could care about a man who would hit the woman who had carried him in her womb for nine months?

It seemed like nobody did, which is why I couldn't understand why I was feeling so much sorrow about what had happened to him. I didn't miss Mr. Zeke. And after I thought about all the pain he'd caused my girl and her family, it was easy for me to convince myself that he got what he had coming.

However, as it turned out, there were people who wanted to know Mr. Zeke's whereabouts, after all. A legion of disgruntled bill collectors that he had left hanging were very anxious to locate him. A few even called on the night he died and left nasty messages on the answering machine. Another one called the house that Sunday. And the only reason they stopped calling was because Miss Naomi had the telephone number changed that Monday. A slew of creditors had sent nasty letters addressed to Mr. Zeke threatening him with lawsuits. They'd arrived that Tuesday. After school that day, I helped Valerie write *MOVED* on the envelopes so we could return them to the post office. On one she "accidentally" wrote *DECEASED.* I spotted it in time, and as soon as she looked away, I balled it up and stuffed it into my backpack. I saw no reason to tell her about her slipup, and I made a note to monitor her actions. I was too involved in her mess not to be concerned.

It bothered me to know that my best friend had had to resort to murder so that she could enjoy a normal life like me. I didn't know it at the time, but I would eventually lead a life that would be anything but normal.

CHAPTER 18

A few days after I'd helped Valerie return the letters to Mr. Zeke's bill collectors, she started treating me like I was a bill collector! Each time I called the new telephone number I was told that she was either too "busy" to talk to me or that she was "gone somewhere." I stopped trying to reach her when I called after midnight one Wednesday and was told, "she's gone somewhere." I couldn't even catch up with her at school. And under the circumstances, I didn't even try that hard. Besides, with just a few days left until graduation I had more than enough loose ends to tie up myself so I was "busy," too.

When I saw Valerie on graduation night heading toward the auditorium in her cap and gown, with her mother and several of her relatives trailing behind her, I didn't try to get her attention. For one thing she saw me anyway, so I figured that was enough.

She looked me straight in the eye, and then strolled right past me without acknowledging me, as if I were a straight-up stranger. I didn't know what she was thinking or feeling about what she'd done, so I had no way of knowing why she didn't want to talk to me. I thought that if anything, despite my promise that I'd never tell that I'd witnessed her crime, she'd have wanted to keep me on a short leash to make sure I didn't blab. The night seemed twice as long as any other night. Somehow, I managed to get through it with a smile on my face.

We had received our diplomas and suffered through long-winded speeches made by our principal and vice principal. I was about to leave the auditorium when Valerie came up to me. I had no idea why she had such a strange look on her face. She looked uncomfortable, embarrassed, and confused. If anything she should have been looking sorry. There was no excuse for the way she had been avoiding me. I was glad that Floyd and Viola were with me because their presence made me feel less awkward. Both of them knew that I had not communicated with Valerie in a while. And since I'd told them both the same stupid story about me canceling my prom date because Valerie was sick, they couldn't understand why. About the only thing that Viola and Floyd had in common was that they usually didn't stick their noses in my business. I was glad that the situation with Valerie was one that they stayed out of. But tonight it couldn't be avoided.

"Where you been keeping yourself, stranger?" Viola asked Valerie as soon as she got close enough to us where we were standing in the hallway outside of the auditorium. "I thought you'd left town, too. Like Zeke."

At the mention of Mr. Zeke's name Valerie shot me a nervous look. I blinked and cleared my throat.

"Oh, I've just been busy trying to help Mama with Paw Paw," Valerie said in a weak voice. "Hi, Floyd. Long time no see."

I heard Floyd snicker under his breath before he responded. "Likewise." Floyd shifted his weight from one foot to the other and folded his arms. He looked good standing there in his cap and gown. I was more proud of him than I was of myself. For one thing, Glodine and a few other people had not expected him to even make it to high school, let alone graduate. And the fact that he had a job at the mall, too, had a lot of people scratching their heads.

"Lo, you going to be home tomorrow?" Valerie asked, her voice cracking. She didn't seem like the same girl who had killed a man and buried his body. Now she seemed, looked, and sounded fragile and frightened.

"As far as I know," I told her in a strong voice. I wanted to make sure I didn't sound as pitiful as she did.

"I wanted to stop by for a little while. I'll be going away for a while," Valerie revealed. I looked at Floyd. He gave me a dumb look and a shrug. Then I looked back at Valerie. She looked away. If I was having nightmares about Mr. Zeke's murder, I could only imagine what was going through her mind.

"Where you going, Valerie?" Viola asked before I could.

"Oh, I'm going to go to Tennessee where most of Mama's folks still live. Y'all remember my goose-necked, long-legged Uncle Dobie that came to visit that time when Mama had her hip replacement surgery?" We all nodded and mumbled. "Well, Uncle Dobie had a fit when Mama threatened to put Paw Paw in a home. He said that as long as there was a breath left in his body, bag of bones that that body is, nobody was putting his daddy in no old folks' home. Mama told him if that's the case, he needs to bring Paw Paw to Memphis to stay with him." Valerie paused and sucked in her breath.

I didn't like the way she was looking at

me. It seemed like she didn't want to take her eyes off mine, and that made me nervous. I also didn't like the way she *looked,* period. Her appearance was disturbing. She'd lost at least ten pounds since that night and resembled a bag of bones herself. Her face looked bony and hollow, like the face on a skull. "I'm going to escort Paw Paw back to Memphis. We're leaving tomorrow around noon." I hadn't seen such a desperate look on her face since the last time I saw Mr. Zeke slap her for sassing him. Valerie suddenly looked away and took her time facing me again when I spoke.

"When are you coming back?" I asked. I had other female friends, and I had Floyd, but I had a special relationship with Valerie. Especially now.

"I . . . I don't know," she said with uncertainty, and a heavy sigh. She looked at me and shook her head. "I might not come back this way. Binkie and Liz are moving in with Aunt Hazel in Compton." Valerie gave me a strange look. I had asked her time and time again why her mother allowed the younger kids to remain in that house with Mr. Zeke when they had relatives they could move in with. This was not the time, or the place, to ask her why they were finally moving out now that Mr. Zeke was gone and no longer posed a threat. But I think I knew why they had stayed and experienced and witnessed so much abuse. It was the same reason that Valerie stayed. They wanted to be there to support and protect their mother. I blinked back a tear. Things were happening too fast for me. What had happened on prom night had already made me lose my grip on reality. Now I'd have to deal with the absence of my best friend. "And with me on my way, Mama's thinking about closing up the bar and coming to Memphis herself."

"What about your mama's house?" I asked. Miss Naomi had inherited the house from Paw Paw. Like the bar, the house was Miss Naomi's, free and clear. As slovenly and mean as Mr. Zeke had been the last few years of his life, he had contributed a lot in the upkeep of the house. He'd even painted the whole thing all by himself two years ago. And he'd been good about maintaining the lawn and trimming all the trees in both yards. I shuddered when I recalled how much time he'd spent trimming the fig tree that he was buried under. With all the work that he had done, it was no wonder that that house was still the most attractive one on the block, even after all these years. Viola often said that Miss Naomi could probably sell the house for several times more than Paw Paw had originally paid for it.

"What about my mama's house?" Valerie asked sharply. I knew that she knew what I was thinking. And that was — that pretty house had an ugly story to tell that Valerie didn't want anybody else to hear. For the record, I didn't either. What if some new tenants decided they wanted a pool in the backyard? Or what if they wanted to uproot that fig tree? It wouldn't take a sharp forensics investigator long to identify Mr. Zeke's body and to determine how he died! I'd watched enough crime shows on television to know that even though I had not even touched Mr. Zeke, I was still an accomplice. And even if I was lucky, at the very least I could get a couple of years in some women's prison.

"Your mama finally going to sell that showpiece of a house?" Floyd asked, clearing his throat. I knew that he was uncomfortable standing in front of Valerie. They had never been that close. As a matter of fact, the only connection they had was me.

"I wish I was in financial shape enough to buy it." Viola swooned. "I'd trade your mama's house for that ramshackle mess I'm in any day. Course I wouldn't get to enjoy it that long, and the one that would benefit

153

the most would be my nephew in San Diego."

"Mama's not selling our house. Not now, not ever," Valerie said with a quick and firm nod. "As long as I live, it's going to stay in our family. That way, I can make sure it's, uh, kept up the way my real daddy would have wanted." Valerie looked at me and blinked hard. "Dolores, I'll write to you when I get settled."

"I'll still be here," I said, squeezing Floyd's hand.

Valerie cleared her throat and turned to Floyd. "You better take care of my girl while I'm gone." He gave her a bear hug and patted her on the back.

"Take care of yourself, V," he said, giving her a quick peck on the cheek and a firm squeeze around her narrow waist. Then just like that, she was gone.

I was glad that Floyd had to work later that night. It was just as well. Not only did I not want to attend any of the after-graduation parties, but I didn't want to spend the night with him, either. Romance and the "good fucking" that Floyd had been threatening to give to me for the past two nights was the last thing on my mind.

Thanks to Valerie, all I wanted was to be alone. I had too many things to think about, and getting fucked wasn't one of them. For one thing her recent behavior toward me had put me in a royal blue funk that seemed to intensify with each day. What she'd just told me sent me to an even lower level of sadness. In addition to everything else, now I had to worry about Valerie confessing her crime to somebody in Tennessee and dragging my name into it.

Valerie had a big mouth, and a conscience. After a few too many drinks, or a few puffs on a strong blunt, she usually shot her mouth off like a Gatling gun. I could easily believe that with her conscience combined with alcohol or weed, there was a chance that she might eventually confess to every murder since Kennedy's. And I had no way of knowing how big a role she'd claim I played in her mess. For all I knew, she could put more of the blame on me to lessen her own. She, along with her mama's support, could say whatever she wanted to say about me, and it would be their word against mine.

There was no telling how big a can of worms Valerie could open in Tennessee with her long tongue and loose lips. Should that happen, I wouldn't hear about it until it was too late for me to prepare a defense, or sneak my ass on down to Mexico and live the rest of my days as a fugitive. I knew that if I went to a good lawyer and told him everything, it might do me some good. However, I wouldn't do that until, if and when, Valerie or her mother broke down and confessed first.

One thing I knew for sure was that I'd *never* be the one to spill the beans. Not even on my deathbed. And it was not just because I was only *slightly* involved. Like a lot of black folks in L.A., I was skeptical when it came to the police — and had every reason to be. Especially after that Rodney King mess that we'd all struggled through — not to mention the fact that Mr. Zeke had once been a policeman.

I planned to live each day like it was my last, because one day it would be.

CHAPTER 19

That Floyd. That boy was one person who usually didn't stop trying until he got what he wanted. Especially when what he wanted was something I had. And that usually meant what I had between my thighs.

That night of graduation, Floyd got his way with me, again. After he left his usher job that night at the Tri-Plex Cinema a couple of miles from our street, he called me up from his cellular phone as he stood on the front porch of Viola's house. Mumbling profanities under my breath the whole time, I threw on my housecoat and tiptoed downstairs. Except for a howling dog, it was quiet outside when I cracked open the door and peered out. I gave Floyd an exasperated look. "What's wrong with you?" I snarled.

"It took you long enough to answer that door," he grumbled, pinching my ass as he followed behind me across the living room floor. He wore a pair of tight black jeans, ripped on both knees, and a loose-fitting blue shirt, unbuttoned all the way down the front. It was hard to believe that this was the same brother I'd admired a few hours earlier in his cap and gown. "I wanted to see you," he whined. "With a lady like you, what else could I do? I couldn't help myself."

"I was in the bed," I snapped, whirling around to face him, slapping his hand. "And I'd like to get back in it." Viola always kept fresh flowers in the living room. There was a large vase on one of the tables at the end of her sofa that was filled with red roses. There was an even larger vase on the other end table. It contained an elaborate bouquet that that manipulative nephew of hers had dropped off earlier in the day. Despite the floral fragrance that filled the living room, I could still smell what was left of the last batch of tea cakes Viola had baked just before she went to bed.

"That's good because your bed would be a lot more comfortable than that mother-fucking couch! And the sooner the better. My dick's about to bust through my jeans, girl." Floyd looked around the room. He lifted his chin as he looked toward the kitchen and sniffed. "And I know you need me to help you get rid of the latest batch of them tea cakes Miss Viola cooked up."

"Keep your voice down, fool! The only man that's welcome in Viola's house this time of night is that nephew of hers and Reverend Carter. You should know that by now," I said under my breath. "That poor woman would have a complete breakdown if she ever found out about me fucking in her house with all these Bibles, and religious knickknacks, and pictures of Jesus scattered all over the place. And as good as she's always been to me, she is the last person in this world I want to upset."

Then I started sniffing in Floyd's direction. Right away I sneezed. The potent smell of all the flowers in the room and the smell of those tea cakes coming from the kitchen seemed to permeate the air. But all that was nothing compared to the stench coming from Floyd. The smell of weed was so overwhelming I couldn't tell where on his body it was coming from. His breath was so foul it almost blew me across the room. I cussed under my breath some more and fanned the air with both hands. Nobody liked to spark up a doobie more than me, but I knew that Viola had a major problem with anything illegal. That's why I never indulged myself in her house. I plucked the thick, lopsided joint that Floyd had propped behind his ear and slid it into my bra.

"See, that's what happens when we go too long without some pleasure. You get all cranky and shit," he complained, leering at me so hard I almost lost my train of thought.

"I'm not cranky," I insisted, letting out an exasperated breath. "I just don't appreciate uninvited company in the middle of the night. And especially company high on weed."

"You want me to leave?" He knew which of my buttons to push when he wanted to get his way, and he was pushing every single button I had on my body. "Graduating was a big deal for somebody like me. I wanted to do something to make it special. It was bad enough that none of my folks came to see me get my diploma. And I thought that since we didn't get to go party like everybody else, it'd be nice for us to celebrate. I know it's late, but I couldn't get out of going to work. And you know I need my job." He blew more bad-smelling breath into my face. Then he started taking slow, tentative steps toward the door, which was part of his plan to get his way. I lunged at him and clamped my hand around his arm. Just like I usually did in similar situations.

"Baby, I'm just a little on edge because of

Valerie's leaving. She's been my girl ever since I came to live with Viola," I told him, my bottom lip stuck out like I'd just dipped a pound of snuff.

"Let me see what I can do about getting rid of that edge," he said wrapping his arms around me and guiding me toward that well-used couch.

If the sex had not been so good, it would have been a lot easier for me to send Floyd back out the door with his pants still zipped up, no matter how much he whined. But he was the biggest weakness I had, and keeping him happy was at the top of my list. I didn't take him up to my room. I knew that if I did, he would have had me up the rest of the night. He didn't like the couch any more than I did, and when we did use it, we did our business as fast as we could. Sometimes, like tonight, it seemed like a chore that I didn't want to do in the first place. And that was the reason why I was slamming my pelvis and hips into him as hard and fast as I could, so I could get it over with as quickly as possible.

One minute later, I was sliding back into my panties and housecoat. Floyd still had his pants down around his knees and was sitting on the end of the couch staring at me. "Damn, baby. That was good, but it was over almost before it started! That kind of shit can give a brother all kinds of performance problems. Can I get a little head before I go, to even things out? I'll never get to sleep tonight with the bucket-size load of jizz I still got. If I drip all over Glodine's sheets, I'll never hear the end of it," he whispered. "I've been horny as hell all evening. Just seeing you in that cap and gown did something to me. You looked like a nun. I always wanted to bust a nun. All dudes do."

"Floyd, it is two o'clock in the morning and I am not in the mood for fucking, anyway. I need to get some sleep so I can get up early tomorrow and start looking for a job." I stopped talking and looked around the room. "Lord knows I can't stay here forever."

"And you won't have to. Pretty soon we'll have a place together."

"I know, I know," I replied, one hand in the air, the other on my hip. Floyd was wearing down my resistance and he knew it. I could see the satisfied look on his face. "But it's been a long day for both of us," I continued in a voice that was getting weaker by the second. "Let's get together tomorrow night after you get off work. We're both eighteen now and out of school. We don't have to worry anymore about those foster care 'don't give a good goddamn, but nosy as hell anyhow' social workers deciding what's best for us anymore. We can do whatever we want, and we've got the rest of our lives to celebrate, baby. Viola gave me a few dollars for a graduation present. We can use it to get a room."

"That's cool, but what about now? A few more minutes is all I need. Come on, baby," he pleaded.

I rolled my eyes and let out a breath that was so loud and strong it made Floyd rear back and gasp. "Shit! You better come real quick, or you are going to end up doing it for yourself — like you ought to be at home doing in the first place!" I hissed. I dropped to the floor on my knees, with my face inches away from his lap. I never sucked dick as hard and fast before in my life like now.

"Take it slow this time, baby. Sex ain't nothing to play around with. Bad sex don't do nobody no good. That's why we got so many perverts and rapists in this country. It's because of bad sex, or no sex. Dr. Ruth done proved it. How she proved it, I don't know, but I doubt if she knows what she's talking about from experience," Floyd told me, holding my head in place. "Now, let me

hush so I can . . ." He couldn't even finish
his sentence. Two seconds later it was over,
and I promptly zipped him up and sent him
on his way.

CHAPTER 20

I had so much on my mind after I got rid of Floyd, I couldn't get to sleep. For the second time in less than a month, I felt really scared. Other than Floyd, I didn't know what the future held for me.

I was glad that Viola had lived long enough to see me graduate, but eventually leaving the only "mother" I'd ever known was not going to be easy. I didn't have any plans to move to another state or even another city, but not sharing a house with Viola anymore was going to take some getting used to. "Dolores, you can stay on here with me for the rest of your life if you want to," she'd told me more times than I could count. And I knew she meant it. But even if Floyd had not been in the picture and we had not planned on getting married, I still would have moved out, whether I wanted to or not. Once Viola was gone, there was no telling what that asshole of a nephew of hers had up his sleeve as far as the house was concerned. The one thing I knew for sure was that even if the house was twice as big as it was, it would never be big enough for me and that greedy, self-centered punk to live in at the same time.

I hated to speak of the devil because when I got up that morning around eight, there he was. Noble was in the kitchen eating grits straight out of the pan on the stove. He had on some dingy beige Bermuda shorts and a black T-shirt that was so tight I could see the imprint of his navel and the nipples on his titties. "Girl, you must have done some serious partying last night. You look like hell," he mumbled, talking out the side of his mouth. There was such a wad of grits in each cheek, it looked like he had the mumps. There was a large plate on the table with a few pieces of bacon still on it, some half chewed. There was enough bacon grease on his lips and chin I could have fried a chicken in it. His thick, permed, wiry brown hair stuck out in all directions. He looked like a homely Al Sharpton. I couldn't figure out what it was about Noble that that beautiful Mexican woman he married saw in him. And she wasn't the only one. He had the nerve to have other women calling and leaving messages for him at Viola's house. Like Mr. Zeke, he must have had a golden rod between his legs. Just the thought of Mr. Zeke sent sharp pains throughout my chest and head. I had to hold my breath for a moment to stay focused.

"I didn't go to any of the parties after graduation. I came straight home," I told him. I frowned when I saw all the eggshells, bread-crumbs, melted butter, and dirty dishes he'd left piled up on the counter for me and Viola to clean up. I was glad that he'd made a fresh pot of coffee. "Help yourself to some breakfast," I added with a smirk. "Make yourself right at home."

Noble was so anxious to take possession of Viola's house, he already had some of his mail coming to her address. He was moving in little by little. Every time he showed up, he brought a few pieces of clothing or some other possession that he stored in the guest room upstairs across the hall from mine. He had his own key, so hiding and not opening the door when he came knocking was not an option for me when I was in the house alone.

When he finally swallowed the grits, he did it so hard it made his head bob and his eyes water. Then he let out a belch that sounded like a fart. *"I am at home,"* he reminded me, fanning his pudgy face. He sat down at the table with a thud and a groan. "In case you didn't know, I lived here for years before Auntie got stuck with you. She tells me all the time that I'm the son she always wanted." He wiped grease and butter off his lips, cheeks, and his three chins, using a handkerchief the size of a diaper that he'd snatched out of his pocket. Then he gave me an amused look. I poured myself a cup of coffee and then plopped down hard in a wobbly metal chair directly across from him at the cluttered kitchen table. The table had been in the house longer than I had, but the chairs were fairly new. Viola had bought them used from a yard sale in Pasadena, but they didn't come anywhere near matching the table or anything else in the kitchen. But things like that never stopped Viola from taking advantage of a bargain. The chairs had such high backs I felt like I was sitting on a cheap throne.

"Uh, now that you out of school, what you plan on doing next?" Noble asked, wiggling his wide load of an ass in his seat like it was itching. "Aunt Viola's got one foot in the grave and the other on a slippery slope, bless her heart. I know my boobie won't be around too much longer, so I plan on spending as much time with her in her last

168

days as I can. I want her to know she was loved to the end of her days. That way, when she goes, she'll go with a smile on her face. . . ." Like with almost every other thing he said to me, what he said and what he meant were two different things. What he was really asking me now was when I was going to get my ass out of his auntie's house so he could do whatever it was he wanted to do with it.

"That's good because I'm getting married soon," I announced with a proud sigh. "I'll feel better knowing Viola's not in this house by herself."

"Married? You? To who?" he demanded, looking shocked. As dumpy and lumpy as that body of his was, he sat up so straight in that high back metal chair it looked like he'd been impaled.

"I'm marrying Floyd Watson," I said firmly and proudly. I took a sip from my coffee cup, screwing up my face because not only was it weak, it smelled and tasted like Lemon Joy, which meant Noble had washed the coffeepot but he had not rinsed it thoroughly. I couldn't imagine how this man had managed to land a job as a dishwasher at an upscale San Diego restaurant and still be there after so many years.

"Floyd Watson? What in the world — I

know damn well you ain't planning on wasting your life up on a thug like Floyd! A pretty girl like you could do a whole lot better than a scalawag like Floyd. He ain't got nothing to offer you! Ain't he caught up in that gang mess? You keep hanging around with him and we'll read about you in the newspaper — the *obituaries!*"

"Floyd has never been in a gang," I said in a stern voice. "Some of his friends are in gangs, and some of my friends are in gangs. I've never been in a gang, either. He's going to the military so he can get some training and benefits. And I plan on working, too." I heard Viola shuffling into the kitchen, coughing and wheezing all the way.

"Good morning, Aunt Viola. How you feeling? I got breakfast ready," Noble said in a voice so sweet it would have made a Snickers candy bar seem bitter. He rose and wobbled up, and then he waddled across the floor to help Viola to one of her metal chairs. I didn't know what it was about old people that made it so hard for them to do such a simple thing as sit down in a chair. From the tortured look on Viola's face, you would have thought that her body was on fire. Even with Noble holding onto her arm and helping her ease down, she sat down with such a thud the floor shook. But as soon as she got comfortable, she seemed fine. She gave me one of her warmest smiles, then she looked up at her nephew and smiled at him, too. He stood over her like a prison guard. "Dolores was just telling me how she can't wait to get married and get a place of her own. . . ."

Viola, with beads of sweat all over her face, suddenly looked at me with both eyebrows raised. "Lo, I done already told you, just because you and Floyd plan on getting married, you ain't got to move out. I meant it when I said you could stay in this house 'til the day you die. This is your home now and it will be, even after I'm gone."

"I know, I know. But Floyd wants us to have a place all our own, right off the bat," I replied, squeezing Viola's clammy hand. Out of the corner of my eye, I could see Noble looking at me with such contempt I decided to leave the room. I knew that if I stayed around him too much longer, I would not be responsible for my actions. "I'm going to run over to Valerie's to tell her good-bye," I said, walking toward the door. Noble now had a puzzled look on his face. "Valerie's taking her grandfather to Memphis to live with relatives," I explained. I rushed out of the kitchen, but I slowed down once I got to the living room because

Noble had already started running off at the mouth about my ongoing presence in Viola's house.

"She ain't even blood, Auntie. You don't owe her a damn thing. You got other kinfolks that could occupy that room she's been roosting in all these years — rent free!" he snarled.

My blood boiled as I eavesdropped on the conversation taking place at the breakfast table. I got as close as I could to the door leading into the kitchen, pressing my ear even closer to the wall. But I still couldn't hear Viola's response. It didn't matter to me one way or the other now. I knew that Viola was sincere, but I no longer felt at home in her house, even if it was the only place that I'd lived in for the past eleven years. This was a feeling that a lot of kids in foster care shared. That's why so many of us moved on as soon as we reached the legal age. And I didn't care if Floyd and I had to live in a cardboard box as long as we were together.

CHAPTER 21

I sucked in a deep breath of air as soon as I made it outside. The grass was still moist from the morning dew, but it was a typical June day in L.A. There was a bright, warm sun in a bright blue sky, but so was the ever-present smog.

Some of our neighbors, still in housecoats and house shoes, were already out washing cars in driveways or mowing lawns. Most of them clutched either a coffee cup or a tall glass with an iced drink. I even saw one shirtless man walking down the street with a bottle of beer in his hand. I ignored a trio of Jehovah's Witnesses in dull-looking brown suits shuffling toward me with hopeful looks on their faces. Each one held a fistful of those pamphlets they were known to peddle. One even had a bulging briefcase. I held up my hand and shook my head as soon as one made eye contact with me. I glanced to the side. Mrs. Scott was hover-

173

ing over her rose garden, pampering each bush as if it were a cute child. When she looked up, I didn't know if the scowl on her face was for me or the Jehovah's Witnesses.

Jeffrey Wallis, a tall, sad-faced boy who lived in the green stucco house right next door to the church, had been in my graduating class. He was crawling out of a limo carrying his shoes and didn't even see me. That boy was so drunk, he could barely stand. His mother was already fussing at him as she ran out of her house with bare feet to help him into the house. I managed a weak smile. Jeffrey and I had never been close friends, but I was glad to see that he had taken advantage of some of the parties the night before. I slid my tongue across my bottom lip, thinking about what I had done a few hours earlier. Even though I'd fussed up a storm about Floyd dropping in on me, I'd enjoyed his company, after all. And that was a good thing because with Valerie leaving, I'd have to depend on Floyd to keep me company even more now.

Miss Naomi saw me before I saw her, so by the time I stumbled up to her front porch she had already opened the door. I didn't know how to interpret the expression on her face. There was a blank look in her eyes, and her lips were pressed together so tight, it looked like she had one thick lip. She wore a long-sleeved white blouse, tied around her head like a scarf. She wore a green flannel housecoat over her clothes and a pair of Paw Paw's large, backless house shoes that looked like canoes on her tiny feet.

Before I could even speak, Miss Naomi told me in a raspy voice, "You too late. You missed Valerie. She booked an earlier flight. She and Paw Paw are already in Memphis by now."

"Oh," I muttered. "I had wanted to ride along to the airport and say my good-byes there," I managed, blinking hard to hold back my tears. It had been a while since I'd had a good cry, and it took a lot for me to get that emotional. I hadn't shed a single tear the night I saw Valerie kill Zeke. As a matter of fact, Luther's funeral was the last time I'd cried. I suddenly felt dizzy. Before I knew what was happening to me, I was swaying like Jeffrey Wallis just did, crawling out of that limo across the street. Miss Naomi took a couple of steps toward me as I grabbed a hold of the banister. "I'm all right," I assured her, standing up straight, forcing myself to smile.

"Did you party last night after you got your diploma?"

"No, ma'am. I came straight home. I

haven't felt much like partying lately." Our eyes met and I was glad I could not read minds. I didn't even want to know what was on hers, but I knew what she was thinking, anyway. I was convinced that she and Valerie would both be thinking about what they'd done every day for the rest of their lives. I knew I would. What could be more serious than murder? Especially with the body of the victim being under a few feet of dirt in the murderers' backyard. The look on Miss Naomi's face made me dizzy all over again.

"Lo, what you saw here *that night* couldn't be helped. And I hope you realize that," Miss Naomi said, glancing over her shoulder and then mine to make sure we were still alone on the porch. "Zeke had made up his mind to kill me, so having the cops get him out of my house and me getting a restraining order would have done no good. I was a dead woman walking. And I know Valerie must have told you that if I had left him, he would have gone after somebody else in my family. I could have hidden myself and my kids, but what could I do to save the rest of my family? And everybody knows that the cops can't do a damn thing until *after* a crime's been committed. Well, their help wouldn't have done me no good if I was dead."

"I know all that and I might have done the same thing you did, if I'd been in your shoes." I stopped long enough to scratch the side of my thigh and to shift my weight from one foot to the other. At one hundred and ten pounds, I felt like I weighed a ton. "But what if Mr. Zeke was just selling wolf tickets?" I asked in a meek voice.

"What if he was doing what?" Miss Naomi looked at me out of the corner of her eye and folded her arms.

"You know, uh, bluffing. Maybe he was making all these threats just to keep you under his thumb," I explained. "He wouldn't have gotten away with anything. I know he didn't want to spend any time in jail. And that's where he would have spent the rest of his life if he had done something real bad to you, or anybody else in your family."

"Something real bad? What in the — what's wrong with you, girl?" Miss Naomi gasped. "He did something real bad to us for years. You seen him do it with your own eyes. He was already half crazy. He went all the way crazy after they kicked him off the police force. He had nothing else to lose, and according to him, nothing to live for,"

Miss Naomi said with a wave of her hand. "And just so you know, he killed his first wife."

"What? I didn't know —"

"Nobody else knew about it. Just me. I just told Valerie about it last night, so she'd stopped feeling so bad about what . . . about, uh, what she did." There was a faraway look in Miss Naomi's eyes now. And a slight smile on her face as she continued talking. "It happened in Florida years ago. He told everybody that her death was an accident, and everybody believed him. They had no reason not to. He was in the church, and everybody just loved him to death back there. The wife fell off a bridge and was drowned while they were out fishing during a Fourth of July picnic. He told me out of his own mouth that he pushed her off that bridge, then stomped on her hands as she tried to hold on to the ledge. All because she was going to divorce him. If he was still alive today, I probably wouldn't be." Miss Naomi dropped her head, and we just stood there in silence for a moment. She looked back up at me with her eyes narrowed and her jaw twitching. "I hope to God you never have to walk in my shoes. If you do, you'll see why me and my child did what we did."

I gave her a quick nod. "Uh, when you

talk to Valerie, tell her to write or call me up when she gets settled," I said, backing off the porch. "And, I've said it once but I'll say it again, you and Valerie don't have to worry about me saying anything to anybody about what happened . . . uh, that night. I don't care what happens between Valerie and me, I will never ever tell anybody about what I saw. I swear to God I won't."

"I know you won't. *You can't now,*" Miss Naomi told me. Her last comment disturbed me. Not because she had said it in a threatening manner. As a matter of fact, she'd said it in a charming voice and with a smile on her face. What disturbed me was the fact that she seemed to know me better than I knew myself.

CHAPTER 22

When August rolled around and I still hadn't heard from Valerie, I didn't think I ever would again. I rarely saw her mother. When I did, I didn't ask about Valerie, and she didn't mention her, either. I got hired as a cashier at a Walgreens working part-time on the night shift in the same little strip mall where Floyd worked at the Tri-Plex. Between the two of us we didn't even make enough to afford a decent apartment. Therefore, every chance we got, we interviewed for better jobs. Unfortunately, the other jobs that we were qualified to do didn't pay much better than the ones we already had. Almost every place wanted to hire somebody with experience.

"How in the hell do these people expect somebody to get experience if nobody will hire them in the first place?" I lamented to Floyd.

"Dolores, until we get more training and

shit, we still won't get better jobs, anyway," Floyd told me in a tired voice. He was just as frustrated as I was, and that didn't help matters much. When I got frustrated I wanted to mope around and complain. When he got frustrated he wanted to fuck. By now I was so use to him shaking his dick at me, I rarely complained anymore. I had another good reason for not complaining so much anymore and trying to fill all of Floyd's sexual needs. And it was a reason that disturbed me. I had begun to notice that sometimes when I refused his demands, he eyeballed other females in ways that made me uncomfortable — right in front of me! But since his friends did the same thing when they were with their girlfriends, I didn't think that it was anything for me to be concerned about.

I had no intimate interests in anybody but Floyd, and I had no reason to believe he'd cheat on me. But I wasn't naïve. I knew that if God had created a woman who could keep her man from straying, it probably wasn't me. Whenever I had a remote feeling that Floyd was losing interest in me, I paid more attention to him. I supported everything he wanted to do. And I was proud to tell people that he was going to serve Uncle Sam. That was one thing that I ended up wishing I had kept my big mouth shut about.

Floyd didn't join the military like he had said he would. He had told me and everybody else he knew that he'd be gone before July. But he waited until the end of summer to tell me that he hadn't joined because he had flunked the physical. "I guess I had one injury too many when I was growing up. I never got proper medical attention in time after some of these beatings, so I never healed right. You stuck with a cripple, baby," he said, laughing.

I knew that Floyd had been abused a lot before I met him. By men like Mr. Zeke most of the time. That was one of the reasons it was so easy for me to put what happened to Mr. Zeke in the back of my mind.

"Floyd, I would rather have you crippled than not at all," I assured him. I didn't tell him, but I was glad that he wasn't going anywhere. I had a lot of respect for the military, but I didn't agree with a lot of things our government did. It seemed like every time I looked up there was some ruckus going on somewhere in the world. And it was usually men like Floyd who got caught up in all that bloodletting in some off-the-wall country that Uncle Sam should not have stuck his nose in to begin with.

Knowing how dependent I was on Floyd, Viola spent a lot of time trying to encourage me to make more friends. "I see you moping around this house, and I see you standing on the back porch looking toward Valerie's house. I bet she ain't sitting on no porch down south twiddling her thumbs. She done probably latched onto her one of them juicy-butt country boys and got herself married by now."

I didn't attempt to make any more friends, but I did continue to spend more time looking for a better job. After a lot of networking with people I met during some of my dead-end job interviews, I heard about some incentive programs that the state was offering to foster children. The main requirement was that you had to have graduated from high school with at least a B+ average. I was in good shape, but since Floyd had graduated by the skin of his teeth with a C– average, he didn't qualify. "Baby, you go for this. Something else will come along for me," he told me. He couldn't hide his disappointment. And for a minute, he acted like he was jealous that I'd made it. But I didn't let that stop me, because I was working to improve his future as well as mine.

I signed up for one of the programs immediately and took a thirteen-week business course five days a week. One week after I'd completed the program, a dentist who belonged to our church hired me to be his receptionist. Since I worked days for him, I kept my night time job at Walgreens. My income increased considerably, and at my suggestion, Floyd and I opened a joint savings account.

We didn't have a date in mind, but I wanted to get married and move out of Viola's house as soon as we could afford to. I was careful about what I spent my money on. I needed to have enough to fall back on in case I had to move out before I was ready. Viola's health was rapidly deteriorating, and that nephew of hers now reminded me of a vulture, ready to gobble up everything she had that he wanted as soon as she took her last breath.

Now that I was making more money, I didn't mind occasionally covering the cost by myself when Floyd and I checked into cheap motels. He had become my lifeline, so to speak. I honestly didn't know what I would have done with myself if he had not been there for me. The only thorn in my side was the fact that Floyd still "socialized" with some of his friends who spent more time in jail than out. I knew him well and I believed him when he told me that I didn't have to worry about him having any more brushes with the law.

Ironically, I was more worried about me having a brush with the law than I was Floyd. I had panic attacks when cops got too close to me. By not communicating with Valerie, I never knew from one day to the next if it would be my last day of freedom.

On New Year's Eve Floyd took me to the West Hollywood apartment of one of his Mexican friends to spend a few nights. He had offered to house-sit for this friend, who was in Mexico on a mysterious vacation. This friend was a drug dealer whose connections were in Mexico, so I knew that he'd gone down there to do more than romp on the beach and visit his grandmother. Knowing how the friend made his money gave me something else to be concerned about — drugs were a magnet for turmoil. Not just from other thugs, but the cops, for sure. But Floyd had assured me that his *amigo* had a "financial arrangement" with the L.A. cops, so we had nothing to worry about by being in his apartment. Things were fine the first night. We celebrated the arrival of the new year in style with a bottle of champagne and a fuckfest that almost wore me out.

Two days into the new year, while Floyd was out getting more for us to drink, somebody knocked on the door. And they didn't knock the way normal people knocked. Whoever it was, they were banging on the door with something hard. It sounded like they were trying to knock the door off its hinges. When I saw two large, beefy-faced white cops through the peephole I almost had a heart attack. Viola and everybody else knew that I was at this address with Floyd. My first thought was that the cops had accosted Floyd and forced him to tell them where I was. It didn't take me long to realize what a ridiculous thought that was, but I still didn't open the door. By the time Floyd returned, fifteen minutes later, I was hyperventilating. He found me in the bathroom with the door locked, hiding behind the shower curtain.

"Dolores, is there something going on with you that you don't want me to know about? I am not blind or stupid. I've notice for the past few months that whenever we go out somewhere and the cops get too close, you start twitching like you got cerebral palsy," he said, escorting me back to the living room. "You ain't got no reason in the world to be that scared of no cops. If anybody ought to be scared to deal with the cops, it's me." He laughed, pulling me down into his lap on the couch.

"Viola's hairdresser is related to Rodney King. People that used to come to the house to visit Luther knew Rodney's family. A lot of folks I know don't like the cops because of what they did to Rodney, and got away with. I don't like cops," I mumbled, reaching for a glass of the wine he had poured.

"I don't like cops either, but I don't hide from them because I don't have no reason to. And if it'll make you feel any better, they were still downstairs when I walked up. They were looking for my boy. He failed to show up in court for a bunch of outstanding warrants."

"Oh," I mumbled. "Well, I still don't want to be here in case they come back, anyway," I said. "Cops make me nervous." I finished my drink and started gathering my things.

"Dolores." Floyd grabbed my arm and gently spun me around. "Baby, you don't have no reason to be getting nervous about nothing. Or do you?"

"What? Wh-what do you mean by that?" I asked, forcing myself to laugh. "I haven't done anything illegal," I said in a flat voice.

"Do you know somebody that did?"

"What? Why are you asking me all this shit

all of a sudden?" I wailed. My heart did a flip-flop. I could feel sweat sliding down the center of my back, and it felt like hot wax.

"I should have asked you a long time ago. I didn't just start noticing how nervous you get whenever the subject of cops comes up. Now if there is something I need to know, you need to tell me now. We can't even be thinking about getting married if one of us got something to hide."

I sucked in my nervous breath and looked Floyd straight in the eye. "I don't have anything to hide," I assured him. He just stood there with his arms folded, looking at me. "Do me a favor and drop this," I said. "And don't bring it up again," I warned.

CHAPTER 23

A month later I quit my job at Walgreens when Dr. Oglethorpe promoted me from the receptionist position to bookkeeper. Not only did it mean an even higher salary, but there was a lot of overtime. And working for a dentist did a lot for my morale. Days would go by without me thinking about the way my relationship with Valerie ended.

It was a Friday night in March when the bottom fell out of my world. Again. For the second time in less than a year I had to deal with a traumatic situation that could destroy me.

I had worked a full shift at Dr. Oglethorpe's office. And because two of my coworkers had called in sick, everything was behind. I spent several hours during the day filing and doing whatever else I could to help out. The office was located in a quiet, low-crime location, so I didn't mind staying a couple of hours longer by myself. Besides,

Floyd was going to sneak in and keep me company when he got off work.

He helped me do some more filing, grumbling about it all along. But he did it anyway, because he knew that it was the only way he was going to get what he wanted from me that night. There was a vinyl couch in the waiting room, but I didn't want to fuck on it. "Would you want to sit in some doctor's waiting room on a couch where somebody's been fucking their brains out?" I asked Floyd as he ushered me from one spot in the office to another. He was behind me with his arms wrapped around my waist. His dick was so hard against my behind it felt like the tip of a baseball bat.

"Look, baby, I don't care where we do it. I want me some pussy, and I want it now," he said, almost out of breath.

"We can get a room when I get off work," I said with a laugh, slapping his hand. "Now please behave and act like a gentleman. If that's possible with your nasty self."

"We can save that money. And I don't want to hook up at Viola's house tonight. Not the way her nephew comes and goes!"

The last time we'd made love in Viola's house, Noble had let himself in seconds after we'd put our clothes back on. From that day on, I caught him looking at me too

190

long and too hard. Now when he saw me, he usually looked at my titties before he looked at my face. My days were already numbered in Viola's house. I'd been out of school for almost a year now, and even though she kept telling me that I could stay as long as I wanted to, I felt like I had worn out my welcome. As far as I was concerned, I was living on borrowed time. The last thing I wanted to do was aggravate Noble even more than he already was. Despite the fact that Viola loved me, she was a weak old woman, in and out of her mind, and in and out of the hospital. She could be easily persuaded by a shark like Noble. I knew that if he wanted to evict me, it wouldn't be that hard for him to make that happen.

Floyd and I made love on the floor next to the X-ray machine. Then we did it a few times on the swivel chair that I sat in off and on for eight hours a day, five days a week doing Dr. Oglethorpe's books.

Afterward, we cleaned up our mess and locked up. Then we took the bus back across town. With a smile on his face, Floyd walked me to my door. After a tongue-bath of a kiss that must have lasted at least five minutes, he ran off the porch and sprinted across the street to Glodine's house, whistling all the way.

It was Glodine who came banging on Viola's door a few hours later. I was so groggy when I stumbled downstairs to the living room in my housecoat, I stumbled and walked into a wall, even with the lights on. Then I stubbed my toe on the leg of a chair and had to hop to the door on one leg. I looked through the peephole, expecting to see Floyd standing there with his dick in his hand. All I saw was a huge eye peering into the peephole. Since I couldn't tell who it was, I ran to the window and snatched the curtains back. To my everlasting horror, it was that damn Glodine. Seeing her irritated me more than my injured toe. As a matter of fact, the minute I realized it was her at the door, my toe stopped throbbing.

"Glodine! What in the world do you want at this hour?" I hollered, as I flung open the door.

"You don't need to be turning off your phones, girl," she yelled, shaking a finger with a two-inch nail in my face.

"What are you talking about? Where's Floyd? Did something happen to him?" I yelled, looking over her shoulder. I looked toward her house and saw that her porch light and every light in the house was on, except the one in the front upstairs room that Floyd occupied. I also saw two police cars parked in front of her house. "Glodine, what's going on? What are the cops . . . doing in front of your house?"

"I knew Floyd was going to end up in jail sooner or later. He's too sneaky! He was sneaky when they brought him to me, he was —"

"Will you shut the fuck up and just tell me why you are here and why the cops are at your house?" I shouted, looking from her to the police cars parked in front of her house like demons guarding the gates of hell.

"This is it! It's over for your boy! Floyd raped and killed some girl tonight! All this time I been raising a rapist in my house!" Glodine told me, her arms wrapped around her lumpy chest. "It could have been me!" she shrieked.

I almost knocked her to the ground as I ran out the door and across the yard. My housecoat flew open and was flapping behind me like a pair of limp wings. Just as I made it to Glodine's front yard, both of the police cars pulled away from the curb. One had Floyd in the backseat. Even in the darkness, I could see the desperation in his eyes. It was a look that would haunt me for the rest of my life.

I had so many questions running through my head. Like who got raped? When? Where? But the biggest question I had was, "What did this have to do with Floyd?" Floyd was the man I was going to marry soon. Him raping somebody was about as unthinkable as me raping somebody!

I stood there in the middle of Baylor Street in my housecoat and bare feet. I watched until the police car that had my man in it turned the corner. Glodine's husband and their foster daughters stood on the front porch, shaking their heads and mumbling among themselves. The nosy Scotts were peeping out of their upstairs bedroom window. Glodine was standing right next to me now. I could hear her rambling on and on, but she was making no sense to me. The word *rape* and Floyd's name didn't even belong in the same sentence. It was as farfetched as Valerie and murder. But . . . Valerie was guilty of murder, and I had seen her do it. Could Floyd have . . . I couldn't even finish the thought.

CHAPTER 24

It had been less than a year since Valerie killed Mr. Zeke. I was still trying to deal with that mess. I knew that I would never be able to put it completely out of my mind, but I had learned to live with it. As long as Mr. Zeke's corpse remained in the makeshift grave in the backyard of Valerie's house and nobody else ever found out, I could go on about my business. But now I had to deal with another unspeakable horror that involved another person close to me.

If the whole world had come crashing down on my shoulders that night the cops hauled Floyd away for rape and murder, I could not have felt more helpless and confused.

What happened in the next few days happened so fast I couldn't stay focused on any one thing for too long. And none of it made sense to me. From what I'd been able to piece together, based on information dumped in my lap by Glodine and news-paper accounts, some college girl had been snatched off the street, dragged into an al-ley, beaten, raped, and strangled. This hor-rific crime had occurred behind the theater where Floyd worked.

The girl had worked part-time in the ice creamery next door to the theater. Two wit-nesses had identified Floyd as the assailant. He'd been seen talking to the victim earlier that night in front of the theater. From what the witnesses said, he had behaved in an "aggressive and threatening manner." One of the witnesses was a jacked-up hoochie who used to flirt with Floyd at school. She still had a grudge against him because he'd never shown any interest in her. She swore *on the Bible* that she'd seen Floyd in the ice creamery on his break making lewd com-ments to this girl. And for the record, this murdered girl had fucked almost everybody I knew. If Floyd had wanted her, he would not have had to rape her. However, I knew enough about rape to know that even if a prostitute decided at the last minute not to fuck a trick and he forced her, that was rape. Even though I did not witness Floyd's al-leged crime, I refused to believe what I'd been told. He had no reason to rape any-body as long as he had me.

There were other ifs running through my mind. One was the fact that *if* Floyd had pursued other job opportunities as hard as I did, he would not have still been working at that Mickey Mouse movie usher job in the vicinity of the crime scene in the first place. But it was too late to worry about that now. What was important was dealing with the present situation. And it was not going to be easy.

"Baby, you know I didn't do this," Floyd assured me, gripping the bars at the county jail where they'd taken him for further questioning. "I got off work at eight and I was with you from then until after midnight. You know that. They said this girl was raped and killed between ten and eleven."

"Well, did you tell them that? I'm going to tell them myself," I wailed. "You couldn't be in two places at the same time. And if they are right about the time that this happened, there is no way it could have been you."

Floyd gave me a guarded look. "But what if they got the time wrong? What if I was over there when that shit happened? Do you think I could do something like that? You know I don't fool around with nobody but you."

I didn't like the thoughts that quickly

moved from the back of my mind to the front. I couldn't remember all the times I'd caught Floyd ogling other females. If he'd been that bold, right in front of me, what was he like when I was not around? And I couldn't stop myself from recalling all the times I'd practically had to fight him off when he was so horny he didn't want to take no for an answer. There had been several times that he *didn't* take no for an answer. Technically, he had raped me, and more than once. . . .

I blinked hard and sniffed as I looked in his eyes. I hated myself for thinking what I was thinking. I looked at him with these thoughts dancing around in my head, taunting me. My mind said one thing, my lips said another. "Floyd, you couldn't rape anybody," I managed. "I believe you." I *had* to believe him. He was my future.

"Hell no! My sister got raped, my mama got raped. And almost every foster sister I ever had either got raped or came close to it. I know how much pain and suffering rape causes. I could never rape nobody! This is some crazy bullshit!" The longer I stood there talking to Floyd the more desperate he sounded, and looked. From the dark circles around his eyes, and the heavy bags beneath them, I could see that he had not slept. And from his foul body odor, he had not bathed, either. The half-moon-shaped sweat stains in the underarm of his shirt were dripping wet, and so was his hair.

"Look, we got a few dollars in the bank and if that's not enough to bail you out, I'll get the rest from somewhere. I know Viola would lend me some money if I asked her to. What I can't get from her, I'll get from Dr. Oglethorpe."

"No, baby, don't do that," Floyd insisted. "I . . . I don't want you to touch our money. Matter of fact, I don't want you to do nothing right now. I don't want you to get involved in this, if you don't have to. The system works . . . usually." Floyd paused and gave me an uncertain look. That look said a lot. As far as I was concerned, he didn't believe what he was saying any more than I did. His right eye started twitching, and he started breathing through his mouth. Just knowing how scared and nervous he was made me feel even worse.

"Usually? That's just it. This system usually works, but it usually works for white folks — or folks with money! It usually doesn't work for men like you! You know that!"

"Yeah, unfortunately I do know that," he said with a profound sigh. "Baby, I'm innocent. I know the truth will come out," Floyd insisted, his voice cracking. "All we got to do is sit back and wait."

"Well, I'm not going to sit back and do nothing. The least I can do is tell them you were with me in Dr. Oglethorpe's office at the time of the crime," I insisted, stomping my foot so hard on the concrete floor my ankle ached.

Floyd gave me a hard look. Then he shifted his weight from one foot to the other, and exhaled. His sour breath made me flinch. "And then you'll be out of a job," he said, shaking his head. "You know how straight-laced the good doctor is."

"I care a lot more about you than I do that job. I can always get another job. You — I can't replace you," I protested.

"Dolores, I'm not on trial yet —"

"If they've brought you this far, you might as well be! Floyd, we can hope for the best, but we need to prepare ourselves for the worst. Number one, they've got witnesses." I paused and held up my finger, level with his face. He focused his eyes on it, like he was expecting me to hypnotize him. "They've arrested you for suspicion of rape and murder. You are a black man." I paused and held up two more fingers. "A poor-ass black man living in a city that's known for racism! They'll put you up under the jail-house if they find you guilty! You don't have a leg to stand on." I held up five fingers, and then I made a fist and shook it in Floyd's horrified face. He looked at me like I'd suddenly lost my mind, and I felt like he wasn't that far from the truth.

"Well, when you put it like that, I guess I don't have a chance," he said in a weary voice. "If my own woman thinks that my goose is about to be cooked, what's the point? Why don't you just take that money out of the bank and buy me a one-way ticket to San Quentin. I'm a dead man walking. Shit!" Floyd gave me a disgusted look and a dismissive wave. He started to walk away, but he returned his attention to me as soon as I started talking again.

"Baby, you are missing my point. I am just telling you what might happen if things backfire. We are in this together," I insisted.

"I am not guilty," Floyd said in an unusu-ally calm and quiet voice. He gave me a hopeful look, but his eyes were twitching and both his hands were shaking. "I . . . am . . . not . . . guilty!" he repeated, his voice like thunder this time. He wrapped his fingers around the bars to his cell, gripping them hard. After only a few seconds, he let go of the bars and slapped them so hard I was surprised he didn't break the bones in his hand. He moaned and started shaking his head, but from the look on his face I could tell that he was in some serious pain. Pain of any kind was the one thing he didn't need any more of. And neither did I. I reached through the bars and touched his injured hand. Then I held it up and kissed the tips of his fingers. This seemed to do a little good. A faint smiled formed on his lips.

"All I care about is you, and getting you out of this mess!" I snorted and looked around. Behind Floyd in the same funky-smelling cell on the bottom bunk was a Latino man that looked like a big, brown grizzly bear, and he was snoring like one, too.

I knew that most of Floyd's friends were involved in all kinds of criminal enterprises. Most of them had no visible means of sup-port, and even though they dressed like thugs, they all drove big cars, lived in nice apartments, and spent money like kings. Why Floyd chose the friends he did was beyond me. Every time he'd had a brush with the cops it was because of the people he associated with. And now that I thought about it, a lot of the black homeboys that he ran with *looked* like him. Same shade, same height and weight, and same style of dress. I couldn't count the number of times I'd run up to a brother thinking it was Floyd, because from a distance he'd looked like Floyd. A lot of his clonelike friends hung out around that mall where he worked. One of them had probably raped and killed that college girl, and now he was letting Floyd take the heat for it! I didn't want to point that out to Floyd, yet. Mainly because I assumed it would come out in the long run, anyway. "What about some of your homeboys? We can borrow money from some of them! What about that one whose apartment we stayed in while he was in Mexico on vacation."

"Miguel Avalos? Aw shit. My boy got busted while he was in Mexico. They dragged him out of his grandmother's house kicking and screaming. I doubt if he's even still alive. And I don't want to borrow money that would take me the rest of my life to pay back," Floyd told me.

The longer I stood in that spot facing Floyd, the worse I felt about being there. I was ready to start clawing at the walls, and I wasn't the one trapped behind those damn bars. I couldn't imagine what it was like for a free spirit like Floyd. The look in his eyes had become even more desperate. He looked like a caged animal. If just being confined to a cell in County was making him like this, I knew that there was no way he could survive in a more hostile and severe prison environment, like hellholes such as San Quentin or Folsom.

As it turned out, I didn't have to worry about trying to borrow money to bail Floyd out of jail. Things were worse than either of us realized. With all the evidence piling up against him, his goose wasn't just about to be cooked, it was about to be cremated. There was no bail. The district attorney filed formal charges against Floyd for rape and first-degree murder.

There were even stories floating around that claimed Floyd had stalked that girl and had "lain in wait," which was very serious in a case like this. That meant he had planned the crime. As soon as I heard that account, ominous words like *special circumstances* and *premeditated* lodged in my brain like cancers. According to a report in the newspaper, if they found Floyd guilty of this "premeditated rape and murder," he could spend the rest of his life in prison. That would have been punishment enough, but the grand jury didn't think so. The next day the newspaper reported that the DA was going for the death penalty.

CHAPTER 25

Richard Ramirez, better known to the world as the Night Stalker, was on death row, and that was where he belonged. He had raped, tortured, and killed many people in the L.A. area and then he took a "vacation" to San Francisco and killed a man with the unlikely name of Peter Pan and almost killed Mr. Pan's wife. Charles Manson should have been on death row, too, but he was doing life instead. The list of names of people on death row or doing life in the state of California was long. Floyd Watson's name did not belong on that list.

I didn't care what anybody else said, thought, or did. I was going to stand by my man. Even though Floyd wanted me to stay out of it, I told everybody who would listen that he'd been with me at the time of the murder. A woman from church gave me a pitiful look and a hug, telling me how much she admired me for sticking by a rapist/

murderer. This same woman had spent a few months in jail for lying on the witness stand for her two sons, who were both doing time in San Quentin for robbing and killing a paraplegic. Other people just told me to "hang in there and pray" because Floyd's fate was in God's hands, not mine. Even though I had stopped attending church on a regular basis, I took their advice. I prayed for Floyd several times a day.

I didn't lose my job, but I immediately started looking for another one anyway, despite Dr. Oglethorpe's protests. "Dolores, you are a good employee, and I want you to stay on," he said, looking at me over the top of his glasses, his eyes looking like the eyes of a blind man. "You should not have allowed Floyd to be with you while you were on my time, but because of your exceptional record, I'll overlook that this one time. As far as I'm concerned, your only crime was you charging me for overtime for the extra hours you were *supposed* to be working that night, when I know damn well you spent some of that time *with* your fiancé. *If* he really was with you when you say he was. . . ." Even though Dr. Oglethorpe was a dentist and he took real good care of his patients, his long crooked teeth looked like they were about ready to fly out of his mouth. He suddenly reminded me of a vampire, and that made me want to get away from him even more.

The fact that my employer had some doubts about Floyd's innocence bothered me. But he wasn't the only one. Some of the same people who had watched Floyd grow up and spend every Sunday in church would have thrown him to the lions had it been up to them.

Viola was one of the few people I knew who believed me when I told her that Floyd had been with me during the time of the crime. But her ever-present, mean-spirited, meddlesome nephew was beside himself. "You don't know what he did before he got over to you that night! He always did look like a rapist to me, with them sneaky eyes and them tight jeans. Only men with sex on the brain wear their pants tight enough for the world to see how big their dick is. That ain't normal! You ought to be glad you found out what he was before you finished ruining your life by marrying him."

"You hush your mouth, Noble Coleman! You ought to be ashamed of yourself!" Viola said. It was obvious that she was physically weak, but you couldn't tell that from her voice. She sounded strong and determined, and that made me feel somewhat better. She had just come home from the hospital where she'd almost died during an operation on her obstructed bowels. She laid on the very couch that Floyd and I had all but fucked into the ground. There was a loud orange blanket draped across her body. "I been knowing Floyd since he was a itty bitty boy and I know he didn't rape or kill nobody." Viola had to stop talking for a few seconds to catch her breath. Then she patted and rubbed her chest a few times, like she was trying to gather up more steam. And she did. This time when she attacked her nephew, she did it with both guns blasting. "Now you look-a-here, Noble Coleman; I don't believe Floyd done nothing! He ain't raped and killed nobody! And even if I seen him do it with my own eyes, the only thing I'd believe was that my eyes was playing tricks on me! That boy ain't no more of a rapist and killer than I am!!"

Even though Viola repeatedly defended Floyd, Noble talked trash about him every time he came to the house. And he seemed to enjoy it because every time he brought up the subject, he did it with a smirk on his face.

"Oh, them white folks is going to bury Floyd's ghetto ass," he spat, strutting around in Viola's living room with the flip-flops on his ashy, reptilian feet flapping. There was a bottle of beer in one hand and a plate of stale tea cakes in the other. Despite his own health problems, which included high blood pressure, excessive gas, and various heart problems like Viola, this man ate like a hog, and had the flab hanging from his waist like an apron to prove it. His shirt was so tight, two of the middle buttons had popped loose. And the zipper on his dingy gray corduroy pants was threatening to do the same thing. Crumbs decorated his chin like measles. He stopped talking and chewing long enough to take a large, loud swallow from his beer bottle. Then he let out a great belch, which forced him to expel a mild fart. Without excusing himself he started spewing more of his verbal trash. "That nigger is going to get fried like shrimp tempura!"

"I don't care what you say," I said to Noble, looking to Viola for more support, and I got it with a firm nod from her and a scowl that she shot in Noble's direction. "I know Floyd better than you do, and I know he's innocent."

Now that Luther was gone, Noble walked all over poor Viola like he was walking on a beach. But every time he upset her, he crawled back into her good graces like a lizard. There was a contrite look on his miserable face now, but I could see right through it. "Uh, Auntie, I didn't mean to upset you," he muttered. "You know you my boobie. But I'm just going by what everybody is saying. Maybe that boy is innocent after all. . . ."

I had never liked Noble, but right then I despised him. His arrogance was beyond belief. It seemed like he went out of his way to aggravate me. I knew that the sooner I moved out of Viola's house, the better off I would be. If I didn't do it soon enough there was a strong possibility that I'd be the next person to go to jail, with Noble's blood on my hands.

My search for a better job finally paid off. I accepted the first one that was offered to me, and it sounded like the perfect distraction I needed. The other incentive was that it included more money. And if all that was not enough, it sounded like a fun job, too. I was going to be one of three secretaries in the main office in downtown L.A. for a popular cruise ship line called Encantadora. In addition to doing clerical work, I'd get to take cruises from the port in Long Beach to various ports along the Mexican Riviera and occasionally ports in the Caribbean. Health benefits, a credit union, stock options, and a retirement package added more icing to the cake.

I gave Dr. Oglethorpe three days' notice, even though I wasn't going to start my new job for another three weeks. I couldn't continue working for him knowing that he thought that there was a possibility that Floyd was guilty. As a matter of fact, I didn't want to be around anybody else who thought Floyd was guilty.

Just when I thought things couldn't get any worse, they did. Noble had already practically moved into Viola's house. But a week later when his wife left him and returned to Mexico, he did move in. Lock, stock, and barrel. Now I had to put up with his arrogance day and night, seven days a week. I was fit to be tied.

Two days into Floyd's trial, one week into Noble being in the house full time, I ran into Miss Naomi when we got on the same bus coming from downtown. She was coming from the bar she owned and operated; I was coming from the courthouse where I'd sat through several hours of testimony. And none of it was good. Another witness had come forward! This bitch, the best friend of the dead girl, swore that the girl had told her that Floyd had been stalking her. I didn't know how much more of this shit I could take, but I knew I had to be strong for Floyd. I was glad to see Miss Naomi. Seeing her took my mind off my own problems for a while. "Lo, I know that boy didn't rape nobody. And he couldn't kill a fly! You keep on believing in him, and things will work out." Miss Naomi gave me a pitiful look.

I was in such a daze it took me a while to realize I'd never known Miss Naomi to take the bus. She had always had a nice car to get around in. "What happened to your car?" I asked in a feeble voice.

"I sold it. I'm going to be moving to Memphis soon," she told me.

"Oh. Well, when you see Valerie tell her I asked about her," I mumbled. I didn't even care about Valerie anymore. She'd made her choice and it didn't include me. Besides, Floyd's trial and my new job were more than enough for me to deal with.

"You can tell her yourself. She'll be home this Saturday," Miss Naomi told me with a wide smile. "She's going to run the business and keep up the house." At the mention of the house, Miss Naomi gave me a strange look. "She don't like living alone, so she's going to rent out the rooms. One of the waitresses I just hired has already given me a deposit on Binkie's old room."

"Is she going to rent out the rooms and stay there, too?"

"Of course she is! She has to! Why?"

"It'll be nice to have her back in the neighborhood," I said gently. "But I probably won't be around. I'm going to move out of Viola's house as soon as the trial ends. Maybe even before that. Her nephew moved in. . . ."

"That sloppy punk that's been sitting around waiting on her to die so he can take over that house?" Miss Naomi said, almost spitting out the words. I nodded. Miss Naomi gave me a pitiful look and shook her head so hard the flowered scarf she had tied around her head came undone. I turned away for a brief moment, but I returned my attention to her when I realized she had more to say. "You poor child. I feel so sorry for you," she continued, retying her scarf, this time in a double knot. "This thing with Floyd would be enough to drive me to the river. And if you don't mind me saying, from the misery in your eyes, look like you done been to the river and back. You look unhealthy and haggard. No young girl should be in this shape," she said, looking back at me with a look in her eyes so painful you'd have thought Floyd was her man.

213

"But having to live under the same roof with Noble Coleman would finish me off." Miss Naomi grabbed my hand and squeezed it. "Take my advice. Move, girl. *If any woman knows what it's like to live with a devil, it's me.* You'd be happier in a doghouse than in the same house with Noble. Focus your attention on Floyd. Because child, in his case, you got yourself a long hard row to hoe."

Even though I knew that Miss Naomi believed in Floyd's innocence, it didn't matter because his fate was up to a jury. And every day of the trial all twelve of those grim faces displayed so much contempt they would have crucified Jesus all over again.

The next day Floyd called me up. He spent the first few minutes asking me about myself, then he gave me a list of complaints about the jailhouse food. He even laughed about that. Then he got quiet. "Lo, there is something you need to hear from me, not the six o'clock news or the newspaper." I didn't like the serious tone of his voice. It scared me.

With my heart beating so hard I had to rub my chest, I held my breath and braced myself. "What?" I asked, clutching the telephone in my hands like it was going to jump out the window. Floyd was taking too long to answer. "Floyd, what do you have to tell me?"

I heard him suck in his breath before he replied. "Baby, I'm going to change my plea from not guilty . . . to guilty."

CHAPTER 26

"Did you hear me, Lo? I'm going to plead guilty, or no contest. Whichever one will speed this shit up the quickest."

"Floyd, what in the hell are you talking about?" I shrieked.

Of all the things in my twenty years on Earth that my ears had relayed to my brain, this was the one thing that I could not comprehend. I couldn't believe my ears. I held the telephone away from my ear and just looked at it. I wanted to throw it against the wall and then out the window. Had it been a pipe bomb, I could not have despised it more.

I was glad that Viola and Noble were out shopping for a new car, with Viola's money, for Noble to "help her get around town." I almost dropped the telephone as I placed it back up to my ear. "What did you say?" I mouthed, still mad at the telephone for transporting such a shocking message. If I could have "killed the messenger," I would have.

"I'm changing my plea to guilty," Floyd said in a voice that sounded so distant now, he could have been calling me up from the moon.

"You mean . . . you really did do it? You are guilty? *Motherfucker, are you crazy?* You've got me, and you could have any other woman you want and you still went out and raped somebody? Then you killed her?" I still couldn't believe what I'd just heard. I had to hear him say it again. "You are going to plead guilty?"

"Um . . . yeah. That's what I just said," he stammered.

I was so stunned that the slightest breeze could have blown me over. "You did it. You did rape and murder that girl. Just like Noble and most of L.A. said you did!"

"Baby, calm down!"

"Calm down? You admit this shit to me and you expect me to calm down? What the fuck do you think I am?" I didn't even know I was crying until I tasted tears on my lips. "I just want to know why. No, it doesn't matter. You are a sick bastard, and you are right where you should be! What the hell did you need me for?"

"Dolores, I need you to calm down so I

can explain," Floyd said calmly.

"What is there to explain? You did it, and that's that. Do you think I want you to explain how you fucked her? How you killed her? There's nothing for you to explain to me. Any explaining you do, you do it for the jury. I'm through."

"Dolores, I didn't do it," Floyd said, still speaking calmly. "Just listen to me."

"You got two minutes, and then I'm off this telephone," I yelled. "I've been a fool for too long." I couldn't even feel my legs, so I didn't know what was keeping me from falling to the floor.

"I didn't do it. I'd never do something that crazy, and you know I wouldn't."

"Then why the fuck are you going to plead guilty? It sounds like you need to be pleading insanity because the more I talk to you, the crazier you sound."

"They offered me a deal. I am not ready to die, baby. Especially for something I didn't do. The only way I can stay out of that gas chamber for sure is to plead guilty."

"Oh hell no! You didn't do it, and you are not going to say you did!"

"Would you rather see me on death row or doing life? And you know sometimes people who get sentenced to life eventually get out after . . . thirty or forty years. We're young. We could still have a life together in our fifties or sixties."

"Fuck that shit! Do you expect me to wait around for half a century, or longer, worrying about what's going to happen to you in some prison? You are not going to spend one year in jail after this trial — and we'll find a lawyer and sue those motherfuckers to make them compensate you for the time you've already spent in jail! I think you should take your chances and let the jury decide. No, I don't think, I *insist.* You are all I've got now, Floyd. If they find you not guilty, you'll be coming home to me and we can get married and move away from here like we planned. Baby, don't do this to us." I was crying again. Fresh tears and slimy snot glazed my lips and chin. I slid my tongue across my lips and wiped my chin, eyes, and nose with the sleeve of my blouse.

"Lo, I got to go now. Baby, I love you," Floyd said in a low raspy voice.

"Don't you hang up this phone! I am not going to let you plead guilty, Floyd. You can't! Please don't do that. I never begged you for anything until now, and I am begging you with all of my heart not to do this to us. They are putting me on the stand tomorrow, and I'm going to tell the world that you were with me that night." Floyd didn't respond but I could hear him breathing, so I knew he was still on the line. "Floyd, baby, please don't do this to us. There'd be no way I could live knowing you are in prison for life. Don't change your plea. Please, please, please, don't do that." Floyd moaned under his breath, but still said nothing. "Floyd, say something, please. Please take your chances with the jury."

"All right . . ." was all he said.

Floyd didn't change his plea. And my testimony didn't help. Three days after I swore on a Bible and told the court that Floyd had been with me before, during, and after the murder of that college girl, the jury found him guilty. Guilty of rape and murder! The DA didn't get everything he'd asked for. Floyd avoided death row, but he got life, anyway. The *same* thing he would have received had he changed his plea to guilty!

After the two burly bailiffs handcuffed Floyd and escorted him out of the courtroom, people started filing out like they were leaving something as casual as a movie or a play. Other than me, and a young Asian public defender who had fought tooth and nail to get Floyd off, there was nobody there for Floyd. Viola had had a relapse the night before and could barely get out of bed, so I had not expected her to be there to show her support, but I knew she was in Floyd's corner all the way. Miss Naomi had come to court the day before and cried like a baby. But not a single one of Floyd's so-called homeboys, coworkers, or his foster family showed their faces. I don't know how to describe what I was feeling at the moment. But whatever it was, it was too much, and I snapped. I shot across the courtroom floor so fast I lost both of my shoes.

I mowed down three people trying to get to that smug DA so I could give him a piece of my mind. "You son of a bitch! You know Floyd Watson is innocent!" I don't remember grabbing his arm, but before I knew it an armed guard was pulling me away, pushing me toward the door. I didn't even care at that point if they hauled me off to jail, too.

Some of the spectators who had been present during the last part of the trial looked at me with an assortment of expressions on their faces. Some looked amused, some looked horrified, and a few looked downright angry. I even heard a cousin of the dead girl mutter, "She's that killer's girlfriend."

"How will you sleep nights knowing you sent an innocent man to prison for life?" I asked the DA.

He lifted his pointed chin, narrowed his icy blue eyes, and looked me up and down like I was a piece of trash. "I'll sleep like a baby," he said with a snicker, smoothing the sleeve of his expensive-looking blue suit where I'd grabbed him. "What about you?"

CHAPTER 27

There would be no possible parole for Floyd after forty or fifty years like he had predicted. His life sentence was just that: life behind bars until the day he died. People had the nerve to tell me to look on the bright side: "At least Floyd didn't get the gas chamber." Had it been me, I would have chosen that. As far as I was concerned, life in prison for a man Floyd's age until death was a far more cruel and unusual punishment. He could live to be a hundred. And in that case, what good was the next eighty years to him?

I was absolutely devastated. I couldn't eat, sleep, or even think straight. I couldn't even begin to imagine what Floyd felt like. I was so distraught I couldn't start my new job at the cruise ship office when I was supposed to. And I didn't care if they'd hold the job for me or not. But the woman who'd hired me did. "I can give you one more week, but after that I have to fill this position, and we do have two other candidates . . ." she told me over the telephone.

"I have some family problems I need to straighten out first. But I will be there next Monday morning," I assured her. I was glad she didn't ask me my business, because I didn't want her to know that I was the girlfriend of a man who had just been tried, convicted, and sentenced for rape and murder.

Viola was in the hospital again the day I moved from her house into a studio apartment a couple of miles from my new job. I had used part of the money that Floyd and I had saved to pay my first and last month's rent and to pick up a few pieces of cheap, mostly used furniture. "You can take that bedroom suite if you want it," Viola told me when I visited her at the hospital. "And if there is anything else I can do, all you have to do is ask me. As soon as I'm able, me and you will go do something nice. We'll go to Disneyland, or Knott's Berry Farm, and spend the whole day. After all you been through on account of that mess with Floyd, you need a break, baby."

I had no interest in going to Disneyland or Knott's Berry Farm with Viola or anybody else. But I let her think I would, mainly because she was obviously in a lot of physical pain; I didn't want to say anything that might upset her. "That'll be nice," I told her.

I didn't get a chance to get that bedroom suite from my old room in Viola's house. She died an hour after I left her hospital room that dreary day. Since I had not installed a telephone in my new apartment yet, Noble didn't call me to let me know. Knowing him, he probably would not have done it anyway, even if he had known how to get in touch with me. I found out five days later when I rented a U-Haul and picked up two Mexican day laborers off a street in Echo Park to go to Viola's house to help me get the bed I'd slept in for most of my life. I still had a key to the house, so I let myself in.

I was absolutely stunned to say the least. My mouth dropped open as I looked around. There was not a stick of furniture in the living room or anywhere else in the house. As a matter of fact, the only thing in the house was the carpets on the floor. I could see that somebody had already started to remove them. Noble was nowhere to be found, so I called his cell phone from the new cell phone I'd just purchased the day before. He didn't try to hide the fact that hearing my voice annoyed him.

"What?" he said in a voice that sounded gruff even for him.

"Viola said I could take anything I wanted from my old bedroom," I started. I stopped talking when he started mumbling some unintelligible gibberish under his breath. "Please speak clearly. I can't understand a word you're saying."

"I said, my boobie didn't tell me nothing about you taking nothing out of her house," he said casually. It seemed like he was trying to taunt me. I didn't have to see that miserable face of his, but I already knew that there was a smug look on it.

"Is she still in the hospital? I'll call her and have her call you," I offered. "I really don't want to do that because I don't want to upset her. . . ."

"Well, you ain't got to worry about upsetting her no more."

"Excuse me?"

"Aunt Viola's gone. My poor boobie. She had another seizure and died Tuesday evening around five. Now if you don't mind, I got business to tend to." Noble hung up before I could get more information about Viola. But it was just as well. When I got back outside, where I'd left the two puzzled Mexicans standing on the front lawn, I noticed a FOR SALE sign on a stick in the middle of the yard. As soon as I looked toward Glodine's house, she came out onto her front porch in a housecoat, with bare feet and a coffee cup in her hand. She shaded her eyes and stared at me. I ran over to her and started talking from the sidewalk.

"Noble told me Viola died," I yelled with a sniff. I rubbed my nose and shaded my eyes to look at Glodine because the sun was in my face. That didn't irritate me as much as Noble's most recent actions. I had so much anger in me that I didn't have much room for any grief. But I was devastated to hear that Viola had died. "He's selling her house already! And he's already moved every single thing out of the house that she owned!"

"Girl, that ain't the half of it. That greedy buffoon was too cheap to give her a proper funeral. He went online and found the cheapest cremation deal he could find." Glodine paused and slapped her hands onto her hips.

It felt like every word that came out of Glodine's mouth pierced my heart. And my poor heart had been broken in two, thanks to my conversation with Viola's nasty nephew.

"If I had known she was that close to

death, I would have spent more time with her the last time I saw her," I muttered.

"With all of them other busybody kinfolks she had, I don't know how that nigger got away with taking such advantage of that sweet woman all these years. It's mighty funny how fast she left this world after he got that new car and got her to change her will so he gets *everything* now. And another thing, him cremating her so fast was mighty suspicious. I seen a case like this on *Murder, She Wrote.* He must have had something to hide. I bet he poisoned her and had her cremated so they couldn't do no autopsy and find out the truth. If you ask me, I think the DA ought to look into that. Seems like it's a fad to be a criminal these days." Glodine paused again. She glanced at me out of the corners of her fishlike eyes, then she looked past me at the two Mexicans still standing in Viola's front yard. She looked back at me and snickered. "Speaking of criminals, I'm glad you done moved on from Floyd. I see you got you a new boyfriend already. Mexicans make good boyfriends." She leaned forward and lowered her voice. "I heard that when it comes to women, they'll lick everything from the rooter to the pooter. They eat a whole lot of beans and hot peppers, now. I advise you to go to Costco and stock up on some enema bags, some extra strength Beano, and some of them charcoal pills for your *amigo.* Gas can be real annoying, and it'll ruin the most romantic moment at the worst time." Glodine didn't take her eyes off my face as she let out a loud burp.

"I don't have a new boyfriend," I insisted. "Floyd and I are still together," I said firmly, turning to leave.

"Together? Girl, that boy ain't never going to see the light of day no more, just like I told everybody for years. He come from bad stock. I'm just sorry I wasn't able to turn him around."

I didn't respond to Glodine's comments, and I didn't bother to turn back around and waste a dirty look on her. It wouldn't have done any good, anyway. People as callous as Glodine had hearts of stone and skin as thick as an armadillo. There was nothing I could have said to her that would have made her feel any remorse for me, or Floyd.

I drove the confused Mexicans back to the same corner where I'd collected them, and I paid them anyway.

CHAPTER 28

My first apartment was about the size of a large closet, but it was cozy and in a safe and quiet neighborhood. It had thick carpets on the floor, so I didn't mind sleeping in a sleeping bag for the first few nights. I looked forward to shopping for a bed and other items and to learning my new job. I was trying to divert as much of my attention as possible — anything to keep my mind off Floyd.

Floyd's new home was Carson Prison, a brutal, maximum-security facility about two hours north of L.A. Just last month three convicts and two guards died during a violent dispute between some Hispanic and black gang members, against members of a white Nazi-based group that hated all minorities. This was the "bright side" that everybody kept telling me to look on.

Even though I was allowed to visit Floyd for the first time a month after he'd started his sentence, I came up with every excuse in the world not to. Besides, I didn't have a car, and riding on buses for too long made me sick to my stomach. There was no other way for me to get there. My new job was a lot more demanding than I thought it would be, so I volunteered to do a lot of overtime. Working ten hours a day, six days a week didn't leave me much time to visit Floyd in prison, anyway. I had even started making new friends.

The first time that the single woman in the apartment directly across from mine invited me to go out for drinks with her, I jumped at the chance. And it was a good thing I did. Mona Lisa Freeman's favorite bar was Paw Paw's. It was the same bar that Valerie's family still owned. It was a quaint and cute little place wedged between an African bookstore and a Greek deli. Black vinyl booths lined the walls, and tables with red tablecloths surrounded a small dance floor that faced a bandstand. On every wall were glossy autographed pictures of celebrities — famous and not so famous, dead, black, white, unemployed, and everything in between.

Up until now I had been to Paw Paw's only a few times and not as a patron. I'd stopped by with Valerie a few times after school, hoping to catch a glimpse of a celebrity. When I didn't see a single star after five visits, I stopped going, and hadn't been back since.

I had no idea what was happening in Valerie's family these days, and I had not had the time to try to find out. But when I walked into Paw Paw's that evening with Mona Lisa and saw Valerie for the first time since the night of our graduation, I almost cried. She was tending what appeared to be a very busy bar. But as soon as she saw me, she stopped talking to a customer in mid-sentence and ran to me, still holding the bottle of gin in her hand that she'd been pouring from.

"Girl, you are so slim," she squealed, wrapping her arms around me. "Tell me what diet you're on." Valerie had picked up a lot of weight, but it looked good on her. She set the gin bottle on the table and slid into the booth by the door where Mona Lisa and I had seated ourselves.

"It's not a diet I'd recommend," I told her. I gave her a brief update about what had been going on in my life. After she bombarded me with hugs, tears, and comments of sympathy, she shared her own tale of woe, dabbing her eyes and nose with a paper towel the whole time.

"I am so glad to be back in California. Tennessee is a nice place to visit, but I'm a California girl to the bone and I couldn't be comfortable anywhere else in this country but here. I can't get over how good you look, girl." Valerie looked me over as though she were inspecting a cow. "Are you dating someone?" she asked in a tentative voice.

I gave her a dry smile and shook my head. "So you're back here to stay?" I asked. Valerie's eyes searched mine before she answered.

"As far as I know, I'm here to stay. And in the same house I grew up in," she said, clearing her throat and glancing away. Then she looked at me and blinked. The way she screwed up her face a second later, I couldn't tell if it was a sigh she let out or a groan. "My poor mama's days of suffering are over. We buried her last week. Paw Paw's been gone for six months. I couldn't talk Binkie or Liz into moving back into the house, and I didn't want to be bothered with another dog. The girl who's renting Binkie's room is turning out to be the roommate from hell, but I don't know how I'm going to get rid of her," Valerie told me in one long breath. She stopped talking. Then she sniffed and blew her nose so hard that she let out a muffled fart, which I graciously pretended not to hear or smell.

I didn't even need to introduce Valerie to my new friend, because Mona Lisa Freeman was a regular. She was an attractive but frighteningly thin and insecure woman in her late twenties who worked as a claims adjuster for an insurance company in Long Beach. When the oldie but goodie tune "Little Red Corvette" by Prince came on, she leaped up from the table, bobbing her head and snapping her fingers. Like a puppy, she trotted out on the dance floor to dance by herself because none of the two dozen men in the bar asked her to dance. And of the six she'd asked, each one had turned her down.

Valerie shook her head and leaned across the table and started talking in a low voice. "I hope you don't get too close to that one. She'll keep you in the doldrums. She was named after the Mona Lisa, the only work of art that her ghetto-fabulous mother can identify. That's a beautiful name, and the sister is a beautiful girl, but she bitches and moans so much about any and everything, everybody around here calls her the *Moanin'* Lisa."

I laughed, and it felt good to do so. It had been a long time since I'd laughed about something, or had something to laugh about. "Well, I won't be available for her to spend too much time with anyway." I told Valerie about all the hours I'd been putting in at my new job.

"Make sure you give me your address and phone number before you leave," she told me, patting my arm. "We've got a lot of catching up to do."

"Tell me about it," I said, looking at her with my chin tilted. "It would have been nice to hear from you every now and then. Just to let me know how you were doing."

"I didn't call you while I was gone because I had too many things on my plate already." She paused and gave me a sharp look. "I hope you can understand that." I nodded and shrugged. "Well, whatever," Valerie said, shrugging too. "Anyway, I kind of wanted to put my past behind me. I didn't want to deal with anything that would remind me of . . . certain things." At this point she caressed her chin and stared at me for a moment. "Do you understand?"

I nodded again. "I understand. I had a mighty big plate of my own. And it was just as full as yours," I told her, blinking hard. I used my fingers to wipe away a few tears.

"Look, I'm real sorry about Floyd. But I know you'll be all right. With your looks, you'll be back in circulation in no time, if you're not already."

"I'm not really that interested in dating right now," I said. "There are a lot of things I need to sort out first."

"Uh-huh. And the main one is forgetting about that Floyd, right?"

I nodded. "I guess so."

"Lo, did he do it?" Valerie asked in a gentle voice, leaning across the table. She covered my hands with hers.

"No, he didn't do it, Valerie. They got the wrong man."

"Well, it doesn't matter now. He's the one that went down for it, and that's a damn shame. All that good dick going to waste."

"I don't know about that," I said quickly, horrified that she'd made such a crude statement. "The man's not dead."

"That's not what I meant. I mean, Floyd is a hunk and I know he must have served up some good dick for you to be so crazy about him. The best he can hope for now is to claim him a bitch. My cousin Bryce is doing twenty years in Folsom. He tells me that the only way a prisoner can keep the peace and survive is to become somebody's bitch, or make somebody his bitch. Either way, Floyd's 'peace pipe' is going to go to waste."

I was disappointed to see that Valerie still

had a tongue sharper than a serpent's tooth. I didn't care what she had to say about other people, but I didn't want to hear any more comments about Floyd. "Floyd is the past, so if you don't mind, I really don't want to talk about him anymore."

"Well, I can understand that. Anyway, you'll be meeting all kinds of men working for a cruise line. I went on a Caribbean cruise last July and had to beat the men off with a stick. And you don't have to worry about meeting any thugs like the ones we used to fuck around with. You've got too much to offer to waste your time with somebody like Floyd. I hate to say it, but I'm kind of glad he's finally out of your life." Valerie looked at me and shook her head before she rose from her seat. "Let me get you a strong drink. You look like you could use one."

CHAPTER 29

The two thirty-something-year-old secretaries with whom I shared office space loved trying to fix me up with some of their black male friends. Why they were so concerned about my love life was a mystery to me, especially since neither one of them seemed to have much luck with men. Dawn McMurphy, a used-up, dirty blonde with a face that only a dog could love, was involved with a man who came around only to gobble up her food, her pussy, and her life savings. Kathleen Roddy, a Demi Moore look-alike, was dating a married man who had been stringing her along for ten years. To get them off my back, I eventually went out on a few dates. Unfortunately, none of the dates they arranged for me panned out. As a matter of fact, I dodged one bullet after another.

The one man that I had high hopes for was a ship crew member for the cruise line that we worked for. He looked like a young Muhammed Ali. His bronze skin looked so good against his crisp, white uniform, the first time I saw him I swooned. But it didn't take long for me to change my mind about that sucker. As soon as he got me alone in the car that he had borrowed from his estranged wife, who I didn't know about until the night of our date, he told me that he liked to wear women's underwear.

Another one took me out to dinner, speared items off my plate with his fork without asking, and then requested separate checks when it came time to pay. He sold cars for Honda. As soon as he promised that he'd give me a good deal when I was ready to buy a car, I decided to drag along with him until I'd saved up a substantial down payment. The day I drove my Civic off the lot in the Valley, where he worked, the relationship was over as far as I was concerned. He stopped calling after I ignored his next five voice mail messages. The rest of the rogue's gallery included a waiter who worked on the ship. He looked a lot like Eddie Murphy — which was the only reason I agreed to go out with him in the first place. I knew something was wrong with him when I came home one night and saw him crouched behind a bush, peeping in the window of the apartment below mine. I didn't have to worry about getting rid of him. The cops took him off my hands. He had outstanding warrants in three states for everything from fraud to assault and battery.

The more disastrous my love life became, the more I missed Floyd. I couldn't have him, but I wanted somebody in my life. Despite my exciting new job and my new female friends, I was very lonely. I was still a very young and attractive woman, but I felt like a homely, neglected old maid.

I was not the only young black woman in L.A. looking for love and not finding it. Valerie was in the same boat. I didn't know what my problem was, but her fierce independence, needy personality, her successful business, and her drop-dead beauty intimidated the men she wanted. I knew that for a fact, because one of her former fly-by-night lovers told me so one night. I'd caught him hiding behind a tree in front of his apartment building so he wouldn't have to deal with Valerie, who was on his front porch pounding on his door with both fists. I didn't have the heart to tell her, though. I didn't think she would reinvent herself just for a man, because I knew I wouldn't. I figured that sooner or later, we'd both

experience the serious, long-term relationships we wanted.

Unlike me, Valerie eventually took a more
aggressive approach in trying to secure a
relationship, and she took me along for the
ride. Once she started visiting me at work
and at home, she started badgering me to
go out with her to some of the clubs she
liked. And of course, I went. There were
some nights when I enjoyed myself, and
there were some nights when I didn't.

I was so confused. There were days when
I thought I wanted to meet somebody and
develop a relationship, and then there were
days when I didn't. Despite my loneliness,
it was painful for me to even think about
starting up a serious relationship with
another man while Floyd was still so much
a part of me. But I knew that I'd have to let
him go sooner or later. I still had a lot of
years ahead of me, and I wanted to share
my life with someone.

When I finally decided that I was ready to
pay Floyd a visit I didn't discuss it with Valerie, or anybody else. I knew that they
would try to talk me out of it. My emotions
were already on edge, so I didn't need any
more turmoil in my life. But because I
would be seeing Floyd for the first time in
six months, and seeing him in that prison

for the first time, my mind was in a tizzy. I did things I probably would not have done otherwise.

Almost a week before my first visit to Floyd, I met a truck driver named Earl Speakes at Paw Paw's. It was a Sunday night so there weren't many men to choose from. Other than Earl, who had pulled me out on the dance floor a few minutes after Moanin' Lisa and I arrived, there was no other man on the premises who I wanted to spend any time with.

"I should have gone to Blockbuster and stayed home and watched movies, or permed my hair," Moanin' Lisa complained, running her long, neatly manicured fingers through a rope of jet black hair hanging down her back. She looked at her watch with a frown. "I don't know about you, but I'm beginning to think that Paw Paw's has turned into a gay bar." The few men who had approached the table I shared with Moanin' Lisa slunk away as soon as she started moaning about everything from her boring job to her slightly bowed legs. I realized then that this sister could bring down Telstar, and the way the men fled, they must have thought the same thing.

This was one of the few nights that I was having a good time. When I asked Valerie about Earl, she wasted no time giving him her seal of approval. "I heard from five different women that he'll fuck you inside out. If I didn't have my sights set on his friend Dexter, I'd go for him myself," was what she actually told me.

After Earl left the bar with me and Moanin' Lisa, and accompanied us to my apartment, he and I suffered through two hours of her detailed reports about more things that irritated her. It was excruciating.

Even with all the distractions that I had at my disposal that night, Floyd was never far from my thoughts. But with Earl sitting in my living room and me so horny I was ready to hump a doorknob, I managed to push Floyd a little further back in my mind.

I had almost lost interest in Earl by the time we got to be alone. And if one of Moanin' Lisa's old boyfriends had not made a booty call to her cell phone, I might not have had a chance to be alone with Earl at all that night. Once I did get him alone, my feelings changed. He had a musty, metallic smell about him that irritated my nostrils. Whatever it was, it was all over him. His hair, his clothes, and his breath all had the same foul odor. And now that I could see him in better light, he didn't look so good, either. He had droopy, owl-like eyes and lips that were as big as mine and Moanin' Lisa's put together. Kissing him was like kissing a raw kidney. But recalling what Valerie had said about him, I decided to overlook the way he smelled and looked.

Even though I didn't particularly like Earl and I didn't want to pursue a long-term relationship with him, I still needed to get laid, so I did. I was pleased to discover that it was well worth my time. Since Floyd was the only man I'd ever slept with and I had enjoyed sex with him, I didn't think it could get any better than that. But once Earl got down to business, I was all over the new bed I had picked up at Goodwill the week before. Unlike Floyd, Earl didn't have a big dick like all black men were supposed to have — like Valerie had led me to believe. His dick was about the same size and color of a Tootsie Roll. But he knew how to use it. And what he couldn't do with that teenie weenie, he did with his tongue and fingers.

Knowing that Floyd was rotting away in a cell with only his hand to give him some pleasure (at least that was what I hoped), I felt so guilty afterward that I threw away Earl's telephone number. After he left several messages on my answering machine I changed my telephone number.

My one-night stand with Earl didn't stop

me from having more encounters with other men. And even though none of those relationships led to anything substantial (one of the men I dated worked part-time dressed as Mickey Mouse at Disneyland) I enjoyed the distraction. It was important for me to keep myself occupied so I wouldn't spend so much time thinking about Floyd.

CHAPTER 30

There was a part of me that wanted to *forget* about Floyd. And I told myself that it was the reasonable thing to do. That was what I was going to concentrate on now that I knew there would be no future for us. But all that changed when I visited him that Saturday morning. I had booked a room in a cheap motel near the facility so that I could drive up the night before in my new Honda Civic.

I had never been near a maximum security prison so I didn't know what to expect. Even my imagination didn't prepare me for what I saw when I got there. It seemed like everything was funeral parlor gray. The uniforms the guards wore, the walls, the floor, and even some of the white prison officials had pasty gray-looking faces. The few black guards I saw were so mean and evil looking I couldn't tell them from the brooding black prisoners I saw being led from one point to another.

When a grim-looking guard trotted Floyd out to the visiting area, I gasped so hard I choked on some air. For one thing, he wasn't dressed in the same drab gray I'd seen so far. Not that what he had on was any better. He had on a baggy orange jumpsuit with a long number that reached all the way across the top of the one pocket that covered his heart. His hair was matted and dotted with lint. He looked like a scarecrow.

There was a glass partition on the long row of tables in the visiting room. I couldn't touch Floyd, and the only way we could communicate was on a telephone. He didn't seem surprised or particularly happy to see me. He plopped down on the hard-looking chair facing me and picked up the telephone. With a very deep sigh and a weak shudder, he gazed at me with his head tilted slightly to the side. It looked like he was going to burst into tears. That was exactly what I felt like doing myself. Then he bowed his head like he was about to pray.

"How are you doing?" I asked, clutching the telephone, which still had the sour smell of a previous visitor's breath. I had to blink hard and several times to hold back my tears.

"Well," Floyd began. He paused and

shrugged. "Bad." When he looked up, I understood why he'd bowed his head a few moments earlier. He had two black, blood-shot eyes; a knot the size of a large meatball on his forehead; a purple bruise on the side of his nose; and a bandage on the front of his neck. I didn't even want to know the story behind his injuries.

"I miss you," I sniffed, placing the palm of my sweaty hand on the glass. "I miss you so much."

"Is that so?" He asked with a sneer, which threw me off balance.

"Excuse me?"

"It took you long enough to get here. . . ."

"Floyd, coming here was not easy for me —"

"You think it was easy for me?" he hollered, cutting me off in the middle of my sentence. He paused and motioned for me to continue.

I cleared my throat and composed myself. His outburst had startled me. "Floyd, I had to prepare myself to come into this place," I said, knowing that it was a flimsy excuse. But it was true.

"I wish I could have prepared myself," he said with another heavy sigh.

"Like I just said, I miss you, baby. I miss you so much I can hardly stand it. Let's try and make this a pleasant visit for us both," I told him, giving him a pleading look. It must have worked because he immediately changed his attitude.

He cleared his throat and coughed into his hand. "How have you been?" Somehow, he managed to smile in spite of the grim reality of his situation. "It looks like life is treating you good. You still working?"

I nodded. "Not for the dentist, though. I work in the administrative offices for a cruise line now. They're paying me a lot more than Walgreens and Dr. Oglethorpe did. The benefits are good, and I'll even get to take some cruises at the employee discount."

"I see," he muttered, and then gave me a weak nod. He looked down again and when I coughed he returned his attention to me. "I want you to get on with your life, Lo."

"My life includes you," I said firmly. "I promised that I would stand by you, and that hasn't changed."

"Look, I still love you and I always will. But you deserve more than this," he said, making a sweeping gesture with his hand. "I want you to be happy. That's all I ever wanted for you. But I can't do nothing for you no more."

My mouth dropped open and I shuddered. I didn't like what I had just heard. "Are you telling me that you don't want me to visit you? Are you telling me that you don't want to see me anymore?"

"I'm telling you that I want you to move on with your life. If you want to come up here, that's up to you. I'm just telling you that you don't have to. I won't like it, but I can get used to it. I got a lot of time on my hands to get used to you not being in my life no more. You deserve more than what I can give you, which ain't nothing no more."

"Floyd, you can't do anything for me, but I can do things for you to make this . . . this thing easier. I know you don't have any family, or any real friends. I don't either. I *want* to stay in your life. I *want* you to stay in my life. Even like this," I said. This time I made a sweeping gesture with my hand. "I can visit you on a regular basis; I don't have much money to spare, but I'm sure that I can afford to give you a few dollars from time to time to buy things you can't get otherwise. Don't turn your back on me, because I am not going to turn my back on you."

He scratched his chin and looked at me so long I got nervous and had to look away. "I never thought things would end up like this," he said in a voice just above a whisper.

"Neither did I," I replied. "Floyd, it doesn't matter one way or the other now, but I have to know the truth." I had to pause and catch my breath and build up my nerve. He sat up straighter in his chair and narrowed his eyes. I don't know what made me look behind him, but when I did I saw his shadow on the gray, concrete wall. It was so distorted it frightened me. He looked like some kind of monster from behind. When I looked back at his face, he looked like some kind of monster from the front, too. His bloodshot eyes had a fiery glow about them now, and his nostrils twitched and flared as he gritted his teeth. The injuries on his face made him look even more sinister. But I didn't let that stop me from saying what I felt I had to say. "Floyd, I have to know in my heart the truth, and nothing but the truth."

"The truth about what?" he croaked. His lips were so dry they looked like they were going to crack at any moment.

"Did you do it?" I asked, looking him straight in the eyes. The glow in his eyes intensified. His eyes looked like two balls of fire.

"Did I do what?" he hollered into the telephone, rising.

"Did you rape and kill that girl?" I

251

couldn't believe what I was saying and thinking. And from the horrified look on Floyd's face, he couldn't either.

"Get the fuck out of my face and don't you never speak to me again!" he roared. Then he hung up the telephone and signaled for the guard to take him back to his cell.

I fell twice trying to make it back to my car so fast. I broke the heel off one of my shoes when I fell, and scraped both knees. I was the only person who Floyd had to count on, and now I had ruined any chance he had to survive with his sanity intact. If I could have kicked my own ass, I would have.

Instead, I kicked the front tire on my car before I got back into it. Then once I sat down in the driver's seat, I placed my head on the steering wheel and closed my eyes. I had just put both of my big feet in my mouth. Now I didn't know how I was going to patch things up with Floyd. And I didn't know if he was going to let me.

CHAPTER 31

"I saw Eddie Murphy, your favorite star, today. He dropped in for a few drinks this afternoon. Before I knew it, he was all over me! I had to beat him off with a stick to make him get his big head out from up under my dress."

"That's nice."

"He wanted me to spend the night with him. But I told him he wasn't my type."

"That's nice."

"What the fuck is the matter with you? You haven't heard a word I've said!"

It took me a moment to remember where I was. I looked around my tiny living room and back to Valerie. She occupied the cheap plaid sofa that I'd picked up at a flea market. One of her long shapely legs was draped across the arm of the sofa, and she was rotating her bare foot. There was a tabloid magazine in her lap with a grinning Eddie Murphy on the cover. An empty wine bottle, two empty wineglasses, and a fried chicken container from KFC sat on the table next to the wine bottle.

"I'm sorry. I was thinking about something else," I told her. I wobbled up from the red beanbag on the floor facing the sofa and shuffled across the floor to the kitchen area. "Let's pop open another bottle," I said, removing my last bottle of Merlot from the noisy, round-shouldered refrigerator.

"Did you hear *anything* I said in the last five minutes? I asked if you wanted to move into Binkie's old room." Valerie yelled from the across the room.

"In your mama's house? *That house?*" I asked, whirling around. That house with the body of a murdered man buried in the backyard. From the way I screwed up my face, you would have thought that I was referring to the Bates Motel from *Psycho,* one of the scariest movies of all time.

"Yes, in *my mama's* house. My house now. Connie's moving in with her boyfriend."

"Uh, I don't know. I'll have to think about it," I said, returning to the living room area.

I poured myself some more wine. Then I plopped back down on my beanbag so hard that the bones in my back and neck made a cracking noise, like I was being broken in two. In a way I felt like that was the case. I had not heard the first part of Valerie's conversation.

As hard as it was for me to believe, even though she'd repeated it twice, she had told me that she'd rented one of the rooms in that house to Moanin' Lisa. Sharing a house with Valerie and Moanin' Lisa didn't bother me. I was used to Valerie's gossiping by now. As a matter of fact, she was very entertaining at times. The day before, she'd talked about how the star of a prime-time TV show came into Paw Paw's on a regular basis, got so drunk she slid off the stool, and never washed her hands after she'd used the bathroom. She'd even passed that information on to two of the tabloids. And I couldn't count the number of stories she'd shared with me about some of her fly-by-night lovers who flew in and out of her bed. I'd heard so many graphic descriptions of dicks — what they looked like, smelled like, and felt like — that I was beginning to seriously feel that I had been shortchanged in that department. After all, I'd only been with two men.

Then there was that thing with Moanin' Lisa. I had to admit that by now I found her moaning and groaning almost as entertaining as Valerie's gossiping and graphic reports on her sex life. I had reached a point where I looked forward to her ramblings. She was the only person I knew who could turn a simple visit to her gynecologist into a Greek tragedy, which she regaled Valerie and me with while dabbing tears and snot off her face with a soaking wet tissue. "Y'all, I just know that Dr. Hoffman's got something else up his sleeve other than his hairy white arm the way he fingers my pussy during my exams. . . ."

Putting up with Valerie and Moanin' Lisa was one thing. But the situation with Floyd was responsible for the many nightmares and sleepless nights I had to struggle through, and that was more than enough for me. However, the main thing was — moving into a house with such a gruesome history didn't appeal to me at all. Just thinking about it gave me chicken skin. But Valerie wasn't going to take no for an answer.

"Look, Lo, I know Miss Viola didn't raise you to be a fool. I'm serving you up what they call a fatted calf — milk that cow while you can! You'd be living practically rent free. Utilities are included, and so is cable, and furniture. And I know you can find better things to do with your money than keep paying rent on this dump," she said, looking around my living room area with a huge frown on her face. "And to sweeten the pot, you can have the first three months free. I won't even charge you a cleaning or security deposit. Just promise me you won't tell the Moanin' Lisa about our deal, though." Valerie took a deep breath and cleared her throat. She pursed her lips like she was about to speak again, so I waited until she motioned for me to speak.

"I'll have to think about it," I said again.

"What's there to think about? Listen, if you don't like my company, that's fine. If that's the reason you don't want to live with me. But this is a one-time offer." Valerie held up both hands and gave me a guarded look. She took a long drink from her wineglass, and cleared her throat again, coughing like she had swallowed a fist. She shifted in her seat as if she was going in for the kill. In a way I guess she was. "I'm trying to do you a favor because I have a longer history and a more serious relationship with you than anybody else. And to tell you the truth, I thought you'd jump at the chance."

For a woman who had killed a man and buried him in her backyard, Valerie went on about her business like she didn't have a care in the world. By anybody's standards, her killing a man was a lot more serious than my ongoing dilemma with Floyd. But I had a different kind of history and relationship with him than I had with her. And, as far as I was concerned, more of a commitment. Valerie didn't need me as much as Floyd did. Naturally, he was still high on my list of priorities. It had been six months since my disastrous visit to the prison and I had not communicated with him one way or the other. I wanted to, and I planned to do just that as soon as I figured out a way to ease back into his life.

The day after Valerie offered me a room in her house, I got home from work and there was a birthday card to me from Floyd. It was a generic card with a message so neat and elaborately written it looked like he'd practiced his penmanship for days:

Happy birthday, Lo. . . . missing you . . .
I am sorry,
Your fool forever, Floyd

I didn't even take the time to remove my jacket. I called Valerie immediately.

"If that room is still available, I'll take it. I'd like to start saving some money," I told her.

"Good. Then maybe you'll buy yourself a decent wardrobe," she said with a laugh.

"I will," I said back, laughing. I had plans for the money that I was going to save by moving in with Valerie. I had to do whatever I could to make Floyd's ordeal more bearable.

CHAPTER 32

I didn't miss my tacky little studio apartment with its leaky faucets and thin walls. It was good to be back on my old block, even though it saddened me to see new tenants occupying Viola's house. What I saw was enough to make me scream, so I knew that Viola was probably spinning in her grave. Crabgrass had practically taken over the whole front yard, and a rusty old car that looked more like a canoe sat in the driveway, propped up on cement blocks with three flat tires. Two homely, naked boys with bald heads shaped like peanuts were running around in the front yard chasing a cat with sticks.

Glodine and her husband were still in the house across the street from Viola's. But with Floyd no longer under her roof there was no reason for me to ever go into that house again. Not that I would have been welcome, anyway. The one time I tried to reach out to Glodine by paying her a visit to let her know that I had moved back to the neighborhood, she looked at me like I'd stolen her purse. "You the one that got all mixed up with that Floyd, ain't you? Stuck with him even after he raped and murdered that girl to death," she said, glaring at me from her slightly opened front door. "LoReese? That's your name, right?"

"That's right," I said, blinking. "LoReese." I wanted to defend Floyd, but at this point in time, it was no use. His fate was a done deal, and there was nothing I could do to change that. It was bad enough that the system had written Floyd off, but it hurt to know that Glodine had, too. But she was so ignorant she couldn't help herself. However, I liked the way she'd reduced my name from Dolores Reese to LoReese. I even changed my badge I wore at work to reflect my "new" name.

"I still can't believe you got involved with a sad sack like Floyd. I hope you doing better with the men these days," Glodine told me before she closed her door. Despite Glodine's odd reception I was glad to be back on Baylor Street.

Living with Valerie and Moanin' Lisa was not as bad as I thought it would be. They pretty much went their way and I went mine. We all worked various shifts, and even when we were not working, we were rarely in the house at the same time. Other than the backyard, the kitchen was the last place I wanted to be associated with in that house. When I had no choice but to go into the kitchen, I went out of my way to avoid that spot where Mr. Zeke had died. But one morning when I dropped a fork and had to squat down to pick it up, I saw specks of dried blood on the floor! I didn't go into the kitchen for a whole week after that. And when I did, I walked on my tiptoes like I was trying to avoid a land mine.

When I was in the house alone, I turned on every single light and I kept the front door unlocked and slightly ajar, in case I had to get out in a hurry. Moanin' Lisa had mentioned hearing strange noises and smelling a foul odor, all coming from the direction of the kitchen. "And if that's not enough to give me chills and fever, every time I go out on the back porch I feel a cold breeze — even in ninety degree weather! I must be working too hard. . . ." she complained. I agreed with her, but I didn't tell her that I had experienced the same things.

I had to force myself not to think about what I had witnessed on prom night too often. In addition to the fact that Mr. Zeke's body was still on the premises, there were other things to remind us about what had happened to him. The room that he had shared with Miss Naomi was off limits — *way* off limits. It was the biggest of the four bedrooms, and the one with the best view. It was now used for storing things. Valerie kept it locked, and she was the only one with a key. I was glad that it was at the end of the hall so I didn't have to pass it to get to and from my room at the top of the stairs.

Another reminder, and a much more potent one, was the backyard. It was even more off limits to everybody, except Valerie. She had put *two* padlocks on the fence gate so that nobody but her could open or close it. She got rid of the barbeque grill that had occupied a spot by the edge of the porch so there could be no backyard cookouts. She purchased a large wooden picnic table that she had the delivery men set right on top of Mr. Zeke's grave. I assumed that that was her way of making sure nobody disturbed that spot.

Valerie was a typical bartender. She stayed in her customer's business. She liked to listen, but she also liked to dole out advice. And that was why I decided not to tell her about my monthly visits to Floyd. But each time I saw him, she was one of the few people he asked about. That was because I'd told him that Valerie had given me such a great deal on my rent so that I could have more money to help him out with commissary needs and such. "Valerie's a good friend so you need to do whatever you have to do to keep her in your corner," he told me. "It makes a brother feel good to know that there are still some good sisters out there like you and Valerie that can always be counted on. . . ."

Valerie wasn't the only person who I didn't tell all my business. Nobody else knew that I was still involved with Floyd. As far as I was concerned, there was no reason for Valerie or anybody else to know. Floyd would never see the light of day again, so I didn't have to worry about him coming between Valerie and me in any way. And the way she liked to gossip, I didn't want all my business in the streets. I had already told myself that I was a fool for standing by a man in prison for life. I didn't need to hear it from anybody else.

I told Floyd only what I wanted him to know, and even then I could tell from the expressions on his face that he didn't always like what he heard. He rolled his eyes whenever I told him I went out for drinks with somebody. And when I told him that I'd spent a weekend in Vegas with some friends, he looked so exasperated I thought he was going to faint. I didn't see any reason to tell him that I'd been promoted at work. Now instead of spending my days at a desk in a stuffy office, I was working as an assistant to the ship's events coordinator. My work station was the ship *Encantadora* itself.

My new supervisor was the ideal boss. Candace Petersdorf had survived five husbands, breast cancer, and two face-lifts. She was the first woman in her fifties I'd ever met who still had enough nerve to wear a string bikini to the beach. "My motto is: Fuck life, before life fucks you," Candace had told me two minutes into my job interview with her. And she lived by her words. She hid her gray hair with dye and wigs, but she didn't hide her young lovers and her passion for tequila.

Not only was I making even more money as Candace's assistant, but I spent four days a week three times a month floating around on the deep blue sea on a beautiful cruise ship. In addition to a spacious office that I shared with my supervisor, I had my own cabin. As part of my job, I experienced some fantastic shipboard events that the passengers had to pay through the nose to attend. I had grown up watching reruns of that television series *The Love Boat*. I had envied the character Julie McCoy, because she'd arranged all the ship's social events, which was what I helped do now. The first event I helped coordinate, after enjoying a lobster dinner at the captain's table, was a sixties-style dance. It was a huge success. People were still doing the twist after the band had stopped playing. Although my job was not as romantic and as exciting as Julie's, compared to my old job at Dr. Oglethorpe's office, this was heaven.

"Girl, you got a job that I would kill for," Valerie said every time I came home from a working cruise. "And that boss of yours sounds like my kind of woman."

"I hope you don't get drunk and fall off that ship," Moanin' Lisa said, a sour look on her face.

"I know how to swim," I quipped.

"Yeah, but you can't outswim a shark," she said with a smirk.

"I limit myself to one glass of wine when I'm working," I told her, rolling my eyes. Valerie rolled hers, too. "I want to be sober around all those handsome men on board." I laughed.

"Well, I hope some jealous bitch, or some dude you flirted with then rejected, don't knock you out and throw you overboard," Moanin' Lisa said with a nod and a severe frown. "And you better be careful with that boss of yours. I don't care how nice white people treat us, we can't trust a single one of them. They like to set us up to fail, and that's what that Candace woman is plotting, I bet."

"I know," I said dryly, rolling my eyes even more. I had begun to roll my eyes so much since I'd met Moanin' Lisa, sometimes they rolled on their own.

Valerie cleared her throat. "Uh, on the cruise that I went on, the captain performed a wedding," she squealed. "It was so romantic."

Before I could get a word in edgewise, Moanin' Lisa dampened the conversation even more. "Hmmph! I bet it wasn't even legal or religious."

I couldn't think of anything more exciting and romantic than getting married on a cruise ship. But marriage was one thing I didn't allow myself to even think about. I no longer had the option to spend the rest of my life with the only man I ever truly loved. I dated and I slept with more men than I cared to admit, but I had accepted the fact that I'd spend my life alone. That was one of the few things that made Floyd smile. "I don't know what I ever did to deserve such a do-right woman like you. But if you ever do want a real relationship with another man . . . uh . . . I'll understand. Just promise me we'll still be friends," he told me, looking at me with a face that belonged on a puppy dog.

"I don't care about other men, Floyd. You know that," I said weakly. I didn't even sound convincing to myself but from the look on Floyd's face, I'd convinced him.

I gave myself a mild makeover. I improved my makeup and wardrobe, and I smiled a lot more. Before I knew it, men started to notice me in a very big way, and it could not be ignored. It seemed like they were coming at me from every direction — in clubs, parking lots, on the streets, the grocery store. The more I resisted the temptations, the more they came after me. And since there were so many, I could pick and choose. I felt it was safe to date passengers who booked our cruises (even though management discouraged it) because it was unlikely that I would see them afterward. And that worked for a while. As a matter of fact, Valerie hopped on to a few weekend cruises herself just to indulge in a few more fly-by-night flings. Moanin' Lisa came along with her one weekend but didn't like the men who'd approached her, so she vowed she'd never again set foot on the cruise ship I worked for, or any other ship.

Even Candace, who was the most upbeat person I knew, couldn't deal with Moanin' Lisa. "Is your friend always this gloomy?" she whispered to me during dinner on the last night of that cruise, after Moanin' Lisa had refused to dance with Captain Stewart. She was the only woman who had ever turned him down.

"Every day," I whispered back.

Valerie enjoyed her weekend cruises with me for a while but, as usual, she couldn't keep a man's interest for too long. "I don't know what's wrong with me. I'm pretty and I've got everything in the world going for me. My own house. My own business. What's wrong with these men I meet?" she asked me.

"You just haven't met the right man, that's all," I told her. "You just have to be patient."

"That's easy for you to say. I don't know what you say or do, but you always manage to get second and third dates with the same dudes. If I wasn't such a good friend, I'd be jealous," she teased.

"Well, you don't have to be jealous of my relationships. At the rate I'm going I won't meet anybody I want to spend too much time with any time soon, and that's fine with me. Men are too complicated anyway. . . ." I had to eat my words a month later when I met Paul Dunne.

CHAPTER 33

If Paul had not joined me on the Lido deck during a breezy afternoon on our way back from a shipboard Fourth of July celebration in Puerto Vallarta, I would not have given him a second thought. I'd seen him a few times during the past four days, but he always seemed more interested in his male buddies than in me.

"I was hoping to catch you alone before we made it back to the port in Long Beach," he said, standing so close to me I could smell the beer on his breath. "LoReese is an interesting and exotic name," he continued, reading my name tag. "Where are you from? Belize? The Caribbean? Mozambique? Casablanca?" He paused and gave me a dry look. "Am I close?"

I giggled and shook my head. "You're not even on the same planet. I'm from L.A. Not far from South Central."

The handsome stranger reared back on

his legs and gasped. He was so taken aback by what I'd just told him, his jaw dropped open so fast it looked as if somebody had let the air out of his cheeks. "Oh!" He was disappointed, but I couldn't help that. I was not ashamed of where I'd come from. Finally, my admirer told me his name and gave my limp hand a vigorous shake, and then a squeeze. I felt kind of silly standing there in a baseball cap, tennis shoes, baggy shorts, and matching T-shirt all with the American flag design. I must have looked like the most patriotic crew member on board because none of my co-workers, or any of the intoxicated passengers, displayed our country's colors in such a prominent way.

"It's actually Dolores. My friends call me Lo sometimes," I told him, moving back. "My last name is Reese."

"Would it be Miss or Mrs.?"

"I'm not married," I said with a sigh, looking at his fingers. He grinned and held up all ten and waved them in my face. Then as quickly as I could, I looked him up and down. He was just a few inches taller than me with an average-looking body and short curly brown hair. I usually didn't like hair on a man's face, but his goatee was so neat, trim, and attractive it almost made me wish

I had one. He had slanted brown eyes to die for and a smile that wouldn't quit. And those lips! All I wanted to do was cover those juicy, brown, Cupid's bow-shaped lips with mine. Within five minutes I knew more about him than the last three men I'd been with put together. He was a twenty-seven-year-old bachelor who earned a good living as a corporate trainer for a computer company. He helped management employees on all levels develop and improve their managerial skills. This cruise was a celebration for a series of management effectiveness seminars he had just received an award for.

There were several things that I immediately liked about Paul, things that really caught my attention, because these were things we had in common. Like me, he lived in L.A., loved jazz, the Lakers, Eddie Murphy movies, and Chinese food. I had a brief concern when he confessed with a frown that he couldn't stand turnip greens, my favorite dish, or any of the other so-called soul food dishes. I liked the fact that he admitted that his mother called him Sweet P. and that it was fine if that's what I wanted to call him, too. I preferred Paul, and he seemed pleased to hear that.

"LoReese, I hope you don't think I'm too forward, but I'd like to get your phone number."

"O . . . K," I said slowly, trying not to sound or look too eager. But I was eager and I couldn't hide it. I almost twisted my wrist trying to get my hand inside my purse so fast to get a pen to write my telephone number on a napkin.

And the timing couldn't have been better. I had reached a point where I was ready to move forward with my love life. As long as Floyd wanted to keep me in his life on some level, I would be there for him. But the reality was we had gone as far as we could go! What was I supposed to do? Floyd couldn't have been more out of reach had he been sent to another planet. The two of us remaining in a relationship at our age with no physical contact whatsoever was harder than I thought it would be. And unless he broke out of prison, *that would never change.* It had been a while since I'd been with a man I liked as much as I liked Paul. Just from the things he'd said, I could tell that he was going to be a real challenge.

I was ready to jump into a relationship with Paul, feet first. Three times a month I spent four days straight on board the *Encantadora* and then three days off. The rest of the days in the month were off days for me. I had a whole week to myself coming up. For the first time since I'd "lost" Floyd to the system, I had met a man who I was so attracted to, I wanted to give him as much attention and time as I possibly could.

Unfortunately, Paul obviously didn't feel the same way about me. He didn't call me when the cruise was over like he said he would. I couldn't figure out what I'd said, or done, to turn him off. My imagination ran wild. I decided that he'd lost interest because of my weakness for turnip greens and rib sandwiches. Then there was the fact that I had not attended college. He frowned when I'd told him that, too. But he'd frowned even more when I'd told him I had no family and that I'd been raised in foster care.

After three days had gone by, I gave up and was trying to come up with some names nasty enough to call him. In the meantime, I put his name at the top of my shit list. Then I turned his name over to my wrathful female friends. They roasted him good that Saturday night over dinner.

Moanin' Lisa talked about Paul so bad it brought tears to my eyes. "He's a low-down, funky black ass-wipe and you don't need that!" For once, I agreed with her.

"Fuck him! Get yourself a vibrator like the rest of us!" Valerie hollered, chewing on a piece of cornbread. That I wasn't ready for. I wanted a whole man, not a substitute for just part of one.

"I should have known not to trust a man with a goatee. Every picture I've ever seen of Satan, he had a goatee," I complained, tapping my fork against the side of my plate. Valerie stopped chewing and shot me a mysterious look. Her dead stepfather Mr. Zeke had occasionally worn a goatee. I had inadvertently touched upon an extremely sensitive subject. Normally, I would go out of my way to avoid making references to anything associated with Mr. Zeke, but sometimes it couldn't be helped.

"You should have listened to me, LoReese. I tried to tell you that that hound-from-hell was probably just feeding you some bullshit. At least you wasn't fool enough to fuck him," Moanin' Lisa told me with a grimace, spooning mashed potatoes on my plate. I was glad that Moanin' Lisa had diverted Valerie's attention away from Mr. Zeke.

When we did eat together, it was always in the living room at a large card table near the front window, never at the table in the kitchen. As a matter of fact, Valerie used the top of the kitchen table for an ironing board now. Several area rugs covered the side of the floor where Mr. Zeke had died. Since a lot of my time was spent on the ship, Valerie's peculiar house rules didn't bother me.

Since it was so rare that the three of us were ever home at the same time on a Saturday night, I was enjoying our evening. However, I would have preferred Paul's company. I sighed as the attack on his character continued. My roommates seemed to be having such a good time trashing Paul, I didn't have the heart to change the subject. "That slimy devil. That punk. He was probably drunk anyway and thought you were somebody else. Pass the gravy, please. Valerie, I guess you'll be the next one to stumble upon some creep! I just had that little fling with that asshole that helped me pick out my truck. I hope you do better than Lo and I did," Moanin' Lisa snarled.

"I hope I do, too," Valerie mumbled. There was not much conviction in her voice and I was not surprised. Valerie knew more men than any woman I knew, and I knew that she was more than ready to settle down with one. Unfortunately, in her case, knowing a lot of men only meant that she knew a lot of men who didn't want her. She never talked much about what all happened during her stay in Memphis, but as far as I knew, she had not had much luck with the men back there, either.

Valerie's eyes drifted to the side and she stared at the wall for a few moments before she gazed across the table at me with a pensive look on her face. "Maybe we're being too hard on Brother Paul. Maybe you should give him a little more time. Maybe something happened that kept him from calling you when he said he would," she said, her voice gentle and even. It was hard to believe that these words were coming from the same woman who had sounded so hard and harsh a few minutes earlier. "And if you don't ever hear from him again, there's plenty more where he came from."

After a while I got tired of trashing Paul and laughing at jokes about him and the Tootsie Roll of a dick that Moanin' Lisa said he probably had. I had told her about the little surprise that Earl had between his legs. Despite the fact that I still wanted to get to know Paul, I pushed him out of my mind.

However, when he called me up and invited me to dinner two nights before my next visit to Floyd, I was pleasantly surprised and overjoyed. My two roommates changed their tune about Paul as fast as I changed mine. This was the same hound-from-hell that the three of us had demonized. Now they wanted me to find out if he had any single friends.

Despite my previous opinions about Paul, I utilized my prerogative without hesitation. My plan was to enjoy dinner at the upscale French restaurant he had selected, wallow around in bed with him for a few hours, and go on about my business. But things didn't go the way I thought they would. One bedroom romp with him wasn't enough. It was so good I knew I had to see him again. For the first time, my commitment to Floyd bothered me to the bone. And Paul didn't make it any easier. "LoReese, I don't know what it is about you. But for some reason, I feel like I've known you all my life. It feels like we've already shared a past. Now let's concentrate on our future."

"We'll see," I muttered with slight hesitation. "There's no reason for us to move too fast, though."

By the end of that first night with Paul, I looked at Floyd as a burden. But the minute Paul drove onto my street to take me home, which was six o'clock in the evening of the next day, I looked at the house where Floyd used to live with Glodine. That made me feel like shit. As soon as Paul stopped in front of my address, I leaped out of the car while the motor was still running.

"Hey — can I call you tomorrow?" Paul yelled. I turned to see him getting out of his maroon Porsche with a dumbfounded look on his face. I guess he didn't know what to think, especially after the way I'd clawed and pawed all over his body the night before. Neither did Valerie and Moanin' Lisa. Those nosy heifers were looking out the front window in plain view! Valerie had an amused look on her face. Moanin' Lisa looked like she had just finished crying and was about to start up again.

"Yeah!" I managed. I ignored my roommates and ran straight through the living room on upstairs. I stayed in my bedroom until it was time for me to head up to the prison to visit Floyd.

CHAPTER 34

I left the house before dawn the next morning. What was left of my brain felt like it was floating around outside of my throbbing head. During the two-hour drive to the prison, I replayed almost every word that had come out of Paul's mouth the night before. On one hand I was overjoyed and impressed at what he had said to me. But on the other hand, his words had scared me. The way I was already feeling about him scared me. The fact that I had a deep, dark secret sitting in prison for life that I had to keep from him and everybody else scared me, too.

I had no appetite so I had not eaten or even drunk any coffee before I left the house. But as soon as I reached the freeway I wished I had. I was so drowsy I could hardly keep my eyes open and my attention on the road. I even thought about turning around and going back home and jumping into bed and hiding under the covers for the rest of the weekend, and inviting Paul to join me. But every time I thought about doing that, I pictured Floyd sitting in that cold cell counting the minutes to my visit.

I was glad that there were not too many other cars on the road because I was driving like a beginner. Twice I had to swerve to avoid hitting squirrels strutting across the road like they owned it. After those close calls I started driving so erratically I got pulled over twice by highway patrolmen who both made me do that balloon test so they could determine if I'd been drinking. One even made me recite the alphabet backward. After I'd convinced them that I had not been drinking, each one let me go with a stern warning.

I stopped several times at rest stops during the long, lonesome drive, just so I could organize my thoughts. I was so confused about what I wanted to do, and what I needed to do, I could barely think straight. I loved Floyd. There was no doubt about that. But if things went well with Paul, I knew that I could love him just as much. Choosing one over the other was something I didn't want to think about. And wouldn't, if I didn't have to. Under the circumstances, neither one had to know about the other.

As long as I could have them both, I would.

Floyd didn't waste any time cutting to the chase. As soon as I sat down and picked up that prison telephone he got nosy. "What's up with the dark glasses and the turtleneck sweater? You look like a spy." I didn't like that, and I didn't like the cold look on his face. "You trying to hide something?"

"Who me? I don't have anything to hide," I replied quickly. "It's just that I got up at the crack of dawn to drive up here, so I didn't get much sleep. The circles around my eyes are so bad I look like a panda bear," I joked. Floyd gave me a guarded look. And then his eyes roamed down from my face to my neck. I didn't give him the chance to ask me why I had on a turtleneck sweater in the middle of July; I volunteered the information, which was a straight-up lie. He didn't need to know that I'd spent the night with a man who had gnawed on my neck like a vampire and left sucker bites the size of quarters. "Uh, I drove with my window down and that cold air gave me a sore throat," I said, rubbing my throat.

"I'm glad you knew you'd get a sore throat in advance to pack a turtleneck," he said, his suspicious eyes still on my neck. Our eyes met for a moment. He was the first to

283

look away.

"Uh-huh. Uh, you look good. . . . well . . . rested." I stumbled over my words. I was glad he didn't notice how much I was shifting my butt around in my seat. I was still sore between my legs from my workout with Paul.

"So," he continued, crossing his arms. "Tell me something good."

"I'm glad I got a new car. I don't have to worry about renting cars or taking a bus up here to see you. Did I tell you, it's a steel gray Honda Civic?" I said with the excitement of a child.

"Yeah, you've told me all that before. I hear more about that Honda than I hear about you. But you can talk about whatever you want to talk about. Your visits mean a lot to me," Floyd reminded.

"Oh," I muttered. "Well I really like it. I really needed it," I insisted.

"That's nice and I'm happy you got you a new car, Lo. I wish I had one," Floyd said, giving me a stiff look. It was obvious that he had been working out. Everything that I could see on him was more defined, and he looked more handsome than ever. Under the circumstances, I didn't think that a young man looking too good in a prison was a good thing. I knew more than I wanted to know about what went on among convicts who couldn't stick their dicks inside women. That was a subject I had no desire to bring up. The thought of my man becoming some horny bastard's bitch was enough to make me sick. The thought of it being the other way around was twice as bad for me to think about. But it was a thought that I couldn't ignore. Especially since I knew how much Floyd liked to fuck. "How's work on that love boat?" I didn't appreciate his sneer, but I decided to let it slide this time.

"Uh, we hosted a literary cruise a couple of weeks ago. It was two women's birthday, so we had a wild party afterward. My boss got so drunk she flirted with a busboy and then gave the ship's doctor a lap dance." I guffawed. Floyd didn't see the humor. I stopped laughing and resumed a serious tone of voice. "I suggested a costume party on our next cruise. The literary cruise was my idea, too. I wish you could have been there." Floyd looked at me like I was speaking Arabic. I liked to crack open a good book every now and then, but Floyd was the kind of brother who would rather get a whupping than read. "And since it was such a huge success, my boss is going to give me even more responsibilities. That means more money . . . for us." At the mention of money

Floyd's expression changed, and for the better I was glad to see.

"That's good. I'm going to need it if I ever get a new lawyer," he told me, with a hopeful look on his face.

I felt so helpless. I didn't know what to say to make his situation less painful. I decided to let him introduce the subjects we discussed. However, I didn't like the one he had just brought up. "New lawyer? What do you need a new lawyer for? Your trial is over and we lost. Baby, this is the end of road —"

"Thanks for reminding me. I hope you don't mind, but every now and then I like to get a little optimistic."

"Floyd, what do you expect a new lawyer to do? That's all I want to know."

"I need somebody on the outside trying to help me so I —"

"And what do you call what I do for you?" I asked, an exasperated look on my face. "Floyd, I promised you I would stick by you all the way, and that's what I'm doing. Your case is closed. They've sentenced you. What else is there for us to do?" Floyd sniffed and dropped his head. He looked down for so long, I thought he'd fallen asleep. "Floyd, don't make this any harder on yourself than it already is," I pleaded. He looked back up at me with a dry smile on his face. "What is it, baby?"

"Remember all the plans we made about getting married? Those are the thoughts that keep me going," he told me. "I would have been the proudest man on this planet to call you my wife. A straight-up trophy one at that!"

I couldn't speak for a moment. No other man had ever said anything like that to me before, and probably never would. I blinked and then beamed. "And if things were different, I'd love to be your wife," I said with a smile so broad it made my cheeks ache. "If I could marry you tomorrow, I would." Despite the naughty secret that I knew I had to keep from Floyd about Paul, I managed to feel good the rest of my visit.

CHAPTER 35

There were a lot of single men up for grabs in the L.A. area. But a lot of them had as many cracks as a cheap plate. Compared to them, Paul was flawless. He was the man for me. Well, he was one of the men for me. As long as Floyd needed me, I'd be there for him, too.

I had no idea I could fall so hopelessly in love with another man after Floyd. Despite the fact that I felt just a little bit guilty, I was glad to know that at least I still had some love in me to share. My relationship with Paul didn't change a thing between Floyd and me. I was still just as much his woman, as I could be, no matter how far I went with Paul. Bless his heart, he had been around for more than six months, and things could not have been better between us. He liked the fact that I was so independent, and I liked the fact that he didn't badger me about my whereabouts when he couldn't reach me. The relationship was perfect as far as I was concerned. I could not have been happier. And I was convinced that he couldn't have been, either.

Not only did Paul treat me like a queen, he looked at me like I was the only woman on the planet. "Sweetheart, I've been looking for a woman like you all my life. Now that I've found you, I'll never let you go." Paul said those words while he was on top of me, pumping away so hard I was afraid that we would tumble off his bed. I knew that most men said a lot of crazy shit when they were fucking a woman. But he said the same things to me when he was not on top of me. Therefore, I believed every word that came out of his mouth. Why wouldn't I? With him in my hip pocket, and Floyd in my heart, I had it all. I had the best of both worlds. And I was enjoying every minute of it.

Unfortunately, the same things could not be said for my two roommates. I knew that they were jealous of me, but I took it all in stride. In addition to half of Paul's single male friends, and a few of his married buddies, Valerie had gone through several more men in the last six months. As usual, she didn't hear from any of them again after two or three dates. And one even disappeared before the first date was over!

"I must have the most loathsome pussy in the world," Valerie complained, sitting on my unmade bed as she watched me prepare for another date with Paul. He was taking me to Palm Springs for the weekend on the corporate jet! Valerie and Moanin' Lisa were going to spend the weekend painting our living room.

"I wouldn't say that," I told her, wiggling into a loose black cotton dress that hid some of the lumps I'd been trying to get rid of for months. "You just haven't run into the right man yet. Look how long it took me to find Paul."

"And that's another thing. Paul all but fell into your lap. You don't even have to go looking for men, like I do. They seem to find you," Valerie said with tears in her eyes. That poor woman. I felt so sorry for her. Unfortunately, I wasn't the Wizard of Oz, so I couldn't give her the help she needed. I couldn't make a man fall in love with her. If I had that power, none of my female friends would still be single.

"That's the problem," I stated. I paused, hoping I didn't sound smug. I must have, because both of Valerie's eyebrows shot up so high they looked like horseshoes.

I could see that Valerie was close to having an anxiety attack. Her eyes and her body language told me that. She sniffed and swallowed so much air so hard, her chest rose like a balloon. She had to lift her chin and blink hard a few times to compose herself. Massaging her chest, she continued. "Men falling into your lap? You might think that's a problem, but I don't." She held up her hand, and I held up my hand.

"Don't you say another word yet. Let me finish. What I meant was the part about you going looking for men. Stop looking for a man. Let a man look for you," I advised, as I brushed the curly auburn wig I'd been wearing for the past month. I gave Valerie a look that I hoped didn't make me seem smug. "Why couldn't I be as lucky as you and have some decent hair," I said, shaking the wig. "I can't do perms, and I refuse to get a weave. And my own hair gets so frizzy so fast." I could tell by the look on Valerie's face that she was not buying the way I was putting myself down. I knew that she knew I was doing it to try to make her feel better about herself, but I stayed on that track anyway. "With your looks and the fact that you are the sole owner of a highly successful business, you deserve the cream of the crop. None of the men I've been with could appreciate a woman like you," I said. I knew that if I wanted to keep Valerie from getting *too* jealous of me, I had to say something that off-the-wall. From the thoughtful look that slid across her face, she must have fallen for that lame statement. "Relax and things will fall into place."

I did feel sorry for Valerie, but letting her know that wouldn't have done either one of us any good. I knew for a fact that she didn't like to be pitied. And if I had told her that I felt sorry for her because she couldn't get and keep a man, she probably would have cussed me out. And she should have. No woman in America, especially a pretty and successful woman, wanted to be pitied. That was a cloak of shame that most of the people I knew usually reserved for the homely, the poor, and the disabled. Valerie was neither one of those things.

But the reality of romance was cruel — for some women. And that could not be denied or ignored. Not only was the dating game a bitch, it was downright unfair and unpredictable. I was a good example of that. I didn't have a lot of things that most of the men in L.A. wanted in a woman. Like a lot of money, fame, a jazzy car, and a fantastic background. But apparently I had enough. I wasn't Miss America, but I was by no means a plain Jane. A lot of men told me to my face that I was beautiful and that I had a body that they wanted to get some dibs on. So I was all right in the looks department; that was in my favor. I was also loyal, dependable, and sensitive, and I knew how to hold a decent conversation. But all that described Valerie and most of the other women I knew, too. The only other explanation for my success with men had to be luck. And I must have had enough for two women because I had two men in my hip pocket. And I was turning down dates with other men left and right.

I wanted every woman to be as happy as I was, especially my friends. Well, the tide finally turned in another direction. And as hard as it was to believe, Moanin' Lisa had the nerve to get *engaged* to a bodybuilder who also serviced her truck. But that didn't last long. A month after he asked her to marry him, he was gone. I was not surprised. The few times that he'd come to the house to see her, she had whined and complained the whole time about one thing or another. Even the strongest man could only take so much. "I bet he's gay and was just using me to hide it," Moanin' Lisa decided. "Next time I'm going to hold out for a man like Paul, like you did. He's everything I want in a man."

CHAPTER 36

Paul was everything and more of what I wanted in a man. One of the most important aspects was that he was *free*. He was my man in every sense of the word, not just in name only like Floyd had become. Every time I visited Floyd I got so horny when I saw all the new muscles he'd developed from lifting weights every day, I wanted to hump him in the worse way. But with that glass wall between us, I couldn't even fondle his balls or pinch his cheeks like I did Paul when I wanted to cuddle.

"Lo, you don't know how much I look forward to your visits," Floyd told me, a smile on his face and his chin in the palm of his hand. "You're the only thing that keeps me going. And boy do you look good to me. Being in love sure agrees with you, sister. You are glowing like a big candle! What's up with that? That's cool, baby!"

"That's love," I said with a shrug and a

pensive look.

Floyd didn't know the half of it, and I couldn't tell him. Yes, I was in love with him, but I was in love with Paul, too. Knowing that would have destroyed Floyd. I had to let him think what he wanted to think. And right now he thought that the glow on my face was because of him. The lust in his eyes was so thick you couldn't slice through it with a Texas chainsaw. He slid his tongue out real slow and made a sexually suggestive gesture by sticking it in and out a few times. Then he slid it across his lips and made slurping noises into the telephone. The reception on that cheap-ass telephone was bad today, so there was a lot of static. It spoiled the effect.

After Floyd gritted his teeth, he put his tongue back into place, winked at me, and shook his head. "Baby, I know you miss my loving, but this is the best I can do for you right now," he stammered, his voice cracking.

My guilt was already raining down on me in a storm that was gaining more strength by the minute. What he'd just done made me feel even guiltier. I had something he wanted but couldn't have, but another man was getting enough of it for both of them.

"I've lost five pounds since last month," I

announced, hoping to divert his attention. A puzzled look crossed his face, like he was wondering where I was going with this conversation. "I went on one of the diets Oprah used," I added dumbly.

"Why?"

"Why what?"

"Why you need to be losing weight? You ain't fat. You ain't never been fat." Floyd smiled and winked. "You just the right size for me," he said, still smiling.

I shrugged. "Compared to some women I was fat. You know how I love me some pig's feet, greens, and cornbread. I had a few jelly belly rolls, lumps, and knots hanging and bulging and poking out in all the wrong places. My body had begun to look like a pear. Now I can wear all those new string, thong bikinis I picked up in Cabo San Lucas. You wouldn't believe how stiff the competition is on the cruises these days." I let out a loud groan and casually shook my head, closing my eyes the way the women did in those annoying hair commercials on television. I slowly opened my eyes as my fake hair fell down around the sides of my face. I was hoping that I looked as sexy as that little gesture made me feel. My breath almost caught in my throat when I saw how fast Floyd's smile faded. There was now a grimace on his face that made him look as if he'd been sucking on a lemon. "What?"

"And another thing — when did you start wearing wig hats?" he asked in a gruff voice, his eyes looking up at the top of my head and then to the sides. He snorted and looked me in the eyes.

"Huh? Oh this," I said, gently patting the sides of my wig. "You know how humid that L.A. heat can be. It can be murder on a black woman's hair. The wig is so much easier to deal with, and I have to look good these days. There are a lot of pretty younger women jumping off and on my ship."

"How many more times are you going to let me know how great your life is without me? You think I want to hear about how you have to keep up your looks so you can compete with other pretty women? Exactly what are you competing with these other women for?"

"I'm just making conversation, Floyd. What do you want me to say? You brought up the wig. I'm just trying to keep it real. You asked me about it, and I told you. I have to keep myself looking good. It's hard out here for a black woman."

Floyd leaned back in his seat and gave me a weary look. "Want me to have the guard bring you some more nails to hammer into my coffin?"

"What's that supposed to mean?" I threw up my hands and let out an impatient breath. "Look, I don't want to bring up anything that might depress you, so I talk about all the good things going on with me. Would you rather hear about who died, or who else went to jail, or got divorced? Or do you want to hear something worse? I'm trying to give you something to smile about," I wailed. "What do you want to hear? What do you want from me? You need to tell me because I really don't know anymore."

"I'm sorry, baby. I didn't mean that shit. I'm just so fucking — frustrated up in this bitch-ass place!" he hollered, pounding his fist on the counter. "All I want is for you to be . . . I just . . . I just want you to be happy, Lo. When you are happy, I should be happy. Me getting all crazy jealous only hurts me more. So, like I just said, I'm sorry for talking crazy. The thing is, I . . . I don't care what you do while you running around on the Love Boat in them string, thong bikinis you picked up in Cabo. And even if I did, I couldn't do a damn thing about it," he said in a flat voice.

"I am happy, Floyd. I'm happy that I can see you. I am happy that you are where you are and not sitting on death row waiting on the executioner like that prosecutor wanted you to be."

Floyd scratched his chin. "I'm sorry. I need to think before I speak. I know this is hard on you. Maybe even harder on you than it is on me. I want to make love, but I can't. I know you want to make love, but you won't." At this point, a look of uncertainty crossed his face. I wondered just how sincere he was in his belief that I was being faithful. I guess he gave it some thought, too. He shrugged and lifted his chin, looking at me with his eyes half closed. "Baby, I wouldn't be a man if I asked you to do what I know I couldn't do, if I was in your shoes. I can't give you what a woman like you needs. If" — Floyd paused and laughed — "and I do mean *if* you need some . . . uh . . . attention, go for it. I just don't want to hear about it." He gave me a dry look, then a dry smile.

"Are you encouraging me to find another man?"

"Hell, no! I'm encouraging you to do what comes naturally." He paused and laughed some more. "If you are not doing it already," he added with a wink.

"What's that supposed to mean? I don't know what you mean by all that," I wailed defensively.

"I ain't never been on a cruise ship, but I grew up watching *The Love Boat* reruns, and a few of my friends took a few cruises here and there. I know what kind of hanky-panky people get involved in on the high seas on them ships. And I know you still go to the clubs and shit, don't you?"

"Well, yeah. My roommates and I like to get out and let our hair down from time to time," I said, my eyes everywhere but on his face.

"You do more for me than a lot of other women would probably do for a man they'll never be able to call their own again. I appreciate whatever I can get from you. But I can't, and I won't expect you to give up *everything* on my account. I don't want you to forget about me and stop coming to visit. But I do want you to get on with your life, too. Do it for me; do it for yourself, Dolores."

I nodded and offered him a broad smile. The guilt that had been raining down on me in big drops had just turned into hailstones the size of golf balls.

CHAPTER 37

Floyd had been in prison for more than two years before somebody other than me paid him a visit. It was one of several ambitious young lawyers he'd been writing letters to, begging them to help him get a new trial. I had not met Brian Leventhal yet, but as much as Floyd talked about him, I felt like I knew him already. "Brian's a good-looking white boy. Looks a lot like Elvis," he told me.

"Elvis? That's not saying much," I said with my eyebrows raised and a disgusted look on my face. From what I could remember about Elvis Presley, he'd looked like Shamu, the famous killer whale.

Floyd laughed and waved his hand. "Brian looks the way Elvis used to look, before he got hooked on them fried banana and peanut butter sandwiches and got all fat and lumpy. And before he started squeezing into them white jumpsuits."

"Oh. That sounds much better." I laughed. "Elvis Presley was all right for a white boy when he was young." When I met Brian on my next visit the first thing I said was, "You look the way Elvis used to look."

"Before he lost his shape and started wearing those white jumpsuits, I hope," Brian laughed. "I hear that all the time." He rolled his eyes and tossed his head back, making a thick jet-black curl flap across his forehead like a visor. After a few minutes, he left Floyd and me alone.

I liked what Brian was trying to do for my man. "I know I'm probably beating a dead horse, but I have nothing else to lose," Floyd said with a smile so weak his dried, cracked lips hardly moved. It also pleased me to know that Floyd and Brian had become friends. "I never thought I'd see the day that a white dude was the only dude that I could call a friend. And it's my luck that this dude's so rich, he can afford to work for me for free."

"Do you really want to go through another trial, baby? What if things turn out even worse?" I asked, scratching my ashy neck. I had on a brown shapeless flannel dress that I wore when I helped Valerie and Moanin' Lisa clean the house. I had dressed down on purpose. I made myself look like a frump when I visited him now.

One thing I had learned over the years was that Floyd didn't appreciate me looking too "good" when I came to visit. Even though he kept telling me he wanted me to be happy, his demeanor told me something different. If I showed up with a fresh hairdo and a stylish outfit, and my face all made up, he greeted me with a puppy dog look. He greeted me with a smile only when I arrived with my hair in a flat bun and full of lint, no makeup, chapped lips, and in outfits like the one I had on now. He didn't have to worry about me. My appearance didn't provoke some of the convicts and guards enough to make them whistle at me and make lewd comments out the sides of their mouths like they did to some of the other female visitors. Even the most desperate-looking convicts stared at me with disgust, no doubt wondering what a handsome dude like Floyd saw in a dowdy bitch — that's what I'd heard one of the guards call me — like me.

Floyd reared back in his chair and gasped. "Worse? What do you mean by that? What could be worse than where I'm already at? Even if they find me guilty again, I probably wouldn't wind up on death row — but how much worse could things get for me?"

"They could send you to a real bad prison," I muttered.

This time Floyd reared sideways in his seat, gasping even louder. "A real bad prison? Sister, let me tell you something: every prison is a real bad prison."

"I meant the kind of prison where they send the *real bad* convicts. Like Charles Manson or the Hillside Stranglers."

Floyd gave me such a horrified look I thought he was going to scream. But he surprised me by speaking in an unusually calm voice. "I got news for you, girl. As far as the system is concerned, all convicts are *real bad.*" He leaned back in his chair and smoothed his hair back, giving me looks that made me wonder what was really on his mind. "Anyway, I gave Brian your phone number in case something comes up and I can't get in touch with you."

I nodded. "Tell Valerie she could send me a postcard every year or so. I would appreciate hearing from her," Floyd said with a wishful sigh.

"I will," I lied. I didn't have the heart to tell Floyd that that would never happen. I still had not told Valerie or anybody else that I was still communicating with a man in prison for life.

"Now, how's your love life?" Floyd

laughed, then shook his finger at me. "And don't lie because I know better."

"Huh? Who me? Uh, I've been on a few dates, nothing serious," I said quickly and clumsily, the lies spewing out of my mouth like fresh puke.

"Uh, I guess your men friends don't have a problem with you coming to see me every month, huh?"

"Uh-uh. Like I said, I'm not involved in anything serious." That lie left such a bitter taste in my mouth, I had to clear my throat. But it really haunted me the following weekend, when over dinner at the famous Mr. Chow's in Beverly Hills, Paul asked me to marry him.

"Dolores, if you will be my wife, I promise that you will never regret it."

Paul's proposal caught me off guard and startled me. My mouth was full of steamed rice and I almost choked on it. I swallowed the huge lump as fast as I could, which was a mistake on my part. Doing that, I almost choked again. I took a quick sip of water and I wiped my greasy lips with my napkin. "Did I just hear you ask me to marry you?" I asked dumbly.

"You must be deaf because we heard him all the way over here," said a woman's voice from the side. Paul and I turned at the same time. The white couple at the table next to us smiled and saluted us with their glasses. They seemed more anxious to hear my response than Paul.

I cleared my throat first. "Yes. I would love to spend the rest of my life with you!" Right after my eager response, the same nosy couple clapped and insisted on paying our check. I couldn't eat another bite after that. And I had to drink my way through the rest of the night.

I knew that if I wanted to marry Paul and continue my relationship with Floyd, I was going to have to get real creative. And the way things had worked out so far, I didn't think I'd have a problem doing that. Paul was the kind of man that didn't have to have his nose up under my fucking skirt twenty-four hours a day, seven days a week. He had a lot of friends and family who he liked to spend time with. He loved his job and I loved it, too. Mainly because it required him to go out of town a few days each month to conduct training seminars. One thing I was convinced of was the fact that periodic absences in a relationship helped keep everything fresh and exciting.

Paul had no problem with my going to visit a "mentally unstable female friend in Monterey" one Saturday out of each month.

As a matter of fact, he applauded me for being so compassionate and selfless. Early in our relationship, I told him the same lie that I had told Valerie and everybody else. "Dolores, bless your heart. I've never known a woman as caring as you when it comes to her loved ones," he told me. "Your unfortunate friend is lucky to have you give up a Saturday every month so you can visit her," he added.

Paul was a patient and understanding man. I was grateful that he never tried to get too deep into my business. But as understanding as the man was, I knew that he would not tolerate my visiting a convicted rapist and murderer. And since he'd accepted the story about the mentally ill female friend without too many questions, there was no reason for me to tell him about Floyd.

I was surprised that Valerie wanted to be so involved in my wedding plans. She wanted to plan the whole thing — the location, the cake, and everything else. It seemed like odd behavior for a woman as lonely and desperate to get married herself.

I didn't want a big church wedding, or anything else that was too fancy and might attract attention. There was always a chance that I would run into somebody who knew somebody who might get word to Floyd about me. I wanted to trot down to city hall and do the deed there. But Valerie and Paul vigorously opposed that.

"There is no way in the world that my mama is going to let her only boy, and the baby in the family, cheat her out of one more chance to enjoy a big wedding," Paul told me.

Valerie and Paul ganged up on me, but it didn't do them any good. I still didn't want to have a big wedding, especially after I flew up to San Francisco with Paul to meet his mama and some of the rest of his family.

CHAPTER 38

"You don't have *any* folks to speak of, Loretta?" Paul's mama, Miss Thelma, asked me within minutes after we'd first met. We were in her spacious, antique-filled living room with a view of San Francisco's Golden Gate Bridge. Despite all the expensive-looking furniture and other knickknacks, the room had a cold and impersonal feel. I felt like a fish out of water. I had on a simple blue cotton dress and flat heels. Except for Paul, everybody else's attire was as loud and outlandish as a Mardi Gras costume. One man had on a green suit. And they had the nerve to look down on me!

"LoReese," I corrected, forcing myself to keep the weak, fake smile that I had conjured up on my face.

"Say what?" she said, looking at me down her nose. She wore a bright yellow cape over a black-and-yellow striped dress. She looked like a huge bumble bee. Miss Thelma was a more fair skinned, older female version of Paul. Unfortunately, even down to the goatee. Hers was very faint, though. I could tell that she'd just either shaved or used some of that hair removal cream that I used to do my legs and underarms, because I recognized the smell.

"My name is LoReese, not Loretta," I said. My smile got bigger this time because Paul was walking in my direction.

"Whatever," Miss Thelma said with a dismissive wave. "My poor Sweet P. That boy of mine is going to have a hard time dealing with that. He's all about family," she said with a sniff. "Your hair looks real nice. Is it all yours?"

"No, ma'am. I own several wigs and hairpieces. My hair gets really frizzy," I admitted in a stiff voice. I knew then this was going to be a four-glasses-of-wine night, and maybe something even stronger.

"You must have some of that Kenyan African blood. I went on safari in Nairobi, Kenya, last year with my church bingo club members. I swear to God, the hair on the heads of some of those natives looked like barbed wire. I bet they've ruined more pillows with all those naps —"

"Mother, let me get you another drink," Paul interrupted, attempting to rescue me by grabbing my hand.

"Make it a double, Sweet P.," Miss Thelma said, grabbing my other hand. "Let Loretta stay here with me. We were having such a nice conversation."

Paul gave me an apologetic look and shuffled across the floor to the bar.

"Now. Where were we?" my future mother-in-law said. She released my hand, then wiped hers with her napkin. If that didn't make me feel dirty, nothing could. "Your folks from Kenya?"

"They could be. Since I grew up in foster homes, I don't know for sure. My mother told me a lot of things before she left me, but nothing about my ancestors. However, I know that somewhere down the line, I had family members from Africa. Just like you and everybody else." It was my turn to smirk and I did it with style. It must have had a profound effect on this old battle-ax because she gasped and rotated her neck.

"My folks are from Martinique," she snapped.

I nodded. "By way of Africa," I insisted, glancing across the room. I was glad to see that Paul was heading back in my direction with two glasses of wine in his hand.

"And Europe," she said with emphasis. I rolled my eyes and prepared myself to listen

311

to her give me a detailed account of all her mixed blood. People of color must have thought that it was a rite of passage to claim to be of mixed blood. I was beginning to think that I was the only full-blooded black person in America.

"Europe? I never would have guessed that," I said, the sarcasm dripping from my mouth like wax from a burning candle.

"Well, it's true. I can trace our roots back six generations. My grandfather was from Ireland. How do you know you don't have some insanity or hereditary diseases in your background?"

"I don't know any of that," I said meekly, watching Paul out of the corner of my eye. As soon as he handed me my wineglass I took a big gulp. The way he kept fidgeting and glancing at his watch I couldn't tell which one of us was more uncomfortable.

"Excuse me, Loretta. My grandbabies just arrived," Miss Thelma said, leaving abruptly. She pranced across the floor so fast her cape fluttered, and then rose up so high it momentarily hid the back of her head.

Paul immediately gave me another apologetic look. "Mama's a real piece of work," he said. "I hope she didn't say anything to offend you."

"With my background, it takes a lot to offend me," I told him. "By the way, I didn't know you had an Irish relative on your family tree," I said, tilting my chin.

"Oh? Well, did she also tell you that Grandpa Colin, a man who often paid his debts by serving up his retarded teenage daughter for the night, drank himself to death? And that he seduced my grandmother when she was just twelve, as his wife lay in bed dying of cancer? Did she tell you that once his family found out he'd been fucking his black housekeeper and her daughter, they disowned him? Did she tell you that he ended up living and dying in a ghetto in Pontiac, Michigan, in the basement of the house that his housekeeper lived in? Did she tell you all of that?"

"She didn't have to." I sighed. "I've met a few people like your mother."

"My peoples, my peoples," Paul said, shaking his head and rolling his eyes. "Don't let them get to you, baby. Just remember, I couldn't choose my family, but I could choose the woman I wanted to help me create a family of my own. I don't like to brag, but I think I did quite well for myself."

"I think you did, too," I said, wiping sweat off Paul's forehead with my napkin.

Paul looked toward the bar where most of the family members were still holding court.

After giving them a disgusted look, he returned his attention to me. "Just remember, you're marrying me, not them. When you are ready to get out of this . . . this snake pit, just let me know and we'll escape to our room and lock the door."

"I'm fine," I assured Paul, holding up my hand. "I can handle myself. Now let me mingle some more. The last thing I want your family to think is that I'm a snob." I chuckled, walking toward the garishly dressed mob. From the look on Paul's face you would have thought that I was leaping into a lion's den.

Once Miss Thelma took it upon herself to inform the rest of the family that I had no family and had grown up in a lower middle-class neighborhood with foster parents, I became dog meat in their eyes, too. For the rest of that night, I was treated like a bastard at a family reunion.

The fact that I had a good job didn't faze them one bit. "You could get a much better job with a college education," one pie-faced female relative said, looking at me with a frown on her face. I was the most conservatively dressed person in the room, but the way I got stared at by the male relatives, you would have thought that I was naked. The way the females looked me up and down, you would have thought that I was dressed like a streetwalker. One thing was for sure, this was one night that I would remember for a long time. It reminded me of a Freak Night party I'd attended in high school.

About two hours into this "night to remember," the mumbled comments about my glamorous and fun-filled job included one that described it as "a glorified waitress." As painful as the gathering was, I was glad I'd attended. After the way Paul's family had reacted to me, he decided he didn't want a big wedding, either. As a matter of fact, now he was the one who wanted to just trot down to city hall, despite the tantrum his mother threw. But Valerie was still opposed to that. "I'd feel better if you got married in Paw Paw's," she joked. But Paul and I took her joke seriously. Getting married in a popular bar with just a few close friends sounded like a good compromise. Most of Paul's family members didn't go to what they called "low-end" bars like Paw Paw's, so we didn't have to worry about them coming.

I had already moved a lot of my belongings into Paul's apartment. The Friday night before the ceremony, we moved everything else. He lived on the tenth floor in a swank building near downtown L.A. With the huge windows, trendy furniture, and plush green carpets, my new home was like a palace compared to every other place I'd lived in, including Valerie's house. "You can always come back if you ever need to," Valerie assured me, wiping tears from her eyes. She'd waited until she and I were alone in her living room.

"Oh, I don't think I'll have to," I told her, beaming like a lamp.

Valerie closed Paw Paw's to the public that Saturday. And Paul and I got married on the dance floor. The only guests in attendance were Valerie; Moanin' Lisa and her escort, a cab driver she'd met the day before; a few of my co-workers; and a few of Paul's friends and coworkers. I wore a simple off-white silk dress cut just below my knees. Paul looked like a prince in his black tux.

When the power went out on the block, twice in the same hour, we moved the reception to Valerie's house. Things were going fine until one of Paul's co-workers wandered through the kitchen and out onto the back porch to get some fresh air. I didn't know about it until I heard Valerie screaming, "Don't go in my backyard!" The stunned guest came running back into the living room with Valerie behind him, both of them looking like they'd seen the devil. "I . . . I don't want people trampling around in my backyard," she stuttered.

"I wish somebody would tell me what the big deal is about that damn backyard," Moanin' Lisa slurred. "All this time I've been living here, we can't have barbeques back there, or anything else." Moanin' Lisa took a long drink from a tall glass of wine and looked from me to Valerie. "Is there some kind of treasure buried out there or what? One of these days I'm going to find out! My cousin Sonny works for the city digging ditches. He'd be glad to lend me a shovel!"

One of the strangest looks I'd ever seen on another person's face crossed Valerie's. Right there in front of my new husband and our wedding guests, she told Moanin' Lisa she had thirty days to move out.

CHAPTER 39

With my employee discount, Paul and I were able to enjoy a two-week cruise to the Mexican Riviera. I enjoyed it, but I was glad when it was over. I got a glimpse of reality, and it was not a pretty picture.

On the third day into our honeymoon, after Paul had had a few drinks, he showed me a side of himself that I didn't like. While we were enjoying a fun-filled dinner at a long table filled to capacity with strangers, he made fun of the fact that I had *only* a high school education. When I reminded him that I'd also attended a state-funded training program, he took that and ran with it. "That? You think that's something to be proud of? Programs like that are as cheesy as Job Corps!" he roared. He was the only one at the table who snickered. The people, who were close enough to hear him, looked mildly horrified. And if that outburst wasn't enough to make him look like a bumbling idiot, he also made unkind remarks about the fact that I had grown up in foster care. I was outraged, hurt, and embarrassed. Especially after all that shit he had said at his mother's party, apologizing about him not being able to choose his family and how glad he was that he was able to choose me to be his wife.

I was the darkest person at the table, but the way my blood rose, had I been white I would have turned as red as a rose. Despite the effects of the two glasses of wine I'd drunk, I suddenly felt stone-cold sober. I laid down my silverware and turned to my husband, rotating my neck in the true ghetto princess style. Either I overdid it or I didn't do it enough because my neck felt like it was going to break in two. Paul was stunned, but he knew me well enough to know that I was not the kind of sister who took anybody's shit lying down. I'd proven that to him the way I had graciously checked his obnoxious mother.

"Look, baby, I didn't choose to be a member of a dysfunctional family. I didn't choose the woman who gave me life. But I am thankful that she didn't abort me, dump me in a trash can at birth, or sell me to pay off her debts, *like somebody else you know.*" I paused so I could savor the look of agony on Paul's face. But I wasn't through with him yet. I exhaled and took a drink from my water glass. "And another thing, despite all that shit I had going against me, I had a good life, anyway. I didn't choose to grow up in foster care. And I can't help it if I was not able to attend college. But I did finish high school, and that's something a lot of people can't say where I come from. There are a lot of people in this country who had to struggle just to get from one day to the next. Unfortunately, I was one of those people. But I think I am doing all right now." As soon as I paused again, Paul spoke again.

"Are you through?" he asked in a meek voice, looking around.

"No! Hell no, I'm not through!" My lips snapped brutally over every single word that shot out of my mouth. "I've got a few more things to say. You've brought this subject up before, and so has your family. If it's going to be a problem, we need to deal with it now."

From the way Paul squirmed in his seat, I could tell that he was embarrassed. Especially after the distinguished-looking, white-haired gentleman seated on my right patted me on the shoulder. Then in a clipped British accent, he told me how much people like him admired an "underdog overcomes life of despair" story like mine. Our other dinner companions tried to ignore us, but out of the corner of my eye I saw some of them sneaking peeks at us and whispering.

"There is nothing to deal with, Dolores. I don't care where or what you came from. I love you regardless," Paul said with a sheepish look on his face.

"Then let's lay this to rest now. I don't want you to keep bringing this subject up. That's in the past, and I can't change it," I said harshly, and with the nastiest look on my face that I could produce. I snatched up my fork and speared a wedge of potato on my plate, and chewed it to smithereens without taking my eyes off Paul's face.

"This case is closed," he mumbled, barely moving his lips. After he'd finished his drink and dinner, he slunk back to our stateroom. I went to the bar where I enjoyed a few highballs with the British gentleman who had sat next to me at the dinner table and his wife, a frail little woman with diamonds everywhere but on her toes who kept telling me she wished she could be as feisty as I was.

I didn't consider myself a feisty woman, but I was no wimp when it came time for me to speak up for myself. And I was ready to do it again that night, if I had to. But Paul was as meek as a lamb when I returned to our room. He met me at the door with a glass of champagne. After we went dancing in the ship's disco, he escorted me back to our room, carried me over the threshold, and gave me a foot massage. He didn't say anything else stupid about me that night, or at any other time during the cruise. This was the sensitive and gentle man who I had fallen in love with. But something told me that the subject was still on his mind and that it would eventually come up again.

Now that the honeymoon was over, I was anxious to settle into married life. But there was a dark cloud looming over my head. It had probably been there all along, but love had obscured my vision. It had prevented me from seeing certain things, until now. I was still blindly in love with Paul, and I was determined to make my marriage work. But the more I got to know him, the more I could see what he was really like. Despite the foolishness he often subjected me to, he was still a wonderful man. The problem was, I was beginning to think that he thought he was too wonderful for a woman like me.

It didn't take long for me to realize that married life with Paul was not going to be a cakewalk. I didn't involve myself with horoscopes much, but he was a true Gemini. The man was as two-sided as a coin. Dating somebody like Paul was one thing; living with him was another thing.

He complained profusely about my housekeeping skills. He screamed every time I left hair on the bathroom sink. When it was my natural hair that was bad, but when it was the hair from one of my wigs, he flew into a rage. With the exception of breast implants, which his last girlfriend had, Paul was one man who did not tolerate anything fake. He'd had a horrible relationship with another girlfriend. "Every time I wanted to sleep with her, she had to remove her padded hips, her padded bra, her contacts, her fake nails, her hairpiece, and her removable bridgework and drop it all into a chair by the bed. The more time I spent with her, the more pieces she added to herself. There'd be more of her on the chair than in the bed. After a while I didn't know whether to get in the bed or on the chair."

Paul enjoyed regaling me with amusing tales about his former lovers. But he made it clear that he had high expectations for me because I was the one who was going to be with him until the very end. "I am a clean man, Dolores, and I deserve a clean woman." He didn't have to remind me too often, but when he did, he did it with a flourish. The one time that I forgot to flush the toilet after I'd used it, he preached a sermon about the importance of good hygiene and showed me six difference Scriptures, in a Bible that I didn't know he had until that night, where he had marked references to cleanliness.

When I took a bath and didn't clean the bathtub to his satisfaction, he slapped on a face mask and some rubber gloves and did it himself. He also wore a mask and rubber gloves when he picked up my dirty clothes off the floor with a stick. Him doing strange shit like that didn't bother me, but it did when he tried to get me to wear a mask and gloves when I cleaned house. That was one battle he didn't have a chance of winning. "Last time I checked, I didn't have a father," I reminded him. He let me alone after that.

By this time, I knew what was expected of me. I had to vacuum the carpets every day, whether they needed it or not. He got so sick of me leaving dirty dishes in the sink for too long that he took over that chore, which was fine with me. He looked cute in an apron. I didn't have much luck getting him to take over doing the laundry, though.

Paul wined and dined me on a regular

basis in some of the best restaurants in Southern California. He admitted that by taking me out to eat a lot, it was one way to keep me from stinking up our kitchen with turnip greens and neck bones. It got to a point where I cooked my favorite soul food dishes only when he was out of town. He was fine with that as long as I had fumigated our place before he got back home. Paul's remarks didn't bother me any more than the remarks I made about his family bothered him. We both had a sense of humor about the two subjects. I was glad that I had a man who was not afraid to speak his mind.

And not a day went by that he didn't tell me I was beautiful and how proud he was to call me his wife. But that didn't stop him from continuing to point out my flaws. Another one was my choice of friends. Moanin' Lisa had moved into an apartment two blocks from us, so she came over on a regular basis. Paul made it clear that her visits wouldn't have bothered him had she not complained and whined so much. I couldn't do anything about that, so I stopped answering the door when she came. But *that* bothered Paul, too!

"If you don't want to be bothered with that woman, you need to tell her. Why can't you be as honest with everybody else as you are with me?" he said, as I tiptoed back into the living room after refusing to answer Moanin' Lisa's knock on the door.

"I . . . it's not that simple, Paul," I mumbled, reaching for my water mug on the glass-top coffee table. "Sometimes it is better to . . . uh . . . lie." I had my head down because I didn't want Paul to see my eyes. But when I looked up at him, he was staring at me in a way that made my stomach hurt.

"Have you ever lied to me?" he asked point blank, narrowing his eyes in a way that made my stomach hurt even more. "And don't lie to me now, because I will know," he warned.

"I've never lied to you, Paul." It was amazing how I could lie with such a straight face and be so convincing.

"I know you haven't, baby. And your honesty is one of the many things I love about you."

CHAPTER 40

"I've never had a reason to lie to you, Paul," I said quickly, shaking my head so hard everything in it rattled. "When we have to start lying to each other, that's when we'll know our marriage is in trouble." I cleared my throat. "Uh, by the way, I'll be going to visit my friend in Monterey tomorrow morning," I reminded.

"What friend?"

"Baby, don't you remember? The one I visit every month. I told you all about her right after we got together."

Paul shook his head and slapped his forehead with the palm of his hand. "Oh yeah! That friend. The nut case."

"That's a pretty mean way to describe somebody, Paul," I complained. "She's just having some mental setbacks."

"I'm sorry, baby. That was insensitive of me, and I should know better. My mama raised me better. Uh, I'll tell you what — if

I can get out of that card game with Perry and Logan tomorrow, I'll go with you. The last thing I want is for you to think I don't care about your sick friend."

"No, I don't want you to do that. My friend's condition has gotten worse over the years, and I'm one of the few people she'll allow to visit."

A puzzled look slid across Paul's face. "Well, I don't have to visit this friend, per se. I'm sure that I can find something to do to keep myself busy while you visit with her. One of my former college buddies lives near Monterey."

"Paul, one of the few things I really enjoy is that drive by myself. I have never even let Valerie, or anybody else, go with me. I'm around people at work and everywhere else every day of the week. I look forward to spending this little time totally alone." I gave him a pleading look. "Let me have a little space, honey." I held my breath until he shrugged.

"To be honest with you, I didn't really want to go anyway. I just thought that it was about time I offered to do so. If you ever do want me to go with you" — he paused and rolled his eyes — "I guess I'll have to go, huh?"

"Uh-huh," I replied, grinning as I patted

his hand. "Let's go to bed, baby. If you let me play with your, uh, toys, I'll let you play with mine."

Paul and I made love for hours, and the next morning I had the dark circles under my eyes and sucker bites on my neck to prove it. "Baby, I know your friend probably doesn't care one way or the other what you look like when you visit her, but don't you think a little makeup and some brighter colors would be more appropriate than those dark glasses and that ratty turtleneck sweater?" Paul asked with a laugh as I ate breakfast standing up, glancing at my watch every few seconds. Damn! He looked so good to me in his tight jeans and wife-beater T-shirt. I knew that we would make love again as soon as I returned.

"Oh no. I never wear makeup or flashy clothes when I go up there," I explained. I pranced over to his side of the table and nibbled on his ear. "Got to go, babe," I said, glancing at my watch again.

"Hmmm. By the way, what is this friend's name?" Paul asked, grabbing my wrist just as I was about to be on my way. "I think it's about time I started referring to her by name. And, exactly what is her problem? Why is she in this group home, or whatever that place is?"

"Huh? Oh! Her name is Crystal. Crystal Freeman."

"Freeman? Oh shit!" he hollered, releasing my wrist. He took a drink from his coffee cup and stared at me with an amused look on his face. "That explains everything. She's related to your crybaby friend Moanin' Lisa, huh?" Paul stopped talking and gave me a critical look that disturbed me, to say the least. "You do realize that mental illness runs in some families. That's why my mama is so concerned about your not knowing your family history. Some people are already damaged before birth . . ."

"Moanin' Lisa and Crystal are not related. Crystal wasn't born with any kind of mental illness. She had a severe nervous breakdown a few years ago when her husband left her," I said defensively.

"Well, there must have been something weak about her genes. People leave people every day, and they don't end up in mental institutions. If that was the case, as many times as I've been dumped, I ought to be in a padded cell on Scab Island, wearing a straight jacket, and eating my own shit by now."

I gave Paul a disgusted look and he immediately bowed his head, realizing how stupid he sounded. "Crystal is not that

330

bad," I assured him. "But I don't think she'll ever be the same again. Her doctors don't think so, either." I surprised myself at how detailed and extensive this lie had become.

"Shit. That poor woman. What about her family and friends?"

"Uh-uh. She has no family, no friends. Just me. That's why I promised her I'd visit her for as long as she remained in that place. It's the least I could do. She was always there when I needed her."

"That's one thing I admire about you, baby. You are about as loyal as they come. The friends you have are as lucky as I am to have you in their lives. I know I can be a goofball from time to time, and I say a lot of shit I don't mean. But you know the real me by now, though, so I know you don't let my stupidity bother you. Where did you meet Crystal?" Paul asked, giving me that look that made me feel so special.

"Huh? Oh! We used to live in the same foster home." As soon as I mentioned foster home, I knew I'd made a mistake.

"I see. I should have known . . ." Paul poured himself some more coffee. I noticed how he kept his eyes on the coffeepot, not on me.

"Paul, if something had happened to your

family, you could have ended up in a foster home. I really wish you'd stop looking down on it. Just think of where thousands of other kids, including me, would be if there were no foster homes."

Paul lifted his hands above his head, waved them in the air, and gave me an extremely apologetic look. "I did it again! I really am sorry." He sounded truly sincere. "Stop at the mall on your way home this evening and pick me up a muzzle. That's about the only way I'll learn how to keep my mouth shut." He laughed. I laughed, but not for the same reason. The masks that he wore when he cleaned house looked enough like muzzles, and wearing one never stopped him from spewing his gibberish. We stopped laughing at the same time.

I glanced at my watch one more time and finished my coffee. "Baby, I'll see you this evening." I kissed my new husband and then I was out the door before he could get too nosy or make another stupid comment.

Paul offered to go with me to visit my sick friend a few more times, but I was always able to talk him out of it. After a while, he stopped offering.

Things went well for the next couple of years. We moved into a two-bedroom condo on Manchester. We paid off a few bills, bought new furniture, and enjoyed a few more cruises. I didn't see my friends as much as I used to, but a few of Paul's relatives visited from time to time. And to my everlasting horror, it was always the ones I liked the least. Every time his dragon of a mother came, she started cleaning the place ten minutes after she'd come through the door, no matter how clean it already was. And, like Paul, she wore a surgical mask and latex gloves when she cleaned house, too.

Relatives I'd never met often showed up unannounced. "How come you and Paul ain't started no family yet?" asked his obnoxious cousin Bobby, a student at UCLA. Living so close to us, he was the one who caused me the most grief, because I never knew when he'd turn up on our doorstep. "Can't you have no kids?"

"Uh, we want to wait a few years," I told that busybody, glad Paul nodded his approval. But later when Paul and I were alone, he brought it up.

"I'm ready whenever you are," he said, tugging on my see-through gown as we prepared for bed that night. "And I don't care if the first one is a boy or a girl."

"Well, I'd like to wait at least one more

year. I want to make sure I'm ready," I told him.

I couldn't wait to have a child of my own, but I really wasn't ready. I'd seen too many couples break up after two or three years of marriage. I felt that if Paul and I could make it through the first four or five years, we had a pretty good chance of going the distance. And I wasn't going to let my curious secret relationship with Floyd interfere with my plans. Anyway, I had my ruse all worked out. Once I got pregnant, I'd hide it from Floyd by wearing baggy clothes, which was what I usually wore when I visited him now. When and if I could no longer hide the fact that I was pregnant, I'd stop visiting him until after I'd delivered. He knew I had problems with my periods occasionally. There were a lot of common female ailments, and even some surgeries, that I could claim I had, that would make it hard for me to travel for a few months.

CHAPTER 41

Paul and I celebrated our fourth wedding anniversary in Vegas. We'd spent a fortune on a suite at Caesars Palace, one of the most expensive hotels on the Strip. We didn't set foot out of the room until we checked out. We kept a DO NOT DISTURB sign on the door the whole four days. "You don't have to bother us anymore. I'm busy trying to create the first of my three children," Paul told the maid, the morning of the second day when she brought us some clean towels and a bucket of ice.

While Paul was in the shower, I checked my voice mail on an alternate cell phone that I kept turned off most of the time and hidden in a side pocket of my purse. Since Floyd and his lawyer were the only ones who had the number to this service, I knew that the three messages were all from one or both of them. All three were from Floyd. When I played each one, he said basically the same thing: "Baby, I got some great news. I can't wait to tell you! I love you, I love you, I love you!"

My eyes filled up with tears of joy. I had the best of both worlds. Not only was I feeding the cow, I was milking the cow. I rubbed my throbbing crotch as my lips curled into a naughty smile. Despite the fact that I was on a romantic rendezvous with my husband, I had more than enough affection left over that day to be excited about the messages from Floyd. Whatever he had to tell me, it had to be something good. There was too much passion in his voice for it not to be. I smiled again.

I knew that Floyd and a few other convicts had written letters to the prison officials asking them to improve a few things. Like provide better food and more of a variety. Floyd had requested permission to visit the prison library more often, which was one thing I was glad to hear. It seemed so sad that it had to take a life sentence in prison for a bright young brother like Floyd to get interested in reading. He had finally discovered literary geniuses like James Baldwin, Richard Wright, and Langston Hughes, and he loved it. I looked forward to my next visit on the upcoming Saturday.

■ ■ ■ ■

It was a typical Saturday for me. Paul was still in bed when I left the house. I wore a pair of black, flimsy ballerina shoes. They were so thin it felt like I was barefooted. I wore a loose, drab, floor-length gray jumper. I had wrapped and tied a black scarf around my head and neck. I looked like I was on my way to a pilgrimage in Mecca. Everything was going so well, and I was in such a good mood. It pleased me to see that Floyd was in a good mood, too. As soon as he saw me, he started grinning. He was practically beaming. I already had the telephone that I had come to despise in my hand when he sat down. "What's all that smiling for?" I asked. "And what is this great news you got to tell me?"

"Oh, baby, wait until you hear this! God finally came through for me, so I know there is more hope for me after all! I got some damn good news! I didn't want to tell you until I got it all worked out," he started. He was bopping up and down in his seat, like it had suddenly got too hot for him to sit still.

"Tell me what?" I asked, in a fever of nervous anticipation. "Are you going to get a new trial?"

Floyd let out a deep breath, rolled his eyes, and shook his head. "No. But I'm still working on that, too. This is even better. I started working on this about a year ago. Baby . . ." Floyd paused, and there were tears in his eyes. "Baby, *we can get married now*. Brian's helped me work out all the details, and we can do it whenever you're ready. Brian's even bought the ring. It'll be his gift to us. I . . . what's the matter, baby? Your face looks like it just turned to stone. You all right?"

"I'm fine, I'm fine," I said quickly. Hell no, I was not fine! My head felt like somebody had lit into it with a sledgehammer.

Floyd looked relieved. "Good. I can't have you getting sick on me now. I want my bride to be in tip-top shape when I give her my name."

If a bottomless hole had opened up in the floor beneath me and swallowed me whole, I wouldn't have cared. "What did you say?" I asked with a loud hiccup. My words felt like they had attached themselves to the lining inside my throat. I started to hyperventilate.

"Baby, don't get too excited now. I feel the same way you do. Just . . . just get ahold of yourself. Let's get you some water. You want a aspirin, too?" Floyd rose in his seat and was about to signal one of the guards when I held up my hand.

"I'm fine," I whimpered. I swallowed hard and shifted in my seat. Now it felt like I was the one sitting on a hot seat. In a way, I was. "You want us to get married? *Why?*" I asked in a raspy voice.

Floyd's smile faded fast. He looked confused, then disappointed. "Well, I thought . . . baby, you look like you just seen a ghost. I didn't mean to spring this fantastic news on you this way. But I don't have many choices these days. I couldn't tell you in a voice mail. And to be honest with you, this is something I had to tell you to your face, because I wanted to see your reaction. I can see how happy this makes you," Floyd said with a sniff. For a minute I thought he was going to cry.

"I . . . I . . . I." I couldn't even form a sentence. My lips felt like rubber, and I couldn't even feel my tongue. I swallowed hard again and blinked even harder. "I don't know what to say," I admitted. I didn't know what to say, or do. I was absolutely stunned and speechless.

"The warden thinks it's good for the prisoners' morale. Now it won't include conjugal visits yet, but me and Brian are working on that, too." Floyd winked and slid his tongue suggestively across his lips. "All I need to know from you now is when you want to do it. When do you want to become my wife, honey? It took us a long time, but we finally made it, huh? Mr. and Mrs. Floyd Watson. Now, baby, if you want to keep your maiden name at work, that's fine with me. But to the rest of the world, you will be known as Mrs. Watson. Boy, that's got a nice ring to it!" The more excited Floyd appeared to be, the worse I felt.

"Floyd, baby, I love you to death. And you know I do. But . . . but marriage is such a very big step," I began, speaking in a low, tentative voice. "Uh, it's one of the most important things in a woman's life. And in a man's," I told him. With each word my voice cracked a little more. "I never thought that . . ." The hurt look on Floyd's face made me stop talking for a few moments. "Floyd, let's talk about this. I wish you had told me before now."

"I thought you'd be pleased . . ."

"I am! I mean, I will always love you, Floyd. And I know how we talked about getting married before . . . before . . . you know. Marriage would mean a lot of changes in our relationship."

"How is us being married going to change

things?"

"I don't know," I responded, my voice so hollow it echoed.

"Us getting married wouldn't stop you from doing, uh, whatever it is you doing out there now. But it would mean a lot to me. If nothing else, I'd feel better just knowing that we got to do one of the things we talked about doing before this shit happened. If the rest of my prayers get answered, and Brian can arrange for me to have conjugal visits, we can even have a child." Floyd gave me a guarded look as he reared to the side in his seat. "And under the circumstances, I think we should only plan on having one."

"Floyd, we both know what it's like not to have a real family, a loving family. I promised myself that I would not have children if I ever thought I'd wind up raising them alone. Honey, we both know how unimportant black kids are considered. Just being black can be a handicap for every black child born in this country — and those are the ones with two educated and successful parents raising them! We don't need to have children the way things are for us now. We can't do that to a child. Not even one. We can't do that to ourselves." I had to take a very deep breath after the little speech I'd just made, but I could see that it had a

341

profound effect on Floyd.

"Well, I feel you on that. You're right. Us having kids is probably not such a good idea. But I thought marrying me was what you always wanted."

"I did. I mean, I do. But I have to give this some thought! I am not prepared for this."

"I see," he said, blinking hard. "I guess the next time I spend a lot of time and effort on something, I should check with you first, huh?"

"Well, yes, if it involves me. This is one thing that I should have been in on from the get-go." The visit had become so awkward that Floyd looked relieved when I stood up to leave.

I was so dizzy when I left, I almost walked into the wall in the exit hallway. But the way I felt was nothing compared to how depressed Floyd looked when I said goodbye. And it got even worse.

The next time I visited him, he was so depressed he could barely hold his head up. It looked like he was starving himself to death, too, because he seemed at least twenty pounds lighter. The muscles that he had developed had lost their firmness. Loose skin hung from his arms, and his skin looked dull and unhealthy. The circles around his eyes were so severe he looked like a raccoon. His hair was even thinner. I could see several bald spots. I had no idea that depression could ravage a person's body so much. He looked as though he were in the final stages of a terminal illness. I had to save him.

"Floyd, we can get married when I come up next month," I told him. It seemed like such a small price for me to pay to keep him from destroying himself. As soon as he heard that, he perked up. "Did you hear me, baby. We can get married next month."

"Do you mean that?" he croaked. His skeletal hand shook as he held the telephone.

"I mean that." I smiled. He smiled.

In addition to the fact that marriage meant so much to him and would probably save him from self-destruction, there was only one other consolation that I could think of. And that was, other than his busy lawyer, nobody outside of the prison would ever know. . . .

CHAPTER 42

I met up with Floyd's lawyer twenty minutes before Floyd and I stood with him as our witness in front of the prison chaplain in the prison chapel. Even in the dim light, Brian's shiny black hair glistened like new money. Other than the bored-looking warden and a wheezing custodian stumbling around picking up things off the floor, nobody else was present. I immediately slid into a trancelike state. I didn't know what it felt like to be a zombie, but I was convinced that I wasn't too far from it.

I had cried so much the night before that I looked like a Cabbage Patch doll now. I had even left the house an extra hour early so Paul wouldn't see my puffy face. I had to come up with an explanation soon to tell Paul when I got home. While I was standing there committing a crime against man and God, a brainstorm suddenly formed in my mind. I decided that as soon as I could get to a place where I could have a private conversation on my cell phone, I would call Paul. I planned to tell him that I was stuck in a major traffic jam, due to an accident, and that I would be delayed by several hours. Then I would spend the night in a motel with an ice pack on my face to help the swelling go down. I didn't come out of my trance until Floyd slipped the ring that Brian had brought onto my trembling finger. It was the first time I'd been able to touch Floyd since this mess had started, and it was like touching a dead man. He was just that cold and stiff. I knew what dead men felt like because I'd kissed my late foster father's cheek as he lay in his coffin.

I must have said "I do" somewhere along the line, because the next thing I was conscious of was Floyd wrapping his arms around me and kissing me like I'd never been kissed before. He lifted me off the ground, and probably would have kissed me for the next hour if the warden hadn't pulled us apart. The warden shook Floyd's hand and hugged me. Brian kissed me, almost as passionately as Floyd. That made everybody, except me, laugh. Instead, I broke down and cried like an injured baby. My legs felt like jelly, and the rest of my body felt like it weighed a ton. It took Brian and Floyd to hold me up to keep me from falling to the floor.

Floyd's hands were as cold as ice, and he had a smell that I could not identify. It reminded me of something sour and stale. Like some old clothes that had been stored away in a closet for too long. Then it dawned on me that everything else in the prison visiting area — the vending machines, the hellacious ladies' room, and the dimly lit hallways — all had the same foul smell.

Floyd had told me that other prisoners had had to get married in their prison attire, those hideous orange jumpsuits, but because the warden liked Floyd, he had allowed Brian to bring a suit for Floyd to wear.

I wore a plain white linen suit. I'd left home in a plaid shirt and a pair of jeans to keep Paul from getting suspicious. I'd checked into a Motel 6 and changed, shaking so hard I could barely walk in the new heels I'd purchased from Payless for the occasion.

"I'm sorry I wasn't able to work out something so you two could spend some time together," Brian told me after the three-minute ceremony, with an apologetic look on his face. "But I won't stop until that happens, too." He gave me a hug and he shook Floyd's hand. "Good luck to you both." Then the guards led my new *husband* — I assumed that's what he was — back to his cell. I wasn't sure what he was to me because I was already married to another man. But as far as Floyd was concerned, he was my husband, period. He was happy, and if anybody deserved some happiness, it was Floyd. That was all that mattered. For now, at least.

It was one of the most uncomfortable weekends in my life. When I got home that evening, Paul was so horny he literally grabbed my hand and led me to the bedroom as soon as I entered the condo. "Oooh wee! I've got so much sap in me to unload, I'll be surprised if you don't get pregnant with triplets tonight."

I wasn't going to get pregnant with triplets or anything else, anytime soon. I was on my period, so I got out of fucking Paul that night. The following Monday morning, I made a special trip to the drugstore to refill my birth control prescription.

The last thing I needed right now was a baby to complicate matters even more. It was going to take me a while to get comfortable about what I'd done. Especially if

Floyd's lawyer worked it out for Floyd to get conjugal visits. I still planned on having children. But now I didn't know when, or with which husband!

As if things were not complicated enough, Paul's company offered him a major promotion that would almost double his salary. They wanted him to manage two dozen high-level corporate trainers. The only thing was, the job was in the Bay Area city of Alameda, which faced San Francisco across the Bay. "Honey, I'd be a fool to pass up an opportunity like this," he told me, calling me from his office as soon as he'd received the news.

Paul didn't have to admit it, but I knew that one of the reasons this job offer was so attractive to him was because he'd be able to spend more time with his relatives in San Francisco. And knowing the way those snooty fools felt about me, there was no way I was going to move anywhere to be closer to them. At least not without a fight. As soon as I heard Paul's news, I prepared myself to lock horns with him if I had to.

"Paul, I love my job and I love L.A. I don't want to move," I wailed. "As a matter of fact, I am not moving up there." Things were happening too fast for me. I didn't want to "lose" Paul, and I didn't want to give up my job, either. I was glad that it was one of my off weeks. It had been three weeks since I'd married Floyd, and I was gearing up for my next visit to him in a week.

"You don't have to move, baby. I would never expect you to give up that job you love so much for me. You can stay down here, keep an eye on our place on Manchester, and be with me on your off days. And I will still be spending time in the L.A. offices a few times a month. As a matter of fact, we probably won't be apart too much more than we already are now. I think this is the way all relationships should be! They say that absence makes the heart grow fonder."

"They also say, 'out of sight, out of mind,' " I said with a dry laugh. Then I got real serious. "I can live with us being apart even more, but maintaining two residences will be expensive."

"Baby, let me finish. Here is another reason why we can't pass this up. The job includes an expense account that won't quit. The company will provide me with a leased car, and a leased apartment, all at their expense!"

"My God," I mouthed, my heart beating a mile a minute. "You're right. We can't pass this up," I said, feeling extremely relieved. "When is this going to happen?"

"As soon as possible. Now look, I want you to fly up there with me next Saturday."

"Next Saturday?"

"Next Saturday. I'm sure that sick friend of yours won't die if you skip a visit from time to time. And I don't want to bring this up now, but shouldn't this friend be better by now? Is she ever going to be well enough for me to meet her? This is a strange setup, if you don't mind me saying so . . ."

"Uh, um . . ." I was groping to try to find the right words, but I wasn't having much luck. I paused and pretended that I had something caught in my throat. I had to cough for a few moments, and that allowed me a little more time to come up with an appropriate response. "Some air went down the wrong pipe," I said, blinking hard.

"When was the last time you took your vitamins?"

"I don't remember. I'll take some tonight."

"Make sure you do. This is not the time for you to be getting sick. This new job situation is going to be stressful enough for us both."

"You're right. That's what we need to concentrate on right now — your new job and the move," I agreed. "This has nothing to do with Christine."

"Christine? What? You said — I thought her name was Crystal . . ." Paul said in an accusatory voice.

"It is! Didn't I say that?"

"You just referred to her as Christine." Paul got real quiet. All I could hear on his end was his heavy breathing.

"Paul, if it's that important to you, you can go with me the next time I do visit Crystal. I just don't see the point. You have a lot of friends that I've never met, and I don't want to. I can't expect you to share every little aspect of your life with me. We both agreed that our individual independence was one of the things that attracted us to each other in the first place. It's just that, well, Crystal was finally beginning to make some progress. You, um, kind of resemble the man she lost her mind over. If your unexpected presence upsets her, I will just have to deal with her relapse, I guess."

"Girl, stop messing with me!" I was glad to hear Paul laugh. "I don't really want to meet that loony friend of yours."

"Paul, I wish you'd be a little more sensitive. The woman can't help herself," I said in a plaintive voice.

"I'm sorry, baby. I should be ashamed of myself, and I am. But I have to be honest about this peculiar situation. Now don't take this the wrong way, but I just ask about your sick friend from time to time so you won't think I don't care. And to tell you the truth, I asked you to go with me to the Bay Area so I'd have a good excuse not to let my family make a fuss over the new place, and me, when I go up there next Saturday."

"What I could do is drive up there after I visit Crystal. It should take me only three or four hours, if I don't get lost," I offered.

"Now you know I don't want you to do that. I don't want you driving on that highway alone any more than you already do. I would never forgive myself if something happened to you. You're the most important thing in my life, Dolores. You do know that, don't you?"

"Uh-huh," I mumbled. "I know that."

"Other than death, I can't think of anything that I wouldn't challenge to keep you. And I hope you feel the same way about me."

"I do . . ." I muttered.

CHAPTER 43

There were a couple of women on the ship who pestered me to socialize with them every time they saw me. They also tried to tag along with me when I went shopping in every port we cruised to, and when we were not on board the *Encantadora.* Sue Ann Thomas managed the ship's gift shop. She was old enough to be my mother, and so loud and brassy I was embarrassed to be seen in public with her. She was a nasty piece of work. One time she'd almost got us arrested in Cancún because she'd insulted a Mexican policeman by calling him a spic to his face.

The other pest, Donna Minger, was a couple of years younger than me. She was a cute, redheaded waitress in the ship's main bar. Other than work, I had nothing in common with these two women. However, they were a little more fun to be around than the two matchmakers who I'd previously worked with in the corporate office.

The strange thing about all four of these white women was that they often said things that sounded racist to me. Their targets were usually the Latinos who we came in contact with when the ship cruised into the Mexican ports. I avoided these women whenever I could. As far as I was concerned, anybody who was stupid enough to display a racist attitude toward another race with me could just as easily do it to me. I couldn't understand why these women wanted to hang around with me in the first place. They had become such pests that I started avoiding them. It was women like them that made me appreciate Valerie.

One of the reasons I had such a strong friendship with Valerie was because we didn't see each other that often now. I was glad to see her when I did, and it was usually at Paw Paw's, with me slumped on a stool at the bar and her mixing me one complimentary drink after another.

A few nights ago, I'd sat at the bar and sucked up four drinks as I listened to her complain about how dull and empty her life still was. "I have so little to look forward to," she whined, sounding more and more like Moanin' Lisa. This foolishness was coming from the mouth of a beautiful young woman who owned her own house and her own business. If that was not something to look forward to, what was? I didn't have the nerve to ask her, but I wondered how much of Valerie's gloom could be blamed on her dark secret.

I also wondered if her conscience ever bothered her, and if she had nightmares about her stepfather from time to time. But to hear her tell it, her biggest disappointment was not having what I had. "You've got it all, Lo. Other than children, you've got everything a woman wants." Valerie gave me a thoughtful look. "And with your luck, you will have nothing but the most beautiful and most intelligent kids in town."

Since I had two handsome husbands, a nice condo, and a job that I enjoyed more and more each day, I didn't know what to say — that I hadn't said already — to make Valerie feel better.

I had come to her house today because she had invited me. She still did not like to be in that house alone. And I didn't blame her. I didn't believe in ghosts, because I'd never seen one. But I had never seen the Grand Canyon, either. And if ghosts did exist, the last one I wanted to see was Mr. Zeke's. I understood Valerie's fears about being alone in that house. One of the two women who had taken over the rooms that Moanin' Lisa and I had vacated had moved out the day before to get married. And the other one was threatening to move out, too.

"I just wanted some company today and you were the first person that came to mind," Valerie told me, handing me my favorite drink — a large glass of white wine. "This old house seems like a big old scary castle when I'm here by myself. I've been begging Binkie and Liz to move back home, but they don't want to come near this place."

"You still don't want to sell it and move into a condo?" I asked, knowing the answer to that question, and why.

Valerie shook her head and scratched the back of her neck. "I got a call from Moanin' Lisa the other day. She wanted to know if she could move back in after Toni moves out." I knew that Valerie had evicted Moanin' Lisa because of that comment she'd made about the backyard during my wedding reception. However, she later admitted to me that she'd regretted that decision. "I told her I already had a new tenant lined up. I just might break down and let her move back in, though." Valerie cocked her head to the side and gave me a pensive look. "Some days I can't walk into the kitchen without a Bible held against my bosom." Valerie rarely entered religious territory these days but when she did, she was serious. I didn't know if she had prayed for God to forgive her for killing Mr. Zeke like I had, but she and I both still needed some serious spiritual guidance in other areas. "But you, you can always move back up in here. And, if you have to, you can bring Paul with you. It might be nice to have a man in the house again." Valerie paused and laughed, but it was a short, weak laugh. "At the rate I'm going, it might be the only way I ever get to live under the same roof with a married man."

Valerie looked so sad and lonely when I left her house that night. I felt the same way when I got home myself, even though I had spent an hour talking to Paul on the phone earlier that day, and I was going to see Floyd that Saturday.

I felt better after my visit with Floyd. And things got better as time went on. I spent days at a time with Paul in the new apartment in Alameda, when I could. He was happy, I was happy. And now that I was Floyd's wife, he was happy, too.

Paul came to L.A. often enough so I didn't really miss him the way I thought I would. I usually visited Floyd once a month.

But every now and then I visited him twice in the same month, just to keep his spirits up.

My life became so routine that I got a little too comfortable. As a matter of fact, I got so comfortable, I got careless. I went for days without checking my voice mail on the other cell phone that I had bought to use only to communicate with Floyd and his lawyer.

On a Monday morning there was an urgent telephone message left for me with the ship's receptionist. It was from Brian, Floyd's lawyer. I stumbled to my stateroom and called him back right away.

"I've left several voice mail messages for you," Brian told me, talking so fast and loud it frightened me. The first thought that came to my mind was that something bad had happened to Floyd. He had told me about a few altercations that he'd had with some of the other prisoners. And last year two convicts had been attacked and killed by other prisoners.

"What's wrong?" I asked, my voice just above a whisper. "Is Floyd all right?"

"Mrs. Watson, *your husband Floyd is coming home to you,*" Brian told me. The news hit me like a ton of bricks. I got so light-headed and dizzy I fell across the bed, shaking like a leaf, and babbling gibberish like an idiot.

I don't know how long I remained on the bed like that. But the next thing I was conscious of was Brian's voice ringing in my ears like a bell. "Hello? Hello? Mrs. Watson? Mrs. Watson, are you all right?"

The telephone was still in my hand, even though I couldn't feel it. Somehow I managed to sit up on the bed and speak again. "What did you just say?" I croaked. "What in the world is going on?"

"I've been trying to reach you for three days. Floyd and Warden Beale have also tried to reach you by telephone. I didn't want to call you at your work, but I didn't want you to hear the good word on the six o'clock news!"

"Did the real killer confess or something?" I had to squeeze my thighs together to keep from losing control of my bodily functions. I wanted to vomit, pee, and shit all at the same time. But I couldn't even move from the bed.

"Are you familiar with DNA procedures?"

"Uh, a little," I whimpered.

"Well, DNA was still in its infancy back when Floyd got arrested. Through DNA, we've been able to prove — beyond a shadow of a doubt — that Floyd Watson was not the man who raped and killed that girl. The real culprit is currently in custody for another crime. Not only will Floyd be released soon, with the settlement I am sure we will receive, he will never have to work again a day in his life. That won't make up for the years he spent in prison, but that's about the best we can hope for. I am so happy for you!" There was a long pause before Brian spoke again. "Mrs. Watson, are you still with me?"

"I . . . I'm still here," I managed. A million and one thoughts were swimming around in my aching head. I didn't know what to say, think, or do. "When?"

"When will he be home? Well, he's free to leave at any time now. But, as you know, he has no home to go to, except with you. Can we get together this evening?"

"Uh, can I call you back?"

"Well, yes, but it has to be soon."

"I will call you back later today. I have to call somebody right now." I hung up before Brian could say anything else. Then I dialed Valerie's number at Paw Paw's. I was so stunned, confused, and frightened that when she answered I could barely speak. "Valerie . . . I need," I began, struggling with the words. "I need to talk . . ."

"Lo, what's the matter? You sound

strange," Valerie said, sounding alarmed. "Hold on, let me get Tiny out here to cover for me, so I can take this call in my office." I waited about three minutes for Valerie to return to the telephone. "Now, what's the matter?"

"Val, I don't care what you are doing. I have to see you right now. I need to talk to you."

"Well, whatever it is, I hope it can wait." Valerie paused and started whispering in an excited voice into the telephone. "Listen up. Two of TV's biggest stars strutted up in here a little while ago. As we speak, they are huddled in a booth, carrying on like newly-weds. They are married, but not to each other. I just left a message for my contact at *Star* magazine." Valerie cleared her throat, and the excitement in her voice increased. She hissed the next few words. "Anybody that famous and married ought to know better! Dude is a primetime asshole and Miss Thing calls herself a Christian!"

"Valerie, I don't care if you've got Jesus, Joseph, and Mary sitting in your bar right now. I need to talk to you," I insisted. *"Now."*

I could tell that Valerie was caught off guard and taken aback by the way she gasped. "Dolores, I've got a business to run. . . ."

"I know that!" I snapped. It bothered me that Valerie considered something as frivolous as gossip about two TV stars more important than what I had to talk to her about.

"And aren't you at work yourself?"

"We are, uh, we are in dock for the next two hours. Then the ship will be heading out for Puerto Vallarta again, but I won't be on it." Then I burst into tears. My breakdown was so sudden and aggressive, I squawked like a parrot for the first minute. Then I sobbed softly for the next two minutes while Valerie yelled and begged me to tell her what was wrong.

"Oh shit! Girl, is it that serious?" I was glad to hear some real concern in Valerie's voice now. "You sound like a woman on the verge of a nervous breakdown."

"I'm fine," I told her. I actually managed to laugh. It was not the way I usually laughed. *I was braying like a jackass.*

"Well, you don't sound fine to me. You sound like a fucking creature. What in the hell is going on?"

I held my breath and vigorously rubbed my chest. But the only thing that did was make my chest ache. "Can you get away from the bar for a little while?" I croaked. Even though I was breathing through my mouth, it felt like I was letting air out through every opening on my body, including my stupid black ass.

"I could, but I don't really want to. Can't we talk here? I've got a bachelorette party coming in a couple of hours, and I want to be in on the festivities. Who knows, one of those heifers just might have a man that's got a buddy I might like."

"Can you meet me at The Ivy in an hour?"

"You want me to drive over to Beverly Hills? Girl, what is this all about? Is this about your husband?"

"Uh, you could say that."

CHAPTER 44

It was over. I had confessed to Valerie everything that there was to confess about myself, Paul, and Floyd. Each word had rolled out of my mouth like a rock and now my lips felt bruised. But I felt so much better! Whoever it was that said "confession is good for the soul" was right. Not only did it seem like I had just shed my skin, it felt like a huge stone had been lifted off my chest, too. I felt ten pounds lighter.

I knew it was my imagination, but now it seemed like everybody at The Ivy was looking at me. Even Ryan Seacrest from the TV show *American Idol,* sitting two tables away. I lowered my voice even lower. "Valerie, I don't think I can get through this without your help," I admitted.

She agreed with me by nodding. "I know I owe you big time for, uh, being there *that night* for me. Whatever it is you need me to do to help you pull this thing off, I'll do,"

Valerie told me. "I guess I can live with having a bigamist for a best friend." She laughed. I didn't. She cleared her throat and gave me a serious look. "Just tell me what you want me to do."

"Well, like I already said, I need to move back into your house. I don't know for how long, but that's the most important thing I can think of right now. I will need to use you for alibis from time to time," I said in a stiff tone of voice. "Another thing is I can't have you sharing this information with anybody else."

"Look, with that cold case of mine that I've got to deal with every day of my life, blabbing somebody else's crime is not on my agenda. You feel me?"

I nodded.

"But even with my help, do you seriously think you can pull this off?" Valerie asked. "Have you given any thought to the fact that you might slip up sooner or later? What if you run into one husband while you're out with the other? What if you leave some incriminating shit in the wrong place one day? Like a letter or some other document. What if a friend of one husband sees you out with the other husband? And what if you get —"

I held up my hand and cut Valerie off in

mid sentence and gave her a frustrated look. "I've thought about all of that. I've thought about everything else that could happen, too. But if I'm smart and lucky, it won't. At least not until I come up with another plan. I will figure this shit out as I go along. Like I said, I am going to remain in the condo on Manchester for when Paul comes to visit. But I am going to give up my job."

"What? You *love* that job. Listen, you are talking crazy. Other than being Miss America, what other job could be more fun and exciting than yours?"

"I can't keep the job and both husbands. I can for a while, but eventually my job would get in the way. I'll use the time that I'm *supposed* to be at my job to do some serious juggling. If I don't, I'm bound to get caught. Until I come up with a better plan, I have to let them both think I still work on the *Encantadora.* They both know about my down time. Now all of my time will be down time. When I'm up in Alameda with Paul, Floyd will think I'm out to sea. When I spend some time with Floyd, in your house, Paul will think I'm out to sea. It can work, but I need your help now. Please, Valerie. I never ask you for much, and I wouldn't ask for your help now if I didn't really need it."

"Girl, I already told you that you can move back if you want to. To be honest with you, I'm glad you're coming back. I love your company. If you think Floyd is such a prize, he must not be that bad," Valerie said, looking and sounding so serious it made me squirm. Then her expression and her voice softened. "And as long as Floyd doesn't start any mess up in my house, and respects me, he can come, too. I really mean that, and under any other circumstances, I wouldn't even charge you and him the same rent I'd charge anybody else. But with him about to get paid big time when his settlement comes through, I expect to get paid, every first of the month."

"Thanks, girl. I really appreciate this, and it will only be for a little while. Maybe it'll be just a couple of weeks or months — only until we can get a place of our own."

"What? Fuck that 'couple of weeks' shit. Look, you know I don't like to live alone, and I've been trying to get you back in my house for years. You got me all worked up and now you're telling me you'll only be there for a minute?"

"Valerie, I just need a place to bring Floyd to until I know what he wants to do. You know that if it was up to me, I'd stay on with you forever. And that just might happen. But with him getting that settlement, and it must be fat if his lawyer said that nobody — especially Floyd — wants the amount made public. He'll want a place eventually, and I will have to go with him."

"You are making me dizzy. Let me try to get all this shit straight in my head." Valerie ordered another drink. "You have a home up in Alameda with Paul. You spend a few days a month up there with him. When he has business down here, he stays with you at the Manchester address. You will move back to my place and then you want to eventually move to some other location with Floyd. And, you want to quit that fantastic job? Did I leave anything out?"

I shook my head. "One more thing, tell me again you won't ever tell anybody about any of this." I was teasing Valerie at this point, but I knew that she knew I was also very serious.

Valerie's mouth dropped open for about the tenth time since we'd entered The Ivy. "Why would I? What would I have to gain by blabbing your business?"

"Well, with all due respect, girlfriend, I know how you like to chat while you're working that bar. And even when you are not behind that bar, you do talk out both sides of your mouth."

"If you don't think you can trust me to keep quiet about all this, why the hell did you tell me? Yeah, I've got a big-assed mouth, but I know when to keep it shut."

"I know, I know. I'm just so fucking nervous! I don't know what to say to Floyd when I see him." I sighed, shook my head, and rolled my eyes. "The first thing he's going to want to do when I get him home is fuck the hell out of me!" A strange look slid across Valerie's face like a dark shadow. "Why are you looking at me like that?" I wanted to know.

"Maybe I shouldn't say this . . ."

"Say it!"

She exhaled deeply first. Then she started talking fast, but in a low voice. "Well, the man has been cooped up behind bars for a bunch of years. I never got to know Floyd that well, but he didn't strike me as the type to spread his ass. I doubt if his dick has felt any real pleasure since he got locked up, other than his hand. Even so, his dick must be like cobalt steel by now!" Valerie took a sip of her wine and gave me a look that could only be described as envy. "Hell yeah, he's going to want to fuck the living hell out of you. And don't worry about embarrassing or disturbing me. I'll be in my room, wishing I was in your shoes."

I gave Valerie a sad look and shook my head. "No, you don't want to be in my shoes. Even I don't want to be in my shoes these days," I told her.

CHAPTER 45

When I got back to the condo on Manchester, the first thing I did was stumble to the
wine rack in the den to pop open a fresh
bottle. I drank half of it straight from the
bottle. I still had on my sweater and my
purse in my hand.

After a series of long, loud burps, I
dropped my purse on the table and listened
to some of my voice mail messages. Floyd's
voice made my skin scrawl as he yelled his
good news. "Dolores, baby, it's finally over!
I'm coming home! We can finally be together
as man and wife!"

After I listened to three more messages
from Floyd, each one making my flesh crawl
even more, I listened to two from the
warden. There were three from his lawyer. I
was sorry that I did not share their enthusiasm about Floyd's release. I was happy for
Floyd. I prayed that he would be able to get
over what had happened to him and live a

normal life. What scared the shit out of me was the fact that as Floyd's wife, I'd be expected to help him restore his life. Under the circumstances, I didn't know how the hell I was going to do that and still keep everything intact with Paul.

I had to finish that bottle of wine before I checked the voice mail messages on the telephone in my living room. Paul had called twice. I screamed, between belches, when he told me that he would be in L.A. in a couple of days for just a few hours to attend a business meeting. Then I checked my primary cell phone for messages. Paul had also left me a message on it, too, telling me the same news. I didn't know what to do next, but I knew what I had to do. I called Floyd's lawyer. Even with all the alcohol in my system and the false courage that came with it, my voice was so weak, shaky, and hoarse that he asked me if I needed to see a doctor.

"I . . . I'm fine," I stammered, rubbing my nose. I felt myself about to belch some more, but I held that off by taking a few deep breaths. I was glad that I had a buzz, but drinking so much wine in such a short time did me more harm than good. There was the taste of sour grapes in my mouth and a painful, throbbing sensation on both sides of my head. And since I had not eaten much, my stomach felt queasy. I tried to picture all of that wine sloshing around in my nearly empty stomach, pickling my insides.

"I was beginning to wonder if I'd hear from you today, Mrs. Watson. Floyd is champing at the bit to fly out of that cuckoo's nest, so to speak. For a man who has gone through the hell he's gone through, he's in a remarkably good mood. However, he wants absolutely nothing to do with the media. Not after the way they had tried and convicted him before he even went to trial. And I can certainly understand that. I've turned down three local TV station interviews, four newspaper interviews, and offers are still coming in. I've heard from everybody but Oprah. I just told my secretary that when and if they call, she's to tell Oprah's people the same thing we're telling everyone else: no interviews."

I froze. All of this shit being public was another can of worms! I hadn't even thought about that! I knew how relentless reporters and photographers were. If they wanted a story bad enough, they didn't stop until they got it. If worse came to worst, the whole world would know what I'd done. *I could end up behind bars next!* I had to keep my name and picture out of this mess. "Brian, I don't care what you have to do; you have to keep the media out of this. I don't want anybody to know about me and Floyd."

"Well, like I just said, Floyd will not give any interviews, and I am behind him one hundred percent. Even though I personally think that this would make an incredible human interest story. The public needs to know about these things. It could give some other wrongfully convicted individual hope. I believe that there are a lot more 'Floyds' rotting away in prison for crimes they did not commit."

"I know and I agree with you. But I don't care about all that right now. I am more concerned about my privacy," I hollered. "You can't tell anybody about me. This kind of attention could cost me my job!"

"I don't know how it could make you lose your job, but you don't have to worry about me revealing any information about you to anyone. However, if news about his marriage to you leaks, you might have to make a statement, at the very least."

"It's my ass if I fix my lips to do any damn interviews! Hell no! I am not talking to any newspaper reporters or anybody else! You're a lawyer. Can't you put a stop to all this? I don't want to talk to anybody, period. I don't even want anybody to know that I've been visiting Floyd all these years," I wailed.

"And you won't have to if you don't want to. Let me handle everything. Now, moving forward. It's rather late in the day, but I don't mind making the trip with you."

"Trip? What trip?" I asked dumbly.

"Mrs. Watson, your husband is a free man now, and he wants to come home to be with you. He has nobody but you. I am sorry that I was not able to prepare you better, but it was not easy to get in touch with you. If you don't feel up to it, I can collect Mr. Watson on my own. But under the circumstances, I think he deserves to spend his first hour back on the outside with his beautiful bride."

I was speechless.

"Mrs. Watson, are you still there?"

"Uh-huh."

"Did you hear what I just said?"

"Uh-huh. Well, okay. But first I have to take care of a few things. I will call you as soon as I'm ready," I said. I hung up and called Valerie immediately. She must have been sitting by the telephone because she answered it two seconds into the first ring. "Get over here now and help me haul as much of my stuff to your house as we can."

"We need to discuss something first." Valerie sounded uncertain and a bit frightened. That made me even more nervous. She was the only person I could count on. Just like I was the only person who Floyd could count on.

"What?" I wanted to know, my hand over my heart. The way I was feeling, I was surprised that I was still able to talk, stand, or do anything else.

"Have you turned on the TV? Floyd is all over the news."

"No. I don't want to see it. I just got off the phone with his lawyer, and he promised me that we wouldn't have to deal with the media. He also promised that he would do all he could to make sure that information regarding my jailhouse marriage to Floyd would not be made public. You know goddamn well I can't do any interviews!"

"Well, you won't have to, but that won't stop those assholes from doing the story with whatever information they do have. They just showed a clip from the trial. There you were sitting in the courtroom. They also showed you going at the DA . . ."

"Shit. I forgot all about that damn shit. Well, did they say anything about me visiting Floyd all these years?"

"No, nobody has said anything about you

and Floyd having any contact at all after the trial. Listen, maybe now is not the time for me to say this, but I don't want any attention."

"What do you mean?"

"You and Floyd can stay with me as long as you want, as long as I don't get dragged into your mess. I don't want any punk-ass reporters digging into my background. You know . . ."

"Valerie, I can understand why you don't want any media attention. You can understand why I don't want any either, so we don't have anything to worry about." I let out a heavy sigh and looked around the room. "Get over here as soon as you can."

"Before we do anything, I need to let you know that your husband called my house a few minutes ago."

"Which one?" I couldn't believe what I was saying. Floyd knew nothing about me staying with Valerie these days. He thought I had my own place. It would be one of the first things I told him when I saw him. "Oh, Paul called there for me?"

"He said he left you a message or two."

"I know." My voice was trembling and getting hoarse. "Girl, he's going to be down here in a couple of days."

"No, he won't. That's what he called to

tell me to tell you. There was some crisis up there in his office that he needed to take care of."

I let out a huge sigh of relief. "That's good. I can't tell you how glad I am to hear that."

"Listen up. There is one more thing we need to discuss before you bring Floyd into my house. If you don't keep this shit under control, we could both suffer. I don't want too many people, including Floyd, to know *all my business* . . ."

"Valerie, you should know by now that if anybody can keep a secret, it's me. You wouldn't know anything about me and Floyd being married all this time if I hadn't told you."

As far as I was concerned, I was the one with the most to lose if everything got out. Not only was I an accomplice in a murder case, I was also a bigamist. Valerie might have been lucky enough to get off by claiming self-defense, but what excuse could I use? There was no justification for committing bigamy.

CHAPTER 46

I threw up twice before I called Brian back an hour later to tell him that I was in no shape to make the trip to the prison to pick up Floyd. His reply made me feel slightly better immediately. "I didn't think you'd be able to go, and please don't beat yourself up about it. I know how traumatic hearing all this was for you. I've already communicated this to Floyd and he totally understands."

"What time do you think you'll bring him?" I asked in a meek voice. Valerie was standing in the middle of her living room floor with her arms folded. She had helped me haul two suitcases full of my stuff to her house and arranged it in the old bedroom I'd once called mine. Now it was mine again.

"Under the circumstances, I think it'd be best to move a little more slowly. Floyd and I will check into a room tonight and make the drive back down here some time tomorrow. I'm still fighting off reporters. A slew of them would no doubt follow me from the prison to your place."

"Oh Lord, I hope they don't do that!" I hollered.

"Well, they've been known to do a lot worse. Another one of my clients discovered a reporter and a photographer hiding behind a bush in her backyard."

"Shit! Well, this is private property. If they come over here they might get hurt," I said. That made Brian laugh, but I didn't think it was funny at all.

"That's all the more reason why we should take this more slowly. Now. Listen to me. You get some rest. I will be in touch with you tomorrow."

"Wait! I have to give you my home address."

"I beg your pardon? Your husband doesn't have your address?"

"Uh . . . yeah. But the one he's been sending mail to is one of those private mailboxes. I've had it for years. My job takes me away from home so much, a private mailbox is so much more convenient and secure."

"I see."

I gave Brian the address to Valerie's house and then I ran to the bathroom to throw up some more. I had puked up so much already, I was surprised that I had anything left in my stomach.

When I returned to the living room, Valerie was standing there with her hands on her hips. I didn't like the look on her face. "I don't know if I should stay here," I told her, wiping my lips with a damp towel.

"What's wrong now?"

"I don't like what I'm hearing from Floyd's lawyer about how bad these reporters want to get his story. I don't want to get you in any trouble, Val. If you want me to leave, I'll go back to the condo."

"Girl, you can't take Floyd *there!* Even though Paul is up north, his shit is all over that place. And what if Paul decides to pay you one of his surprise visits?"

"I don't know what I'm saying," I said, shaking my head and waving my hands. I could have sworn that I heard things rattling around inside my head. It sounded and felt like marbles. Maybe I was losing my marbles and didn't know it. "Uh, I can get a cheap motel room and keep him there for a while." I stumbled to the wine cabinet to pour myself some wine, but just looking at it made my stomach heave again. I decided I'd had enough to drink for a while. And besides, I was really going to need a few

381

drinks when I had to face Floyd.

"How would you explain a motel to him?"

"Oh. Then I can still bring him here?"

Valerie nodded. "You'll get through this. I'll see to it."

I don't know how I made it through the first night of Floyd's return. Had Valerie not been there, I wouldn't have. Just seeing him outside of that dank prison was a shock to my system. His eyes looked so sad and empty. And it looked like it hurt his face for him to smile. He gave me a mild hug and a hungry little kiss on my cheek. Then he leaned back on his legs and looked at me. His gaze was intense, like he was trying to stare straight through me. "I didn't think I'd ever get to do this again," he said, his voice cracking. Then he turned to Valerie standing behind me. "Val, you're as beautiful as ever." Then he looked around the room with a puzzled look on his tortured face. "I didn't know your house was the setup," he remarked to Valerie, turning to me with a questioning look on his face. "I thought you had a place all to yourself these days."

"Uh, I've been renting a room here for a few months now. They sold my old apartment building, and the new owner raised the rent too high for me," I offered. I was so used to lying by now, I did it with such ease; I often believed my own lies.

"Well, we'll be able to live anywhere we want to live as soon as I get myself situated," Floyd said with a nod and turning to Brian, who was still standing near the door with a proud grin on his face. "Thanks for everything, man," Floyd said, walking over to Brian. They shook hands, hugged, and patted each other on the back, and then Brian left.

"You look like you could use a drink, Floyd," Valerie offered, already walking toward the portable bar in the corner. "I know I could use a few."

"Not now, but a little later for sure," Floyd mumbled, looking at me with a mysterious smile. I smiled back when he winked.

I took Floyd upstairs to our room, and that's when he broke down. I held him in my arms like a baby as he cried on my shoulder, but it was only for a very short time. "Look at me. I ought to be running up and down that street shouting for joy," he said, crying and laughing at the same time.

"No, you did just what anybody else would do," I said, guiding him to sit down on the bed. "Why don't you get comfortable, and I'll bring you that drink." By the time I returned to the bedroom with a glass of tequila, Floyd was fast asleep on top of the bedspread, still fully clothed.

"You want more privacy? I can spend a few nights with Binkie, or one of my crazy cousins in Compton," Valerie whispered, walking into the room and handing me yet another glass of wine.

"No, please don't leave me here alone with him." That must have sounded crazy because Valerie gasped. "You know what I mean. I've got to get used to him and all this."

Floyd slept until noon the next day. I wasn't due back at work for another two days. I called the receptionist and told her to tell my boss that I was as sick as a dog and that I would be off for a while.

I didn't even know that Valerie had left the house to go open up Paw Paw's until a few minutes later when I went downstairs. Contrary to what I'd been told to expect, Floyd hadn't been that anxious to make love to me, and it was just as well. Sex was the last thing on my mind. However, a few hours after he showered, shaved, and had a light breakfast, he practically dragged me back upstairs and attached himself to me like a conjoined twin.

CHAPTER 47

"Dolores, what the hell is going on? I've left six messages at the condo, and the girl at your work told me you've been out sick for several days. I was just about to call the cops and have them go check on you."

"Paul, I'm fine, baby."

"Why are you whispering? Why are you at Valerie's house and not at home?"

"Uh, Valerie's got company. I'm whispering so I won't disturb her. I'm over here because she's sick." As far as I knew Valerie was at Paw Paw's. Floyd was upstairs in our bedroom, splayed on top of the bed, still horny. I had just pried his arms from around me and come downstairs to catch my breath.

"You're sick. Now you're telling me she's sick, too? What the hell is the matter down there? She must not be too sick if she's entertaining company."

"Huh? Company? Oh! It's just Dr. Lawson. He still makes house calls. He thinks it's some kind of virus. I can barely talk." I managed a few quick coughs. "My head is spinning so bad, I didn't want to be at home alone in case I faint . . ."

"I'm coming home as soon as I can get a flight."

"No! I'm not *that* sick," I said, still whispering.

"Look, if your being so sick you can't go to work or be alone in your own home is not *that* sick, I don't know what is. I'll try to get there before midnight. I can only stay overnight, though. I need to be back up here in time for an important meeting tomorrow afternoon. Don't even try to come pick me up from LAX. I'll take a cab." My first husband hung up, and I was glad he did when he did. Floyd walked up behind me while the telephone was still in my hand.

"Who was that?" he asked, rubbing the stubble on his chin. I could smell his scent from across the room — a combination of sweat, alcohol, underarm funk, and sex. He pursed his lips and gave me a quick, sour, sloppy kiss. I grimaced. He grinned. Then he placed his hands on my shoulders and held me firmly in place as he looked at me, his red-rimmed eyes blinking like streetlights as he gazed into mine. "I know I smell and taste pretty foul right now, but you sure don't," he leered, sliding his tongue across his teeth. I held my breath so I wouldn't have to smell his, then I kissed him.

"You taste all right," I assured him.

"Who were you just talking to on the telephone, Lo?" he asked, releasing my shoulders and rearing back on his legs. His eyes looked straight into mine some more, searching for something that I was determined not to let him find: the truth.

"Who me? Oh, I was talking to a girl from work. Uh, I really hate to do this to you, baby, but I am going to have to go in to work, even though it's my day off. My boss fell down some steps at her building and sprained her ankle. That's what my co-worker called to tell me."

"Baby, you do whatever you have to do. I know you've still got a life out here that you need to keep up with. I'll be fine. What time will you be home?"

"Uh, that's another thing. The ship is cruising into Ensenada tonight. But it's just for this one night. We'll be back in port in Long Beach tomorrow."

"Oh." Floyd shrugged. "I wish I could go with you. A cruise would suit me fine right about now."

"I wish you could go with me, too, baby,

but this is work." I kissed Floyd long and hard on the lips again. He got aroused so fast, we barely made it back upstairs to the bedroom.

"Lo, it's not going to be easy for us to get back to a normal life after all these years, after all that's happened. I am not sure when the settlement is going to come through, but in the meantime, Brian's going to front the money for us to get a place. And I . . . what's wrong, baby? You are as stiff as a plank. You were the same way when I made love to you last night — and just now." He sat up and looked at me. I was naked and spread-eagled on the bed, staring at the ceiling.

"I'll be fine once I get used to you being with me," I muttered.

"Tell me something, Dolores. Is there somebody else you need to talk to about me?"

"What do you mean?" I sat bolt upright, squinting my eyes as I looked into his. He looked as tortured as I felt.

"I'm not stupid, Lo, and you know I'm not. I grew up on the streets. If you didn't have you a boy out here while I was in the joint, you should have. I told you a long time ago that I didn't expect you to, you know . . ."

"I did have a few dates from time to time," I replied with a shrug, looking away. "But there's nobody special in my life right now except you." I don't know how I was able to keep telling one lie after another with a straight face. And it seemed like every time I told a new lie, I had to cover it with even more lies.

"What about after we got married? Did you continue to date other men?"

"Uh-uh. That's when I stopped dating," I said, touching the tip of my nose to make sure it wasn't growing the way Pinocchio's nose grew every time he told a lie. From the look on Floyd's face, I could tell that he didn't believe that barefaced lie. "Other men never appealed to me that much, anyway," I added.

"Whatever," he mouthed, giving me a curious look.

I leaped off the bed like a frog, and Floyd wasn't too far behind me. "Uh, I have to shower and be on my way in a little while. First, I'll show you around the house," I offered. "You could get lost in this big old barn." I cackled. "Valerie's kind of touchy about her backyard. That's where her grand-daddy had his stroke . . ."

"Pffft!" Floyd snickered, waving his hand

dismissively. "I don't have no reason in the world to be roaming around in nobody's backyard. Just show me where the liquor is, that's all I want to know," he said, winking and grinning.

After we got dressed, he followed me back downstairs. I was already wondering in advance if I'd have sucker bites on my neck that I'd have to explain to Paul in a few hours.

"Uh, there's that little portable bar in the living room, but we keep a lot of beer in the refrigerator." I moved across the living room floor like a robot, praying that my legs wouldn't buckle. Floyd was so close behind me, he was stepping on the back of my heels. He grabbed me from behind, cradled me in his arms, and hauled me back upstairs and tossed me on the bed.

When I left the house an hour later, I had on a turtleneck sweater. There were so many love bites on my neck, it looked like I had a purple necklace. All I could think about was how I was going to explain that to Paul.

CHAPTER 48

As soon as I crawled into my car, I made a beeline to the condo that I shared with Paul. I went straight into the bedroom and messed up the covers on the bed, and then I flopped up and down on the pillows to flatten them. I took off my bra, panties, and ankle stockings and dropped them on the floor in the bathroom. I knew that as soon as Paul saw that, he'd slap on one of his masks and pick up everything with a stick. And I knew he would lecture me about being such a slob, but I didn't care. All I cared about was keeping him distracted.

Next, I ran into the kitchen and stuffed half a loaf of bread and some beef patties down the disposal. I emptied out every container of milk and I hid two packets of instant coffee in a bag in the broom closet. By the time I got through, that place looked more like I'd been lounging around and kicking back than it did when that was true.

Paul was so tired when he stumbled in the door a few hours later, all he wanted to do was take a long hot bath, have a drink, and go to bed. He didn't comment on the turtleneck sweater I had on, but he commented on the fact that I didn't look sick at all.

"I'm feeling much better," I told him. "So is Valerie."

"Well, whatever it was, don't pass it on to me," he said, holding up his hand. "I just had to come down here to make sure you didn't need a doctor or something. You know I can't let anything happen to my favorite girl." He leaned over at the waist just far enough to kiss my forehead. "Hmmm. Damn, baby. You look fine, but you sounded like hell when I talked to you."

"I . . . I am feeling much better," I said weakly, pushing him away. "But I don't think we should get too close. I don't want you mad at me for making you sick, too." I coughed into my hand. "You can't miss that meeting tomorrow."

Paul gave me a strange look and shrugged as he felt my forehead with the palm of his hand. "You don't have a fever, either. But you sure sounded like hell on the telephone. If you get any sicker, I want you to call Dr. Peterson. Do you hear me?"

"Uh-huh."

I didn't sleep at all that night. When Paul opened his eyes before dawn and tried to get nasty, guiding my hand to his hard dick, I started coughing and groaning. "Aw shit. I don't have time to be catching whatever it is you and Valerie's caught!" he hollered, rolling as far away from me as he could get.

I offered him a fake pout when he refused to kiss me on the lips before he left for the airport. As soon as he made it out the door, I called my supervisor at her home in Pasadena and told her that I was going to have to terminate my employment. "Now that's the last thing I wanted to hear, LoReese! Please tell me you're joking," she shrieked. "You can't do that! I won't allow it!"

"No, Candace. I really hate to do this to you, but I need a break. I'm really sorry."

"Then take a break. You're the best assistant I've ever had. And I need a pretty young woman like you to help us keep the youngsters interested in return trips. What can I do to make you stay?"

"Well, it's my husband. He wants me to spend more time with him."

"Is that all? You don't have to quit your job to do that. How about returning to a position in the main office? That way you can go home to your sweetie every night like normal women do."

I frowned and shook my head, even though I knew Candace couldn't see me. "I don't want to go back to a secretary's salary," I said with a chuckle.

"And you won't have to. As a matter of fact, I will put it in writing if you want me to."

"Oh. Well, can I still take a little time off to think about it? Can I get back to you next week?"

"LoReese, I adore you, and I think you are one of the most important employees we have. But I can't promise you the moon. I can't hold a position open for you indefinitely. It wouldn't be fair to my other employees."

I was glad to hear that I was important to the cruise line. I felt myself getting choked up. It was a struggle to keep from crying. Now was not the time that I wanted Candace to know just how weak I was. "OK. Let me take the rest of this week off. I'll come back to work, but only in the main office. For now, that is. If things change, I'd like to go back on board."

I felt like I was running from pillar to post, and in a way I was. As soon as I was able to get showered and dressed, I returned to Valerie's house. Floyd greeted me at the door and covered me with wet kisses. There was a surprised look on his face. "I didn't expect you to be back so soon. How was Mexico?" he wanted to know, leading me to the sofa where he pulled me down into his lap. I squirmed when I felt his erection poking my butt.

"Huh? Oh! Well, it was just one of those turn-around trips. A lot of people who can't be gone for more than a day take these mini-cruises," I said, all in one breath. That was another lie. I didn't know about any of our rival cruise ships, but the *Encantadora* never went from California to Mexico and back in one day. "Oh! It was nice," I said quickly. "Mexico is always real nice!" I didn't have any luggage with me, not even an overnight bag, even though I'd left the house with one. It was still at the address on Manchester that I'd just left. I realized that as soon as I got back to Valerie's house. "I am so glad to be back home," I said, prepared to tell Floyd that I'd left my overnight bag in my cabin on the ship in case he asked.

"Good. Because this is where you belong." Floyd grabbed my wrist and squeezed so hard, I grimaced; the pain was just that intense. I rose from the sofa and he rose with me, gripping my wrist so hard it felt like I'd been handcuffed. "Baby, you look so good to me. Not a day went by that I didn't think about you. Even when I was at my lowest." Floyd paused and glanced off to the side. When he looked back at me, there was the most extreme look of torture on his face that I'd ever seen. He had not looked this hopeless when he was in prison.

"What's wrong?" I asked, alarmed.

"You probably know what jail is like for rapists . . ."

"Yeah, but you didn't rape anybody. They've got proof now," I said, wondering where this conversation was going.

"Another thing is, everybody in prison is innocent."

"Well, now we know that at least one convict really was innocent: you. And I am sure that a lot of the others really are innocent, too. Your lawyer even said so." He glanced off to the side again. "Floyd, I know how bad it must have been for you, but it's over. And if you don't want to talk about it, that's fine with me." I knew where rapists and child molesters ranked on the prison hierarchy. And I knew what the other prisoners often did to them: the same things that rapists and child molesters had done to their victims. But I didn't want that information in my face, especially when it involved my husband. "Let's try not to talk about *that* unless we have to."

He nodded. "I just want you to know another thing on that subject. While I was in lockdown, I got my ass kicked more than once, but that was all. I want you to know that. I am still as, uh, *straight* as I was before I went in there. Case closed." He parted my thighs with his knee. Then he pressed his dick against me and humped real hard a few times. Even though it felt good, I was glad when he suddenly stopped. "And before we change the subject, there is one other thing I've been meaning to discuss with you," he volunteered, twisting his lips. I had a feeling that whatever it was he wanted to discuss, it was probably something else I didn't want to hear.

"What?"

"I know that you heard rumors about Glodine getting jiggy with some of the boys she took in."

"That? Yeah, I heard the rumors," I said with a clumsy nod. "Valerie mentioned it a time or two when we were still in school. Why are you bringing that up now?"

"Because I want you to know everything there is to know about me. You've always been honest with me, that's the least I can do for you."

"Uh-huh," I mumbled, biting my bottom lip because I didn't like the way that lie tasted. As nasty as it was, it was sweet compared to the bile rising in my throat.

"It was true." He paused and held his hand up to my face. "But not with me. It was nothing but rumors and gossip that got started after she had a fling with one of the boys years after he'd moved out of her house. Dude was a grown man by then." Floyd dipped his head and looked up at me. "I never had nothing to do with that woman, *like that*. She was a poor excuse for a mama, but she treated me better than my own mama did and I will always be grateful for that. You do believe me, don't you?"

"I believe you, Floyd. Look, we don't have to talk about things like this —"

"That's where you are wrong, Dolores. This is our second chance at a real future. We can't build much of a future if it's based on secrets and lies. Now like I said, you love me enough to be open and honest with me. I want to do the same for you. Understood?"

"Understood," I said, barely opening my mouth. We spent the rest of the afternoon in bed.

Valerie didn't come home that night. When I checked the voice mail, I was surprised but glad to hear the reason why. "Girl, I've met the cutest little ex-sailor boy in the world. His name is Russell and he's been doing some DJ gigs around town. He was part of that bachelorette party we had here a few days ago. I think he's the one! Lo, you and Floyd have a good evening. There's plenty of booze, some new CDs, and everything else you need to enjoy yourselves. I will see you two sex maniacs when I get home — whenever that is!"

I was so happy for Valerie, tears flooded my eyes. It was about time. She hadn't spent the night with a man in more than a year! I prayed that this Russell would make this a very special night for her. On the other hand, if he hurt her in any way, he'd have to answer to me.

CHAPTER 49

Only God knows how I made it through the first month with Floyd in Valerie's house. Running from that location to the condo on Manchester when Paul came to L.A., then up to Alameda to be with him and back, felt like a game of cat and mouse. I was both the cat and the mouse. Valerie found all of this amusing, but she covered well for me.

I was glad to see that her love life had *finally* picked up and seemed to be going in the right direction. My girl was so anxious to get married she had already scoped out a Vera Wang wedding gown. "Girl, when are you going to slow down long enough to meet my sweetie? Russell is dying to meet you," she told me, sounding as lovesick as a schoolgirl.

I couldn't wait to meet Russell. But as luck would have it, I was always out whenever he came to the house. "Soon I hope," I told her. "If he's the one, I need to let him know as soon as possible that you and I are a package deal. I've already promised myself that if he makes a fool out of you, he'll have to deal with me."

"You are too funny for words! If anybody should be worried about being made a fool of by some man, it's you, *Mrs. Dunne/ Watson.*" Valerie laughed.

"I just want to make sure you know I'm looking out for you," I said sternly. "What all did you tell him about me? Does he know I'm married?"

"Of course he knows! I had to tell the man something. He spent two hours playing cards with Floyd the other day while you were with Paul." Valerie laughed again when I gave her a horrified look and covered my mouth with my hand. "He only knows about Floyd. When you do meet him, just remember to keep things straight. He knows you work on a cruise ship and that you're onboard when you're not here. Don't worry; I've got your back, girl."

Paul had never called me at work. I had told him that the company was very strict about us receiving personal phone calls, unless it was an extreme emergency. That was why we all used cell phones, I'd told him. There was no reason for anybody to call me at work these days, so I didn't have to worry about that. That was one less thing to worry about, because I quit my job. I had even changed my mind about taking a job in the main office like I had told Candace. There was no way I could do any job and still keep both husbands.

With Paul, I had to come up with something a little more elaborate than the "sick friend in the mental institution" to explain why I had discontinued my once-a-month jaunts to Monterey. The next time he asked about the phantom friend that I'd invented, I was ready. "Oh, Crystal is doing so much better. Her doctor thinks that it would be better for her if I stopped visiting for a while. That way she can regain her independence faster, and more control of her life."

One thing that my beloved foster mother had taught me was to never let my right hand know what my left hand was doing. Knowledge was power and could be deadly if it got in the wrong hands. What Paul and Floyd didn't know didn't hurt them — or me.

The allowance and money for household expenses that I received from Paul and Floyd was enough to cover the rent that I paid Valerie, my car insurance, my ten credit cards, and other necessities. I was doing all right in that area, and as long as I watched my step, I didn't have to worry.

I still didn't know the amount of Floyd's settlement, and he made it clear that that was one thing he wasn't ready to discuss, yet. Not even with me. But it had to be sweet for him to be able to buy a three-bedroom condo in Beverly Hills.

"This is going to be our dream home, baby," he told me. Such a huge knot formed in my throat, it felt like I was being strangled. I was overwhelmed. "Baby, don't cry. Everything is going to be all right now. I keep telling you that, but every time I look up, you crying like a baby." He was right.

I had been doing a lot of crying lately. Not just in front of Floyd, but the last time I was with Paul, I'd boo-hooed so much he offered to take off a month from work and spend it with me somewhere exotic. "You pick the place, baby. Belize, Cancún, Maui. Anywhere you want to go, we'll go. And first class all the way," Paul told me, as we shared a bubble bath together a few nights ago. "The world is yours. Once we get to wher-ever it is you want to go, I am going to do everything but hog-tie you to a bed so I can give you the loving you *need.* I don't have to be a psychic to see that you are feeling neglected. . . ."

I squalled like a panda just listening to

him talk about the romantic rendezvous he wanted to arrange. As tempting as it was, there was no way I could go. After practically pouring a few glasses of wine down his throat, and a two-hour session in bed after we got out of the bathtub, I talked him out of that notion. There was only one way to do it at such short notice. I brought my bogus friend Crystal back into the picture. I told him she'd had a sudden relapse when she'd heard that her ex-husband had remarried and now she was back in the institution. I needed to be close by, in case she needed me. "Baby, I've told you before, but I'll tell you again, I hope your friends appreciate all you do for them."

"I hope they do, too," I said.

I knew at least one friend did. Valerie appreciated everything I did for her. And there was nobody I felt more comfortable with than I did with Valerie. I had just run into her house in such a frantic state of mind, I had on two different shoes. I had just dropped Paul off at LAX. As much as I loved that man, he had driven me to distraction the night before. He'd stayed two days longer than he'd originally planned. While he was shampooing the carpets, I'd slipped out to go spend a couple of hours with Floyd. He had surprised me that night with a filet mignon dinner that he had prepared by himself. I ate as much as I could, sexed him up for a few minutes, then I was out the door again — going to work "to attend an emergency security related meeting and to cover an overnight cruise to Mazatlan for a sick co-worker." Now that Paul was out of my hair, I could concentrate on Floyd. But first, I needed a break.

"Valerie, please fix me a very large, very strong drink," I said, plopping down on her living room sofa, rubbing my sore thighs. I groaned from all the pain I was in. I wondered how prostitutes could fuck several men a day and still walk. I kept my legs spread open so much these days, I was getting bowlegged. Just fucking on a regular basis had taken a heavy toll on me. And in my case, both of my men were good in bed, so I usually enjoyed it as much as they did. My sex life had become a double-edged sword. "If I live through this shit, I will become a nun and spend the rest of my life douching with vanilla."

"Lo, I can't tell you how to live your crazy life, but as your best friend, I have to tell you that you need to do something about this. You can't go on like this too much longer. You are coming apart at the seams, girl. I can see it happening right before my

405

eyes. And to be honest with you, these two husbands of yours must be some stupid-ass motherfuckers to believe all the shit you tell them. I've never seen a woman shove as many lies down a man's — two men's — throats the way you do and get away with it. Are men really that fucking gullible?"

"They must be," I said with a shrug. "But I do love them both, and that's the important thing."

"I don't know what this world is coming to. But I still worry about you. . . ."

"I'm fine," I insisted, even though there was a noticeable tremor in my voice. Valerie handed me a large glass of white wine and a shot glass filled with tequila. I gave her words some thought. And I sincerely appreciated her concern. But that didn't change anything.

She shook her head and gave me a worried look. "You might think you are fine, but at this rate you won't make it to your thirty-fourth birthday coming up next month," she told me.

"At this rate, I won't make it to next week. Girl, I don't know what I was thinking! Shit, shit, shit — I'm covered with shit! How the hell did I get myself into this mess?!"

"That's what I'd like to know. I've been meaning to ask you, what the hell were you thinking? Did you honestly think that you could get away with being married to two men at the same time?" Valerie sat on the arm of her sofa, sipping from a glass of red wine.

I gave her a thoughtful look. "All I ever wanted in life was to be happy. I wanted Floyd to be happy. We deserve to be. I promised him when we were kids that I'd marry him." I sighed and drank the entire shot of tequila in one big gulp. It burned like hell going down my throat, but that didn't even faze me. I handed the glass to Valerie for another shot.

"But you didn't count on him going to jail. And when he did, that cancelled out your promise," Valerie told me as she got me another drink.

"Whatever," I said, shaking my head and staring at the refilled shot glass in my hand like it was a magic wand. "I just thought of something. I know a way I can straighten out this mess."

Valerie looked at me like I'd just sprouted a beard. "After all the stupid shit you've already done, I'm afraid to ask what," Valerie told me in a stern voice, shaking her head.

"What if I up and disappear?" I asked sharply. "I don't have any family who would come looking for me. I could even go to another country and assume a new identity."

Valerie gave me a stunned looked. "That's just as crazy as everything else you've done. In case you didn't know, husbands are considered family. And you've got two. They'd both report you missing and there'd be newspaper reports. It would be just a matter of time before Paul found out about Floyd, and vice versa."

"There is more than one way to disappear. If I wrote a farewell letter to each one and then took off, neither one would have any reason to come looking for me. I could even say that I'm dying, or that I'm in love with another man and running away with him."

"Now you listen to me! Don't *ever* mess around with death. Faking something like death is not something to play around with," Valerie scolded. "That would open the door to bad karma so fast your head would spin off."

"Well, what about a story about me running away with another man? Somebody I met in one of the ports I went to. A foreigner."

"I don't know about that," Valerie quipped, a thoughtful look on her face. "It could work, but is that what you really want to do? These two men love you. You'd be hurting them. Probably as much if not more than you would if they found out the truth." Valerie fanned the air with her hand. "Uh-uh. I advise you not to go there. A lie about a disappearing act to be with another man could create even more problems. You can always divorce one and stay with the other. If you do it right, neither one will ever know about the other. Which one do you love the least?"

I blinked and thought about what Valerie had just said. But I couldn't answer her question, because I didn't know the answer myself.

CHAPTER 50

I had a comfortable life with Paul, but it could not compete with the life I suddenly had with Floyd. Because of his sudden wealth, thanks to his settlement with the state of California, the man was able to live the lifestyle of the rich and famous and he wanted me to share that lifestyle with him.

I had never considered myself a gold digger. However, now that wealth was there for the taking, I wanted to enjoy it, too. And I deserved it. I had bent over backward to support Floyd. As far as I was concerned, that support had also been an investment. Now it was time for me to reap the benefits.

Other than his dedicated lawyer, Brian, I was still the only close friend Floyd had. However, once some of his former "homies" from the hood got word of his windfall, they all started trying to crawl back into his life. None of them had his new address or phone number, but when Floyd finally paid a visit to Glodine, she handed him two sheets of paper with the names and numbers of "friends" who wanted to hear from him.

I was disappointed when Floyd told me that he had visited Glodine. "I just wanted to tie up another loose end. As mean as she was to me, living with her was better than what I had before. She never let me forget that, and it bothered me. Besides, if she hadn't took me in, I wouldn't have met you. I greased her palm with a few thousand dollars, but it was more to clear my conscience than it was to finance her latest shopping spree or a trip to a casino. My debt to her for raising me is paid in full, as far as I'm concerned."

I admired Floyd even more for compensating that heifer. Glodine hadn't done such a lousy job, after all. I was glad that he had no intentions of breaking off any of his former friends with a dime, though. After most of the excitement had worn off, I even felt a twinge of guilt about taking money from him. But I reminded myself that if anybody deserved to share his windfall, it was me. However, this new development was so bittersweet, I really could not enjoy it like I thought I would. And I wouldn't, as long as I was living the double life of a bigamist.

In addition to a lot of new clothes from some of the most exclusive boutiques on Rodeo Drive in Beverly Hills, Floyd wanted to replace my aged Honda Civic with a brand-new BMW, or something more appropriate for our Beverly Hills address. He was the proud owner of a brand-new champagne-colored Jaguar. We'd been in the new condo for only a month. Under normal circumstances, I would have jumped at the chance to own a luxury car. "Only if I can keep my Civic," I told Floyd. We stood on the terrace that night looking out at all the bright lights below, wondering what celebrities were hiding behind the tinted windows of the many stretch limos crawling down our street.

"I don't know why you want to hold on to that old *jalopy,* but that's fine with me," Floyd grinned, holding me around my waist so tight you would have thought that he was afraid I was going to stumble over the railing.

I wanted to hold on to my old car. It had too much sentimental value for me to remove it from my life. Besides, there was no way I could explain a brand-new BMW to Paul. But I accepted it anyway, just to shut Floyd up. As long as Paul didn't see me batting around in that fancy ride, he'd never know about it. My plan was to keep the Honda until it stopped running, no matter how many new vehicles Floyd insisted on buying for me. It was one of the important props I still needed to keep up appearances with Paul.

Valerie was still driving around in her three-year-old Altima, so she was more than happy to put some miles on my new steel gray BMW. I eagerly left it with her when I flew up to Alameda to spend time with Paul and when he was in town. She was doing me a favor by helping me keep it out of Paul's sight. Each time I handed it over to her, she snatched the keys out of my hand like a child snatching a piece of candy. "Girl, when my honey saw me pull up to his apartment in style, he about shit his pants. He thinks I'm doing so well with Paw Paw's," Valerie told me with a misty-eyed look. "Russell is not perfect, but he's perfect for me," she swooned.

I still had not met the man who had opened Valerie's nose so wide I could drive a car through it. But I couldn't wait to do so. She had reluctantly mentioned that he was "a little younger" than us and that he shared a two-bedroom apartment with three other people. One was his mama. "Him being so young, I can still mold him to my liking," she decided.

"Is this Russell really the kind of man you want?" I asked. "Young, broke, and still living with his mama? Is he with you for the right reasons?"

"Since when did *you* become an authority on this kind of shit? We can't all hook up with *two* gorgeous, well-heeled men, like you did. Some of us have to settle for what we can get." I didn't like the hopeless look on Valerie's face, or what she was saying. And she wasn't through with me yet. "You, of all people, know what my love life has always been like. I'd like to think that you'd be happy for me, no matter who I hooked up with, as long as I was happy."

"Val, I didn't mean to hurt your feelings. It's just that I don't want to see you get hurt. You've got your own business and your own home. But you are not that young anymore. Those are the facts of your life. Stir in a young, handsome, broke-ass man with a big dick, and you've got a recipe for disaster. I —"

"Girl, shut the fuck up! You with your two husbands! All right! Enough is enough. Let's change the subject before one of us says something she will regret." There was complete silence for a few moments as Valerie and I regrouped our thoughts. I was about to speak, but she beat me to it. "And by the way, did you hear about Moanin' Lisa getting engaged? She brought him into Paw Paw's two nights ago. He looks like a flying monkey, but she was beaming like a lighthouse she was so happy. And for the first time in all the years I've known her, she was not moanin'. Dude works as a custodian at the Greyhound bus station, but that didn't seem to bother our girl." I was glad that Valerie had steered the conversation in a different direction.

"That's nice. I hope she will be very happy," I said.

Valerie gave me a steely-eyed look. "You want her to be happy? Don't you think *I* deserve to be happy, too?"

"I want you to be happy with your young honey, but I don't want you to get hurt, or used in the process."

"Dolores, I'm in love with Russell, and if being used feels this good, I hope he doesn't stop until he uses me up."

"You sound like that old Bill Withers song," I commented. I could tell from the puzzled expression on Valerie's face that she had never heard of it. "Anyway, I can't wait to meet this man that's got you smiling so much these days. When are you going to hook up a party so you can introduce him to all your friends?"

"Well, it was supposed to be a surprise, but I'm planning one for your thirty-fourth birthday this month. Paw Paw's will be closed for the evening, and I know that's not going to set too well with some of my regulars. But, fuck 'em. What the hell! My friends come first!" Valerie gave me a playful pinch on my arm. "Don't get confused and bring the wrong husband."

"Which one is the wrong one?"

"Russell has met Floyd, but he knows nothing about Paul. The only thing we have to do is coordinate the date. We need to make sure that Paul will be up north."

"Oh shit. I just remembered something. He's taking me to dinner at Alioto's in Frisco on my birthday."

"Then we can have the party before you go up there, or when you return. What about Floyd? I know he'll want to spend your birthday with you."

"I've already got that covered. I told him that I have to do the Puerto Vallarta cruise that weekend."

There was a slight smile on Valerie's face as she looked at me and shook her head. Then she grabbed me by my shoulders and shook me, all the while giving me a look of playful contempt. "You bitch. Sometimes I hate you so much I want to beat the dog shit out of you! You're pretty, but you are not drop-dead gorgeous. You've got big, flat feet and hair that looks like it belongs on a rag doll. You are not even particularly intelligent. On top of all that, you are already showing your age," she said, adding a smirk. "I don't know what the hell you do to deserve so much. But one day I hope you will share your strategy with the rest of us."

"Well, if I ever figure it out, I will," I muttered. Valerie released my shoulders and gave me a big hug.

CHAPTER 51

I knew that I was not the first woman to commit bigamy, and I would not be the last. And trying to juggle two husbands in two different cities was one of the hardest things I had ever done before in my crazy life. That was why I could not explain why I got involved with *another* man!

It all started when my Honda ran out of gas on the freeway. I reluctantly accepted a ride with a handsome young stranger. He was tall. I could tell that even though he was sitting in the driver's seat of his noisy, battered Ford. His seat looked as if it was pushed back as far as it could go, and even then his long legs still looked scrunched up. He had small, intense black eyes and a smile that lit up his coconut brown face. Short black hair covered his head like a skullcap. He had nice teeth, even though they were slightly crooked. I liked what I saw, and I couldn't stop myself from thinking about how lucky some woman was. Besides Paul, he was the only other man I'd met with a goatee who I found attractive. A shiver went up my spine when I realized that this brooding stranger looked like a younger combination of my two husbands!

"You look safe," I commented. "How do I know you're not a serial killer?" I teased, already in the front passenger seat. Even though I was making light of a potentially serious situation, getting in a car with a stranger could have been a fatal mistake.

"You look safe, too. How do I know you ain't no serial killer?" he chuckled, and slapped the steering wheel with the palm of his hand. "Sister, you can relax. I'm not going to hurt you in any way. As a matter of fact, you can use my cell phone to call somebody and tell them who you are with."

There was so much junk piled up on the backseat, I could barely see out the window. I couldn't tell where the musty smell was coming from, the junk on the backseat or the young man's body. His hands were covered in dust and grease, and so was the denim jumpsuit he had on. I had always found blue-collar men attractive, and the one sitting next to me was the cream of the crop. He looked cash strapped, and couldn't have been more than twenty-three.

He leaned over, jabbing into my lap with his elbow. With a grunt, and a sexy grunt at that, he removed his car registration from the glove compartment and dropped it into my lap. I managed to hold back a gasp, but that caused a lump to dance a James Brown jig down my throat. I had to cough hard to clear my throat. I was sitting so close to the door, I had to shift in my seat so that I could pick up the document.

"Marvin R. Meecham," I read aloud. "So is that what they call you?"

"They call me a lot of things. Some I won't repeat." He laughed. "You can call me whatever you want to call me." He had a gentle voice, and that made me feel more comfortable.

"Mr. Meecham, you can just drop me off at the nearest gas station," I told him.

"Nobody has ever called me Mr. before," he told me. Even though he was young enough to be my baby brother, there was an air of maturity in his demeanor that I thought was just as attractive about him as everything else.

"What do you do?" I asked, looking his dingy jumpsuit up and down.

"I do a lot of things, baby," he told me, glancing at me with a hungry look in his eyes. There was something suggestive about the way he'd answered my question. Him being so young and luscious, there was no telling what he meant.

"Uh, I meant what kind of work do you do?" I asked, clearing my throat and then biting my bottom lip. My whole head suddenly felt like somebody had wrapped a steamed towel around it. The air got so hot I was surprised I didn't see some smoke. I didn't know if the heat wave caressing my face was embarrassment or lust. Being this close to a man like Marvin made me nervous. Without thinking I glanced at his crotch, and what I saw made me grin like a Cheshire cat. If that wasn't bad enough, he saw me looking at his lap. He parted his thighs slightly so I could get an even better look. I replaced my grin with a stony look, pressing my lips so close together they felt as though they'd been glued shut. I sat up straighter in my seat and aimed my eyes at the road in front of me. If I could have moved closer to the door, I would have. But I was already so close to it, the door handle was jabbing me in my side.

"I work on cars mostly," he said. "And anything else I can get. That's what I get for dropping out of school in the ninth grade," he said in a sorry voice. "And, I get by with a little help from my friends," he added in a mysterious tone, spoken in a voice almost as low as a whisper. I had no idea what he meant by that, and I didn't *even* want to know.

I had just dropped Paul off at LAX. With all of the running around I'd been doing this particular week, nightclub visits with Floyd and his lawyer and the brassy blond he'd just married, shopping and having lunch with Valerie, and other particulars, I had overlooked a lot of the little things. One just happened to be gassing up my car. I hadn't bothered to check the gas gauge until the car stopped. And this was one of the few times I'd left one of my residences without my cell phone. Valerie had my BMW, and I had just gassed it up before I handed it over to her.

"You live in L.A.?" Marvin asked, glancing at me as he swerved around an eighteen-wheeler. He drove like an escapee in a stolen car. It felt like we were on a roller coaster. Each time he passed another vehicle, or changed lanes, my knee hit against his.

"Uh-huh."

"Family? Husband? Kids?"

"Uh-uh. Just me." One thing I had learned was not to give too much information about myself to people I didn't know that well. Especially people I didn't plan on seeing again. Things had a way of coming back to haunt me.

"Here we go," he said, pulling into a Chevron station. As soon as he stopped the car, he ran into the office and came out with a gas can and ran straight to one of the pumps. After he filled the can with gas, he beckoned for me to roll down the window on my side. "Do you want me to take you back to your car or do you want to call somebody else?" he asked.

"It's just down the freeway a few miles. I can walk," I said, forcing a smile. He gave me a dry look and climbed back into his car, gently placing the gas can on the back-seat floor.

"Unless you got a death wish, you don't walk along no freeway in L.A." He started the car and zoomed back onto the freeway.

"I don't have but a few dollars cash on me. Will you give me your address so I can send you a check when I get home to settle this?" I said.

"I'd rather settle for a drink," he grinned, glancing my way again with his lips parted. "I only drink beer, so it won't set you back too much."

"I think I should just send you the money I owe you for the gas. I don't go out drinking much these days."

"Whatever," he said with a hint of disappointment in his voice. He put a CD in the player and we listened to Toni Braxton all the way back to my car.

After he poured the gas into my tank, he waited until he was sure my car would start. Then he started walking back to his car. I honked my horn and he ran back. "You forgot to give me your address so I can send you a check," I told him. Not only did he give me his address, he included his telephone number. I planned to put a check in the mail as soon as I got back to the condo I shared with Floyd, and that's just what I did. Why I called him, too, was a mystery to me. "This is Dolores," I stated.

"Dolores who?"

"Oh. I'm the woman who ran out of gas on the freeway. I just wanted to let you know that I put the check in the mail a little while ago. And I wanted to thank you again for helping me. That was a nice favor you did for me."

"Well, would you do a favor for me now?"

"What?" My heart rate increased and my mouth felt bone dry inside. Given my history with men, and me with my weak self, I should have hung up and disposed of this man's telephone number immediately. But I didn't, and it was a mistake that would cost me dearly. . . .

"Hold on to my phone number, in case you change your mind about buying me that drink."

I wanted to blame everybody but myself for what I eventually did. First of all, I was upset with Floyd, because he was wearing me down to a frazzle. When I was with him, we went nightclubbing two or three nights a week. He'd made a few new friends who I didn't like — loud, coarse men he'd met in the clubs we went to. I didn't like them hanging around the condo, usually looking for handouts. These leeches included a wannabe rap singer looking for a financial sponsor, a wannabe actor looking for a financial sponsor, and a few wannabes who hadn't decided what they wanted to be. But they were still looking for a financial sponsor, too. Then, on a regular basis, I had to listen to Floyd's detailed, tear-filled account of how the system had failed him. It did me no good to remind him that he was now a free man, his name had been cleared, and because of his tragedy he now had more money than he could have earned in three lifetimes.

Paul had started to get on my nerves even more than Floyd. It was bad enough that I had to put up with his family when I visited him in Alameda. Now he was bringing various relatives from the Bay Area to our home in L.A. who I had to wait on hand and foot — and clean up after them like a maid.

Oh, that Paul, and that Floyd. I still loved both my husbands and I knew they loved me. What Floyd saw in me was obvious. We had so much in common — the foster home experience, no biological relatives in our lives, limited education, and the fact that we had both endured the lower middle-class experience.

What Paul saw in me was another story. To him, I was a challenge. He had told me that more than once. I represented everything his family had tried to protect him from. He even told me once that I was a refreshing change from all the hissy prissy debutantes who had attended UCLA with him. Those were the only kinds of women he had dated and almost married before I "took advantage of him," said his mama. Paul had confessed that marrying me was the only time he'd defied his mother and that it felt good. However, that old biddy was so certain that our marriage wasn't going to last she referred to me as Paul's "first wife." Well, I had news for her: I would be Paul's first wife and last wife — as long as he didn't find out about my second husband.

Paul was more of a challenge to me than Floyd was. Even though Paul had begun to get on my nerves, I absolutely adored the man, despite the many obstacles I had to deal with. I continued to overlook the fact that he still took it upon himself to educate me in the housekeeping department. Our bathrooms were major thorns in my side. Thanks to him, I probably knew more about grout, lime scales, and rust stains than Mr. Clean. When I didn't want to be around Paul, I ran into Floyd's arms, and vice versa. However, there were times when I didn't want to be in the arms of either one. Like now. I was undergoing some emotional issues that only another woman could relate to.

I was disappointed that Valerie's shoulder was not available for me to cry on much lately. When she wasn't tending the bar, she was with that new boyfriend that she bragged about all the time. I was glad that she was in love with somebody, but this duckling was already on my shit list and I hadn't even met him yet — and wasn't sure I wanted to. For one thing, I didn't like the fact that she was helping him out of one financial difficulty after another! There had been a few times when I'd had the nerve to lend her money to lend to him! And according to her, he was fucking the living daylights out of her. "Now I know what real love is," she told me, after giving me a blow-by-blow account of her latest bedroom tryst. I just smiled. If Valerie thought that what she had was real love, and it made her happy, that was all that really mattered. But I prayed that she would not lose her perspective and do something really foolish in the name of love. She didn't need to screw up her life over a man. I was screwing up enough for the both of us.

I thought about booking myself on a cruise, a real one. And on any ship but the *Encantadora*. I missed my old job, but being on that particular ship would have brought back too many painful memories. It represented a life that was no longer mine. For the sake of my sanity, I had to do something for myself. It felt like the world was closing in on me. I had to get away from everybody and everything. That was when I remembered that handsome young stranger who wanted to have a drink with me. Without giving it much more thought, I called him up.

CHAPTER 52

"I ain't never been to The Ivy before," Marvin said, looking around the patio area of my favorite restaurant. He was in awe. The slack-jawed look on his face embarrassed me. I was horrified when he blew on a spoon, then wiped it with the tail of his shirt. It was almost like being out with one of the Beverly Hillbillies. "I've heard a lot about this place, though. I read about it in the tabloids, and it was in that movie Jane Fonda did with J. Lo." Marvin rotated his neck to look around some more, rolled his eyes, and then shook his head. "I knew that any place that the stars hung out at was way out of my price range." He paused again and looked me straight in the eye. "Thank you. I really appreciate you being so good to me." He kept his eyes on mine, and a thousand and one thoughts ran through my mind. I was ashamed of every single one of them.

"Uh, you look nice today," I said after an awkward moment of silence. I was disappointed to see that Marvin had on the same dusty jumpsuit that he had on the first time I met him. But I was glad to see that there was no dirt, grease, or oil underneath his fingernails. He looked so out of place sitting one table away from a rap star I used to fantasize about. I promised myself that if I ever agreed to see Marvin for drinks again, it would be in a truck stop off the freeway, or one of those dimly lit little bars where the bikers and construction workers hung out. I scolded myself for entertaining such thoughts. The fact that Marvin seemed so ordinary, in appearance and personality, made him even more appealing to me.

"I don't know about that. But I'm glad to see that I'm not the only one not sitting up in here in a three-piece suit. I expected a bunch of Hollywood studio suits with fat wallets to be here, cutting deals and talking all kinds of shit about making or breaking the next American idol."

"Marvin, you'd be surprised at how many regular working people come here. I started coming here when I was still living paycheck to paycheck, so it can't be that expensive," I assured him, gently squeezing his large calloused hand. He seemed to like my touch.

He gave me a mysterious look, and then he smiled. It was the first time I noticed the slight dimple in his left cheek. Then he flipped his hand, covered mine, and squeezed. That smile was still on his handsome face. I smiled back. "And don't worry, this is on me. I owe you that beer." I eased my hand away from his and looked around to make sure I didn't see anybody I knew. Other than Valerie I didn't know anybody else who visited The Ivy. But that didn't mean that other people I knew didn't visit it, too.

When the waiter took our order for drinks, Marvin ordered the same white wine and the same grilled garden salad that I'd ordered. I could not remember the last time I'd felt so relaxed. I refused a third glass of wine because my buzz was already at a point where I could not be held responsible for my actions. Two hours later, while Marvin was in the men's room, I checked my cell phone for messages and returned a call to Paul. I was glad he didn't answer so I could leave him a voice mail message. Then I called up Valerie. I must have looked suspicious as I whispered into my cell phone. That rap star gave me an amused look, like he thought he was the subject of my conspiratorial phone call. Had I been alone, he would have been. But there was a bigger "star" in my book in the men's room, and he was with me.

"Woman, where the hell are you?" Valerie asked as soon as she heard my voice. "Floyd has called me twice looking for you. He really wants to look nice for you at your party, so he wants you to go shopping with him for a new suit."

"Listen, Paul left me a message on my cell. I just called him back and left him a message that you and I are going to spend the evening at a spa and go to a wedding shower afterward."

"You didn't answer my question."

"I'm with a friend. We just had lunch, and a few drinks . . ."

"Dolores, what are you up to now? You sound like you are either drunk or delirious."

"I've never felt better," I said proudly. "I'm just taking a break from my exciting life as a *biggie mist,*" I slurred, having trouble saying the word right. I cleared my throat. "I just needed to regroup, that's all. It's hard out here for a bigamist."

"What's his name, and where did you meet him?" Valerie seemed to be enjoying this new development. "You nasty little slut!"

"His name is Marvin!" I snapped. "And he's gorgeous. But you don't have to worry about me marrying him. I don't think he's the marrying kind. He's the strong, silent type," I bragged.

"So was King Kong," Valerie reminded.

"I'm serious. He seems like the fun, no-strings-attached kind; and that's what I need right now."

"All I can say is, get enough for me. I have a lot of catching up to do in that area. Where will the sensuous encounter take place?"

"I never said I was going to fuck him, but I probably will, sooner or later. He's cute, and fun to be with. Especially for a man his age."

"Oh shit. Please don't tell me you've latched onto one of those old geezers who lives in one of those mansions in your new neighborhood."

"Not exactly. He's younger. Younger than us."

"Younger, huh? Uh-huh. Well, I hope you and your hypocritical ass will enjoy this young piece. Maybe you'll think twice about dogging me when I mention Russell the next time."

I spent the afternoon in the arms of a man

I didn't plan on ever seeing again. And that was why it didn't bother me to whip out one of my platinum credit cards and pay for the room at the Marriott near LAX.

"You had on a different wedding ring the first time I saw you," Marvin commented, right after we had fucked like two dogs in heat. I gasped and balled my hand into a fist. One thing I had always been careful about was switching to the right wedding ring at the right time. When I was not going to be around either Paul or Floyd, it didn't matter. "I know you're married, Dolores, but if it doesn't bother you, it doesn't bother me. Next time I won't even mention it."
Next time?

"Um, I love my husband to death. And this is the first time I've done something like this. I don't know if there will be a . . . next time," I responded, my hand still balled into a weak fist. I had already slid back into my clothes, but Marvin was still naked on the bed, with his dick propped up on his thigh, ready to spring into action again. Having sex with Floyd and Paul was still good and exciting. And the variation between the two of them kept it that way. But this additional variation was more exciting than I had imagined it would be, and that scared me. Despite what I'd just told Marvin about a next time, I was already thinking about a return visit.

"Well, if we ever do have a rematch, like I said, I won't mention marriage again. I have a lady friend myself, and she's dying to get married."

"Oh? Are you going to ask her?"

Marvin let out a loud breath as he sat bolt upright. "I guess I should," he replied with hesitation. "Ever since I met her, she's been like a mother to me."

My mouth dropped open, but I closed it right away because I didn't want to startle Marvin the way he'd just startled me. "Marvin, let me give you some advice. As long as you live on this planet, don't ever tell a woman who loves you that she's like a mother to you — unless it is your mother."

Marvin gasped and gave me a confused look. "What's wrong with that? My woman *is* like a mother to me! She even irons my underwear when I spend the night at her house."

This woman, who was like a mother to Marvin, was making it hard for the rest of us. No wonder some men were so spoiled and expected so damn much from women! "I don't care if she is or not. Don't tell her that."

"I hear you, and I know you must be right.

Anyway, I think she'll be good for me. As a matter of fact, I was going to pop the question this week."

"If you are getting married, then there won't be a next time for us," I stated in a stiff voice.

"Whatever. That's cool with me. No hard feelings. That's why we should get all we can now." Marvin patted my crotch and took a deep breath. Then he covered my body with his so completely, if somebody had walked into the room, they would have thought that he was humping the mattress. It was only after we'd both come all over the place several more times that it dawned on me: we had not used a condom the second time.

"Shit!" I yelled, reaching for the towel on the nightstand and rubbing his juices from the insides of my thighs. "You forgot to put on a condom this time!"

"Baby, you ain't got a damn thing to worry about. You don't have to worry about me infecting you with nothing. I just got tested last month and I'm as clean as a monk," he replied, sitting up. He put on another condom. I didn't protest when he climbed back on top of me again.

It was around nine when I finally untangled myself from Marvin's arms and legs. He gave me a very long, very wet kiss, and if I had not pulled away from him when I did, there was no telling when I would have left. I gave him the number to the cell phone that only Floyd called me on now, but I didn't expect to hear from him. And then I left, sneaking out the door of the room like a burglar.

I wasn't sure if Floyd was at our condo, but I knew that Paul was up north, so I went to the condo on Manchester. I planned to chill out for a couple of hours before I had to face Floyd. And with my luck, he'd want to fuck my brains out as soon as I hit the door.

After a long hot bubble bath, I wiggled into some fresh underwear and my white terry cloth bathrobe. Then I poured myself a glass of wine, plopped down on the sofa, and called Valerie.

"How was he?" she asked, giggling.

"Just what the doctor ordered."

"You . . . you . . . you — HO!" Valerie laughed.

"Jealous?"

"Damn right!" She guffawed. "No, I am not jealous. I'm happy that you're happy. You know, this is the first time we've both been this happy at the same time."

"And I hope we stay this way," I said,

meaning every word.

"We will. Lo, can I ask you something? I've been wanting to ask you this for a long time." The serious tone in Valerie's voice made me hold my breath. I had no idea what was coming.

"You can ask me anything, Valerie," I told her. "What is it?"

"What is it really like to be married to two men at the same time?" Valerie's voice sounded dull and listless. "I know I'll never be in that position, but I'd still like to know what it's like."

I blew out a silent sigh of relief. "Is that all you wanted to ask me?" I chuckled. "Well, except for all the lies I have to tell, and all the running from pillar to post to be with them, it's nice. I feel so special knowing that two gorgeous men loved me enough to want to marry me. That neat freak thing about Paul drives me crazy. But it keeps me on my toes. And that's a good thing because I've always tried to be a clean woman. Floyd, well he's got that 'bad boy' thing going for him. And after the drama that Whitney Houston starred in with Bobby Brown, we know how sprung a woman can get when it comes to a bad boy. Girl, I lucked out. Not only are both my husbands handsome and fun fucks, they both have money."

I paused and let out a long, loud sigh. "I wish every woman could try it once in her lifetime. It's a damn shame that it's not legal to have more than one spouse."

"It is legal. Idi Amin had several wives, and other men all over various parts of the world have several wives at the same time. I read in the *National Enquirer* about some sultan in one of those desert countries who has eleven wives. Whew! I bet his dick looks like a raw hot-link sausage by now. Unfortunately, I've never heard about a woman who was able to get away with having more than one husband at the same time. Not in anyplace in the world. You should —"

"I should change this subject. Now can we get back to the subject we were discussing earlier?" I suggested. "Now, what's up with my surprise birthday party?"

"Yeah, right," Valerie said, the spark back in her voice. "We need to get together to go over the details."

"What's there to go over? And if this is supposed to be a surprise, why am I involved in the planning?" I yawned. "You of all people know that I have more than enough going on in my life to keep me busy."

"Don't rub it in, bitch. I just thought you'd like to see the guest list and meet the DJ. But if you don't want to, that's fine with

439

me. Just don't complain to me if you don't like something."

"Valerie, whatever you want to do is fine with me." I sighed and took a drink from my glass. "By the way, how's your lover boy?"

"Things couldn't be better." Valerie swooned. "He's not as dapper as Paul, or as rich and handsome as Floyd, but he's good enough for me. You'll see. He'll be at your party. And I am warning you in advance to keep your roving eyes to yourself."

"Now you know you don't have to worry about me flirting with any of your men. I've never stooped that low, and I never will. I do have a few scruples."

"I know. I'm just tripping. It's just that Russell is so fine. Everywhere I go with him, women look at him like he's something good to eat. It's obvious that he's younger than me, so a lot of these heifers are schoolgirls. And you know how bold and brazen those bitches can be."

"Like I said, you don't have to worry about me. I'm not a schoolgirl. Floyd will be there, and I'll be busy keeping my eyes on him."

CHAPTER 53

Paul was not at the San Francisco airport to pick me up when I flew up to the Bay Area to celebrate my birthday with him. I had to take a cab. He didn't answer his cell phone, and he wasn't in his office when I called him up. And none of his relatives knew where he was when I tried to pry the information out of them.

I was just about to start calling the hospitals when he stumbled in the front door at our swank, beachfront condo in Alameda. His clothes and hair were so disheveled and unkempt that it looked like he'd been in a fight with a bear. The tails of his white shirt had been tied into a clumsy knot. And he had the jacket to one of his fifteen hundred dollar suits tied around his waist like an apron!

"What happened to you?" I yelled. "You look like hell! Where the fuck have you been?" I demanded. He dismissed me with a wave and kept walking. He didn't stop until he reached the liquor cabinet next to the plasma TV. "I broke my neck trying to get up here in time for you to take me out for my birthday and you are nowhere to be found. Do you think I enjoyed taking a cab all the way from the airport? And look at you! You are as drunk as hell!" I was right up in his face, trying to wrest the wine bottle out of his hand. He jerked his hand away and threw the bottle against the wall, spilling wine and broken glass onto the light beige carpets and the back of a plush white love seat. Then he viciously kicked over a large green plant on the floor by the sofa, spilling coal-black soil and leaves. I dreaded the clean-up frenzy I knew he'd involve me in once he calmed down.

"You no-good, whoring-ass bitch!" he shouted through clenched teeth. "My mama told me I should have married Councilman Hardy's daughter. But did I listen? No! I had to tie myself down with your cheesy, ghetto, black ass! You cocksucking bitch!"

"What?" I shrieked. "What's the matter with you?"

"You! You are what's the matter with me! With your nasty self!"

I stood there blinking at him with my mouth hanging open. My ears were ringing with disbelief, confusion, and fear. There was red hot rage all over his face. His eyes looked as if they were on fire. His nostrils were twitching and his lips were trembling. I moved back a few steps, because it looked like he was about to throw a major hissy fit. "What are you talking about?" I asked, moving back a few more steps until I was against the wall. Now he was in my face. "Paul, what —"

"Whore!" he hollered. The word hit me like a baseball bat.

"Paul, will you tell me what this is all about?" I demanded, now moving sideways against the wall. He moved right along with me. He swung at me with his fist, but I ducked and he missed. He hit the wall with his fist. When he swung at me again, I grabbed his arm and held it in place. The man was so drunk, he could barely stand. Had he not been so drunk I would have been in serious trouble. "Baby, you're drunk. Let's have a cup of coffee and talk."

"Fuck a cup of coffee! Fuck talking! Fuck you, bitch!!" he boomed.

"Well, then let's just talk," I begged, trying to lead him to the sofa. He took a few steps back and slapped his hands onto his hips, glaring at me with so much contempt I feared for my life. "Paul, please tell me

443

what this is all about!" I wailed. My heart was beating so hard, I thought that if he didn't kill me first, I'd have a fatal heart attack.

"Do you know how many seminars I've conducted at the Marriott?!" he roared.

"Huh?"

"I know everybody that works in that damn hotel. I've flashed your picture around that damn place so many times, they know every inch of your face. Did you think that you could take your whoring ass into that particular hotel and me not find out about it? I ought to kill your bitch ass right here and now!" Paul shook his fist in my face. Then he untied his jacket from around his waist and flung it across the room.

"Calm down! Baby, let me explain!"

"Calm down? Calm down my ass! What the fuck is there for you to explain?" He sucked in his breath and folded his arms. "I'm listening!"

"It wasn't anything. It didn't mean anything to me."

"I bet it didn't! Did you suck his dick as good as you suck mine?" At this point, Paul grabbed me by my hair and started dragging me across the floor toward the sofa. I was glad I didn't have on one of my wigs. When he got me to the sofa, he plopped down. With my hair still wrapped around his hand, he forced my head between his legs. With his other hand he unzipped his pants. Then he made me suck his dick so long and hard I got the hiccups.

When he was finally satisfied, he pulled me up to his lap. I braced myself because I had no idea what he was going to do to me next. What he did do surprised me. He gently placed his head on my shoulder and cried like a baby. "I . . . I'm sorry. I'm sorry for everything. I love you, Dolores. I don't want to lose you. . . ." We stayed that way for about ten minutes without speaking, with him patting my shoulder and moaning under his breath. His pants were still unzipped, and he was still aroused. The tip of his rock-hard dick stuck out like the barrel of a gun.

"I'm sorry. I don't know what else to say, Paul. I had no reason to cheat on you. . . ."

He gave me the strangest look before he burst into tears again. There was nothing more disturbing to me than to see a grown man cry. Floyd had cried after he got out of prison, but that was different. He'd had every reason in the world to cry. He still did from time to time. But Paul was just straight-up drunk and disappointed in me because I'd been unfaithful. "I was glad when I found out what you'd done. . . ." he said in a low voice. My mouth dropped open again. He sniffed. "It made me feel better about what I'd done. I was taking my guilt out on you just now."

"You cheated on me?" I reared back and gave him a hard look. Now I was ready to take a few swings at his face with my fist. But I knew better.

There was a contrite look on his face as he nodded. "Baby, it just happened. That heifer came at me with both guns blasting. TWICE! That no-good wench took advantage of me in my own office, right there on the top of my desk with your framed picture just inches away! And if that wasn't bad enough, a few weeks later she lured me to her tacky apartment in Half Moon Bay and made a fool out of me again! My mama was right. You're not the only jezebel in my life." His last comment made me flinch, but I let it slide because it was true. Paul sniffed again and gave me a pleading look. "She meant nothing to me. She wasn't even that clean! I . . . I could still smell her on me even after I'd bathed and scrubbed myself raw."

I started to rise from the sofa. "Paul, you can do whatever you want, but I'm going back to L.A. tonight." My luggage was still on the floor by the door.

"And I'm coming with you, baby. We need to be together so we can fix things," he said, rising, too. I grabbed his wrist and pulled him back to the sofa. I put my arm around his shoulder and patted his back affectionately, like he was the one who needed to be comforted. "Let me throw a few things into a suitcase and we can be on our way."

"Paul, I need to be alone for a few days," I said, talking slowly. I rubbed my scalp where he had pulled my hair. "Please stay up here. When things settle, we can talk and decide what we need to do."

"What do you mean by that? I know what we need to do! We need to get some counseling or have a baby, or anything else you want. This can be fixed," he insisted, looking completely desperate now. It hurt to see how much my tryst with Marvin had hurt my husband. I couldn't imagine how he would feel if he knew about Floyd. I knew now, more than ever, that Floyd was one "indiscretion" that I had to do whatever it took to conceal.

CHAPTER 54

I am not the kind of person who likes to use a lot of clichés. But if there ever was one that applied to me now, it was "when it rains, it pours." Shit was raining down on my head so hard I needed a hard hat.

Paul insisted on going back to L.A. with me. I had tried to talk him out of it, but I'd failed. I gave him another blow job, hoping it would make him change his mind. But that didn't do any good, either. We had to wait several hours to get on the next flight. By the time we got home, we were both more than a little cranky. And then there was that business of my affair with Marvin, and his with some nameless bitch he would only refer to as "that heifer." We agreed not to discuss our affairs again until we got in front of a marriage counselor. Despite everything that had happened, I didn't believe in divorce. Therefore, I was determined to save my marriage to Paul, and to Floyd.

Shortly after we got home, I dragged Paul to bed. After I made sure he was asleep, I closed the bedroom door and went into the kitchen to check all my voice mail messages. Valerie had left me a message to call her back ASAP. Floyd thought I was on the ship on my way to Puerto Vallarta, so I had not expected him to call. But there was a message from him, too, telling me that he loved me and couldn't wait to see me again. I shook my head and let out a deep, loud sigh.

I called Valerie up. "Will you be my bridesmaid?" she cooed.

"Oh my God! Russell proposed?" As bad as I wanted to talk to her about my confrontation with Paul, I didn't. This was her moment, and I didn't want to spoil it.

"Yes! No, not exactly. I proposed. But he admitted that he was planning to do it soon, anyway. Oh, I wish that Mama and Paw Paw were here to experience this. Here I am, a woman nipping at the heels of middle age. Both my baby sister and my baby brother have been married for years. I was beginning to think that it was never going to happen for me." Valerie released a muffled sob. "Lo, I've been jealous of you ever since we met. But I didn't mean any harm. Now that

I finally got what I've always wanted, I'll never be jealous of you, or any other woman, ever again. I . . . I am finally where I want to be!"

"Oh, Valerie. Honey, I am so happy for you. Have you made the announcement yet?"

"That's one of the things I wanted to talk to you about. Do you mind if Russell and I share our good news at your party? Now if you don't want us to, that's fine. I don't want to steal any of your thunder. But there will be a few bitches that I can't stand at your party, and I would love to rub this in their smug faces."

"Of course you can make the announcement there." I let out a loud tired breath.

"Lo, is everything all right? Your voice just cracked."

"It did? Uh, I'm fine."

"Where's Paul? How was dinner? How's the weather up there? Are you going to do much shopping in Frisco?"

"Valerie, I'm back in L.A. and so is Paul. We had a little misunderstanding. I want to talk to you about it, but I don't think this is the right time. I need to get Paul's black ass back up to the Bay Area tomorrow. I'll call you then." I cleared my throat, but now even I could hear my voice cracking. "Valerie, I am really and truly happy for you. I can't say it enough. If anybody deserves to be happy, it's you. I never gave up hope on you. Whatever you do, don't make as big a mess out of your life as I've made out of mine."

"Lo, do you want to meet me somewhere tonight? I'm worried about you."

"I'll talk to you tomorrow," I said. "Now if you don't mind, I'd like to get some sleep. And you should do the same. We're both going to need it." I hung up, but I held the telephone in my hand for a few minutes just looking at it. I needed to talk to somebody, but not Valerie. I closed my eyes and recalled a telephone number that I had dialed only once and memorized without even trying. But there it was, right in front of my mind. All of a sudden, it seemed like my fingers had taken on a life of their own. I couldn't control them. I felt disembodied as I watched my fingers tip and tap around on the telephone pad until they tipped and tapped Marvin Meecham's number. The same man who was responsible for the mess that I had stepped into with Paul!

"Yeah," he said, in a sleepy but still sexy voice.

"Marvin, this is Dolores. Listen, I don't want anything. I just want to talk."

"What about?"

"Uh, just to say hi. I just had a rough evening with my husband, and I was feeling kind of down in the dumps."

"Oh. Well, I am sorry to hear about that. Is there anything I can do for you?"

"Some nosy busybody that works at the hotel recognized me. They told my husband about us checking into a room," I revealed, speaking in a quiet and level tone of voice, despite the fact that I was slightly nervous.

"Oh shit!"

"He didn't take it too well."

"*Pffff!* I guess not! I wouldn't either. But it's too late to worry about that now. Is that the reason you called me up? Isn't this kind of like closing the barn door after the mule has been stole?"

I laughed. "I guess you could say that. Well, I wasn't the only one creeping on the side. He had a confession of his own."

"That's a man for you." Marvin laughed. "Where is your old man now?"

"So fucking drunk he wouldn't know if the house was on fire. He's sleeping it off. I'm going to put him on a plane back to the Bay Area, first thing in the morning." Marvin's silence told me that he had some questions about my marriage. I decided to answer a few before he asked them. "He works up in Alameda, and we have a pretty liberal marriage. He cheated on me with some heifer he works with. Twice!"

"Well, what do you feel worse about? You cheating on him with me or him cheating on you with that heifer?"

"I don't know what I feel right now. Listen, I'll let you get back to whatever it was you were doing. I am sorry for disturbing you."

"Let me ask you again — is there anything I can do for you?"

"Well . . ."

"Dolores, let's cut out all this bullshit. All of my roommates are in Vegas. Why don't you come over to my place? Shit."

I gasped. "What? My husband is here."

"So drunk he wouldn't know if the house was on fire, ain't he?"

"I don't think so, Marvin. I've already crossed a line I should not have crossed in the first place."

"So did your old man. TWICE! Don't you want to make things even? Look, baby, he already knows what you did. What else have you got to lose? You sound like you're in a lot of pain. The least I can do is listen to you. Talking helps, you know. That's why you called me in the first place, ain't it now?"

"I guess. I needed to talk to somebody, and you were the only person I could think of. That's all . . ."

"Talk? That's all? Well, let's talk face to face. I'll leave the porch light on . . ."

"Can I think about it for a little while?"

"Dolores, listen to me. You get in your car and get over here now, before I change my mind."

It took me five minutes to get out the door.

CHAPTER 55

I couldn't figure out what it was about men that made me such a fool for them. Just loving them the way I did was all it took for me to lose my perspective. I had never talked to a professional, but I had a feeling that my foolishness had something to do with my biological background. I knew enough about my mother to know that she had no use for me. But I knew absolutely nothing about my father, and that emptiness had a lot to do with my wanting a male in the highest possible position in my life. I had no brothers to speak of, or any male children. So for me the next best thing was a husband. Or in my case, a couple of husbands. However, I knew that sooner or later, something would happen that would bring me to my senses. It was bound to happen because of all the stupid shit I pulled. Juggling two husbands had become a full-time job. I wanted to keep Paul and Floyd, but I knew that this fling with Marvin was temporary. I didn't need Marvin, but I wanted him. Therefore, I decided to enjoy his goodies while I still could.

I knew I couldn't spend the entire night with Marvin. For one thing, I had to be back in my condo before Paul came back to life. The other thing was, Marvin lived in a seedy neighborhood, and I didn't feel safe there at night. His building had an enclosed garage so I was able to hide my car from thieves and what not. But before I could get out of the garage, after I'd parked facing a graffiti-filled wall, I noticed a few shady-looking individuals lurking about. What was so odd about that was that it seemed like they had come out of nowhere. Like they either dropped from the garage ceiling or sprung up out of the ground. Anyway, they were in my presence now, and I was uncomfortable and frightened. I ended up barreling back out of the garage and parking on the street after all. At least I could see my car from Marvin's living room window.

As soon as I took my windbreaker off, he grabbed me by my arm. Then he snatched me into his arms so fast and hard, the bones in my neck popped. I had the nerve to try to resist — very weakly, though. My protests didn't do a damn bit of good. He was all

456

over me, covering my face and neck with kisses. But when he tossed me over his well-defined shoulder like a sack of flour and hauled me to a bedroom about the size of a large closet, I didn't resist any more at all.

"I hope you don't think I just called you to come over here just for *this,*" I said, licking up and down his chest as we lay on a twin bed, cluttered with a few of his dirty undershirts. Our legs were twisted around each other like pretzels. With the exception of his soft, luscious lips, everything else on his body was solid muscle. His chest felt like a heated rock. And when I placed my face against it, as I continued to lick on him, I felt so safe. Why? I didn't know. It just seemed like I had escaped all of my problems. And for the time being, the only care in the world I had was pleasing Marvin, and myself.

I was pleased to see that he had some condoms in the top drawer of a scarred nightstand by the side of the bed. Unfortunately, he broke through the first condom at the worst time. He shot a load of his hot sperm into me like a bullet. As soon as I realized what had happened, I pushed and kicked him until he was on the floor. "Shit!" I hollered, leaping off the bed. I hopped up and down for a few moments like I was stomping out fires, hoping to shake out as much of his juice as I could. With the rest of his thick juice streaming down my thighs, I ran into the bathroom right outside the bedroom door. I was already in the shower trying to wash it away when he appeared in the doorway, puffing on a joint.

"I shouldn't have called you," I said.

"But you did, and you can call me again if you want to," Marvin said, standing there naked and blowing thick smoke in my direction. I shook my head when he offered me a few puffs, even though I could have used it, and something even stronger. Like a shot of tequila.

"What about your lady friend?" I asked. The hot water felt good on my skin. But when I spotted a water bug sliding up the stiff, dingy shower curtain, I gasped. I couldn't get out of that bathroom fast enough. Marvin was right behind me, squeezing and slapping my ass like he was inspecting melons.

"What about my lady friend?" We were back on the bed, and my head was back on his chest.

"I don't want to mess up things for you. Just like my husband found out about us, she might find out about us." I lifted my head so that my face was close to his. He gave me a quick, dry kiss on the tip of my nose.

"*Pffft!* I wouldn't worry about her," he said, waving his hand. "I don't. She's one of those slightly older sisters, so desperate she'd marry Shrek. I got her in my hip pocket, see."

"I see," I said, glad that I wasn't the woman that this man seemed to take for granted and was so blasé about. "I'm one of those slightly older sisters," I reminded. He didn't respond to my comment. All he did was giggle and play with my titties some more.

As much as I enjoyed making love with Marvin, I was glad when he fell asleep. While he was snoring like a moose, I slid off the bed and took another quick shower. I slipped out of his apartment on my tiptoes because I didn't want to wake him up. I knew that if I did, he'd be on me again. That would have been fine with me, but under the circumstances, time was not on my side.

Speaking of time, it was a good thing I left Marvin's place when I did. As soon as I got home and walked into the bedroom, Paul opened his eyes, yawning and growling like a bear. Despite the suspicious look on his face, he motioned with his hand for me to join him in the bed. I was glad to see the suspicious look disappear with the next yawn. That look was replaced with a mischievous twinkle in his eyes and a smile that looked so loving and sincere, it overwhelmed me. He was looking at me in a way that made me feel like I was for his eyes only. It was the kind of look that would have made me feel guilty, even if I had nothing to feel guilty about.

CHAPTER 56

"Honey, where have you been?" he asked, yawning some more. I ignored Paul's request to join him in bed. I was glad to see that it didn't bother him. That haunting smile was still on his face. Slime had dribbled from his mouth onto his goatee, glazing it.

"I had to run to the store," I said, picking up clothes off the floor, trying not to let him see my face.

"Oh. What did you buy?" he asked, roughly wiping his chin with a tissue he'd snatched from the box on the nightstand.

"Nothing. I wanted some hog head cheese." I gave him a big smile.

"LoReese, baby, this is not Compton or South Central. These folks out here wouldn't know hog head cheese from mincemeat pie."

"Well, at least one of them does. Last week I found some at that deli on the corner."

"But not today?" he asked with a nod and a puzzled look.

"But not today," I answered, clearing my throat.

"Lo, baby, is everything all right now?" He sat up with a wan look on his face. "It seems like something is still bothering you. I know we had a rough night . . ."

"There is nothing wrong," I told him. I couldn't lie straight and I couldn't walk straight. I bumped into the edge of the dresser facing the bed and almost fell. "Everything is going to be just fine between us," I assured him, sitting down gently at the foot of the bed. I thought I would fall to the floor when he winked, nudged my hip with his bare foot, and patted a spot on the bed next to him. I rose so fast I stumbled. "Listen, you get up and get ready so I can take you to the airport. You've got a plane to catch this morning. And you know what a zoo LAX can be this time of day."

"Huh? I thought we were going to talk things through some more," he pouted, rubbing the back of his knotty head. His hair looked like a briar bush. His body odor was such an unholy stench it made my eyes water, and I was standing a few feet away from him.

"We did. We sorted out everything last

night. And everything's fine. I won't mention that heifer you performed that little comedy with, and you won't mention that punk that I was stupid enough to check into the Marriott with. That's what we agreed on."

"Oh? We did? Baby, I was so drunk last night I don't remember much of anything. And I'm paying for it now," he said with a groan, rubbing the back and side of his head. "Shit! I have to be in Frisco for a meeting with my boss this afternoon!" Paul jumped off the bed like a flea. The flap of his shorts flew open and his dick looked as limp as a piece of raw bacon. "Did I take you to dinner for your birthday?" He frowned as he rubbed the back of his head. Then he laughed. "I can't remember much of anything!"

"Uh, yeah. Don't you remember? We went to Alioto's after that little ruckus we had. I enjoyed it. You did, too. You were feeling so good, you gave the waiter a 50 percent tip."

"Shit!" He guffawed. "That's the last time I want to feel *that* good!"

I nodded. "I won't argue with that. Now get showered, and dressed so I can put you on that plane." I looked at my watch. "Uh, remember I have to be on the ship myself by four P.M."

"Honey, that's what I've been meaning to ask you about. What name do you go by at work?"

I froze. "Why?"

"I wanted to send you some flowers, but when I called, that dumb-ass bitch on the switchboard said she didn't know anybody by the name of Dolores Dunne."

I breathed a sigh of relief. "Because that's not the name I go by. Everybody there knows me as LoReese. But please don't try to send anything to me at work, or call me. Always call me on my cell phone."

"I know that much, but why can't I send you flowers?"

"It's a security thing. The terrorists are coming up with all kinds of ways to wreak havoc. Somebody sent a mysterious box of candy to the ship's doctor, and inside was a threatening note. And last week we got a bomb threat."

"Shit!"

"Uh, I'll fix you some coffee, but you'll have to drink it lickety-split. We don't have much time." I glanced at my watch again.

While Paul was in the shower, I called up Valerie. "It's me. I'm all right now."

"What was it you didn't want to talk about last night?"

"Oh, it was nothing important. What time

do you want me and Floyd to be at Paw Paw's for my surprise birthday party this Friday?"

"I want things to be in full swing by the time you guys get there. I've got two of the most rocking DJs in L.A. — one also happens to be my honey — and a birthday cake that will be so potent with rum, you won't be able to drink anything else." Valerie let out a soft sigh. "Then after you've had your moment, Russell and I will make our announcement. This will be a night for us all to remember. I promise."

Right after I dropped Paul off at the airport, I went back to the condo on Manchester where I remained until the day before my party at Paw Paw's. When I returned to the condo in Beverly Hills, Floyd was so glad to see me he picked me up at the door and swung me around the room until I got dizzy. "Baby, you look so well rested. But how did you manage not to soak up some of that Mexican sun?" he said, comparing his arm to mine.

"I always wear the strongest sunblock," I told him, standing up straight as soon as he released me.

"I know you're tired, baby, so I won't bother you. Not yet," he said with a wink. "But tomorrow night after the party, I plan to bring your fine ass back here and fuck you inside out." I ducked when Floyd attempted to nibble on my ear. "Is something wrong?"

"Uh, I'm just tired. Do you mind if I take a long, hot bath?"

"You do whatever you have to do, baby. Pamper yourself for a change. You deserve it. I'll have a drink ready for you when you get out."

I stayed in the bathtub so long that when I got out, Floyd was in bed asleep. I drank the glass of wine he had left for me on the living room coffee table. It helped me relax, but I still couldn't get to sleep. I knew that if I wanted to hold on to Paul, I was going to have to work on my marriage. I just didn't know how I was going to find the time. One thing I had decided to do was break off the relationship with Marvin. I promised myself that no matter what, I would never see him again. It was time for me to do something right for a change.

The next morning Floyd took me to Rodeo Drive again so he could pick out what I was going to wear to my party. We settled on a yellow silk dress with a low neckline and a high hem. He had decided to wear a white linen suit, a white hat, and white gloves, even though I told him he would look like a pimp.

As the evening wore on, I realized that a party was the last place I wanted to be. Even though I was the guest of honor. But it meant so much to Valerie and Floyd that there was no way I was going to back out now.

It did me no good to argue with Floyd about us rolling up to Paw Paw's in a white stretch limo. And if that wasn't pretentious enough, there was a poster on the wall by the front entrance with a blown-up picture of me on it. As soon as I stepped into the dimly lit place, a man blew out the happy birthday tune on a trumpet. There was only one candle on the elaborate cake sitting on a table that had been placed in the middle of the dance floor. One candle was all I had the strength to blow out. I was pleasantly surprised to see so many people.

Valerie was all over the place in a pale green hostess gown, floating around like a butterfly trying to make sure that everything was running smoothly. She was frantic because one of the two DJs she had hired was running late. But the other DJ made up for it. He kept the music going nonstop. One tune came on the tail end of another. Men of all sizes, shapes, and colors pulled me out on the dance floor so I was totally occupied for the first hour.

I was on my way to the ladies' room when I bumped into a tall man who had his back to me. Then he turned around. Marvin was the last man in the universe that I wanted, or expected, to see at my birthday party. Before I knew what was happening, he hauled off and kissed me. All I could do was scream and take off running.

CHAPTER 57

"Dolores, what in the world is the matter with you? Are you all right?" Valerie was beside me, looking puzzled. As soon as I'd screamed, she had run behind me into the ladies' room. I stood in front of the counter on legs that felt like jelly. Valerie handed me a wet paper towel to wipe sweat off my face.

"I'm fine," I assured her, pushing her away. With each second that passed, the puzzled look on her face intensified.

"Lo, you are scaring the shit out of me. You need to tell me what the hell is going on, and you need to tell me now," she hollered, hands on her hips and a serious look on her face now. "I put a lot of time and effort in setting things up for tonight, and I don't want any other drama to fuck things up. I know that this party is for you, but the man I plan to marry is here, and I want to make a really good impression on him."

"Valerie, remember that guy I spent some

time with at the Marriott?" I said, wiping my face and neck some more. I couldn't remember the last time I'd sweated so hard. Marvin had just smeared my lipstick so I had to apply some more. He had kissed me so hard my lips were still throbbing. "Remember when I called you up and said I needed to get away for a minute?" I held my breath for a few seconds and pressed my lips together to even out the fresh coat of lipstick.

Valerie nodded and dabbed at a smudge of lipstick in the corner of my mouth. I loved this woman. Had she been a blood relative, I could not have loved her more. It pleased me to see that she was genuinely concerned about me. "What about him? Are you still seeing him?" She paused, and then gave me a critical look. "He'd better not be mistreating you or he'll have to deal with me," she assured me. "And you can count on that."

I nodded. "I know, I know." I cleared my throat and started talking in a low, controlled voice. "I spent some time with him at his place the other night after I put Paul to bed. I couldn't help myself. I needed to talk to somebody, and he was the only person I could think to call."

Valerie looked hurt for a brief moment.

"You could have called me . . ." she said with a pout.

"I know that, but I didn't want to burden you that night. You had enough going on at the time. Well, anyway — *he's here!*"

An amused and excited look appeared on Valerie's face. "What? Well, did you talk to him? Does he know you're with your husband? How did he know about your party? Does he know that I own Paw Paw's?"

"That's what I was going to ask you!" I swallowed hard and stared at myself in the mirror. I was glad to see that my makeup still looked okay, despite all the sweating I'd just done. "He must be one of your regulars, or maybe he came as the guest of one of your regulars. Shit. As long as he keeps his distance, nobody will be embarrassed here tonight."

Valerie nodded. "I hope not. I hope he's not one of those thug-ass niggers that'll tear my place up. I can't have the cops coming up in here. If you think he's going to cause trouble, you point him out and I'll politely ask him to leave. If he even acts like he wants to get belligerent I will make my bouncers, Tiny and Bobo, physically remove his ass. What's his name? What does he look like?"

"His name is Marvin. He's a tall young

dude in a yellow nylon jacket and black jeans. He's standing by the DJ booth. He must be the other DJ."

Valerie gave me a look that made her look three times as confused as before. When she started talking again, it sounded like her voice was coming from beyond the grave. "A . . . yellow jacket and black jeans? Are you sure that's what he's wearing?"

Now it was my turn to look confused. "Of course I'm sure," I said, adding a lot of emphasis to my words.

"There's only . . . can you peep out the door and show him to me?" Valerie suggested. I couldn't figure out why she was acting so odd. I was the one with the problem!

Just as I cracked open the ladies' room door, he was there. His face was just inches away from mine. Before I knew what was happening, he snatched open the door and pulled me into his arms and kissed me again. This time it was so long and hard, my jaws felt like they were going to lock up on me. I pulled away, gasping for air. I used my tongue to feel around inside my mouth to make sure all my fillings were still in place. I couldn't believe the nerve of this man! It must have occurred to him that my husband might be with me, and here he was slobbering on me like I was his main squeeze!

"Happy birthday! I didn't know you were going to be here tonight, and that you were the Lo or LoReese — or whatever name you want to be called — that this party was for, baby," Marvin said. Then he looked behind me and froze. "Valerie!" The word shot out of his mouth like a torpedo.

"WHAT THE HELL IS THIS SHIT?" Valerie screamed. The words were coming from her mouth, but they didn't sound human. She sounded downright beastly. She snorted and then shoved me to the side with both hands. "What the fuck is all this?!" Her face was scrunched up so tight, it looked like she had only one eyebrow.

"This . . . this is Marvin," I stammered in a low voice, looking out into the crowd to make sure Floyd was not too close by. Valerie looked from me to Marvin. By now he was looking like he'd seen Caesar's ghost.

"This is the man you've been fucking? This is *Marvin?*" Valerie asked, looking at me with so much contempt in her eyes, I almost lost my breath. *"This is the bastard I was going to marry!"* She whipped her neck around to look at Marvin. "So you told her your name was Marvin, huh?"

"It is! My middle name is Russell," he

said, holding up both hands. By now a small crowd had gathered and Floyd was in the front of the crowd, taking all this in. He looked like he didn't know if he was coming or going. He stood there with his mouth open so wide, I could see almost every tooth in his mouth. "Listen, let's go somewhere and talk. I don't want to make a scene!"

"Look, Russell or Marvin, or whatever the hell your name is, you've already made a scene!" Valerie then turned to me. "Two husbands weren't enough for you! You had to have my man, too? You no-good slut! I never want to see you again! Don't you ever call me, don't you ever set foot in my house or my bar again! If you do, I will kill you! Now you get the hell up out of my place!"

I held up both hands in protest, but also as a means of defense. I had to protect my face, in case she decided to bitch-slap me. "Valerie — sister-girl, I didn't know! I didn't know he was the one!" I yelled. Floyd finally walked over to me. There was a look on his face now that words could not describe. I couldn't tell if he was going to laugh, faint, scream, or cry.

"Will somebody tell me what is going on around here? Is this some kind of hidden camera shit for TV?" He looked at Valerie, then around, then up at the ceiling, and then at me. "What was that about two husbands? I'm Dolores's husband. Will somebody let me in on this joke?" He glanced around some more, still looking for a candid camera.

"Floyd, why don't you ask your bitch? Ask her about Paul Dunne and the condo she shares with him over on Manchester. Ask her about the place up near Frisco where she goes to visit him when you think she's working on that cruise ship — a job she quit a long time ago." Valerie looked at me again. I was glad that looks couldn't kill, because if they could I would have dropped dead on the spot. I knew it was just my imagination, but her eyes looked like they were on fire. "I can't wait to hear what Paul's going to say when I tell him everything. You — you no-good, backstabbing, cocksucking slut!" Valerie was shaking so hard her body was vibrating. "Get out of my place now while you are still able! Get the fuck out before I throw you out with my own hands!"

CHAPTER 58

By now everybody in the bar had witnessed my downfall. The party people, most of them too drunk to know any better, formed a perfect circle around me, Valerie, Floyd, and Marvin. Valerie lunged at me and swung at my head. If I hadn't ducked, she probably would have knocked my brains out. The only other time I'd ever seen her this mad was the night she killed her step-father. . . .

I had to plow through the crowd like a linebacker to make it to the door. Valerie was nipping at my heels, calling me names I had never heard before. Floyd was right behind her, cussing and yelling at me that he wanted to know everything. Every other person in the bar must have wanted to know everything, too, because they were all stumbling along behind Floyd. Most of them were even cussing at me, accusing me of trying to scam them out of birthday gifts

I didn't deserve. The only person I didn't see in the nosy, agitated crowd following me was Marvin/Russell.

I ran out of Paw Paw's and sprinted down the street. I broke the heels on both of my stilettos, but that didn't slow me down. I didn't stop until I saw an empty taxi sitting at a corner. I went straight to the Beverly Hills address that I shared with Floyd, and I immediately started throwing clothes into my suitcases. I was just about to haul my luggage out to my Honda when Floyd stormed in. He looked like a monster. His eyes were stretched open wide, and spit was foaming out both sides of his mouth. In spite of the fact that he had not killed the girl who he'd spent so many years in prison for, I had every reason to believe that he was going to kill me.

"I want to know what the fuck is going on, and I want to know now, Dolores!" he boomed, spraying spit all over my face.

"It's over, Floyd," I told him, surprised at how calm my voice was now. "I can't keep this shit up. I can't go on like this. I had no right to marry you and drag you into this mess." I set my suitcases down. "The keys to the BMW are on the dresser in the bedroom. So is the checkbook to our joint account." He stood in front of me with his hands on his hips, blocking my way. "If you don't mind, I'd like to leave now," I said, still speaking in a calm voice.

"Do you think I'm going to stand by and let you walk out of here without telling me what the fuck is going on?" He lunged at me, and I jumped back, but not in time. He grabbed me by my arms and gripped so hard it hurt. I squirmed, trying to free myself. But he held me in place. It felt like I'd been cemented to the spot. "Who is this motherfucking Paul? And don't lie to me because I'll get the truth one way or the other. Even if I have to stomp it out of you!"

"Motherfucker, if you hit me you better kill me, or you will regret it for the rest of your life," I warned.

"Look, lady, I don't have time for any more games, lies, or tricks. I asked you a simple question, and I am not letting you out of here until I get some answers. Now, who is this motherfucker Paul?"

"He's my first husband," I replied in a meek voice, twisting and turning until he released me. "I married him years ago. I didn't think you'd ever get out of prison, and I didn't want to spend the rest of my life alone." I was dog tired, and it showed in my voice. Now all I wanted to do was go someplace where I could decide my next move. And it had to be a safe location where I could find some temporary peace. But the way everybody had ganged up on me, I wasn't even sure that the moon would be far enough away for me.

Floyd looked profoundly hurt. It broke my heart to see him that way. "Why did you marry me? Why didn't you tell me you were already married? Do you know what a fool I feel like now?" he asked, his voice trembling, his hands back on his hips.

"I tried to get out of marrying you, but you were so . . . I . . . I felt so sorry for you . . ." I stammered. "I still feel sorry for you."

He gasped. "Why you uppity black bitch! *You* married *me* because you felt sorry for me? Sister, I don't need your pity now, and I didn't need it then. You could have at least been woman enough to tell me you were already married. I would have got over you eventually. And what's up with that youngster back at the club? Exactly where does *he* fit into this mess?"

"You mean Marvin? Uh . . . I . . . I had a little fling with him, that's all that was! He didn't mean a damn thing to me! I didn't know he was the man that Valerie's been bragging about and planning to marry. With him, it was just . . . *sex*." Just the mention of the word made Floyd cringe. He dipped his head and squeezed his eyes shut for a few moments.

"Shaddup! Shaddup your mouth! I don't want to hear nothing else out of that hole in your face, woman," he advised, shaking a finger in my burning face. I would have stopped talking and slunk on out the door at this point, but he was the one who kept the conversation going. "In other words, my loving wasn't enough for you? You had to have two backups?!"

"It wasn't like that!" I shouted, raising my hands in protest and for protection, the same way I had done when Valerie lit into me.

"Then why were you with that other nigger?"

"Which one? Oh, you mean Paul? I stumbled upon him during a weak moment. On the ship during a holiday cruise. He said everything I wanted to hear. He did everything I wanted a man to do for me. He was . . . he was just there at a time when I couldn't help myself. I was not looking for love . . ."

"Other than him and that young punk, were there any others?" Floyd asked, rotating his arms like a windmill, his lips trembling. To this day, I don't know why that man hadn't killed me by now. He was so angry and hurt, I thought he might snap at any minute. I was glad, and lucky, that he could still control his actions.

"What? Of course not! It was just you three," I admitted.

"Three?" Floyd spat the word out like poison. "You must be one nasty-ass whore for it to take three motherfuckers to satisfy you!"

"You got some fucking nerve calling me a whore when I was the only person you had to fall back on for years! You could be a whore yourself, for all I know! I know about all the shit that goes on in prisons! How do I know you didn't become some bald-headed motherfucker's bitch?"

"I want you out of my sight!" he informed me, pointing toward the door. I ignored the dumbfounded look on his face, but I could not ignore what he said next. "If you don't get out of here now, I am going to kill you. And this time, *I'll be glad to go to prison for killing a bitch!*" I knew that Floyd didn't mean that. I knew in my heart that he could not kill me, or anybody else. However, I didn't want to find out if I was wrong.

"I'm going. And don't try to find me," I said, gripping the handles on my luggage. I still had on my party dress but a pair of Nikes were on my feet, in case I had to do some more running.

"You don't have to worry about that!" Floyd slammed the door so fast and hard behind me, the doorbell rang. Once I made it outside, I flung my suitcases into the back seat of my Honda, the only thing that really belonged to me. Then I fell into the driver's seat. I sat there for a few minutes, trying to compose myself.

I still loved Floyd, and if nothing else, I still wanted him in my life as a friend. But I knew that it would be a while before he cooled off enough for me to talk to him again. I had not given up on him during his prison crisis, and now it was his turn to not give up on me. I felt that I had a better chance of coming to some kind of a truce with him than I did with Valerie. I had a feeling that there was nothing I could do, or say, that would make that sister want to be friends with me again.

Without giving it much thought, I leaped out of my car and ran back toward Floyd's building. I no longer had a key to get into the building lobby, so I had to ring the buzzer to his condo. He did not respond. And after all we'd been through together it didn't seem fair. But it was what it was, and I couldn't change anything now. I let out a defeated breath and returned to my car.

I looked up toward the front of the condo that I had loved so much. Floyd was peeping out at me from the living room window. Our eyes locked and for a brief moment, he smiled. Then he did a strange thing. He raised his hand and saluted me! But that was all he did. A moment later, he closed the curtains and removed himself from my view. That was when I knew for sure that I would never see or hear from him again. I started my car, and then I shot off down the street like a stray bullet.

CHAPTER 59

As soon as I got to the condo on Manchester, I called Paul up at our place in Alameda. I prayed that Valerie had not already called him up and told him everything like she had threatened to do. This was one thing that I wanted him to hear from me. He didn't answer. I left him a message just telling him to call me back because something extremely important had come up that we needed to address. I had not heard from him by midnight, so I called him up again. He answered on the fifth ring.

"Paul, I need to talk to you," I started.

"What? Baby, it's late. Is there something wrong? Can't this wait until morning?" He sounded groggy, but he didn't sound drunk. I was glad that he had not been drinking. This was one time that I needed this man to be stone-cold sober.

"No, we have to talk about this now. You won't be able to reach me in the morning."

"Well, whatever it is, it is going to have to wait until morning. After what we've already been through lately, I am not in the mood for any more drama. Enjoy Mexico."

"I'm not on the ship, Paul. I'm at the Manchester address. I haven't been on that ship for a long time. I quit my job so long ago I don't remember when I did it. Now if you don't want to hear what I have to say, that's fine. If you don't want to talk to me right now, just remember one thing: I did love you, I still do, and I tried to be a good wife. But there were so many things going on in my life . . ."

"Dolores, where are you? Why are you talking like this? Have you been drinking again?"

"I just told you. I'm at the Manchester address. And no, I am not drunk."

"Can I call you back in a few minutes? I was on my way to the bathroom. I had lunch at Hop Sing's today . . ."

"Yes." I hung up and called the last person on the planet that I ever thought I'd turn to for help. Moanin' Lisa was glad to hear from me.

"Oh, LoReese, I thought you had forgot all about me. I wanted to call you and come see you, but Paul didn't make me feel welcome." I had prepared myself for the usual moaning and groaning that usually accompanied almost every sentence that slid out of this woman's mouth. "Valerie sent me an invitation to your birthday party, but I was too depressed to come tonight. Did you get that punch bowl I sent? I wrapped it myself."

"Uh, thanks. I appreciate that."

"Did the party end early?"

"It did for me. Listen, I can't explain it all right now, but I need a place to stay. I don't know for how long. I have enough in my savings account to pay rent for at least a few months if I have to stay that long." I paused and took a few deep breaths. I could hear Moanin' Lisa gearing up on her end. Her loud breathing told me that she was in a fever of anticipation.

"Have mercy Jesus! What's wrong? What's going on, Lo? Did somebody —"

"Hush for a minute and let me talk," I ordered. I hated to cut Moanin' Lisa off midsentence. But if I hadn't, I would have been up all night listening to her pain. It was my turn to moan now. "Can I stay at your place for a while?"

"*You* want to come live with *me?*" she gasped. Her enthusiasm concerned me immediately. I was trying to run away from some major emotional issues, not run to some more. I knew that this woman was the kind of person who could reduce me to a nub if I let my guard down.

"I promise you that it will be just for a short time. A few weeks, I hope."

"Oh. I thought you said a few months." Moanin' Lisa sounded disappointed now.

"It could take me a few months to get things straightened out," I admitted, a headache already blazing a deadly trail throughout my head.

"Dolores, you could live with me for the rest of your life if you want to. You are the closest I ever came to having a real true best friend. I had a boyfriend for a minute a few weeks ago, but he took off after he maxed out my credit card, and I haven't heard from him since. That's what I get for hooking up with a custodian who works for Greyhound. What about Valerie? What about your husband?"

"Valerie and I are no longer friends and I am no longer with my husband," I reported in a stiff voice.

"Say what? You and Valerie were practically joined at the hip. What happened to —"

"I'll tell you all about it when I see you," I replied, the stiffness gone from my voice.

"My goodness. When are you coming? You

can move in any time you want to. I live on Figueroa now. This is a kind of rough neighborhood, and the complex is not the Trump Towers, but I like it. I'm so glad you called. I've been dying to get somebody up in here to keep me from getting bored. As a matter of fact, I didn't have anything better to do this evening so I applied some roach paste in every room just before you called. That's how bored I was."

"I'll call you when I know for sure. What's your address?" I wrote down Moanin' Lisa's address, and then I sat down on the sofa and waited for Paul to call me back. During the twenty minutes that I sat there with the telephone in my lap, praying that he would call, I ignored the wine bottle across the room. This was one time I wanted to be stone-cold sober when I talked to Paul.

"Dolores, what is going on now?" he asked as soon as I picked up the phone, halfway through the first ring.

"Paul, I don't want anything from you. No alimony, no nothing. I'm leaving with only what I came with — my clothes and my Honda." I couldn't believe how the words rolled off my tongue with so much ease.

"What did you just say?"

"I think you heard me," I said in a stony voice.

"I heard you all right. But I don't believe my ears."

"Well, you'd better believe them."

"Dolores, are you telling me that you are *divorcing* me? I love you, woman, and I will fight to the bitter end to keep you! Didn't I tell you that that bitch didn't mean a goddamn thing to me! Look, baby — what do I have to do to prove that?"

"Paul, before I met you I was involved with another man. He was in prison for something he didn't do: rape and murder." I heard Paul gasp, but other than that he remained silent as I continued. "He was serving a life sentence without the possibility of parole, so I never thought he'd get out. I, uh, married him." I could hear Paul mumbling profanities under his breath, but I was glad that he let me finish speaking before he spoke again. "Then, through DNA testing they found out that this man had been telling the truth all along. He never raped or killed anybody. They released him. He got a ton of money from an out-of-court settlement against the state, and he bought a fancy condo in Beverly Hills. I . . . moved in with him. Whenever I wasn't with you, I was with him."

489

"I'm sitting here, wide awake, and you are talking gobbledygook! Gibberish! I don't believe any of this shit! Woman, what in the hell are you telling me? How in the hell were you living with this other nigger and living with me, too?"

"Oh, Paul. I didn't want it to end this way. But the way things have been going lately, I knew it was just a matter of time before it came to this."

"Slow down. There is a piece of this puzzle missing. What was that thing about in the Marriott? Is that the man you married?"

"No. That was somebody else," I said in a meek voice.

"Let me get this straight. You married another man while you were married to me. Then you fucked some other asshole in the Marriott, too? What else do you have to tell me? Why are you telling me all this shit now?"

"Because something happened tonight and you are going to hear it from Valerie, anyway. I wanted you to hear it first from me," I told him.

"Oh? Did you fuck somebody else tonight?"

"No, I didn't. I was at a party tonight. I was celebrating, well, I was going to celebrate my birthday with some of my friends.

As it turned out, the same man I'd spent time with in the Marriott turned out to be the man that Valerie is going to marry. One thing led to another, and it all came out. Floyd, my uh, other husband was there."

"Where is this other husband now?"

"His name is Floyd."

"Daffy Duck, Mickey Mouse, or Goofy — I don't give a shit what that motherfucker's name is! I want to know where he is now! Is he there with you? Put his ass on the phone!"

"He's not with me now. We had it out, so I won't be seeing him again, either. He . . . he threatened to kill me."

"Not if I see your black ass first! Dolores, how could you play me like this? I ought to jump on a plane and come down there tonight and maul your head! You . . . you . . . you bitch!"

"Are you threatening me, Paul?"

"Hell yeah, I'm threatening you! I want to talk to that . . . that . . . my husband-in-law!"

"The man's name is Floyd," I told him again. "And I just told you, I won't be seeing him again."

"Well, you won't be seeing me again, either, you no-good whore! That's one thing you don't have to worry about — or I will kill you myself! When I get back to L.A. you better be as far away from my property as you can get! And let me tell you one more thing, bitch! I wasn't stupid! I wasn't one of those pea-brained niggers you grew up around. I had your number a long time ago. My whole family did. I figured you were fucking around on me on those damn cruises and shit. But guess what? I was having my fun, too! The fine-ass honey I was with last week makes you look like Biggie Smalls!"

"Paul, I don't need to hear all that now. It's over. None of that matters anymore, anyway."

"You're damn right it's over, but not before I finish saying what I have to say! I've listened to you, now you listen to me!"

"I'm listening," I said calmly. I saw no reason to scream and holler and cuss. Paul was doing enough of that for both of us.

"Everybody told me that I could do better than you. Nobody in my family wanted me to marry you. Do you know that the women I can pick and choose from include a diplomat's daughter? She's the one I was with last week! I hope you will take your foster-care-raised black ass back to Watts or South Central where you will be around your own kind. You were way out of your league with me, lady!"

"If you thought that, why did you marry me?"

"Because I was a damn fool! Any man who gets involved with you is a damn fool!"

"Paul, have a nice life."

"And another thing —"

I hung up before Paul could complete his last insult. I was through with him, and he was through with me. That was all that mattered.

Paul, Floyd, and Valerie had been the most important people in my life for years. And they had all been deleted in one night. But unlike them, I was not bitter. I had nobody to blame but myself. And as painful as it was for me to admit, I got what I deserved. No matter what happened to me now, it could only be an improvement.

I folded the scrap of paper with Moanin' Lisa's address and stuffed it into my wallet. And then I left the apartment on Manchester for the last time.

CHAPTER 60

Paul wasted no time filing for a divorce. I had sent him my new address as soon as I got settled into Moanin' Lisa's place. Two weeks later, a process server knocked on the door and presented me with the papers. He hired a sour-faced, high-powered pit bull of a lawyer, which was a waste of his money because I wasn't going to contest the divorce or ask for a damn dime. Except for my freedom, that man had nothing else I wanted now.

However, I did appreciate the fact that Paul had not even mentioned my marriage to Floyd during our day in court. In his final voice mail message to me, the day before we went to court, he had issued a chilling threat. "If you broadcast this news about how you duped me to any of my relatives, friends, or co-workers, I will make sure you suffer for the rest of your life. There is no place on this planet you can hide, because I will pay somebody to find you," he'd warned. I didn't see how I could suffer any more than I already was.

It didn't take long for me to realize that Paul keeping his own lips zipped about my committing bigamy was more for his benefit than mine. With his proud and cocky self, I couldn't imagine him putting up with rude comments and sly grins from his friends, co-workers, and especially that snooty family of his. It was not hard for me to imagine what his mother would say if she ever found out that her baby boy had married a woman who had married a convicted rapist and murderer: "Sweet P., what did you expect from that rootless foster care heifer?"

But Paul had to have the last word with me. "I pity the *next* fool you marry," he yelled as I strutted out of the courtroom with my head held high. I was not proud of what I'd done, but I had accepted the consequences with dignity.

I'd also sent my new address information to Floyd, but I never heard from him again, nor did I ever see him at any of the clubs and other places that we used to go to. And since our marriage had never been legal in the first place, there were no marriage issues for us to resolve, or dissolve.

I never heard from or saw Marvin/Russell

Meecham again, not that I wanted to, or expected to. I never heard from Valerie again, either. But I heard from at least a dozen other people about all the nasty things she said about me that night after I'd run out of Paw Paw's. I was especially not happy with the way my relationship had ended with her. I felt that there were a few loose ends left between us. I just didn't know how to tie them up by myself.

Knowing Valerie the way I did, I knew that she had written me off completely. But that didn't stop me from wanting to see her at least one more time. I didn't expect her to "kiss and make up" with me, but I wanted to formally apologize for all the pain I'd caused her. I'd done that for Floyd and Paul, so it was the least I could do for her. But the problem was, I had no idea how I was going to make that happen. However, I was determined to come up with a way.

A few weeks after that disastrous night in Paw Paw's, while Moanin' Lisa was preparing dinner, I decided to go out and drive past Valerie's house. For some reason, I thought that if I saw her house one more time while everything was still fairly fresh, I'd feel some sense of closure.

"I need to run to the liquor store to pick up some Italian wine to go with our Italian

dinner." I headed for the door before Moanin' Lisa could respond, but there was a
puzzled look on her face and I knew why.
Wine was one thing that we never ran out
of. There had to be at least half a dozen
bottles in our wine cabinet.

I drove around like I was lost for about
twenty minutes so I could build up my
nerve. It was a good time for me to do some
more serious thinking about my situation,
and what I was going to do about it. I was
now thirty-four years old. My life was as
raggedy as a bowl of sauer-kraut. Everything
that I had accomplished over the years was
gone. I had no man, no network of friends
to speak of, and no place to call my own.
Nothing. It was like I was back at square
one, just starting my life from the gate.

I had a lot of thoughts to sort through
about other things, like what I was going to
do about my future? I had already tried to
get my job back at the cruise line, but it was
too late. The supervisor that I had admired
so much had accepted a position with the
Princess Cruise Lines. I had to laugh when
I heard that. Princess was a fierce competi-
tor that she and I, and most of my former
co-workers, used to talk trash about to the
point of no return. The new events coordinator for the Encantadora cruise line had

come from the mighty Royal Caribbean line and had brought an assistant with him. However, they'd told me that they'd keep me in mind for future opportunities.

The folks at Encantadora had kept their word. When a suitable position became available a few weeks later, they called me up. I immediately accepted a secretary position in the main office, exactly where I had started. I had come full circle. I didn't know if that was a good sign or a bad sign. I was just thankful to have a job. These thoughts danced around in my head as I continued to drive around.

When I finally reached Baylor Street, I got to Viola's house first. I had not paid too much attention to it during the times that I was in and out of Valerie's house during the recent years. There was no reason for me to do so. I didn't know the large Hispanic family that Viola's greedy nephew had sold her house to. I glanced down the street toward Valerie's house. Right away I felt a sense of dread. I refused to think about what she'd do or say to me, if she saw me. However, I knew what she was capable of doing. And I was not ready to join Mr. Zeke in a home-made grave.

I was not brave enough to park too close to Valerie's house. So as a security measure,

I decided to park for a few minutes in front of the house where I'd grown up with my late foster parents. I changed my mind as soon as I saw Glodine prance out onto her porch when she saw me. The years had not been kind to her. Her hands looked like meat hooks; her bare feet looked like hairless puppies. She beckoned me with both hands. I backed up and parked in front of her house, forcing myself to smile, something I had not done in a while. It hurt my entire face to do so now.

Like Valerie, Glodine had always been a major source of juicy or useless information. The information she shared was usually unflattering and unreliable, but as long as it wasn't about me, it held my interest.

"Girl, I ain't seen you in a coon's age," Glodine greeted, opening my car door with hands shiny and dusty with grease and flour. Why such a slovenly woman wore a white apron over a plaid housecoat was beyond me. There was so much sauce, grease, and flour on the front and sides of the apron where she'd wiped her hands, it looked like an abstract painting. There was an anxious look on her moon face, so I knew she had some stories to share that would curl my limp hair. "I just made a fresh pot of coffee to go with my fried chicken dinner," she said with a proud sniff. She stood in front of me with her arms folded, looking me up and down like I was something for sale. "I'm glad to see you done put on some weight. Black men love women on the heavy side. All that extra meat looks good on you. . . ." There was a smug look on Glodine's face as she continued to look me over.

I had gained more than ten pounds in the last few weeks, and I didn't like it, no matter how good the extra weight looked on me. "Thanks," I muttered, sucking in my stomach, glancing down the street toward Valerie's house. I couldn't stop myself from wondering who had rented the room I once occupied.

I followed Glodine into her neat living room. One wall was covered with pictures of all the foster children who had once lived in her home. There had to be at least a dozen. I had to look away when I saw one of Floyd, sitting on the back of somebody's motorcycle with Glodine frowning in the background like a gargoyle. There were still no pictures displayed anywhere of Glodine's three deceased children. At least not in the living room, which was as far as I ever got in her house.

"Too bad you show a lot of your weight gain in your face. I do, too." Glodine grinned. "What you been up to?" Glodine didn't even give me a chance to respond to her anxious question. With a sniff so aggressive it made her nose wiggle, she launched a one-sided verbal assault on everybody she knew, and a few people she didn't know. Her husband had run off with an Asian woman. Her last two foster daughters had run off with thugs. The Mexicans who had bought the house that I'd grown up in *had* to be drug dealers — how else could they afford to buy a house? Her sister's only son had been arrested for showing his dick to some little kids on a playground. She frowned every time I glimpsed at my watch. "I know you ain't got no place else to go, or you wouldn't be here." She laughed. She poured me another cup of her weak coffee, my fourth, and then she continued. By the end of the second hour I was so exhausted I didn't care how rude it was to look at my watch.

"I'm meeting somebody for dinner," I lied, rising from her lumpy sofa. My "fishing" trip to Glodine's house had done nothing for me but waste my time. Even though she had left no stone unturned, the only person she had *not* mentioned was Valerie. The only reason I didn't bring her name up was because the last thing I wanted Valerie

to know was that I'd been in the neighborhood asking about her.

CHAPTER 61

My life quickly became routine. I went to work, came home, listened to my room-mate's latest tale of woe, then I went to bed. I did a little socializing, but I avoided most of my old friends and didn't attempt to make any new ones. A lot of interesting men asked me out, but dating was the last thing on my agenda these days. But eight and a half months after my sordid secret had been exposed, a new male came into my life that I could not ignore. My precious son, Martin Luther. I gave him my last name, because Reese was the only name I wanted to be associated with these days.

"He doesn't look like Floyd or Paul," Moanin' Lisa noticed right off the bat. And he didn't. He looked like his father, Marvin Russell Meecham. There was no doubt in my mind about who my baby's father was. Despite the fact that I'd been on the pill during my foolishness, I'd still gotten pregnant. There was the time that Marvin/ Russell had forgot to put on a condom, and there was that one other time when he'd broken through the condom at the most dangerous moment.

Each day Martin Luther looked more and more like his father, so there was no way I could not think about Marvin/Russell on a regular basis. But I had no desire to try to locate him. I felt the same way about him now that I felt about Paul and Floyd: I wanted nothing else from him, either. However, I did wonder from time to time if he and Valerie had been able to restore their relationship and get married, anyway. In a sad way I hoped that they had been able to. In all the years that I'd known Valerie and all the men she'd been with, Marvin/Russell was the only one who had made her happy, and the only one who stayed interested in her after a couple of dates. The fact that she had insulted me in the worst way in public because I had inadvertently turned her dream into a nightmare didn't change the fact that we'd once been best friends.

I missed Valerie, but I knew in my heart that we could never be friends again. All I could do was wish her well.

My son was a little more than a year old

when I decided it was time for me to move on. I scolded myself because I should have left Moanin' Lisa's apartment a long time ago. She was a lousy housekeeper, and I was tired of cleaning up behind her. I had to laugh to myself when I thought about how crazy her sloppiness would have driven Paul. She had no friends left except me, so there was nobody for her to visit or cling to. She was beginning to make me feel like her hostage. Despite the fact that it bothered Moanin' Lisa when I left her alone, I went out on a few casual dates, and I do mean *casual.* She hadn't been asked out in more than six months.

And the only people who visited Moanin' Lisa were some of her relatives. That was another irritating mess, because most of them whined as much as she did! It got to a point that whenever Cousin So and So, or Uncle What's His Name came in one door, I bundled up my son and went out the other. I still had a few options. I visited a few co-workers and a couple of sisters from the church I used to attend on Baylor Street.

But Moanin' Lisa's life outside of her dreary apartment was about as empty as it could get. As hard as it was to believe, her unnecessary complaining had gotten even worse over the years. Other than the job at that insurance company that she'd hated from day one, and somebody's funeral, she rarely went anywhere. It did me no good to advise her to get some hobbies, change jobs, stop attending so many funerals, and find other things to do with her time. The woman thrived on misery. She was getting old before her time, and I was not going to let her drag me along with her. Every little ache and pain she had had to be cancer or some fatal disease. If that wasn't bad enough, now she was at a point where she'd burst into tears and howl more than my baby boy did, when I least expected it. When my son stretched open his mouth when he had no reason to, I shut him up by sticking a pacifier into his mouth. Well, the day that my son stopped crying and took his pacifier out of his mouth and stuck it into Moanin' Lisa's mouth during one of her outbursts to shut her up, I knew that it was time for me to make a change. I had enough bad habits that he was probably going to eventually pick up. He didn't need to pick up any of hers.

I moved into a one-bedroom apartment only a few blocks away from Moanin' Lisa's, but that was not far enough away. I realized that immediately when I came home from work one day after picking up my son from his sitter's and found her sitting in her car parked in front of my building waiting for me to come home. I knew I had to move again, and beyond her reach this time.

Two months after I'd moved into a small house in Anaheim with a fenced-in backyard for my son to play in, I retrieved a message from my cell phone voice mail. Candace, my beloved former supervisor from the cruise line, had called me and offered me another job on a cruise ship. She didn't leave a lot of details, but from the excitement in her voice, I knew it had to be something she knew I'd be interested in. It was too late that night for me to return her call, but by the time morning arrived, I had decided that I would accept the job, even if it was sweeping the ship's deck.

"LoReese, it's so good to hear your voice again," Candace squealed as soon as she answered her phone. "What have you been up to? All kinds of fun things I'm sure."

"Lady, you don't know the half of it," I said, more to myself than to her.

"Excuse me?"

"Nothing."

"So, let me try again. Have you been doing all kinds of fun things, or not?"

"Oh, not much," I said, making a face. I had to wonder if she'd still be interested in me working for her again if she knew all the stupid shit I'd done during the past few years. "You said something about a shipboard job?" I asked anxiously.

"I heard you were back with the Encantadora — working in the front office."

"Well, yeah. The new events coordinator already had an assistant, so I took whatever I could get," I said sheepishly. "How are things at, uh, the Princess Cruise Line," I said. "Are the big boys treating you well?"

"Like an ugly stepsister," Candace snarled.

"I guess that means you're not happy there."

"Hell no! Don't mention those assholes! That's why I am no longer with them. Had I known what I know now, I'd have stayed where I was. But things happen for a reason." Candace paused and cleared her throat. Then she started speaking in a much louder and more eager voice. "Are you familiar with the DreamBoat cruise line?"

"Of course." One thing that employees of cruise lines kept up with was news that involved rival lines. "They are a small independent line like Encantadora, but aren't they based in Miami?"

"The main office is. The cruises primarily cover the Caribbean area with an occasional jaunt to ports along the Mexican Riviera."

"Like us. Except we do Mexico the most, and the Caribbean from time to time. Is that where you work now?" I asked with an envious gasp.

"It pleases me immensely to say that that is true! I organize the entertainment and all other social events. And, I need an assistant. Patty Boone, the girl who's going to leave me, couldn't keep her legs together, or her hands off those island studs, and now she's jumped ship and run off and married one. If I don't get another assistant soon, I just might 'jump ship' myself." At this point, Candace started sounding frighteningly serious and her voice got so low I could barely hear her. "Now I don't know why I feel the way I do, but you've been on my mind a lot lately. LoReese, uh, for some mysterious reason I have a feeling that you are ready for a big change in your life."

CHAPTER 62

"Candace, are you offering me a job?" I was glad that I was already sitting down on the sofa because the news was so incredible I almost passed out, and almost dropped my son off my lap. I held my breath because this sounded too good to be true. From my experiences in life, I had learned the hard way that anytime something sounded too good to be true, it usually was. I braced myself and wondered what the catch was. "What's wrong with this job?" I asked with a heavy sigh.

"What's wrong with the job? Why would you ask an odd question like that?"

"It sounds too good to be true," I mumbled. "Is the ship haunted or something? A person would have to be crazy to give up a job like that in the first place . . . like I was."

"You're awful gloomy today. Is this a bad time to discuss employment opportunities?

Or are you just not interested? I am sure I'd be able to fill the position in a flash, but you are my first choice . . ."

"I'm sorry, Candace. I guess I'm just being cautious," I said, swallowing hard.

Candace didn't reply right away, and that made me wish I had sounded more enthusiastic, because I really was. "Anyway, I'm sure you remember all the fun we had working together. This will be just as much fun, if not more. Now the pay won't be that much more, but it'll be enough for you to enjoy a fairly comfortable life. And to sweeten the pot, my retirement is just around the corner, which means you'd be the most likely one to replace me." Candace paused. I heard her suck in some air, then clear her throat with a hearty cough. "All you have to do is clear it with your husband."

"Uh, we are no longer together," I said in a low voice.

"Oh my word! What did he do?"

All five of Candace's husbands had cheated on her, abused her, and used her for her money, and she was still bitter about it. It was easy for me to understand why she assumed all men were the ones at fault when a relationship fizzled out.

"We just grew apart," I said, responding

in a detached voice.

"Aw, that's too bad." Candace didn't sound the least bit sorry to hear that my marriage had failed. If anything, she sounded happy about it. "Shit happens when you sit on a toilet! Then it shouldn't be a problem at all for you to move to Miami. A single, pretty young woman like yourself will get a lot of attention down here. Do you have a problem relocating? One of my best clients, and new best friends, manages several apartment buildings in south Florida. Nothing on the Palm Beach level, but something I'm sure you'd like. I could have a place lined up for you within a week that you could afford. And I'll even help you furnish it, at my expense."

"Well, me moving to Miami wouldn't really be a problem. Not a big problem, I mean," I said with some hesitation as I caressed my son's cheek. "Uh, I'm not exactly single anymore, see."

This time Candace was the one to gasp. "Don't tell me! Please don't tell me that you dumped one husband and picked up another already? Are you going to have to sift through five like I did and still end up alone when you could have been using your time more productively?"

"I'm not married, but I have a child to

512

take care of now," I chirped. I followed that with an extremely proud sigh. I wanted it known that I was delighted to finally be a mother. For the first time in my life, I had somebody that belonged to me in every sense of the word.

Candace breathed a loud sigh of relief, and her doing that made me do the same thing. I loved my son to death, but the last thing I wanted was for him to hinder my progress in any way. I knew women who couldn't work, date, or do much of anything else because of their children, and they ended up resenting them. I didn't want that to happen to me. I'd lost too much already, and at this point, my child was all I had left.

"Is that all? I don't see how it would be a problem. As a matter of fact, I'm the only crew member who doesn't have any children, and that's only because no man in his right mind wants to wade into this sixty-year-old pothole of a pussy anymore. Thank God for male escort services and vibrators." Candace laughed. "Boy or girl?"

"Boy. His name's Martin Luther. Named after Dr. King and my late foster father," I said. I looked around the room at all the cheap furniture I had purchased. Then I looked at my son's face. I was no longer a happy resident of California. I didn't think that I was going to be happy in the state of California any time soon after all I'd been through. As for me staying in the same area, just moving from one apartment to another, that was not going to help much, mainly because I would still be too close to the things I needed to put behind me.

It was when my son smiled, cooed, and reached for the telephone that I knew what I had to do. It was almost like he wanted to take over the conversation and say what I knew I needed to say. But he didn't have to. "Candace, I'll start packing as soon as I get off this telephone," I told her. And I did.

I didn't tell anybody I was leaving town. I decided that it would be better just to go. Once I got settled, I'd write or call up the people I wanted to keep in touch with. I had packed everything I wanted to take with me. I had donated my furniture to Goodwill. Then I rented a booth at a nearby flea market and sold almost everything else. I was just about to pack up my leftovers and drop them off at the Salvation Army drop-off location when one more customer stopped at my booth.

"Dolores? Is that you?" It was a voice that I would have recognized anywhere, and it was just as harsh and irritating as ever. Glodine Banks, the wicked witch of the west, stood there with a familiar smirk on her face and a bulging plastic shopping bag in her hand.

"Glodine?" I said, whirling around. "How have you been?"

"Oh, I'm too blessed to be stressed, but I heard you been having a lot of ups and downs." She cackled, her eyes sparkling with excitement and mischief.

"I don't know who told you that. I'm doing just fine," I said, with a proud sniff.

"*Pffftt!* Well, you sure don't look it," she sneered. Her eyes, wide and cold, roamed all over me, looking for distress.

"You can believe what you want to believe. I'm doing real well and that's all that matters," I insisted.

"I heard you done got yourself pregnant!" Glodine hollered, giving me a sly look. She kept right on talking before I could respond to her outburst. "Whose is it? I seen Floyd and I asked him and he said it wasn't 'no telling' who . . ." Glodine picked up a cheap camera off the counter, one I hadn't been able to sell even though I'd reduced the asking price to almost nothing. "This thing work?"

"It works," I said, ignoring what she'd said about Floyd. "You can have it if you want it."

"How come you never told me about that riot you caused at Paw Paw's a couple of years ago?" Glodine demanded, fiddling around with the camera. You would have thought that it was a rare diamond the way she was inspecting it. "I had to hear it from three other people. You know how these L.A. niggers like to yip yap." She let out a loud breath, stopped inspecting the camera, and then looked me in the eye. She shaded her eyes with her hand. "I didn't know nothing about you fooling around with so many men, marrying *three* at the same time! Then, playing oochie coo with Valerie's fiancé! Eeeyow!"

I glared at Glodine, refusing to let her make me crack. "That's all over and done with. And it was two men I married, not three. And for the record, I didn't know that Valerie was involved with that man. I told her that that night, and when you see her, you can tell her I said it again."

At this point Glodine reared back on her legs like a steed and looked at me with her mouth hanging open as wide as a big dipper. "Didn't you hear about Valerie? Her life ain't worth a used condom these days."

"Oh?" Now I was the one with my mouth hanging open. "What did she do now?" I

516

asked. I was more than a little curious. "Valerie in jail, girl."

CHAPTER 63

"Valerie is in jail?" I mouthed, shaking my head. The words felt so hot on my tongue, I had to gulp in some cool air to ease the burning sensation in my mouth. I leaned forward and narrowed my eyes to see Glodine better. I didn't like what I saw. She was gloating. Of all the things I expected to eventually hear about Valerie, this was not one of them. After all the years that had passed since she'd killed her stepfather, she'd gotten away with murder as far as I was concerned.

"Uh-huh. And let me tell you something, that sister won't be sitting her happy ass up in that Ivory restaurant over there in Beverly Hills no time soon. Uh-uh. Her Ivory restaurant eating days is over!" Glodine paused and released a massive grunt. She had on plum-colored lipstick, mascara, and powder that hid the deep lines on her face. Her hair, now all completely gray, looked like it had been freshly done. I didn't want to tell her what I was sure she already knew — she looked quite nice for a change, for a woman her age. She cleared her throat and hawked a huge wad of spit onto the ground, missing her own foot by inches. "Yeah, honey. That sister is going to be in jail 'til times get better. Are you standing here telling me you didn't know that? You used to be her best friend!"

"Well, I am not her best friend anymore, so I don't keep up with what's happening in her life." I gave Glodine a thoughtful look. "That's the way she wanted it. What . . . what is she in jail for?"

"She killed a man!" Glodine reported. I could see that she was in her element. She slapped a hand on her boxy hip and looked me straight in the eye. "Ain't it funny that the two people that you was in cahoots with ended up in prison. First Floyd, now Valerie. When it comes to friends, you sure know how to pick 'em."

"Who . . . who did she kill? Did she kill the man she was supposed to marry a while back?"

"Girl, don't you read the newspapers, or watch the news on the TV? It's been all over the news all week."

"I've been busy preparing to relocate," I

explained.

"Oh. Where you moving to? Done found you another man?"

I ignored Glodine's questions. "Who did Valerie kill?" I asked again, not even trying to hide my impatience.

"Remember that mean-ass stepdaddy of hers? Zeke."

For a split second everything went dark. The blood rushed to my head and I thought I was going to pass out. If I had not placed my hands firmly on the counter of the booth, I would have. "I remember Mr. Zeke. After the last time he beat on Miss Naomi, he disappeared," I said in a weak voice. Glodine was so excited about sharing this juicy piece of information with me, she didn't even notice how it was affecting me.

"He disappeared all right. In a hole in Naomi's backyard, and Valerie was the one that put him there with her own hands. Hmmm. Looking at her, you'd never guess she was that strong . . ."

"Who said that?" I mouthed, surprised that I was still standing and not stretched out on the ground.

"She said that! It was in the newspaper. I don't know all the details, and I ain't running around trying to find it out. The last thing I want people saying is that I don't know how to mind my own business. The newspaper said that she cut up that nigger she was supposed to marry. The same one you stole from her. Anyway, she allowed that punk to hang around after you messed him over. That's how desperate she was for a dick. One thing led to another, and she finally figured out he wasn't worth shit. Last Saturday night they fought in her house. She sliced him across the neck like she was gutting a catfish. But that wasn't enough for her. Then she stabbed him below the breast-bone and sent him to the hospital in critical condition. While she was in that dark dreary jail cell for that, she must have got the spirit in the dark, because she broke down and confessed to killing Zeke. You can run and you can hide, but the one thing that'll always find you is that spirit in the dark. That's God's way of showing us he ain't blind. He's the only spirit that can see everything. Even in the dark. . . ." Glodine's spiritual words gave me a sudden warm feeling. I felt calmer than I'd felt in years. My only regret was that she had not said something like this to me years before. I could see that what she'd just said had a profound effect on her, too. She had never gotten along with Mr. Zeke, but her emotions got the better of her. She paused, looked off to the side, and wiped a few tears from her eyes.

After sucking in a few loud breaths of air, Glodine looked at me again. The makeup hid her age and flaws, but not her pain and sadness. I wondered if a woman who'd lost all three of her children could ever not feel some level of pain. Thinking about that made me feel sorry for her. She seemed surprised, but pleased, when I smiled and leaned over the counter and gave her a brief hug.

There was a noticeable lilt in her voice when she continued. "Me, if I was Valerie or her broke-down mama, I would have killed that booger a long time ago and it wouldn't have took no spirit in the dark to loosen my lips. I hate to speak ill of the dead, but I like to be thorough." Glodine paused again. This time she raised a fist in the air and shook it. "If any man ever had it coming, it was Zeke Proctor. And I think the DA thinks the same thing, because he knew what a motherfucker Zeke was when he was still on the police force."

What I had just heard about Valerie made my head spin. I was totally overwhelmed. "What are they going to do to her? Did she say anybody else was involved?" I asked in a shaky voice.

Glodine shook her head. "Just her and her mama was involved, may she rest in peace. But I got a notion that there was a whole lot of other folks that would have eventually cooked Zeke's goose. I'll give you two dollars for this camera," Glodine said, holding the camera up to the light.

"No, you can have it," I insisted, pushing it toward her. "Uh, have you talked to Valerie since the news broke?"

"Have I talked to Valerie?" Glodine gasped and stabbed her chest with her crooked finger, looking at me like I was just as crude as she was. "What's wrong with you, girl? I ain't going up into no jailhouse to talk to Valerie, or nobody else. We ain't got nothing to talk about no more, no how. All them years she lived down the street from me, she thought her shit didn't stink. Half the time I seen her, she didn't even speak to me. But I am a Christian so I do feel for her regardless of her sins. I prayed for her when I heard about her backsliding situation. . . ." Glodine let out a loud breath and then looked at me out of the corner of her eye. "Girl, you better not tell the new people that you meet all this shit you been caught up in. They might think you bad luck. Most people ain't as scientific as I am. I don't believe in bad omens, but a lot of people do." Glodine looked at her watch. "Where you moving to?"

"I'm moving to Florida. I just accepted a job offer," I announced.

"Florida? Aw shuck it! You moving to Florida with all them hurricanes and bugs — some big as me? Girl, you might as well move to some jungle in Uganda. Bah!" I was not surprised that Glodine was more interested in the Florida weather and bugs than my new job. She didn't even ask what my new job was. She fanned her face with one hand, and stuffed the camera into her bulging, plastic shopping bag with the other. "Well, call me when you get settled. I'd like to keep in touch. I been itching to see Florida all my life, but I never could go to Florida because of them highfalutin hotel prices. But now that you're going to be out yonder, I'll have a place to stay for a few weeks." Glodine let out a mild belch and then gave me one of her most sincere smiles. "What else you got to give away, LoReese?" It was the end of the day in more ways than one. Once Glodine realized I had nothing else to give her, she left.

I watched until this sad and mysterious woman was out of sight. Despite my delayed feelings of sorrow for her, I had no desire to keep in touch with her. It was too late. And

I had no desire to visit Valerie in jail. It was also too late for that. But I was glad that she had not dragged me down with her when she made her jailhouse confession. She had made it clear that she never wanted to see me again, anyway. And even if she did, there was nothing I could say, or do, that would help her get through the mess she was in this time. Besides, jail was one place I didn't want to visit again anytime soon. After all of the years that I had spent comforting Floyd while he was incarcerated, our relationship had still blown up in my face, even though it was my fault and I could have avoided it by not marrying him.

I had already made arrangements to leave for Florida the next day, that Sunday afternoon. After I'd packed up and left the flea market, and retrieved my son from the sitter's, I went straight home. As soon as I got inside, I called the airline to see if I could change my travel arrangements. They had *one* flight to Miami that had only *two* seats left, and it was leaving at midnight.

When that plane roared out of LAX, my son and I were on it.

■ ■ ■ ■

A READING GROUP GUIDE

SHE HAD IT COMING

MARY MONROE

■ ■ ■ ■

ABOUT THIS GUIDE

The suggested questions are intended to enhance your group's reading of SHE HAD IT COMING by Mary Monroe.

DISCUSSION QUESTIONS

1. Miss Naomi's brutal husband had promised her that he would kill other members of her family if she left him. And since the police said they couldn't do anything to him until he committed a crime, was his murder justified?

2. Was Dolores wrong for helping Valerie and Miss Naomi conceal their crime? If you think so, what do you think Dolores should have done when she innocently entered the crime scene?

3. Dolores was the only friend Floyd had after he went to prison. But do you think he expected too much from her? Do you think that she let him manipulate her too much or do you feel so sorry for him that you were glad he had a friend like Dolores?

4. With Floyd in prison, Dolores's relation-

ship with him had a lot of limitations. Were you glad that she got on with her life and married Paul? If so, why?

5. Dolores knew that it was a crime to marry Floyd while she was still married to Paul. But since she didn't think Floyd would ever get out of prison and getting married meant so much to him, she gave in. What would you do in the same situation?

6. When Dolores heard that Floyd was going to be released from prison, should she have immediately come clean with him and Paul or should she have disappeared from both men's lives?

7. Dolores was already having a hard time juggling her two husbands but she still got involved in an intimate relationship with another man at the same time. Do you think that she was stupid, out of control, or just plain greedy?

8. Did you suspect before it was revealed that the third man in Dolores's complicated love life was the man that Valerie was planning to marry?

9. Valerie had promised Dolores that she would never tell anyone that she had committed bigamy. But when Valerie found out Dolores was sleeping with her fiancé, she snapped and spilled the beans in front of almost everyone they knew. Do you think she was justified?

10. Floyd had pressured Dolores into marrying him. Should he have been more sympathetic and understanding as to why she had committed bigamy?

11. Despite the fact that Valerie blabbed on Dolores, Dolores kept her word and never told anybody that Valerie had killed her stepfather. Do you think that Valerie felt guilty about betraying Dolores?

12. Do you think that Valerie turned herself in for killing her stepfather because of her conscience or because she thought that Dolores might pay her back by turning her in?

13. Do you think that Dolores should have paid at least one visit to Valerie in jail, just to clear the air?

14. Despite the fact that Dolores lost both

husbands and her best friend at the same time, she still landed on her feet. She had a beautiful son and had been offered another dream job in another state. She had a lot to look forward to. Do you think she deserved to be happy after all she'd done?

ABOUT THE AUTHOR

Mary Monroe is the *New York Times* best-selling author of *Deliver Me From Evil, God Don't Play, In Sheep's Clothing, Red Light Wives, God Still Don't Like Ugly, Gonna Lay Down My Burdens, God Don't Like Ugly, The Upper Room,* and the novella "Nightmare in Paradise" in *Borrow Trouble.* An avid traveler, Mary currently lives in Oakland, California. She loves to her from her readers via e-mail at AuthorAuthor5409 @aol.com.